Scandalous single St Claire males—
ready to marry!

Tall, Dark &
Scandalous

Three fabulous novels
from international bestselling author

CAROLE MORTIMER

CAROLE MORTIMER'S
TALL, DARK & HANDSOME COLLECTION

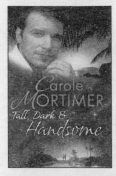

August 2013

September 2013

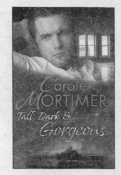

October 2013

November 2013

December 2013

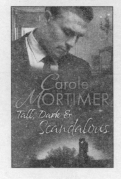

January 2014

A beautiful collection of favourite Carole Mortimer novels.
Six seductive volumes containing sixteen fabulous
Modern™ and Historical bestsellers.

Carole MORTIMER
Tall, Dark &
Scandalous

MILLS & BOON

Published in Great Britain 2013
by Mills & Boon, an imprint of Harlequin (UK) Limited, Eton House,
18-24 Paradise Road, Richmond, Surrey TW9 1SR

TALL, DARK & SCANDALOUS
© Harlequin Enterprises II B.V./S.à.r.l. 2014

Jordan St Claire: Dark and Dangerous © Carole Mortimer 2011
The Reluctant Duke © Carole Mortimer 2011
Taming the Last St Claire © Carole Mortimer 2011

ISBN: 978 0 263 91027 8

024-0114

Harlequin (UK) policy is to use papers that are natural, renewable and recyclable products and made from wood grown in sustainable forests. The logging and manufacturing processes conform to the legal environmental regulations of the country of origin.

Printed and bound by
CPI Group (UK) Ltd, Croydon, CR0 4YY

Carole Mortimer was born in England, the youngest of three children. She began writing in 1978 and has now written over one hundred and eighty books for Mills & Boon. Carole has six sons, Matthew, Joshua, Timothy, Michael, David and Peter. She says, 'I'm happily married to Peter senior; we're best friends as well as lovers, which is probably the best recipe for a successful relationship. We live in a lovely part of England.'

Jordan St Claire: Dark and Dangerous

CAROLE MORTIMER

PROLOGUE

'I THINK I should warn you, Miss McKinley—at the moment my brother is behaving like an arrogant lout!'

Must run in the family, Stephanie thought wryly as she looked across at Lucan St Claire, who was sitting behind his desk in the London office of the St Claire Corporation. Tall, dark, and aristocratically handsome, with a remoteness that bordered on cold, he wasn't loutish at all—but this man had to be the epitome of arrogant!

The fact that he showed absolutely no interest in her as a woman might have something to do with Stephanie's unkind thoughts—but, hey, a girl could dream of being hotly pursued by a mega-rich, tall, dark and handsome man, couldn't she? That Lucan St Claire had more money than some small countries, and reportedly only dated leggy blondes—as opposed to women like Stephanie, with her average height and flame-red hair—probably had something to do with his lack of interest. Also, if that weren't enough strikes against her, she was merely the self-employed physiotherapist this man intended hiring—she hoped—to aid his younger brother's recuperation.

She steadily returned the piercing darkness of his

gaze. 'Most people in pain tend to become…a little aggressive in their behaviour, Mr St Claire.'

The sculptured lips curved in a humourless smile. 'I believe you will find that Jordan's a *lot* aggressive.'

Stephanie mentally sifted through the relevant facts she already had on the man who was to be her next patient. On a personal level, she knew Jordan St Claire was thirty-four, and the youngest of three brothers. Medically, she knew Jordan had been involved in some sort of accident six months ago, resulting in his having broken almost every bone down the right side of his body. Numerous operations later, his mobility still impaired, the man had apparently retreated from the world by moving to a house in the English countryside, no doubt with the intention of licking his wounds in private.

So far Stephanie found nothing unusual about his behaviour. 'I'm sure that it's nothing I haven't dealt with in other patients, Mr St Claire,' she said confidently.

Lucan St Claire leant his elbows on the leather-topped desk to look at her above steepled fingers. 'What I'm trying to explain is that Jordan may be…less than enthusiastic, shall we say?…even at the mere thought of having yet another physiotherapist working with him.'

As Stephanie had never thought of herself as 'yet another physiotherapist', she found the remark less than flattering. She was proud of the success she had made of her private practice these past three years. A success that had resulted in almost all her clients coming as referrals from doctors or other satisfied ex-patients.

From what Stephanie had read in the medical file that now sat on top of Lucan St Claire's desk—a confidential file that she was sure he shouldn't even have had access to, let alone a copy of—the surgeons had done their work, and now it was up to Jordan St Claire to do the rest. Something he obviously seemed less than inclined to do…

Her eyes narrowed as she studied the aristocratically haughty face opposite her own. 'What is it you aren't telling me, Mr St Claire?' she finally prompted slowly.

He gave a brief appreciative smile. 'I can see that your professional reputation for straight talking is well earned.'

Stephanie was well aware that her brisk manner, along with her no-nonsense appearance—her long red hair was secured in a thick braid down her spine, and there was only a light brush of mascara on the long dark lashes that surrounded cool green eyes—invariably gave the impression she was less than emotionally engaged. It wasn't true, of course, but inwardly empathising with her patients was one thing, and allowing them to *see* that empathy something else entirely.

As for her professional reputation…

Thank goodness Lucan St Claire didn't give any indication that he had heard any of the rumours concerning Rosalind Newman's recent accusation—that Stephanie had been involved in an affair with her husband Richard whilst acting as his physiotherapist. If he had, then she doubted he would even be thinking of engaging her.

'I've never seen any point in being less than truthful.' She shrugged. 'Especially when it involves my patients.'

Lucan nodded in agreement. 'Jordan wouldn't accept anything less.' He sat back in his black leather chair.

'And…?' Stephanie pierced him with shrewd green eyes. If she was going to work with this man's brother then she needed to know everything there was to know about him—and not just his medical background.

He gave a heavy sigh. 'And Jordan has absolutely no idea about my intention of engaging you.'

Stephanie had already had a suspicion that might be the case. It made her job more difficult, of course, if the patient was hostile towards her before she had even begun working with him, but she had worked with difficult patients before. In fact most of Stephanie's patients were difficult; her reputation for being able to deal with 'uncooperative' patients was the reason there had been no shortage of work since she had opened her small clinic.

'Can I take it from that remark it's your intention to present him with a *fait accompli*?'

He grimaced. 'Either way, he's as likely to tell you to go away—impolitely—as he is to let you anywhere near him.'

Stephanie pursed her lips. 'If you engaged me we would just have to make it impossible for him to tell me to go away—impolitely or otherwise. I believe you said that the house where he's staying in Gloucestershire is actually owned by you?'

Lucan eyed her warily. 'It's part of an estate owned by the St Claire Corporation, yes.'

'Then as the head of that corporation you obviously have the right to say who does and does not stay there.' Her gaze was very direct.

He looked at her appreciatively, those dark eyes gleaming with hard humour. 'You wouldn't have a problem just turning up there and facing the consequences?'

'If my patient leaves me with no other choice, no,' she assured him bluntly.

He smiled slowly. 'I do believe that Jordan may have more than met his match in you!'

Stephanie brightened. 'You've decided to engage me to work with your brother?'

'Working *with* Jordan might be an exaggeration,' Lucan drawled ruefully. 'He's been very vocal in not wanting anyone else "poking and prodding" him about, as if he's a specimen in a jar.'

'I never poke or prod, Mr St Claire,' Stephanie said dryly, her interest in the case deepening as she considered the hard work ahead of her. 'I can begin next week, if that would suit you?' She had absolutely no intention of allowing this man to even guess how relieved she felt at the thought of getting out of London for a while.

Away from Rosalind Newman's nasty—and totally untrue—accusations that Stephanie had had an affair with her husband…

'Very much so.' He looked relieved that nothing he had told her about his brother seemed to have succeeded in deterring her.

Stephanie understood that relief only too well—knew that very often a patient's inability to deal with their illness affected close family as much as it did them. Sometimes more so. And, for all that Lucan St Claire was known for his coldness and arrogance, he obviously loved his brother very much.

'I will need a key to the house where he's staying, and directions on how to get there,' she said. 'What happens next you may safely leave to me.'

Jordan St Claire didn't know it yet, but the immovable object was about to meet the unstoppable force!

CHAPTER ONE

'WHO the hell are *you*? And what are you doing in my kitchen?'

Stephanie had arrived at the gatehouse of Mulberry Hall an hour or so ago, and had rung the bell and knocked on the door before deciding that either Jordan St Claire wasn't in or he was just refusing to answer. Either way, it left her with no choice but to let herself in with the key Lucan St Claire had given her. Once she had walked into the kitchen and seen the mess there she hadn't bothered going any further. The dirty plates and untidiness were a complete affront to her inborn need for order and cleanliness. She doubted Jordan had bothered to wash a single cup or plate since his arrival here a month ago!

'*This* is a kitchen?' She continued to collect up the dirty crockery that seemed to litter every surface, before dropping it gingerly into the sink full of hot, soapy water. 'I thought it was a laboratory for growing bacterial cultures!' She turned, her gaze very direct as she raised derisive dark brows at the unkempt man who stood in the doorway, glaring at her so accusingly.

Only to feel the need to steady herself by leaning against one of the kitchen cabinets as she instantly recognised him. Despite the untidy overlong dark hair, the several days' growth of beard on the sculptured square jaw, and the way the black T-shirt and faded blue jeans hung slightly loose on his large frame, there was no mistaking his identity.

It took every ounce of Stephanie's usual calm collectedness to keep her expression coolly mocking as she found herself looking not at Jordan St Claire but at the world-famous actor Jordan Simpson!

Admittedly, the shaggy dark hair and the five o'clock shadow that looked more like an eleven o'clock one managed to disguise most of his handsome features— which was perhaps the intention. But there was no mistaking those mesmerising amber-gold eyes. Reviewers' descriptions of the colour of those eyes differed from molten gold to amber to cinnamon-brown—but, whatever the colour, the descriptions were always preceded by the word *mesmerising*!

As a fan of the English actor, who had taken Hollywood by storm ten years ago when, as a relative unknown, he had been given the starring role in a film that had been an instant box office hit, Stephanie knew exactly who he was. She should do, when she had seen every film this man had ever made—twenty or so to date. A couple of them had even resulted in him winning Oscars for his stunning performances, and she would have recognised those chiselled features in the dark. In her many fantasies involving this man it had always been in the dark...

Added to which, she knew Jordan Simpson had fallen from the top of a building six months ago, whilst on the set of his last film. The newspapers had been full of sensational speculation at the time, hinting that Jordan had been severely disfigured. That he might never walk again. That he might never work again.

No doubt about it, Stephanie accepted, as her heart continued to beat rapidly and her cheeks started to feel hot, he might be walking with the aid of a cane, but the man in front of her really *was* the incredibly handsome actor she had obsessed over for years. A little fact that Lucan St Claire had forgotten to mention to her the previous week, she thought with annoyance. She'd rather have been forewarned!

'Very funny!' Jordan rasped in response to her remark about the kitchen. He stood in the doorway, leaning heavily on the ebony cane he had necessarily to carry around with him everywhere nowadays if he didn't want to end up falling flat on his face. 'That still doesn't tell me who you are or how you got in.'

Jordan had been in an exhausted sleep, lying on the bed that had been brought down to the dining room because he could no longer walk up the stairs, when he'd heard the sound of someone moving about in the kitchen. His first thought had been that it was a burglar, but intruders didn't usually hang around long enough to wash the dishes!

'I have a key.' The redhead shrugged.

His eyes narrowed. 'Given to you by whom, exactly?'

A slight indrawn breath and then another shrug. 'Your brother Lucan.'

Jordan's glare turned to a scowl. 'If my interfering brother sent you here to act as housekeeper, then I think you should know I don't need one.'

'All evidence is to the contrary,' the redhead drawled, and she turned her back on him to once again move efficiently about the kitchen, collecting up yet more dirty plates and stacking them on the draining board. Giving Jordan's narrowed gaze every opportunity to notice how a short white T-shirt clung to the firmness of her breasts and flat stomach, ending a couple of inches short of the low-slung jeans that moulded to narrow hips and the perfect curve of her bottom.

Great—the only part of his body that didn't already ache from his injuries was now engorged, throbbing and ached like hell!

It was the first time Jordan had felt the least bit of sexual interest in a woman since the accident six months ago—but, considering the pitiful condition the rest of his body was in, it wasn't an interest he particularly welcomed now. 'Most of that stuff will go into the dishwasher, you know,' he muttered resentfully as the redhead began to wash the dishes already in the soapy water in the sink.

'They *could* have gone in the dishwasher after they were first used,' she corrected without turning. 'Now they need to be soaked first.'

'Implying that I'm a slob?'

'Oh, it wasn't an implication,' she commented pertly.

'It may have escaped your notice, but I'm slightly impaired here!' Jordan defended angrily; he didn't have much of an appetite nowadays anyway, but on the occasions he did feel hungry his hip and leg ached so much by the time he had finished preparing the food and eating it that he didn't feel up to doing the dishes.

The redhead stopped washing up to slowly turn and look at him with wide green eyes. 'Wow.' She gave a rueful shake of her head. 'I have to admit I didn't expect you to play the "I'm crippled" card right off the bat!'

Jordan drew in a harsh, disbelieving breath even as his fingers tightened about his cane until the knuckles showed white. '*What* did you just say?'

Stephanie's gaze continued to calmly meet Jordan's fierce amber eyes even as she quickly registered the way his already pale cheeks had taken on a grey tinge, along with the resentful stiffening of a body that obviously showed the signs of being ravaged by pain and illness.

Normally a complete professional when it came to her job, Stephanie was finding it difficult to deal with Jordan's dark and sensual good-looks with her usual detachment. In fact, she had deliberately not looked at him for some minutes in an effort to regain her equilibrium! Usually level-headed when it came to men, Stephanie had dragged her reluctant sister along to see every film Jordan Simpson had ever made, just so that she could sit in the impersonal darkness of the cinema and drool over the big screen image of him before she was later able to buy the film on DVD and drool over him in private. Her sister Joey was just going to fall over laughing when she learnt who Stephanie had taken on as her patient!

Her expression remained outwardly cool as she inwardly acknowledged that thankfully the sexy and ruggedly handsome actor was barely recognisable in the gaunt and pale man in front of her. Except for those eyes!

'I'm sorry. I thought that was how you now thought of yourself? As a cripple,' she said evenly.

Those eyes glittered a dangerous gold. 'Forget who you are and what you're doing here, and just get the hell out of my home!' he ordered furiously.

'I don't think so.'

He frowned fiercely at the calmness of her reply. 'You don't?'

Stephanie smiled unconcernedly in the face of the

fury she could see he was trying so hard to restrain. 'This is your brother's home, not yours, and the fact that Lucan gave me a key to get in shows he has no problem with me being here.'

Jordan drew in a harsh breath. '*I* have a problem with you being here.'

She smiled slightly. 'Unfortunately for you, you aren't the one paying the bills.'

'I don't need a damned housekeeper!' he repeated, frustrated.

'As I said, that's questionable,' Stephanie teased lightly as she moved to dry her hands on a towel that also looked as if it needed to come face to face with some hot soapy water—or, more preferably, disinfectant! 'Stephanie McKinley.' She thrust out the dry hand. 'And I'm not a housekeeper.'

A hand Jordan deliberately chose to ignore, breathing deeply as he looked down at her from between narrowed lids. Probably aged in her mid to late twenties, the woman had incredibly long, dark lashes fringing eyes of deep green, and the freckles that usually accompanied hair as red as hers were a light dusting across her small uptilted nose. Her lips were full, the bottom one slightly more so than the top, above a pointed and determined chin. She also had one very sexy body beneath the casual white T-shirt and denims, and—as he was now all too well aware—a tongue like a viper!

No one—not even his two brothers—had dared to talk to Jordan these last few months in the way Stephanie McKinley just had...

'How do you know Lucan?' Jordan probed suddenly.

'I don't.' With a shrug, the woman allowed her hand to fall back to her side. 'At least, not in the way I think you're implying I might.' She gave him another mocking glance.

Jordan had been standing for longer than he usually did, and as a result his hip was starting to ache. Badly. A definite strain on his already short temper! 'Is paying a woman to go to bed with me Lucan's idea of a joke?'

Stephanie smiled in the face of the deliberate insult— at the same time as she wryly wondered whether the coldly remote man she had met the previous week even had a sense of humour! 'Do I *look* like a woman men pay to go to bed with them?'

'How the hell should I know?' Jordan scorned.

'Implying you don't usually need to pay a woman to go to bed with you?' That was something she was already well aware of—Jordan Simpson had trouble keeping women out of his bed rather than the opposite!

'Not usually, no,' he ground out.

Stephanie realised that he was deliberately trying to unnerve and embarrass her with the intimacy of this conversation. He was succeeding, too—which wasn't a good thing in the circumstances.

She raised an eyebrow. 'I assure you I would have absolutely no interest in going to bed with a man who is so full of self-pity that he's not only shut himself off from his family but the rest of the world, too.'

Jordan's face darkened ominously. 'What the hell would *you* know about it?' he snarled viciously. 'I don't see *you* suffering pitying looks every time you so much as go outside, as you stumble about with the aid of a cane just so that you don't completely embarrass yourself by falling flat on your backside!'

Stephanie hesitated slightly before answering. 'Not any more, no...'

Those golden eyes narrowed to dark slits. 'What exactly does *that* mean?'

Stephanie calmly met that furiously glittering gaze. 'It means that when I was ten years old I was involved in a car crash that left me confined to a wheelchair for two years. I couldn't walk at all for all of that time, not even to "stumble about with the aid of a cane". You, on the other hand, still have mobility in both your legs, which is why you won't be receiving any of those pitying looks from me that you seem to find so offensive from the rest of humanity!'

Ordinarily Stephanie didn't tell her patients of her own years spent in a wheelchair. She saw no reason why she needed to, and wouldn't have done so now, either, if the challenge in Jordan's tone hadn't touched on a raw nerve.

'You were lucky enough to get up and walk so now you think anyone else who finds themselves in the same position should do the same?' he said.

'So you've had the bad luck to receive injuries that have left you less than your previously robust and healthy self. Either live with it, or fight it, but don't hide yourself away here, feeling sorry for yourself.' She was breathing hard in her agitation.

Jordan looked down at her with sudden comprehension. 'If Lucan didn't send you here to go to bed with me, then who the hell *are* you? Yet another doctor? Or perhaps my arrogant big brother now thinks I'm in need of a shrink?' His top lip turned back contemptuously.

Stephanie McKinley quirked dark brows. 'I had the impression from reading your medical notes that your skull escaped injury when you fell?'

'It did,' he bit out tightly.

She raised auburn brows. 'Do *you* think you're in need of a psychiatrist?'

He scowled darkly. 'I'm not playing this game with you, Miss McKinley.'

'I assure you I don't consider this a game, Mr Simpson—'

'You know who I am?' Jordan interjected.

'Well, of *course* I know who you are.' Irritation creased the smooth creaminess of her brow. 'You're a household name. Obviously you're feeling less than your usual…suave and charming self,' she concluded tactfully, 'but you're still *you*.'

Was he? Sometimes Jordan wondered. Until six months ago he had enjoyed his life. Living in California. Doing the work he loved to do. 'Suave and charming' enough to be able to go to bed with any woman who took his interest. Since the accident all that had changed. *He* had changed.

'In that case, Miss McKinley, what I need is for someone to find a screenplay that calls for a male lead who limps! Know of any?' Jordan growled his frustration as he moved away from her, favouring his right side as usual, as the damaged muscle and bones in his hip and leg protested at the movement. Hell, he hurt no matter if he moved or not!

'Not offhand, no,' the redhead said tartly. 'And you wouldn't need one if you concentrated your energies on getting back the full use of that leg instead of wallowing in self-pity.'

'Damn it to hell!' Jordan gave a groan of disgust, his eyes lifting to the heavens in supplication. 'You're another sadistic physiotherapist, aren't you? Come to pound and massage until I can't stand the pain any longer.' It was a statement, not a question; Jordan had

had one physiotherapist or another working on his leg and hip for weeks, months, since the surgeon had finished putting his shattered bones back together. None of them had succeeded in doing more than sending him to hell and back.

'The fact that the leg still hurts could be a positive thing, not a negative one,' Stephanie McKinley retorted.

'I'll be sure to think of that at two o'clock in the morning, when I can't sleep because the pain is driving me insane!'

When Lucan St Claire had warned Stephanie that his brother was 'a *lot* aggressive', he had forgotten to add that he was also stubborn and unreasonable! 'In this case pain could be a good thing—it could mean the muscles are regenerating,' she explained patiently.

'Or it could mean that they're dying!'

'Well, yes…' No point in trying to deceive him concerning that possibility. 'I'll be able to tell you more once I've worked with it—'

'The only part of my body I would be remotely interested in having any woman work with is a couple of inches higher than my thigh!' he shot back wickedly.

There was no way, complete professional or not, Stephanie could have prevented the heated flush that now coloured her cheeks. Or the way her gaze moved instinctively down to the area in question. That particular part of his anatomy certainly seemed to be working normally, if the hard and lengthy bulge she could see pressing against his jeans was anything to go by!

Jordan St Claire—no, Jordan *Simpson*—was obviously physically aroused. By her.

No, not by her in particular, Stephanie rebuked herself impatiently. She very much doubted that this man had allowed a woman within touching distance since his accident, and after six months of celibacy she was probably just the first reasonably attractive female he had seen in a while—consequently he would have been aroused by a nun, as long as she had a pulse and breasts!

'If you're trying to embarrass me, Mr Simpson—'

'Then I've succeeded.' He eyed her flushed cheeks triumphantly.

'Perhaps,' she allowed briskly. 'Does knowing that make you feel good?' She eyed him speculatively as he gave a hard and unapologetic grin. A slow and sexy grin that reminded her all too forcibly that this man was the actor she had lusted after for years.

Oh, help!

He gave a casual shrug. 'It doesn't matter whether it did or it didn't. I intend to forget you even exist as soon as you've walked out the door.'

This time it was Stephanie's turn to smile slowly. 'You're an altogether arrogant family, aren't you?'

Jordan gave a huff of laughter. 'How many of us have you met?'

Stephanie blinked. 'Just Lucan and you...'

'And you think *we're* arrogant?' He snorted. 'Believe me, you don't know what arrogance is until you've met Gideon.'

'Your twin?'

That golden gaze sharpened. 'You seem to know a lot about me.'

She shrugged. 'I believe it's public knowledge that Jordan Simpson has a twin brother.'

He grimaced. 'Gideon and I are only fraternal twins, not identical ones.'

Thank goodness for that! Stephanie wasn't sure the

world—or she—could stand there being two men in the world with Jordan's devastating good-looks.

She had yet to decide whether or not this man posed a problem as regarded her working with him—other than the need she felt every time she so much as looked at him to rip his clothes off and jump into bed with him, of course. But surely that was normal? Hundreds—no, *thousands* of women must feel the same way about the actor Jordan Simpson. Except none of those women were supposed to act the complete professional and treat this man like any other patient—which he most certainly wasn't to Stephanie!

She gave a weary sigh as she pushed back some loose tendrils of hair that had escaped the plait down her spine. 'Look, Mr Simpson, I've had a long drive up here from London, and on top of that I could do with something to eat, so do you think we could call a truce to this argument long enough for me to cook us some dinner?'

Jordan's eyes narrowed contemplatively. On the one hand he wanted this woman gone from here, but on the other the mention of food had reminded him that he was hungry—a side-effect of those damned sleeping pills he had to take in order to get any rest at all. 'That depends,' he finally murmured slowly.

Deep green eyes looked across at him suspiciously. 'On what?'

'On whether or not you can actually cook, of course,' Jordan drawled. 'Put another plate of baked beans on toast in front of me and I may just throw it at you!' He had been living off something on toast since he'd moved here a month ago, in too much pain and lacking the appetite to bother to cook anything else.

Lucan had gone to the trouble of sending this woman

here, but Jordan had no intention of even allowing her to look at his injuries. Sex didn't appear to be on her agenda either. So she might as well make herself useful in some other way—before Jordan went ahead and threw her out anyway!

'I think I can do better than that,' Stephanie McKinley told him. 'I wasn't sure what the situation was for having groceries delivered, so I brought some things with me,' she continued brightly. 'I'll just go out to the car and get them.' She collected her black jacket from the back of one of the kitchen chairs and slipped it on, releasing her braid from the collar before moving towards the door. 'I hope you like steak?'

Just the mention of red meat was enough to make Jordan's mouth water. 'No doubt I could cope,' he said gruffly.

Stephanie was smiling slightly to herself as she went out to her car. He was allowing her to stay long enough to cook dinner, at least. Unsurprising, when she knew from the dirty plates she had collected up earlier that Jordan hadn't been exaggerating about the amount of baked beans on toast he had eaten since coming here. What happened after Stephanie had fed him was still in question, of course; she wasn't fooled for a moment by his sudden acquiescence in allowing her to cook dinner for them both.

She was going to have dinner with Jordan Simpson!

Admittedly he was a Jordan Simpson much changed from the charming, sensual man she had read about so much in the newspapers over the years. Or the one she had gazed at so longingly on the big and small screen, but still…

Stephanie had barely had time to open her car door when she heard her mobile ringing. Bending down to pick it up from where it lay on the passenger seat, she checked the number of the caller. 'Joey?' she breathed thankfully as she pressed the receiver to her ear and took her sister's call. 'I'm so glad you rang! I think I might be in trouble. *Big* trouble!'

CHAPTER TWO

'I THOUGHT you had decided to get in your car and leave after all,' Jordan rasped when Stephanie McKinley finally came back into the kitchen, carrying a box of groceries.

She put the box down on the kitchen table before answering him, her face slightly flushed, and even more of that long fiery-red hair having escaped the confining plait. 'I stopped to admire how beautiful the big house looked in the distance, with the sun going down behind it.'

'Mulberry Hall?'

She nodded. 'Is it a hotel, or something?'

'Or something.' Jordan nodded tersely. He had sat down at the kitchen table while he waited for her to return, and stretched his leg out in front of him now as he watched Stephanie take steak, potatoes, asparagus and salad from the box with hands that were long and slender, the nails trimmed capably short. No doubt in readiness for the sadistic pummelling she gave her patients!

'Either it is a hotel or it isn't,' she reasoned with a slight frown as she paused in the unpacking.

'It isn't,' Jordan supplied unhelpfully. The sight of all this fresh food reminded him of just how long it had been since he had last eaten. Yesterday some time, he thought. Maybe.

Besides which, he had absolutely no intention of talking about Mulberry Hall, or its function, with a woman who was going to be gone from here in a few hours.

'Your brother Lucan said this whole estate was owned by the St Claire Corporation.'

Jordan's mouth twisted. 'Did he?'

She raised dark brows. 'If you don't want to talk about it then just say so.'

He shrugged. 'I don't want to talk about it.'

Well, she had definitely asked for that one, Stephanie acknowledged ruefully. 'I was only trying to make polite conversation.'

Jordan looked at her coldly. 'I agreed to let you cook dinner, not talk.'

Stephanie bit back her angry retort as she resumed unpacking the box of groceries. Maybe he would be more amenable after he had eaten? And maybe he wouldn't! she thought dryly.

His medical file had stated that the broken bones in his arm and ribcage had knitted back together well, but the lines of strain grooved beside his mouth and eyes were evidence of the pain he still suffered in the hip and leg that had been fractured and obviously hadn't healed as well. Stephanie's fingers itched to explore that damaged leg and hip, to check for herself what could be done about restoring this man to full mobility.

Or maybe they just itched to touch all six foot four inches of lean, male flesh that was Jordan Simpson...

Her sister had been first incredulous and then amused when Stephanie had explained her dilemma to her, dismissing her misgivings regarding having the actor as her newest patient.

Joey had also reassured Stephanie concerning her worry over her unwilling involvement in the Newmans' divorce. Her lawyer sister had advised Stephanie to 'just get on and do what you do best, sis, and leave me to deal with the Newman situation.'

That the 'Newman situation' even needed dealing with still rankled with Stephanie.

'Could you lay the table while I cook?' she prompted sharply.

His jaw clenched. 'I'm not a complete invalid, damn it.' He gritted very white teeth as he rose awkwardly to his feet before grasping the ebony cane to balance himself.

'It was a request for you to actually lay the table, not a question as to whether or not you're capable of doing it,' she elaborated.

'Of course it was,' he said sarcastically.

Stephanie watched him as he limped across the kitchen to open the cutlery drawer, determinedly keeping her gaze professional. The muscles in his leg were obviously weakened from months of disuse, but that didn't explain the amount of pain he seemed to be suffering. It might be an idea to have someone else look at him—

'What the hell are you looking at?'

Stephanie raised her gaze to find Jordan scowling across the kitchen at her, and the look of savage anger on that handsome face warned her to opt for honesty. 'I was wondering if you should have that leg and hip re-X-rayed.'

'Forget it.' He threw the cutlery noisily back into the drawer before slamming it shut. 'And while you're at it take your food and just get out!' He walked stiffly towards the door that led back into the hallway.

Stephanie frowned her dismay as she realised his obvious intention of leaving. 'What about dinner?'

Those amber eyes were glittering furiously as he turned to glare at her. 'I just lost my appetite.'

'Just because I talked about your leg?'

'Because you talked at *all*,' Jordan told her insultingly. 'Men just shut up and get on with it—whereas women, I've learnt, feel the need to dissect everything.'

'If by that you mean that men prefer to bottle up their anxieties rather than—'

'The only anxiety I have at this moment is *you*!' he cut in viciously, able to feel the nerve pulsing in his tightly clenched jaw. 'A situation that will resolve itself the moment you walk out the door.'

This man really was an immovable object, Stephanie recognised in sheer frustration. Well, two could play at that game! 'I'm not going anywhere,' she told him levelly.

Those glittering amber eyes turned icily cold as his gaze raked over her from head to toe and back again. 'No?'

'No.' She stood her ground. 'And I very much doubt that you're capable of making me leave, either.'

His face was once again unhealthily pale as his mouth tightened to an angry grim line. 'You don't pull your punches, do you?' he muttered harshly.

Stephanie sighed. 'It isn't my intention to upset you, Mr Simpson—'

'Then get the hell out of my house!' He turned and left the room without a backward glance, his dark hair long and unkempt on his shoulders, and his back stiff with the fury he made no effort to hide.

Leaving Stephanie to sink down wearily into the kitchen chair Jordan had just vacated. She was used to difficult patients—actually relished the challenge of working with them. But dealing with Jordan Simpson was going to be so much harder than Stephanie could ever have imagined a week ago, when she had unknowingly agreed to help Lucan St Claire's brother...

'Changed your mind?' She looked up hopefully an hour later, when she heard the slight unevenness of Jordan's gait as he walked back down the hallway.

'No.' Jordan couldn't say he hadn't been tempted by the delicious smells emanating down the hall from the kitchen and into the study, where he'd sat as this stubborn woman obviously prepared her own dinner. Or that his mouth hadn't watered at the thought of sinking his teeth into a medium-rare steak and a fluffy jacket potato smothered in butter, possibly with a nice light French dressing on the green salad on the side. Tempted, maybe, but there was no way he would give Stephanie McKinley the satisfaction of joining her. 'I thought I told you to leave?' The pristine tidiness of the kitchen showed that she had finished cleaning before even attempting to cook her meal.

She remained comfortably seated at the kitchen table, where she had obviously just finished eating her meal—washed down by a glass of decent-looking red wine if the label on the open bottle on the table was anything to go by. 'Your brother wants me to stay.'

Jordan clenched his jaw. 'You've spoken to him?'

'Not since last week, no.'

'Well, it may have escaped your notice, but Lucan isn't here right now.'

'I have no doubt that he could be here in a matter of hours if I should decide to call him,' Stephanie McKinley came back unconcernedly.

Knowing his arrogant brother as he did, Jordan had no doubt, either, that Lucan was quite capable of climbing into his private helicopter and flying up here if he felt there was a need for him to do so. If Lucan thought that Jordan was being difficult. Which he undoubtedly was!

Jordan limped over to get a glass out of one of the cupboards, poured himself a glass of red wine from the open bottle and then took a sip before answering this increasingly annoying woman. 'If that was a threat then I'm not impressed.'

'It wasn't, and you weren't meant to be.' She grimaced. 'And should you be drinking wine if you're taking medication for pain?'

'This *is* my medication for the pain!' One thing Mulberry Hall did have was a decent wine cellar, and Jordan had helped himself liberally to its contents this past month. A cripple and a drunk; how the mighty had fallen! he thought derisively.

Stephanie McKinley eyed him frowningly. 'Alcohol causes depression—'

'I'm not depressed, damn it!' The glass landed heavily on the table-top as he slammed it down, spilling some of its contents over his hand and onto the wooden surface.

'Okay. But you're angry. Frustrated. And rude.'

'How do you know that I wasn't angry, frustrated and rude before the accident?' Jordan asked.

'You weren't,' Stephanie said quietly as she looked up at him. 'The press would certainly have made something of it if the famous Jordan Simpson were known to be any one of those things.'

Instead of which the media had always written glowing reports of the handsome and charming actor as he escorted leggy blondes to film premieres, or out to dinner at one exclusive LA restaurant or another. Usually looking devastatingly handsome in a black tuxedo or casually tailored clothing, his dark hair still overlong but expertly styled to make the most of his hard and chiselled cheeks and jawline, and the lazily sexy smile that curved those sculptured lips. Not to mention, of course, those mesmerising amber-gold eyes!

A complete contrast to *this* savagely acerbic man, in the crumpled T-shirt and denims he wore this evening, with that growth of beard on his chin and his too-long untidy hair.

'When did you last go to a barber or have a shave?' Stephanie asked.

Jordan picked up the glass and took another long swallow of red wine. 'None of your damned business,' he growled.

'Taking a pride in your appearance—'

'Isn't going to make a damned bit of difference to the fact that my leg is shot to hell.'

'We need to find out why that is,' she pressed.

'No, Stephanie, *you* need to find out why that is if you want to keep what I have no doubt is a very well paying job,' Jordan pointed out. 'But, as I have no intention of letting you anywhere near me or my leg, that's going to prove rather difficult, don't you think?'

Impossible, actually, Stephanie admitted with frustration. Being able to actually assess a patient's disability was more than half the battle. It also affected any and all treatment. Treatment this man had assured her he definitely wasn't going to allow her to give him. She stood up to collect her dirty plates, and carried them over to begin loading them into the dishwasher. 'Would you like me to cook your steak for you now?'

'Tell me, Steph, which part of *get the hell out of my home* didn't you understand earlier?' Jordan St Claire snarled cruelly.

Stephanie drew in a controlling breath. 'As I am neither stupid nor deaf, I understood all of it. I also prefer my...my clients to call me Stephanie or Miss McKinley,' she added primly. Only her family and very close friends were allowed to shorten her name in that way. Besides which, the formality of her full name sounded more professional. And she freely admitted she was having more trouble than usual in keeping her relationship with Jordan Simpson on a professional basis.

Considering the threatened scandal of what Joey called the 'Newman situation', Stephanie definitely needed to keep her relationship with this man—with *all* her patients—on a completely professional basis. If Rosalind Newman's accusations concerning her husband and Stephanie had been true, she knew she would deserve the other woman's vitriol. As it was, she had actually found Richard Newman one of her *least* likeable patients.

Unlike Jordan Simpson, despite his disgraceful temper...

Jordan eyed her mockingly as he refilled his wine glass. 'Why won't you just accept that you're wasting your time with me, *Stephanie*? That I don't want or need you here?'

She raised an eyebrow. 'I agree with the first part of that second statement, at least!'

Jordan's jaw tightened as he saw the challenge in the slight lift of her pointed chin and sparkling green eyes. As he acknowledged once again that his mouth and brain were pushing this woman away at the same time as his body wanted to pull her into his arms and kiss her senseless. He hadn't so much as felt a flicker of physical interest in a woman these past six months, and had wondered in some of his darker moments if perhaps the accident had robbed him of that ability too. The stirring of his thighs just looking at this woman had at least reassured him that wasn't the case, he thought ruefully.

Jordan wondered just what the determinedly professional Stephanie McKinley would do about it if he were to follow through on his instinct to kiss the hell out of her? Run screaming bloody murder into the night, probably, and never darken his door again!

Which, thinking about it, was precisely what Jordan wanted her to do...

He carefully placed his cane against the kitchen table before turning to walk—damn it, hobble!—the short distance that separated them, so that he stood only inches away from the suddenly wary Stephanie McKinley as she pressed herself back against the kitchen cabinet to look up at him with wide apprehensive eyes. 'Not so confident now, hmm, Stephanie?' Jordan deliberately moved closer still.

Stephanie inwardly panicked. She could actually feel the heat of Jordan's body as he stood mere centimetres away from her. She instantly responded to that heat, her breasts seeming to swell, and the nipples becoming hard and full against the thin material of her T-shirt, to her dismay.

Shaved or not, untidy overlong hair notwithstanding, he was undoubtedly every inch the sexually mesmerising A-list actor at that moment!

Stephanie moistened dry lips with the tip of her tongue, at once realising her mistake as she saw the way that seductive golden gaze followed the movement. 'This isn't funny, Jordan—'

'It isn't meant to be.' He moved the small distance that separated them. The aroused hardness of his thighs pressed against Stephanie's own, causing that heat to flare into an uncontrollable flame. 'Is this natural?' Jordan lifted a hand to touch the deep red hair at her temple.

Stephanie frowned. 'You don't seriously think any woman would deliberately dye her hair this colour?' she scorned, in an effort to dispel her discomfort at his close proximity. At having Jordan Simpson touch her in this way.

'It's beautiful,' he murmured appreciatively as he caressed several silky tendrils against his fingertips. 'Unusual.'

Stephanie knew exactly what Jordan was doing. She'd already realised that he was deliberately playing with her as another tactic in getting her to leave. But knowing that didn't make the slightest difference to the way she was responding to his closeness and the light caress of his fingertips as he touched her hair. She could barely breathe—didn't dare breathe—when her aroused breasts were already brushing against the hardness of Jordan's chest and making her ache for even closer contact! 'It's just plain old red.'

'No,' he murmured huskily. 'I've never seen hair quite this colour before. It's auburn and cinnamon, with highlights of red and gold.'

The colour of Stephanie's hair had been the bane of her childhood, and certainly wasn't the feature to mention if he was serious about this seduction. Which he obviously wasn't! 'It's red,' she insisted flatly.

That golden gaze moved slowly over the fullness of

her breasts, lingering appreciatively on those hardened nipples before travelling over the flatness of her stomach and down to her thighs, to linger there speculatively. 'Are you the same—?'

'Don't even go there!' Stephanie interjected sharply, the heat having burned up her cheeks now. 'Just step away from me, Jordan,' she warned.

That golden gaze taunted her. 'Or...?'

She met his gaze challengingly. 'Or I'm afraid I'll have to make you.' Stephanie had taken Ju-Jitsu lessons in self-defence several years ago. She had no doubt she could make him stop, but she wouldn't enjoy doing it to this particular man.

Unnerving Stephanie McKinley, making her too uncomfortable to want to stay on here, had started out as a game to Jordan. It didn't feel like a game any longer, as he saw her physical response to his deliberate seduction. As his erection literally throbbed, so full and hard that it actually hurt as he imagined stripping those figure-hugging jeans from her shapely bottom and thighs, sliding her panties down her long legs before releasing himself, pushing her back against one of the kitchen cabinets and sinking his fullness into her hot and welcoming warmth!

Jordan wanted to do those things so badly—wanted to hear Stephanie McKinley screaming in ecstasy rather than bloody murder—and he could feel the sweat dampening his forehead as he fought against giving in to that impulse.

This physical response to her—the second in an hour or so—had to be because Jordan had been too long without a woman in his bed. With that long red hair, impishly attractive face, and slender if curvaceous body, she wasn't in the *least* his type, damn it!

Jordan's gaze was deliberately mocking as he looked down into her overheated face. 'You just might have been amusing to have around, after all, Stephanie.'

She arched dark brows. 'Might have been?'

'Hmm.' He deliberately moved away from her to limp across the room and pick up his cane. 'Despite your pert little breasts and curvaceous bottom, I still want you out of here,' he bit out contemptuously.

Stephanie eyed him in frustration. Although she had to admit she was relieved Jordan was no longer standing quite so close to her. Or touching her. Or making her completely aware of the thick hardness of his arousal. A physical response that had been undoubtedly because of her!

She ran the dampness of her palms down denim-clad thighs. 'I'm still willing to cook you that steak if you're hungry?' she said huskily.

'That would just be feeding the wrong appetite, Stephanie,' he jibed back.

'Your brother is paying me to take care of your leg, not to go to bed with you!' she exclaimed.

He shrugged. 'That's a pity, when I've decided that right now I need a woman in my bed more than I need a physiotherapist.' Jordan knew he had never needed physical release more than he did at that moment!

'Don't you have a girlfriend you could call?' Stephanie asked curiously.

His face hardened. 'Not any more, no.'

Stephanie looked at him searchingly. Because his parents had divorced when he was a child, Jordan Simpson had never made any secret of his own aversion to the married state. But that hadn't prevented him from having a constant stream of women in his life. Beautiful women. Sophisticated women. Women as unlike Stephanie as it was possible for them to be. Which was the reason she knew that his interest in her wasn't genuine.

'Why not? There must be plenty you could call who would come running.'

He gave a humourless smile. 'Look at me, Stephanie,' he demanded. '*Really* look at me,' he pressed.

Stephanie had already looked. Several times! And, yes, he was obviously thinner, gaunter, grimmer than he had been six months ago, but as far as she was concerned none of that detracted from the fact that he was a compellingly handsome man.

'What am I looking for?'

Jordan gave an impatient snort. 'What was it you called me earlier? A cripple, wasn't it?'

She gasped at the bitterness in his tone. 'No, what I actually said was that *you* obviously believe yourself to be a cripple,' she corrected firmly.

'Maybe because that's what I am?' he said harshly. 'I certainly don't want any woman to be with me just because she feels sorry for me.'

'That's ridiculous—'

'This from the woman who just refused me?' he taunted.

Stephanie rolled her eyes. 'We both know you weren't being serious.'

'Do we?'

'Yes,' she snapped. 'You were just trying to make me leave.'

'Is it working?'

'No,' she told him firmly, determined to ignore the traitorous responses of her own body to this conversation; her breasts felt full and aching, and there was a burning warmth between her thighs...

Knowing that this man was deliberately playing with her in an effort to make her leave made absolutely no difference to the way Stephanie's body responded to him. 'How do you think Lucan will react if I have to call him and tell him I had to leave because you were sexually harassing me?' She looked at him challengingly.

Jordan gave a feral grin. 'He would probably be relieved to know that something has aroused my interest at last.'

Remembering how deeply concerned Lucan St Claire had been about Jordan the previous week, Stephanie thought that might be the case, too!

'*Aroused* being the operative word,' Jordan jeered, and had the pleasure of seeing the blush that re-entered those creamy cheeks.

Stephanie McKinley was really quite beautiful, he realised with a frown, her face impishly lovely, her body feminine and shapely. And his fingers actually itched to release that red-cinnamon-gold hair from its confining braid. He could imagine all that hair splayed out across her luscious nakedness as he feasted hungrily on the fullness of her breasts, before going lower...

He wasn't going to get any sleep tonight, either, if he continued to allow his imagination free rein. In fact a cold shower sounded as if it might be a good idea! 'I'll wish you goodnight, Stephanie.' He gave her another lazy grin before he turned and left the kitchen.

Heading straight for that cold shower.

CHAPTER THREE

'WHERE have you been?' Jordan demanded the following morning, as Stephanie unlocked the kitchen door and let herself back into the house accompanied by a gust of chilling wind, the plastic shopping bags she carried in her hands necessitating she gently nudge the door closed behind her with her foot.

The cold shower Jordan had taken the night before had briefly succeeded in dampening some of his arousal. Unfortunately that arousal had returned with a vengeance the moment he had heard Stephanie making her way up the stairs to use one of the bedrooms for the night.

Because Jordan could no longer negotiate the stairs, Lucan had had the dining room converted into a bedroom before Jordan had moved in, and he'd lain on the bed, staring up at the ceiling, aware of nothing but the throb of his own arousal and easily able to imagine Stephanie McKinley stripping off in the room above his. Jordan had got up to impatiently pull on his clothes before going back out to the kitchen. In the circumstances, the nearly full bottle of red wine on the table had seemed very appealing!

Which had turned out not to be such a good idea on an empty stomach. Consequently, Jordan was like a bear with a sore head this morning, his temples aching almost as much as another part of his anatomy had continued to do for most of the night.

He had already made a pot of strong coffee and brought it to the kitchen table, and had drunk half a cup of the rich and flavoursome brew before he'd become aware of the silence in the rest of the house. Unable to go up the stairs himself, to check on whether Stephanie had left or not, he had instead looked out of the kitchen window to see that her car had gone from the driveway. Leading Jordan to believe that she had taken his advice and left, after all.

Which, strangely, hadn't given him as much satisfaction as he had thought it would. Making him wonder if Lucan could be right when he said Jordan had been here on his own for too long. And now, if he actually felt pleased at the return of the physiotherapist his interfering big brother had hired without even consulting him, he knew he probably had!

'Where does it look like I've been?' Stephanie said sarcastically—a question that required no answer as she dumped the heavy bags of shopping on top of the wooden table before removing her jacket to reveal she wore a yellow fitted T-shirt today, with those low-slung faded blue jeans.

Another short T-shirt, that once again revealed a tantalising glimpse of her flat abdomen and clung to what Jordan was pretty sure were completely bare breasts above...

'Why don't you pour me some of that delicious-smelling coffee while I find the croissants I bought for our breakfast?' she suggested lightly, and she began to look through the bags, that thick braid of red-cinnamon-gold hair falling forward over her shoulder as she did so.

'Yes, ma'am,' he murmured dryly, and he leant back in the wooden chair to snag a clean mug from the side before sitting forward to lift the coffee pot and pour the hot and aromatic brew into both mugs.

'It was a request, not an order,' she sighed.

Jordan raised dark brows as he placed her mug down on the other side of the table, frowning his irritation as he realised he was actually enjoying having his verbal sparring partner back in the house. 'I telephoned Lucan last night,' he informed her coolly.

She continued to search through the bags for the croissants. 'I know.'

Jordan became very still as his gaze narrowed on her suspiciously. 'You *know*?'

'Yep.' Stephanie smiled her satisfaction as she found the box of freshly baked pastries and took it out of the bag, putting it on the table along with the butter and honey she had obviously bought to go with them. 'I telephoned and spoke to him before I went out shopping. He didn't seem too happy about the fact that you woke him up at two o'clock this morning to tell him how much you didn't appreciate him sending me here.'

She lifted the rest of the bags unconcernedly down onto the floor to be unpacked later, moving to take out the plates and knives they needed to eat the croissants before sitting down at the table in the chair opposite his.

Jordan's already frayed temper hadn't been improved the night before by his consumption of two-thirds of a bottle of red wine, and he hadn't even noticed what time it was when the idea to telephone Lucan and take his temper out on his brother had occurred to him. Lucan's growled responses to Jordan's complaints had left him in little doubt as to his big brother's displeasure at the call.

'Then maybe he should have thought of that before he sent you here without asking me!' he snarled.

Stephanie gave a dismissive shrug as she helped herself to one of the deliciously buttery croissants. 'He obviously completely underestimated just how rude and unreasonable you've become.'

Jordan's mouth twisted derisively. 'No doubt you took great pleasure in enlightening him.'

'I didn't need to after you had called him at such a ridiculous hour to complain.' Stephanie took a bite of the butter- and honey-covered croissant, almost groaning at the sensory pleasure she experienced. After being assailed with the delicious aroma of the croissants, first in the supermarket and then on the drive back to the gatehouse; they tasted just as wonderful as she had imagined they would. 'Try one of the croissants, Jordan,' she advised him. 'They might help to get rid of your hangover,' she added naughtily, before taking another delicious bite.

It had been obvious from the used wine glass and the completely empty bottle of red wine she had found left on the table this morning that Jordan must have returned to the kitchen some time during the night. From the look of the dark shadows under his eyes and the pallor in his cheeks the red wine had done little to dispel whatever pain had been keeping him awake.

Although he had at least brushed his hair and shaved this morning, his cleanly shaven jaw revealing its perfect squareness and the beguiling cleft in the centre. A beguilement that Stephanie resisted responding to by concentrating on the fact that he was also wearing a clean white T-shirt and faded jeans, hopefully meaning he wasn't completely bereft of the social niceties, after all. Although she wouldn't like to bet on it!

Stephanie hadn't slept that well herself the night before, aware as she had been of Jordan's presence somewhere in the house, and discovering this morning that there was nothing she could eat for her breakfast— not even bread for toast!—hadn't improved her mood.

A quick telephone call to Lucan St Claire, to confirm that she had arrived safely and so far hadn't been bodily thrown out into the Gloucestershire countryside, had resulted in his informing her that Jordan had already telephoned him during the night with the same news. Although in Jordan's case it had obviously been in the nature of a complaint. A complaint that the older St Claire brother didn't appear in the least concerned about. In fact, his comment had been the one Jordan had predicted—that any response from Jordan was better than the uninterest he normally showed to everything and everyone nowadays.

Stephanie waited until Jordan had taken one of the croissants onto his plate, smothered it in butter and taken a bite before speaking again. 'I decided to refrain from telling your brother that you had decided on sexual innuendo as the best way of getting rid of me.'

Jordan continued to slowly chew the first mouthful of food he'd had for a couple of days, swallowing the buttery pastry before answering her. 'Only because you knew Lucan wouldn't be interested.'

She shrugged. 'Or maybe I'm just saving that complaint for another day.'

Jordan decided there was a lot more to Stephanie McKinley than that unusually coloured hair and a taut and supple body. It surprised him how curious he was to know exactly what that lot more was.

He leant back in his chair. 'I should have asked last night whether or not there's a Mr McKinley waiting for you at home.'

She glanced down at her bare left hand. 'No ring.'

'Not all the married women I know wear a wedding ring,' Jordan drawled.

'That's probably because the married women *you* meet don't want you to know that they're married,' Stephanie pointed out.

Jordan's eyes narrowed. 'I don't get involved with married women.'

'No?'

His mouth firmed. 'No.'

'Because of your parents' divorce?'

Jordan drew in a sharp breath. 'And what do *you* know about my parents' divorce?'

She shrugged as she stood up to place her empty plate neatly inside the dishwasher. 'Only that during interviews you use it as an excuse for never having considered marriage yourself.'

'It happens to be a fact, not an excuse.' He pushed his empty plate away to stand up abruptly.

Stephanie knew she had annoyed Jordan intensely with her mention of his parents' divorce. Not quite the reaction she'd wanted from him, but it was probably better than no reaction at all!

She gave a knowing smile. 'I can't imagine any woman ever daring to be unfaithful to the famous Jordan Simpson.'

His eyes glittered a bright, intense gold. 'My father was unfaithful, not my mother.'

Reason enough, Stephanie decided, for Jordan

never to know that she was being named—albeit completely falsely—as the 'other woman' in an ex-patient's divorce!

He thrust a hand through his hair. 'I'll be in my study for the rest of the morning.'

'Doing what?' She moved so that she was standing in front of the door that led out into the hallway.

He frowned at her. 'None of your damned business!'

'Maybe I could help?'

'And maybe you could stay the hell out of my face!' He glared down at her.

Maybe getting in his face hadn't been such a good idea, Stephanie recognised uncomfortably, as she became aware of the heat of Jordan's body and the glittering intensity of those mesmerising gold-coloured eyes. 'When I spoke to Lucan this morning, he mentioned that there's a heated indoor pool at Mulberry Hall...'

Jordan raised a brow. 'And?'

'And a swim might be fun.'

Those gold eyes hardened. 'Am I right in thinking it might also be regarded as good exercise to strengthen the muscles in my leg?'

Stephanie felt the guilty heat of colour in her cheeks and her expression became defensive. 'What's wrong with that?'

He shrugged those wide and powerful shoulders. 'Absolutely nothing.' His mouth thinned. '*If* I wanted to exercise the muscles in my leg. Which I *don't*,' he added emphatically.

She sighed. 'Why don't you?'

A nerve pulsed in his tightly clenched jaw. 'Get out of my way, Stephanie.'

She gave a firm shake of her head, her chin raised.

She refused to move. 'Not until you explain to me why you don't even seem to want to *try* to get back the full mobility of your leg.'

A red haze seemed to pass in front of Jordan's eyes as this woman's persistent questions managed to pierce his armour once again. 'Don't be so stupid!'

'So you *do* want to get back the use of your leg?'

'What I want and what I've got are two different things,' he said pointedly.

Stephanie put a hand on his arm. 'Then prove me wrong and come swimming with me this morning.'

'Now who's playing games?'

'Come on, Jordan, it will be fun,' she cajoled.

'Don't force me into making you move, Stephanie,' he bit out between gritted teeth.

'Could you do that?' Her chin rose another determined notch. 'Do you really think you're physically capable at the moment of making me—or anyone else— do anything?'

Jordan's fingers tightened about his cane as the taunt struck him with the force of a blow. 'You vicious little—!'

She gave an unconcerned shrug. 'No one said you had to like me in order for me to help you.'

'I don't remember asking for your help,' he ground out as his eyes glittered down at her in warning.

'Whether you ask for it or not, you certainly need it.'

Jordan breathed deeply as he continued to glare down at Stephanie McKinley's five feet six inches of slender shapeliness. And stubbornness. Let's not forget the bone-deep stubbornness so evident in her determined expression, Jordan told himself.

He deliberately, slowly, allowed his gaze to move lower, to where her breasts pressed against her T-shirt.

Having him staring so intently at her breasts wasn't exactly conducive to her feeling as if she were in control of this situation, Stephanie acknowledged. And she had decided during her own virtually sleepless night that being in control was going to be necessary from now on, if she was going to get anywhere in bringing about this man's recuperation.

Especially as that gaze alone was enough to cause her nipples to harden noticeably beneath the soft material of her T-shirt, so that they now stood out like ripe berries begging to be eaten!

Stephanie could never remember feeling this sexual tension with any of the men she had dated. Or the flare of electricity that seemed to spark between herself and Jordan whenever they were in a room together. Or the need to halt the impulse she felt to wrap her arms protectively over those betraying breasts!

She determinedly continued to resist that impulse as she kept her gaze fixed steadily on Jordan's arrogantly handsome face. Instead, she drew in an irritated breath. 'I'm here on a professional basis, Mr Simpson—or Mr St Claire—whatever I'm to call you—not to provide you with amusement!'

Jordan wasn't as sure of that as Stephanie appeared to be. For days, weeks after the accident, there had been dozens of visitors to the hospital where he had been taken for treatment—many of them women he had been involved with in the past or who would have liked to have become involved with him in the future. Not a single one of them had succeeded in arousing the heated response in him that Stephanie McKinley had almost from the moment he'd first looked at her. Nor given him the perverse enjoyment he felt during their verbal exchanges...

Admittedly, he had been in even more pain immediately after the accident than he was now, and so hardly in the mood for physical arousal. But he was still in a lot of pain, and he only had to look at Stephanie to know he wanted to strip her bare and lie her down on the nearest bed, before kissing and caressing every freckled inch of her.

He focused his gaze on the fullness of her provocatively pouting mouth. Lips that Jordan could all too easily imagine taking him to the heights of pleasure...

'Parts of your body don't seem to be in agreement with that statement,' he taunted, with a knowing glance at her full and obviously aroused breasts.

Stephanie's cheeks burned uncomfortably as she felt an increase in the sexual tension that had flared so suddenly between the two of them. 'It's cold in here,' she excused lamely.

Jordan chuckled softly. 'Strange...it feels the opposite to me.'

To Stephanie too. The sexual heat between them was enough to make her cheeks flush even hotter. 'I won't delay you any longer,' she muttered as she finally stepped aside to allow Jordan to leave. Willing him to leave so that she could try to calm her overheated body.

Jordan leant on his cane and walked slowly over to the door. 'Let me know if you decide to leave, after all.'

'Why, do you intend to come and wave me off?' she shot back dryly.

'No, I'd just like to have the key to the door returned before you leave,' came his parting shot, and he gave her one last challenging glance before leaving the kitchen.

Stephanie sank back down into the kitchen chair once she was alone, and poured herself another cup of the deliciously strong but now cooling coffee Jordan had made earlier.

What *was* it about the male patients she had worked with recently? She was pretty sure she hadn't suddenly turned into some sort of sex siren or temptress, so it had to be that her job brought her into such close proximity to those patients that it made her an easy target.

Whatever the reason, Stephanie knew she was going to have much more trouble resisting Jordan's advances than she ever had the lecherous and totally obnoxious Richard Newman's!

CHAPTER FOUR

'WHAT do you want now?' Jordan asked impatiently as he looked across the desk to where Stephanie loitered in the open doorway of the study where he had been working for the last hour.

She was completely undeterred by his obvious lack of enthusiasm. 'I was thinking of going for a walk, and wondered if you would care to join me?'

Jordan's eyes narrowed as he sat back in the leather chair behind the desk. 'I'm not sure if you're being deliberately insensitive again, or just a pain.'

'Neither.' Stephanie smiled.

She had tidied and cleaned the kitchen after breakfast, dusted and vacuumed the sitting room—which didn't look as if anyone had sat in there for some time— and made some fresh chicken soup for lunch and left it simmering on top of the Aga. On the basis that seeing that Jordan had a healthy and varied diet was part of her job of restoring him back to full health.

With nothing else left to do, Stephanie was becoming a little bored with her own company. 'We don't have to go far, Jordan,' she added cajolingly. 'You could just take me up to Mulberry Hall and show me around if you don't feel like going any further than that.'

Jordan eyed her suspiciously. 'Does this I'm-a-little-girl-in-need-of-company routine usually work?'

'I'm not in need of company, and it isn't a routine,' she denied. 'I just thought some fresh air might be nice.'

'And exercise,' he drawled derisively. 'Let's not forget the exercise!'

'God, you're a grump.' Stephanie sighed with frustration as she turned away.

'Hey, I don't remember saying I wouldn't go with you.'

Stephanie turned back slowly. 'Does that mean you will?'

'Why not?' Jordan said, and he picked up his cane and stood up. He doubted he would be able to get any more work done on the film script this morning now anyway, knowing that Stephanie was wandering about the estate. 'Although showing you round Mulberry Hall might prove a little difficult when I can't get up stairs,' he added with a scowl.

'You can always wait downstairs while I go and take a look upstairs,' she reasoned practically.

'You might have a sudden urge to try one of the four-poster beds!' Jordan teased.

'Oh, give it a break, Jordan,' the little redhead growled.

He shrugged. 'I can't see any point in you staying on here if I can't make life uncomfortable for you.'

Neither could Stephanie at the moment, but she lived in hope that she might eventually be able to change Jordan's mind about accepting her professional help. In the meantime, getting him to take a walk with her was better than nothing.

'I'll just go upstairs and get my thicker jacket. It's quite cold outside for October.'

'If that was your subtle way of telling me that I need to wrap up warm too, then I strongly advise you not to treat me like a child,' Jordan told her.

'I wasn't treating you like a—' She stopped, frowning as she realised that was exactly what she had been doing. In an effort, perhaps, to try and keep their relationship on a professional footing rather than the flirtatious one Jordan kept reducing it to with his questionable remarks. 'I—' She broke off again as the telephone began to ring.

Well…one of them. There was an extension for the landline on the desktop, as well as two mobiles—one black and one silver. Stephanie could understand the landline, but who needed two mobiles, for goodness' sake?

Jordan picked up the black mobile, checking the caller ID before taking the call. 'Hi, Crista,' he said, and he turned his back on Stephanie to look out of the window.

Stephanie stared at the broad expanse of that muscled back, at the way the white T-shirt stretched tautly over his shoulders, and debated whether she should go or stay. The call was obviously private. From Crista Moore, the woman Jordan had been reportedly involved with before his accident.

'Stay!' Jordan barked as he turned and saw that Stephanie was about to leave.

'Woof, woof!' She wrinkled her nose at him before going ahead and leaving anyway.

Jordan found himself smiling as he watched the sway of those curvaceous hips and taut bottom as Stephanie walked down the hallway. She really was the most—

'No, I wasn't talking to you, Crista,' he said lightly into the receiver as the caller queried his last comment. 'Oh, just a—an associate of my brother's,' he said evasively, easily able to imagine the tall, slender blonde actress as she sat in her apartment in LA.

Of all the people Jordan had known before the accident, Crista was definitely the most persistent—calling him at least once a week to see how he was and when he would be coming back to LA. As Jordan had no intention of ever resuming their relationship, any more than he had immediate plans to return to LA, he usually kept those telephone calls short.

Even so, Stephanie was sitting at the kitchen table impatiently waiting for him by the time Jordan had ended the call and collected his coat. 'Hmm, something smells good.' He sniffed appreciatively at the saucepan he could see simmering on top of the Aga.

'Soup for lunch,' she supplied economically as she stood up to pull on a heavy black jacket. 'No, I *don't* see that as acting the housekeeper,' she defended irritably as Jordan raised mocking brows. 'For your body to be healthy you need to eat healthily, that's all.'

He smiled. 'So you're saying you only made lunch because you consider feeding me a part of my treatment?'

Those green eyes narrowed. 'Exactly.'

'If you say so.'

'Jordan—'

'Stephanie?'

She wasn't fooled for a moment by Jordan's too-innocent expression, knowing he was just trying to irritate her again. And obviously succeeding! 'Why do you need two mobile phones?' she asked, as she pulled on a pair of black gloves to keep her hands warm.

A slight frown appeared between those amber-gold eyes. 'What?'

She shrugged. 'I noticed earlier that there were two mobiles on the desk in the study, and I was just curious as to why you would need two when most people manage fine with just one?'

'Maybe because I'm two people?' Jordan finally replied, deciding that Stephanie McKinley was far too observant for his comfort sometimes.

She arched auburn brows. 'Because you're both Jordan Simpson and Jordan St Claire?'

'Yes.'

'Why did you change your name when you became an actor? Jordan St Claire is quite a charismatic name—'

'Are we going for this walk or not?' Jordan's mouth thinned as he stepped forward and pointedly opened the back door for her.

'We are.' Stephanie nodded as she stepped outside. 'So you actually consider Jordan Simpson and Jordan St Claire to be two distinctly different people?' she persisted as he locked the door behind them before joining her on the path.

Jordan didn't *consider* them to be anything—they *were* two distinctly different people! As different as night and day. And non-interchangeable. 'Could we just get this walk over with, do you think?' he barked, before striding off in the direction of Mulberry Hall.

'Of course.' Stephanie deliberately measured her strides so that they were in step with his much slower ones. 'You never considered working in the St Claire Corporation?' she prompted curiously.

It was a curiosity that was probably understandable in the circumstances. Except Jordan wasn't presently known for his understanding! 'Have you ever heard of maintaining a companionable silence when out walking?'

Of course Stephanie had heard of it; it just wasn't something that was ever likely to happen between herself and Jordan! An awkward silence, perhaps. An uncomfortable silence, even. A totally physically aware one, certainly. At least on her part... The scowl on Jordan's arrogantly handsome face as he stomped along beside her didn't give the impression that he was in the least aware of her, or anyone else for that matter.

'Wow!'

Jordan leant tiredly against one of the four marble pillars in the magnificent hallway of Mulberry Hall as Stephanie gazed up in awe at the huge Venetian glass chandelier hanging down from the frescoed ceiling high above them. Jordan's leg was aching too much from the half-mile or so walk over here for him to share her enthusiasm. Besides, he had seen the inside of Mulberry Hall dozens of times before.

'This is... I mean, *wow*!'

'I get that you're in awe,' Jordan drawled dryly as he watched her wandering around the cavernous hallway, admiring the beautiful marble floor and statuary.

'And you aren't?' Her eyes were wide with accusation.

'Not particularly, no,' Jordan muttered as he pushed himself away from the pillar to lean heavily on his cane and walk towards the main salon at the front of the house.

Stephanie trailed slowly along behind him, her eyes bright with pleasure as she came to stand on the threshold of the room, looking at the beautiful gold and cream decor and delicate Regency furniture. 'Has Lucan never thought of opening this up to the public?'

'Definitely not.' Jordan almost laughed at the thought of the expression of disgust that would appear on his eldest brother's face if anyone dared to suggest he should open the doors of Mulberry Hall to all and sundry. 'I don't recommend that you suggest it to him, either— unless you want to feel the icy blast of his complete disapproval.'

'But it seems such a waste.' Stephanie frowned. 'The building itself must be very old.'

'Early Elizabethan, I believe.'

Stephanie crossed the room to lightly touch the beautiful ornate gold frame about the huge mirror above the white fireplace. 'Did Lucan buy it completely furnished like this?' There were ornaments and lamps on the surfaces of the many side tables, and a large dresser along one wall, as well as a beautiful Ormolu clock on top of the fireplace.

Jordan gave an uninterested shrug. 'As far as I'm aware some of this furniture has been here for a couple of hundred years at least.'

'I wonder what happened to the family that lived here?' Stephanie murmured. 'It must have been someone titled, don't you think?'

Jordan nodded. 'The Dukes of Stourbridge.'

Stephanie sighed. 'It's such a pity that so many of the old titles have either become extinct or fallen into disuse.'

'Yes, a pity,' Jordan drawled dryly.

'Do you suppose Lucan intends to live here once he's married? It was just a thought,' she defended as Jordan gave a shout of laughter. 'You say that he doesn't intend opening it to the public, but he must intend doing something with it, surely?'

'Sorry, I was just trying to imagine Lucan married,' Jordan gasped, his shoulders still shaking slightly. 'No, I just can't see it, I'm afraid.'

Stephanie couldn't imagine the cold and self-contained man she had met the previous week madly in love and married, either. 'I wonder why he bothered to buy it, then?'

'I never try to second-guess Lucan, and I'd advise you not to bother trying, either,' Jordan suggested as he turned away. 'Do you want to see the pool at the back of the house now?' he offered, when he saw Stephanie hadn't moved from in front of the fireplace.

'Philistine,' she accused him good-naturedly as she followed him back out into the incredible marble hallway.

Stephanie had visited several country estates in the past that had been open to the public, but never an empty one that looked quite so much as if someone still lived there. There were paintings on all the walls, ornaments and antique mirrors everywhere, and there was even a silver tray on the stand in the hallway that looked as if it were waiting for visiting cards to be placed upon it. In fact the whole house had the look of expecting the master of the house—the Duke of Stourbridge—to walk through the front doorway at any moment.

'Lucan has a caretaker for the grounds, and his wife keeps the inside of the house free of dust,' Jordan explained when Stephanie said as much to him.

'Even so, it seems a shame that no one actually lives here...' Stephanie looked about her wistfully.

'It's really not the sort of place you could ever call

home, now, is it?' Jordan scorned. 'That you would ever really *want* to call home,' he added.

Stephanie stood at the bottom of the wide and sweeping staircase that led up the gallery above, wondering how many beautiful women had stood poised at the top of that staircase, in gowns from the Elizabethan period to now, to be admired by the men they loved as they floated down those stairs and into their waiting arms. Dozens of them, probably. And now Mulberry Hall stood empty, apart from the caretaker and his wife who obviously lived somewhere else on the estate, when it should have been full of love and the laughter of children.

'I suppose not,' she agreed slowly, before following him.

Jordan had nothing more to add to that particular conversation. Had no intention of telling the already over-curious Stephanie McKinley that Lucan hadn't bought Mulberry Hall at all, that he was in fact the current and fifteenth Duke of Stourbridge. Which consequently made *him* Lord Jordan St Claire and his twin brother Lord Gideon St Claire—a little known fact that his using the professional name of Simpson had helped keep from the public in general.

The three brothers had spent their early childhood growing up at Mulberry Hall. Until their Scottish mother had discovered that their father, the fourteenth Duke of Stourbridge, had been keeping a mistress in the village. After the separation Molly had decided to move back to her native Edinburgh, and had taken her three sons with her.

Obviously the three boys had come back to Mulberry Hall on visits to their father, but they had all much preferred the rambling untidiness of their home in

Edinburgh to the stiff formality of life at Mulberry Hall. Besides which, none of the three brothers had ever really forgiven their father for his unfaithfulness to their gentle and beautiful mother.

As a consequence, when the three boys had reached an age where they could choose to visit or not, they had all chosen not to come anywhere near Mulberry Hall or their father again. That aversion to the place hadn't changed in the least when their father had died eight years ago and Lucan had inherited the title.

They had all had their own lives by then. Lucan in the cut-throat world of business, Jordan in acting and Gideon in law. None of them had needed or wanted the restrictions of life at Mulberry Hall. Although it had so far proved an invaluable bolt-hole for Jordan after he had felt the need to leave the States in an effort to elude the press that still hounded his every move months after the accident…

'You wouldn't even realise this was here from the front of the house.' Stephanie stood at the edge of the full-length pool to look admiringly at the surrounding statuary and greenery that made up the low and heated pool room built onto the back of Mulberry Hall.

'I think that was the idea.' Jordan made no effort to hide his sarcasm.

She shot him an impatient glance as she slipped off her jacket in the heat of the room. 'It's really warm in here, and the water looks very inviting; are you sure you won't change your mind about going for a swim?'

He quirked a wicked brow at her. 'I might consider it if you intend skinny-dipping.'

'Stop changing the subject, Jordan.' Stephanie rounded on him. 'You have the ideal facility here for gently exercising your leg, and yet you refuse to use it.'

'Because I don't want to exercise my leg—gently or otherwise,' Jordan stated firmly.

'Why not?'

'And you accuse *me* of being stubborn!' His eyes glittered deeply gold.

'That's because you are!'

'And you really think that your constant nagging on the subject is going to make me change my mind?' Jordan said.

Stephanie gasped. 'I do not nag!'

'Yes. You. Do.' The two of them were now standing almost nose to nose as Jordan glared down at Stephanie and she raised her chin in challenge. 'Oh, to hell with this!' He threw his cane down onto one of the loungers that surrounded the pool, then pulled Stephanie hard against his body before bending his head and savagely claiming her mouth with his.

The forceful kiss was so unexpected that she didn't even have time to resist its sensual pull as her lips parted beneath Jordan's, her coat slipping from her fingers as she moved her hands up to clasp those wide and muscled shoulders in an effort to keep her balance.

Her back arched instinctively, pushing her breasts against the hard wall of his chest, the proximity instantly making her aware of how swollen her nipples were, how they ached for the touch of those same hands that now moved so restlessly down the slenderness of her spine.

Suddenly she realised exactly how inappropriate allowing Jordan to kiss her actually was. Of how easily her behaviour could be misconstrued if he were ever to learn of Rosalind Newman's outrageous accusations.

It was as if a bucket of icy cold water had been thrown over her. She broke the kiss to move back abruptly, her

eyes widening in alarm as she realised that even that
slight movement had unbalanced Jordan—and his hands
took a tight grip of her arms as he began to fall back
towards the pool!

CHAPTER FIVE

'DID you intend that to happen?' Jordan accused as he surfaced and pushed back the wet dark hair that had fallen over his eyes.

His anger was all the stronger for the realisation that he couldn't even do a simple thing like kiss a woman without making a complete fool of himself. Without demonstrating just how incapacitated he was!

Stephanie had been on the verge of laughing at their predicament as she surfaced beside him, but one look at Jordan's grimly annoyed face was enough to kill that laughter dead as she trod water beside him to stay afloat.

Then she recalled exactly what they had been doing before they fell into the water...

Dear God!

How could she have let that happen? *Why* had she let that happen? It made her position here untenable. Almost impossible. She—

'What do you mean, did *I* intend that to happen?' She frowned darkly as Jordan's accusation finally sank into her shocked brain. 'Do you think that I—that we—that I deliberately let you kiss me with the intention of—?'

'Pushing me in?' Jordan finished savagely as he began to swim effortlessly to the side of the pool. 'Yes,

Stephanie, that's exactly what I think,' he said, as he used the strength of his arms to lever himself up and out onto the side of the pool.

Stephanie swam after him. 'You can't seriously believe that, Jordan?'

'Oh, yeah, Stephanie, I can.'

'But—'

'You wanted me in the pool, and that's exactly where I ended up.' Jordan was breathing hard from the exertion, leaving a trail of water behind him as he limped over to the cupboard where the towels were kept, taking one out to rub the excess water from his dripping wet hair. 'If nothing else, I have to give you full marks for professional dedication.' He threw the damp towel down disgustedly onto a lounger. 'In fact I'll be sure to mention to Lucan exactly how dedicated you are when I call him later and tell him I've kicked your shapely little bottom off the estate.'

Stephanie stood on the side of the pool too now, as angry as Jordan. He *really* believed that in the midst of being kissed by him she'd had the presence of mind to deliberately overbalance him as a way of forcing him into the swimming pool? She didn't have that sort of control—in fact much longer in Jordan's arms, being kissed by him, and she would have been completely *out* of control!

'Now, just a minute—'

'I believe I've already wasted enough of my time on you for one day.' Jordan glowered at her from between narrowed lids before his expression turned to a scowl of dark and savage disgust and he looked down to pull the cold dampness of his T-shirt away from his chest.

Stephanie couldn't take her gaze away from the muscled perfection of that chest, which was clearly visible through the wet T-shirt. She could feel her face burning with the memory of how much she had wanted to touch that muscled chest a few minutes ago. Of how much she had wanted to touch and caress all of him.

She turned away to take a towel from the cupboard and dry herself off as a way of hiding the burning in her cheeks, her mind racing with the enormity of what had just happened. World-famous actor Jordan Simpson had just kissed *her*, Stephanie McKinley.

Before accusing her of deliberately encouraging him so that she could push him into the pool! She certainly *hadn't* done it deliberately, but had she encouraged him to kiss her? Stephanie didn't think that she had...although she doubted that Rosalind Newman, for one, would believe that! This was terrible. She was fed up with being portrayed as some kind of scarlet woman. This would surely be the complete end of Stephanie's professional career if Jordan went ahead and voiced his accusations about her to the cold and arrogant Lucan St Claire.

Stephanie felt ill. Nauseous. Could literally feel the heat leaving her cheeks. She stumbled over to one of the loungers to collapse onto it as her knees gave way beneath her.

She might be able to fight one accusation of indulging in sexual indiscretion with a patient—but no one was going to believe two such accusations. Even if Stephanie managed to prove her innocence, some of the mud was sure to stick. Her professional reputation would be in tatters—

'What's wrong, Stephanie?' Jordan had moved so that he now towered over her.

She blinked back the tears that were threatening to fall before looking up at him. God, they both looked

such a mess: hair wet and tangled, their clothes clinging to them damply. Although maybe she should feel
grateful they were still wearing any clothes at all after
the way she had responded to Jordan's kiss!

She shook her head as she murmured heavily, 'That
should never have happened...'

No, it shouldn't, Jordan accepted, disgusted with
himself. He had meant to stay as far away from this
woman as possible, and hope that his non-cooperation
would eventually persuade her into leaving. Kissing her
as if he wanted to eat every delectable part of her could
hardly be called non-cooperation on his part!

Although Stephanie's guilt over a kiss was a little
over the top, wasn't it?

Jordan frowned as he stared down into green eyes
awash with unshed tears. As he remembered how
Stephanie's responses had been so sweet, so addictive...
So much so that Jordan was still aroused, that hardness
clearly visible against the clinging denim material of
his jeans.

Obviously the unexpected swim had been no more
effective in dampening his desire for this woman than
the cold shower had the night before.

Hell!

She blinked back those tears. 'I really didn't deliberately push you into the pool, Jordan.'

Jordan already knew that—just as he knew it was
himself he was angry with and not Stephanie. 'I think
it's better if we both forget the whole incident, don't
you?' he suggested huskily.

'Yes,' she breathed raggedly.

He thrust a hand through his wet hair. 'I suggest we
both go back to the gatehouse now, and get out of these
wet clothes before taking a shower.'

'Before I leave?'

'I think that would be the best thing for both of us,' he confirmed heavily.

'Just as well I didn't unpack completely last night, isn't it?' Stephanie muttered dully as she stood up, giving Jordan a clear view of how the yellow T-shirt clung to the fullness of her bare breasts, clearly out-lining the hard, berry-pink nipples he hadn't quite got around to touching earlier.

He glanced away, but not quickly enough to stop his own arousal from throbbing anew. 'Are you coming back to the house or not?' he bit out, with a return of his impatience.

'I'm coming.' Stephanie picked up her jacket and slowly followed him outside.

She continued to inwardly bombard herself with self-recriminations as they walked back to the gatehouse in complete and uncomfortable silence. No matter how many times she went over the incident in her mind—whether she'd encouraged him or not—Stephanie knew that she shouldn't have allowed that kiss with Jordan to happen. It didn't really matter that she hadn't planned it. Or that it still made her go hot all over just thinking about it!

The heat had completely dissipated by the time they had walked the half-mile or so back to the gatehouse, with the cold wind blowing through her wet clothing, and Stephanie's teeth were literally chattering. Her face felt blue with the cold by the time Jordan unlocked the back door and allowed her to precede him into the warm and delicious-smelling kitchen.

'You need to go upstairs and take a shower and put on some dry clothes,' Jordan said again, as he saw how cold Stephanie was.

'I—yes. Fine.' She turned away to hang her coat on the back of one of the chairs. 'You should do the same.'

'I know what I need to do, Stephanie,' Jordan scowled. 'When you come back we'll sit down and eat the soup you've made.'

She turned, her eyes wide. 'But I thought you wanted me to leave.'

His mouth firmed. 'Not before you've eaten something warm. I would hate for you to get back to London only to be admitted to hospital suffering from pneumonia,' he explained as she frowned.

Stephanie looked at him searchingly before nodding slowly. 'Some hot soup would be nice.'

'Fine,' he said tersely. 'Well?' he added a second later, as she made no effort to leave.

She swallowed hard. 'I—I just want you to know that I really didn't do anything deliberate to make us both fall into the swimming pool,' she told him, one last time before leaving to go up the stairs.

Jordan drew in a deep breath once he was alone, his hands clenched at his sides, his expression bleak, knowing that his accident had obviously robbed him of his sense of humour as well as the mobility in his right leg. At any other time he would have found it funny that the two of them had fallen into the swimming pool.

Stephanie was the first woman he had even attempted to make love to since his accident six months ago. *Attempted* being an accurate description of the fiasco it had turned into!

Stephanie's sensuously lush mouth had been so delicious to kiss. Her body so responsive as it had moulded against his own. Jordan had been totally aroused as he'd kissed her—so aroused, in fact, that he had forgotten everything else. Including the weakness of his right hip and leg...

Jordan knew without a doubt that Stephanie wasn't the one responsible for making the two of them lose their balance and fall into the pool. He was only too aware of why it had happened, and exactly why he had been so angry afterwards. He had unthinkingly put his weight onto his right hip, and it had just collapsed beneath him and toppled them both into the water.

It all went to prove that he couldn't even kiss a woman any more without the embarrassment and utter humiliation of having his leg give way. It was more than a man could stand!

'I've decided I'm not leaving, after all,' Stephanie announced when she returned down the stairs half an hour later. She stood her ground determinedly in the kitchen doorway as Jordan turned to frown at her from where he stood in front of the Aga, stirring the soup.

He had obviously taken advantage of her absence to shower and change into dry jeans and a thin black cashmere sweater. The overlong darkness of his hair looked almost dry too, although there was a grim set to his mouth to add to his icy expression—an expression that Stephanie refused to be cowed by as much as she refused to leave.

She had run herself a bath rather than taking the suggested shower, deciding she needed to immerse herself fully in hot water in order to soak the chill from her bones. She'd had time to think once she had sunk her shoulders beneath the hot and scented bubble bath.

Okay, so she accepted that she shouldn't have let Jordan kiss her. Nor should she have responded to that kiss. She also accepted that those things made continuing to stay on here awkward, to say the least. But awkward in a personal way, not a professional one.

She had no intention of allowing Lucan to actually pay her a wage until Jordan let her work with him professionally. Which meant that technically Jordan wasn't her patient yet. He wouldn't become so until Stephanie actually did something professional for or to him. Her constant arguments with him about his need for treatment really didn't count. Neither did making him a nourishing soup for lunch.

If Stephanie left now then she would be admitting professional defeat. She was guilty of nothing of a personal nature except finding the 'magnetically handsome' Jordan Simpson magnetically handsome! Something that any woman with an ounce of red blood in her veins would have to admit to, surely?

She would be admitting that professionally she was as incapable of getting anywhere with the stubbornly determined actor as all the other physiotherapists who had tried to work with him these last six months. That sort of defeat had never been an option as far as Stephanie was concerned. She wouldn't accept it now with Jordan, either.

She entered the kitchen fully. 'I said—'

'I heard what you said,' Jordan drawled as he considered her through lowered lids. 'I'm just surprised that you still think it's your decision to make.'

'Actually, it's your brother's,' she acknowledged lightly. 'Once I start working for him. Which I'm not doing at the moment,' she added sweetly.

Those gold-coloured eyes glittered icily. 'And you don't believe that attempting to drown his brother is reason enough for Lucan to want to dispense with your services altogether?'

'Attempting to drown—?' Stephanie gave a disbelieving shake of her head, her gaze incredulous. 'Don't you think that's a slight exaggeration?'

'Perhaps. Except you couldn't have known whether or not I could actually swim when you pushed me into the water.' He arched challenging brows.

'I did *not* push you in.'

'Prove it.'

Her cheeks were flushed with temper. 'I can no more prove that than you can prove otherwise!'

Jordan shrugged. 'All of that aside, you must know as well as I do that the two of us staying here together is even less feasible now than it was before.'

'I'm not leaving,' she repeated stubbornly.

Impasse, Jordan acknowledged in sheer frustration. Stephanie was refusing to leave, and this morning had certainly proved that he sure as hell couldn't make her! At least, not physically...

Jordan deliberately crossed the kitchen so that he stood only inches away from her. Close enough to feel the heat of her body in the close-fitting green jumper and blue jeans she had changed into. 'If you stay on here then I guarantee that what happened between us this morning will happen again,' he warned her huskily.

Those green eyes widened in alarm even as her cheeks warmed with colour. Evidence that she wasn't as self-possessed about what had happened earlier as she wished to appear, he thought smugly.

She shook her head. 'Not if I don't want it to.'

'But you *do* want it to, Stephanie.' Jordan held her gaze with his as he curved his hand about one of those over-heated cheeks. He saw with satisfaction the way the blood pulsed at her temples. His gaze moved down and he watched the way she moistened her lips nervously. He glanced even lower and saw the unmistakable signs of her nipples pressing against the soft wool of her sweater. 'Don't you?' he murmured knowingly.

There was a look of panic in her eyes now. 'No, I—'

'Yes, Stephanie,' Jordan insisted gently as he ran the pad of his thumb lightly across the soft pout of her lips and felt the way they quivered beneath his caress. 'Your response to my touch clearly says yes.'

She swallowed hard. 'You're still trying to force me into leaving.'

'Is it working?' Jordan taunted. He knew damn well that it was; he wasn't so out of practice that he didn't know when a woman was responding to him! 'I won't stop at kissing next time, Stephanie,' he warned her. 'Next time I'll kiss and touch you until you're so aching and wet for me that you'll be begging me to make love to you!'

He spoke so forcefully, so graphically, that Stephanie had no trouble whatsoever in imagining them naked in bed together, skin moving on skin, their breathing ragged and their bodies entangled as they caressed and kissed each other to completion.

Just thinking of the possibility of it made Stephanie aroused all over again.

She had made her decision to stay on here when she was upstairs, well away from Jordan's physically disturbing presence. Calmly. Coolly. But they weren't emotions Stephanie could maintain when she was actually in his presence.

She raised her chin stubbornly to meet the mockery of his gaze head-on. 'Just because the tabloids often scream out headlines about the "eligible and sexy Jordan Simpson" as he escorts his latest airhead somewhere, it doesn't mean that every woman you meet is going to fall down adoringly at your feet. Or any other part of your anatomy, for that matter,' she added scathingly.

He gave a hard smile. 'No?'

'No!' Stephanie snapped as she heard the deliberate challenge in his tone.

'Flattered as I am that you've bothered to read those tabloids—'

'I didn't say I had read them, only that I'd seen the headlines,' she defended hotly.

He gave her a knowing look. 'If you say so.'

'I do!'

Jordan shrugged. 'I'm not answerable for what the tabloids choose to print about me, Stephanie. Or to the women I've dated in the past.'

'Don't you mean currently?' Stephanie accused. 'That *was* Crista Moore who telephoned you this morning, wasn't it?'

The name Crista really was too unusual for Jordan's earlier caller to have been anyone else. Which meant he was probably still involved with the beautiful actress...

Which made letting him kiss her even more stupid on Stephanie's part!

'What if it was?' he said.

Her eyes narrowed. 'Maybe you should just stick to one airhead at a time!'

'I wouldn't put you in the airhead category, Stephanie,' he teased.

'*We* aren't dating!'

'We aren't anything yet,' Jordan accepted dryly. 'But if you insist on staying on here we're most definitely going to be something.'

Stephanie's cheeks blushed hotly. 'You can't possibly know that.'

'Would you like me to show you?'

'You arrogant, overbearing, self—'

'Sticks and stones, Stephanie...'

'No, it's the truth,' she maintained forcefully. 'You may have—may have caught me slightly off-guard this morning when you kissed me, but it won't happen again.'

'No?' He moved closer to her.

Stephanie stood her ground. 'No!'

His eyes gleamed with amusement. 'You seem slightly—flustered...'

'I'm getting rather annoyed, actually,' she flared back at him.

Jordan narrowed shrewd eyes. 'Just not annoyed enough to leave?'

'No!'

'Fine.' His mouth firmed as he finally stepped away from her, making her sigh inwardly in relief. 'Have it your own way. Just don't say I didn't warn you.'

It sounded more like a threat to Stephanie than a warning.

A threat of intent.

CHAPTER SIX

'I'M GOING back to my study to work.' Jordan reached for his cane to stand up from the table where they had just sat in total silence eating the warming soup.

It had been an uncomfortable silence. A silence full of awareness. Mental. Emotional. But most of all physical.

Jordan still had no explanation at to why he was even attracted to the determined and difficult physiotherapist. He had never been attracted to green-eyed redheads of medium height and medium build before now. He had certainly never found argumentative women in the least appealing.

Stephanie McKinley was all those things and more.

The 'more' being her mulish stubbornness in refusing to leave Mulberry Hall!

Well, just because *she* wouldn't leave there was no reason for Jordan to have to stay in the same room as her. 'I don't want to be disturbed for the rest of the afternoon, but you can come and get me when dinner's ready,' he said autocratically as Stephanie stood up to clear the table.

'Yes, My Lord.' She turned to give him a mocking curtsy. 'Certainly, My Lord.'

Jordan drew in a sharp breath even as his gaze narrowed on her suspiciously. He had assumed earlier that she knew nothing about the history of the St Claire family. She had certainly given no indication when they'd talked earlier that she had connected Jordan's family with the Dukes of Stourbridge, or that she knew he really was a lord in truth.

There was no indication of that knowledge in Stephanie's mischievous expression now, either—only a glint of mocking laughter in those expressive green eyes to go with that curtsy she had just given him.

Jordan relaxed. 'If I really were a lord, and this were a few hundred years ago, then I would have put you out onto the streets to starve by now for your insolence.'

She gave a rueful shake of her head. 'Then how lucky it is for me that the time of the feudal overlord is long gone.'

Perhaps someone should have mentioned that to Jordan's older brother? Lucan was no more inclined to use his title than Jordan and Gideon were, but there was still no doubting that Lucan was every bit as arrogant as their aristocratic ducal forebears were reputed to have been!

'Yes, lucky for you,' Jordan agreed dryly. 'As for dinner—I believe you said that eating a healthy diet was a necessary part of my treatment?' he reminded her.

She smiled slightly. 'Do I take it from that comment that it's your intention to agree to accept only the parts of that treatment which suit you?'

'Of course.' He looked at her down his gorgeous nose.

Stephanie had never met anyone quite like Jordan St Claire.

Never before had she wanted to slap a man at the

same time as she so desperately wanted to experience the passion of his kisses!

She sighed. 'I'm afraid it doesn't work like that.'

'You aren't afraid at all, Stephanie,' he contradicted her flatly.

He had no idea! 'What work are you doing in your study?'

'None of your damned business,' Jordan said evenly.

So much for trying to change the subject to something less controversial!

The real problem for Stephanie was that even when they weren't engaged in one of these irritating conversations she was still aware of everything about him. Even sitting down and eating lunch with him had been something of an ordeal in self-restraint.

She had found herself looking at Jordan's hands far too often as he ate, easily able to remember those hands caressing her back earlier. Igniting that fire of longing inside her...

Oh, God! she thought, almost groaning aloud. Maybe she should just leave here, after all? Admit defeat and just go. Before she was tempted into doing something she would most definitely regret.

No, she *couldn't* leave.

Between the two of them, Richard and Rosalind Newman had been making Stephanie's life in London a living hell. She simply refused to let her awareness of Jordan force her into returning until Joey could assure her that particular nightmare was over.

'Is there anything you want me to pass on to Lucan when I speak to him later this afternoon?' She arched challenging brows.

Jordan scowled back at her. 'I very much doubt that

my big brother expects you to give him an hour-by-hour report on my progress.'

'Or otherwise,' she shot back.

'Or otherwise,' he confirmed

'No, probably not,' Stephanie accepted lightly. 'But as I have nothing else to do this afternoon...'

Jordan knew the little minx was challenging him. Attempting to hold the threat of Lucan's displeasure over him. A totally useless threat as far as Jordan was concerned. 'I ceased being in awe of my brother the moment I realised that he has to go to the bathroom like the rest of humanity.'

She grimaced. 'I really didn't need that image, thank you very much!'

Jordan shrugged. 'Believe me, it's a good leveller in almost any circumstances.'

'In Lucan's case, it's one I could well do without.'

'Suit yourself,' Jordan drawled. 'I usually like to eat dinner about seven.'

'When you bother to eat at all.'

He gave a mocking smile. 'As you've insisted on staying here, I expect to eat regularly and often.'

Stephanie wasn't totally sure which appetite Jordan was referring to, but she had her suspicions...

She had worked with dozens of patients over the last three years. Young. Old. Female as well as male. Some of them had been extremely difficult to work with, yes—those were the cases she specialised in, after all—but none of them had been as impossible as the man standing in front of her now.

Her mouth firmed. 'At the risk of repeating myself—I am not here for your amusement.'

'Repeat yourself all you like, Stephanie,' he said. 'The only things you can do for me at the moment are feed me or amuse me. I'll leave it up to you which one you want to do at any given time...'

Stephanie stared at him furiously for several seconds. 'Oh, just go away, will you?' she finally huffed irritably. In all of her daydreams, all her fantasies about actually meeting Jordan Simpson, Stephanie had never once imagined herself telling him to go away!

'I'll take that to mean that you want time to think about what to cook me for dinner,' Jordan said.

Stephanie shot him another frowning glare, only breathing a sigh of relief once he had left the kitchen. She heard the sound of him whistling tunelessly to himself as he walked down the corridor and then shut the study door behind him seconds later.

There *had* to be a way for Stephanie to get through to Jordan—to make him accept the professional help Lucan had hired her for. She just had no idea what it was!

'Comfortable?' Jordan asked sarcastically later that evening, as he entered the sitting room to find her curled up comfortably in one of the armchairs, the only illumination in the room coming from the warm and crackling fire she had lit in the hearth.

'Very, thank you,' she answered, and she sat up to swing her bare feet slowly to the floor, still wearing the dark green sweater and fitted jeans she had changed into earlier. 'It isn't seven o'clock yet, is it?'

Jordan's jaw tightened, and his eyes hooded to conceal their expression as he took in how the firelight picked out every amazing colour in Stephanie's plaited hair. 'I've worked long enough for now. How was your afternoon?' He leant heavily on his cane as he came further into the room, the pain in his hip and leg from sitting down all afternoon making his tone harsher than he'd intended.

'Boring,' she admitted.

He raised dark brows. 'Boring?'

She gave a shrug. 'I'm simply not used to sitting around all day having nothing to do.'

Boredom was something that Jordan knew a lot about, after the weeks he had spent in hospital in the States before coming here. 'There's lots of books in here you could have read. Or you could have gone for another walk. Or another swim,' he added dryly.

Stephanie gave a pained wince. 'I'm not going back in the pool until you do.'

'Then you'll be waiting a long time,' Jordan rasped, scowling as moved awkwardly to drop down into the armchair opposite hers, sighing in relief to be off his hip once again. He dropped his head back against the chair to turn and look at her. 'Do you ever wear your hair loose?'

Stephanie put a self-conscious hand up to the slightly untidy plait. 'Not really.'

'Then why bother to keep it long at all?'

'I— I've never really thought about it.' She frowned, very uncomfortable under the scrutiny of that piercingly narrowed gaze.

Jordan looked predatory in the firelight, his eyes an amber glitter, every sculptured angle of his face thrown into sharp relief: the harsh slash of his cheekbones, the long aristocratic nose, his hard, sensual mouth, and the strong lines of his jaw darkened by a five o'clock shadow.

Stephanie sensed a waiting stillness about him. A coiled expectancy much like a jungle cat poised to spring. With Stephanie as its prey!

She stood up abruptly, needing to escape from all that leashed power for a few minutes, at least. 'Would you like a glass of wine before dinner?'

Jordan gave a brief smile. 'I thought you would never ask.'

Stephanie paused in the doorway. 'You're in pain again, aren't you?' She could see by the deepening of the grooves beside his eyes and mouth and the weary droop of his head that he was inwardly battling to keep that pain under his control rather than letting it control him.

He shot her a hard look. 'Just get the damned wine, will you?'

She bit back her own angry retort, knowing by the dangerous glitter in Jordan's eyes that now was not the time to argue with him on the subject of the pain he was suffering. Or the unsatisfactory method he chose to dull that pain. 'Would you like red or white?'

'That all depends what you're making for dinner.'

She shrugged. 'I have potatoes and lasagne baking in the oven, and a salad made up and stored in the fridge.'

'Red, then. Just go, will you, Stephanie?' he urged fiercely as she still hesitated in the doorway. 'When you come back I promise to try and do my best to make polite pre-dinner conversation.' The harshness of his expression softened slightly.

She looked sceptical. 'About what?'

'How the hell should I know?' His snappy impatience wasn't in the least conducive to polite conversation! 'It's been so long since I tried that I think I've lost the art of small talk.'

Stephanie wasn't sure he'd ever had it!

Even as the charming and magnetically handsome

Jordan Simpson, he'd been known as a man who didn't suffer fools gladly—a professional perfectionist, with little patience for actors less inclined to give so completely of themselves.

As Jordan St Claire, a man well away from the public limelight, he didn't even attempt any of the social niceties, but was either caustic or mocking. That mood depended, Stephanie was fast realising, on the degree of pain he was in at the time. Right now she would say he was in a *lot* of pain.

'I've never particularly enjoyed the shallowness of small talk, either,' Stephanie told him.

'Then I guess we'll both have to work at it, won't we?' Jordan closed his eyes to lay his head back against the chair, his expression harsh and unapproachable.

Or just pained…

Stephanie was becoming more convinced by the moment that his hip and leg were more painful than usual this evening. She could see the effects of that pain in the dark shadows beneath those gold-coloured eyes, and in the way his skin stretched tautly over those high cheekbones and shadowed jaw. No doubt wine helped to numb that pain for a while, but it wouldn't take it away completely.

Even though she didn't think drinking wine was the answer, she knew that Jordan accepting some sort of help to manage his pain was better than no help at all. So she turned on her heel and sped off to get some.

'Here you are.' Stephanie returned from the kitchen a few minutes later to hand Jordan one of the glasses of red wine she'd brought, and placed the bottle on the table beside him before carrying her own glass across the room and resuming her seat near the warmth of the fire. 'So, what shall we talk about?' she prompted after a few minutes of awkward silence.

Jordan had sat up to drink half the glass of Merlot in one swallow, knowing from experience that it would take a few minutes for the alcohol to kick into his system and hopefully numb some of the pain in his hip and leg. 'Why don't you start by telling me about your family?' He refilled his glass as he waited for her to answer.

She raised surprised brows. 'What do you want to know about them?'

'You're really hard work, do you know that?' he growled.

'And you aren't?'

'You already know about my family,' Jordan pointed out. 'Two brothers, both older than me, one by two years, the other by two minutes. End of story.'

'What about your parents? Are they both still alive?' Stephanie sipped her own wine more slowly.

'Just my mother. She lives in Scotland,' Jordan answered curtly.

Stephanie seemed to expect him to say more on the subject. But Jordan had no intention of saying any more. He wasn't going to tell her that his mother, the Duchess of Stourbridge, was desperately awaiting the marriage of her eldest son so that she could step back and become simply the Dowager Duchess. That she was impatiently waiting for *any* of her sons to marry and provide her with the grandchildren she so longed for. As none of those three sons had ever had a permanent woman in his life, let alone thought of marriage, she was in for a very long wait indeed.

So instead Molly doted on her three sons. In fact if she had her way she would be down here right now, fussing over Jordan. Much as he loved and appreciated his mother, that was something he could definitely do without!

'Your turn,' he invited Stephanie dryly. 'Start with your grandparents and work your way down,' Jordan prompted as she hesitated.

She gave an awkward shrug. 'I don't usually discuss my private life with my patients.'

'I thought we had agreed that I'm not your patient?'

'Then what am I doing here?'

'Who the hell knows?' Jordan heard the aggression in his tone, and regretted it, but the wine was taking longer than usual to numb the pain this evening—to the point that he was gritting his teeth together so tightly he was surprised he could talk at all!

Stephanie gave him a reproving frown. 'Very well. All four of my grandparents are still alive. As are both my parents. I—'

'I wasn't asking for a roll call,' Jordan sighed. 'Look, Stephanie, this is how it goes, okay? I ask you a polite question, you give me a pleasant answer. With details. *Voilà*—small talk.'

Stephanie knew what small talk was. She just didn't have any patience for it. 'My paternal grandparents moved to Surrey when my grandfather sold his construction business five years ago. My maternal grandparents live in Oxfordshire—my grandmother is a retired university professor, and simply couldn't bring herself to move from the city where she had taught for so many years. My mother and father live in Kent and run a garden centre together.'

'Better.' Jordan nodded approvingly.

'I have one sibling. Joey. She—'

'Joey is a she?'

'Short for Josephine,' Stephanie supplied with a

smile, relieved to see that some of the pained tension was starting to leave Jordan's face. 'But anyone calling her by that name had better be prepared to receive a black eye or worse!'

'Worse?'

'She put a frog down the shirt of a boy at school when he dared to tease her by chanting her full name,' she remembered affectionately.

'And the black eye?'

'A man she dated for a while at university.' Stephanie shrugged. 'Needless to say they didn't date again after that.'

'No, I don't suppose they did,' Jordan chuckled softly as he felt his muscles starting to relax from the effects of the wine and the soothing firelight. 'So how old is Joey and what does she do?'

'She's a lawyer.'

'Aged...?'

'Late twenties,' Stephanie answered evasively before taking a sip of her own wine; she had known exactly where this conversation was going the moment Jordan asked to know about her family!

'Older or younger than you?'

'Slightly younger.'

Jordan gave her a considering glance, sensing there was something that Stephanie wasn't telling him. 'How much younger?' he prompted slowly.

Her eyes glittered in the firelight as she glared across at him. 'About five minutes!'

'Why, Stephanie,' Jordan murmured teasingly, 'does this mean that you're a twin, too?'

Her mouth thinned. 'Yes.'

'And are you identical?'

'Yes.'

Jordan's brows rose incredulously. 'You mean there are *two* of you with that unusual red and cinnamon-coloured hair, those flashing green eyes, a determined chin and an infuriatingly stubborn temperament?'

Those green eyes instantly flashed. 'I do *not* have a stubborn temperament!'

'And the grass isn't green or the sky blue,' he retorted.

'Sometimes they aren't!' she pointed out triumphantly.

'I'm sure that once in a blue moon you aren't stubborn, either,' Jordan jeered. He gave her a considering look. 'Let me guess—Joey has short red hair and tends to wear mainly dark business suits and silk blouses?'

Stephanie gasped. 'How could you possibly know that?

Jordan shrugged. 'For the same reason Gideon and I are completely unalike in our tastes—twin or not, no one really wants to be a clone of another person.'

'But you and Gideon aren't identical.'

'In colouring, no,' Jordan said. 'But we're the same height, and we have a similar facial structure.' He smiled. 'Maybe we should introduce your twin sister to my twin brother and see what happens? As they're both lawyers they already have something in common.'

Stephanie knew exactly what would happen if the fiercely independent and outspoken Joey ever met either of Jordan's arrogant older brothers: sparks would most definitely fly!

'Perhaps not,' Jordan acknowledged dryly, seeming to read her mind. 'Much as they sometimes annoy the hell out of me, I'm not sure I would want to wish that onto either of my brothers.'

Stephanie bristled. 'Meaning?'

'Meaning that having one stubborn McKinley sister

around is more than enough for any man.' He laughed huskily.

The wine had obviously relaxed Jordan. So much so that he was back to tormenting her. Making her less wary of his hair-trigger temper and more aware of the dizzying attraction of him that could be so utterly mesmerising.

Stephanie moistened dry lips as she stood up restlessly. 'I think I'll just go and check on dinner—'

Jordan reached out to grasp hold of her arm as she passed his chair, his fingers like steel bands about her wrist. 'There's nothing in the oven that will spoil, is there?'

She sincerely hoped that the sudden thundering of her heart at Jordan's touch wasn't echoed by the pulse beating beneath his fingers! 'Not really.' She swallowed hard. 'I just thought—'

'You think far too much, Steph. Why don't you just allow yourself to feel for a change?' he encouraged softly.

Stephanie was feeling too much already—that was the problem!

She could feel the strength of Jordan's fingers curled about her flesh, the firm caress of his thumb against that rapidly beating pulse in her inner wrist, the heat of those gold-coloured eyes on her moist and parted lips, then moving lower to her rising and falling breasts. Holding her captive. Drawing her into the deep well of sensuality she could feel rising between them...

'I believe I told you not to call me Steph,' she murmured breathily.

'Your lips have told me several things that aren't echoed by your body language,' he murmured as he placed his wine glass down onto the table. 'You obviously have feeding me well in hand, so perhaps now would be a good time for you to amuse me,' he suggested softly as he tugged firmly on her wrist.

Stephanie tried to resist that tug. And failed. Instead she overbalanced and toppled over the arm of the chair to end up sitting on Jordan's thighs as he took her into his waiting arms. 'Jordan, this is definitely *not* a good idea—'

'I'm all out of good ideas, Stephanie,' Jordan said gruffly. 'Let's go with a bad one, instead, hmm?' he encouraged, as his head began to lower towards hers. 'They're usually much more fun, anyway.'

Jordan was going to kiss her. More than kiss her, Stephanie knew as she became instantly mesmerised by the intensity of his gaze.

'Maybe we'll have more success with this sitting down,' he murmured throatily, his breath a warm caress against her parted lips.

Stephanie attempted one last appeal for sanity. 'Jordan, we really can't do this.'

'Oh, but we really can,' he muttered, and his lips finally claimed hers.

It was a slow and leisurely kiss as Jordan sipped and nibbled at Stephanie's lips, tasting her, tantalising her, encouraging her to reciprocate, groaning low in his throat when her arm finally moved up about his shoulders and she pulled him down to her so that she could kiss him back.

Jordan felt a surge down the length of his spine as her fingers became entangled in the darkness of his hair when the kiss deepened, lips tasting, teeth gently biting, tongues dueling. Stephanie was obviously feeling a desire that was echoed in the pulsing hardness of Jordan's thighs.

He shifted slightly in the chair, so that Stephanie lay back against the arm of the chair as his mouth left hers to trail sensuously down the long column of her throat, his tongue rasping across that silky flesh. She tasted of warmth and sunshine, the lightness of her perfume shadowed by the essence of sweet arousal. An arousal that reflected the hot demand rising inside Jordan to once again hear those panting little cries and breathy groans as he pleasured her.

His hand moved caressingly beneath the soft wool of her sweater as he continued to taste that creamy throat. Stephanie's skin was as smooth as silk and just as delicious. He touched. Cupped her breast. Gently squeezed the rosy-pink nipple and then stroked that sensitive tip. Pushed the softness of her jumper up and feasted his gaze on those small and perfect breasts before lowering his head and claiming one of those roused tips in the heat of his mouth.

'Jordan!' Stephanie's back arched into his caress even as she gasped at the intimacy.

His mouth reluctantly released her, his eyes hot and dark as he looked down at that plump and moist nipple. 'You're too delicious for me to stop, love,' he murmured admiringly, and he stroked his thumb lightly over that plumpness before turning his attention to its twin, his tongue circling rhythmically across that rosy nub before drawing it into his mouth deeply, hungrily.

Stephanie was totally lost to sensation, her hand cradling the back of Jordan's head as his tongue rasped skilfully across her swollen nipple. The rush of pleasure between her thighs moistened her, even as she felt herself ache for him to touch her there too...

Jordan's eyes glowed deeply gold as he raised his head and held her gaze with his. He unbuttoned the fastening on her jeans before slowing pulling down the zip to reveal the black lace panties she wore beneath.

Stephanie couldn't move, couldn't breathe, moaning softly as Jordan lowered his head. She felt the softness of his tongue circling her navel, increasing the heat between her thighs as he plunged into that sensitive indentation even as his hands moved up her ribcage to cup and squeeze her breasts, to capture the swollen nipples once again in a rolling caress.

She was on fire. Hot. Aching. Wet. Needing. Oh, God, needing…!

Jordan answered that need as one of his hands moved to lie flat against the skin just below her waist before moving lower, and then lower still, slipping easily beneath the lace of her panties to seek out the silky damp curls below.

Stephanie cried out as he drew one finger lightly over and around the already swollen nubbin nestled amongst those curls. Over and over again. Round and round. Touching. Pressing. A rhythmic caress that increased the pressure building deep inside her.

Her cries became shaky gasps as she felt herself approaching a climax. Her fingers dug painfully into Jordan's shoulders as his lips and tongue continued to arouse her breasts and pleasure built and built inside her, driving her higher and higher. But he seemed to know exactly when to stop the intensity of those caresses to hold her time and time again on the edge of that release.

'Please, Jordan!' Stephanie finally gasped. She was going insane with need. Immeasurable ecstasy was just beyond her reach.

Jordan's mouth pulled on her breast at the exact moment he slid one long and penetrating finger inside the hot moistness of her, quickly joined by a second, stretching her, widening her to accommodate that invasion, even as the soft pad of his thumb continued to caress her sensitive nubbin.

Stephanie became so wet, so swollen, and those long fingers continued to plunge into her rhythmically, again and again, faster, harder, until the caresses pushed her over the edge into a climax so deep and prolonged it totally took her breath away and she could only cling onto him as she moved her hips into the burning intensity of that pulsing pleasure.

Jordan continued his caresses long after she had climaxed, the hardness of his own arousal continuing to pulse to the same rhythm as the echoing quivers still shaking her inside, and threatening to cause him to self-combust.

He had never been a selfish lover, finding as much satisfaction in giving his partner pleasure as he did in his own, and so he ignored the pulsing of his own body now to continue those caresses, wanting—needing—to give Stephanie every last vestige of physical pleasure.

He was less pleased with the sudden look of panicked awareness that widened those beautiful green eyes minutes later, as she returned to full awareness of where she was and what had just happened between them. 'It's okay, Steph,' he reassured her huskily.

'It is *not* okay!' she groaned self-consciously.

'Believe me, it is,' he soothed, even as he slowly, carefully, disengaged his fingers from her quivering flesh before refastening her jeans and pulling her sweater down. But not before he had given in to the temptation to gently kiss the slight redness of her breasts, where the stubble of his day's growth of beard had rubbed against that delicate skin.

He would have to shave twice a day if he wanted to do this again; he hated seeing even the slightest blemish on that perfect creamy skin.

His gaze was hooded when he finally looked up, to see that her face was flushed and her eyes fever-bright with uncertainty. 'You were beautiful, Stephanie,' he told her.

Her eyes were wide as she moistened dry lips with the tip of her little pink tongue. 'I— What about you? You didn't—'

'We have all night,' Jordan cut in as his hands moved gently from her breast to her thigh.

Her frown was pained. 'We really shouldn't—'

'We really *should*,' he insisted firmly.

She shook her head, her gaze not quite meeting his. 'I'm not sure I'll be able to stay on here if this is going to happen.'

Jordan's arms tightened about her as she struggled to stand up. 'Stay, Stephanie. Please.'

She looked up at him shyly. 'But—'

'If I had known you wanted to be alone, Jord, then I would have just telephoned you instead of flying up here to speak to you in person!' a mocking voice drawled behind them.

Jordan didn't need to turn and look across the room in order to know that the voice belonged to his twin brother Gideon...

CHAPTER SEVEN

'OH, GOD!' Stephanie gave a devastated groan and buried her heated cheeks against Jordan's chest after shooting a single glance across the room and seeing the devastatingly handsome blond-haired, dark-eyed man who stood in the open doorway, looking back at her with a cynical expression on his face.

'Not quite,' the man said derisively.

'Not even close, Gideon,' Jordan retorted.

'I guess you were a little too...preoccupied to hear the helicopter landing fifteen minutes ago?' Gideon said pointedly.

'I guess we were,' Jordan said acerbically. 'Does that mean that Lucan is here, too?' The scowl could be heard in his tone.

'I flew myself up.'

'Why?'

There was a short, telling pause. 'I would rather we talked in private, Jordan.'

'Not yet,' Jordan said grimly, his arms tightening about Stephanie as she trembled against him. 'How about giving the two of us a few minutes' privacy, Gideon?'

'By all means,' the other man murmured. 'Would you like me to continue waiting in the kitchen or—?'

'Will you just go, Gid?' Jordan grated harshly, and Stephanie gave another groan as she burrowed even deeper against his chest.

Stephanie wanted to die of embarrassment! She had never felt quite so much like crawling away and digging a hole before burying herself in it! She had done some stupid things in her life, but surely never anything quite so stupid as this?

Not only had she become totally lost in Jordan's kisses and caresses, but there had been a witness to that loss of control. Not just any witness, either, but obviously Jordan's twin brother!

'It's okay, Stephanie, he's gone; you can come out now,' Jordan cajoled.

Gideon St Claire might indeed have left the room, but Jordan certainly hadn't. And Stephanie was no more eager to look *him* in the face again after what had just happened than she was his brother.

What on earth had possessed her to behave in that totally uninhibited way?

With Jordan Simpson, of all men!

She had no choice now—no more arguments to make to the contrary. She had to leave. Immediately. She couldn't stay on here another minute, another second—

'Stephanie, calm down!' Jordan ordered as she sat up and began to struggle for release from his restraining arms. 'We're both consenting adults and— Damn it, Stephanie, we haven't done anything wrong.'

Stephanie stopped struggling long enough to glare up at him. '*You* may not have done, but *I* certainly have!' She gave a self-disgusted shake of her head, eyes huge in the pallor of her face. 'I have to leave right now, Jordan.'

'Why do you?' His arms tightened about her. 'Gideon never stays long.'

'As far as I'm concerned he's been here far too long already!' Her eyes flashed with the glitter of the emeralds they resembled as she glared up at him. 'Let go of me,' she pleaded, as she attempted to stand up and found the tightening of Jordan's arms once again prevented her from doing so.

His jaw was clenched. 'Not until you calm down.'

Stephanie *was* calm. Or as calm as she was ever going to be when she had just made a complete idiot of herself. Not just with Jordan, but in front of his brother too...

Stephanie inwardly cringed as she thought of how intimately Jordan had touched her. How completely unravelled she had become under the influence of those caresses. How her body, her breasts, were still so highly sensitised she could feel the brush of her clothing against her skin. How the heat of her thighs still quaked and trembled in the aftermath of that earth-shattering climax!

Jordan shrugged. 'I accept it was a little inconvenient, having Gideon walk in on us like that, but—'

'A little inconvenient?' Stephanie gave a humourless laugh as she finally managed to wrench herself out of Jordan's arms and surged forcefully to her feet, straightening and fastening her clothing before turning back to glower down at him. 'How long do you think your brother was standing there? Do you think that he saw—that he heard—?' She broke off with a groan as she thought of the way she had cried out loud as those powerful waves of release had surged through her.

Jordan shook his head. 'Even if Gideon did see or

hear anything, I assure you he's too much of a gentleman ever to mention it.'

'You're just making the situation worse, Jordan!' Stephanie said in protest, and raised her hands to the heat of her cheeks.

Jordan could see that as far as Stephanie was concerned that was exactly what he was doing. But, while he accepted that it was a little awkward to have had Gideon walk in on them in that way, he didn't consider it quite as cataclysmic as Stephanie seemed to. 'Look, just put it to the back of your mind—'

'That's easy for you to say when you weren't the one caught in a compromising position!'

Jordan watched as Stephanie began to agitatedly pace the room, obviously unaware that her hair had come loose during their lovemaking and now fell in a fiery cascade about her shoulders, the firelight picking out the gold and cinnamon highlights amongst the fiery red.

She looked beautiful. Wild and wanton. Like a woman who had just been thoroughly made love to. Only not quite as thoroughly as he'd have liked!

'Oh, I'm pretty sure that I was there too,' he pointed out, the tightening throbbing of his arousal a sharp reminder that he hadn't attained that same release.

Her eyes narrowed to icy-green slits. 'I should warn you, Jordan, I'm not in the mood right now to appreciate your warped sense of humour.'

'Then stop making such a big deal out of this,' he snapped, his expression grim as he reached for his cane and rose awkwardly to his feet. It eased the confines of his painfully engorged arousal, if nothing else!

'It *is* a big deal, damn it!' Stephanie said emotionally. 'Not only do I not normally behave in that—that abandoned way, but I certainly don't do it in front of an audience.'

'I told you—Gideon won't refer to it again if you don't.'

'As if I ever want to *think* about it again, let alone talk about it!' Stephanie exclaimed.

Jordan's mouth tightened and he suddenly became very still. 'Why is that, exactly?' His voice was silky soft. Deadly.

'Why?' she repeated incredulously.

'Yes—why?'

'Surely it's *obvious*?'

A nerve pulsed in Jordan's tightly clenched jaw. 'You wanted it. I wanted it. And as I said we're both well over the age of consent—so what's your problem?' he snarled.

'My problem is that Lucan hired me to be your physiotherapist, not to go to bed with you,' she told him heatedly.

'I don't need a physiotherapist—'

'Oh, yes you do—'

'And we didn't go anywhere near a bed,' Jordan continued coldly.

He just wasn't getting this, Stephanie realised impatiently. And why should he? Gideon was his brother, and if his closeness to his twin was anything like her own to Joey, then Jordan felt none of the awkwardness at his brother's intrusion into their lovemaking that Stephanie did. But then, he wasn't the one who had totally lost control. Who had screamed in ecstasy as he found release—

Oh, God, Jordan's hands had been all over her body! *In* her body!

Stephanie sat down abruptly in one of the armchairs,

putting her hands completely over the heat of her face as she felt the tears well up before falling hotly down her cheeks.

Jordan stared down in utter frustration at Stephanie's bent head as he heard her quiet sobs, having absolutely no idea what he should do or say next. In his experience women didn't usually cry after he had made love to them!

They didn't usually cry after they had made love with world-famous actor Jordan *Simpson*, he reminded himself grimly; the crippled, useless Jordan St Claire was obviously something else entirely. Some*one* else entirely!

God, how he hated feeling so damned helpless. So unlike himself. It was—

'I've been thinking...'

Jordan turned fiercely at the sound of his brother's voice. 'Get *out* of here, Gideon!'

'That I'm probably an unwanted third,' his brother finished unhurriedly, and gave a pointed look in the direction of the obviously upset Stephanie. 'I can easily book into the pub in the village for the night and come back in the morning.'

'No!' Stephanie looked up to protest, hastily drying her cheeks as she stood up. 'Of course you mustn't leave, Mr St Claire—'

'Gideon,' he invited coolly. 'Mr St Claire makes me sound too much like my older brother.'

'Whatever,' she dismissed uncomfortably. 'You have as much right to stay here as Jordan does. I'm the one who should leave.'

'Oh, I doubt my baby brother would be too happy about that,' Gideon said, after a swift glance in Jordan's direction.

The two brothers were like two sides of a negative, Stephanie suddenly realized: Jordan's hair was long and dark, whereas his brother's was the colour of gold and styled ruthlessly short. Jordan's eyes were the same gold as his brother's hair, and Gideon's eyes were so dark and hard they appeared almost black. And the contrast in the way they were dressed was just as extreme. Jordan's clothes were casual; Gideon St Claire wore tailored black trousers and a black cashmere sweater over a grey shirt unbuttoned at the throat, his black leather shoes obviously handmade.

They were also two of the most devastatingly handsome men Stephanie had ever set eyes on!

'You're right. He *wouldn't* like that,' Jordan answered his brother. 'Let's get the introductions over with and go on from there, shall we?' he suggested. 'Stephanie, meet my brother Gideon St Claire. Gideon, this is Stephanie McKinley.'

Stephanie didn't know quite what to make of the fact that he didn't add anything else to his introduction to explain what she was actually doing there. Although *she* didn't feel too inclined to explain what she was doing there to the haughty Gideon St Claire, either, after the intimacy of the scene he had walked in on only minutes ago!

'Mr St Claire,' she said with a stiff nod.

'Miss McKinley,' he murmured, his features every bit as hard and chiselled as his twin's.

Stephanie had no doubt this cynically tough man was a formidable lawyer. She would have to ask Joey if she had ever met him in court...

'McKinley...?' Gideon St Claire repeated slowly, his dark gaze narrowing on her in shrewd assessment. 'Red hair. Green eyes. Hmm.' His mouth compressed. 'You wouldn't happen to be related to Josephine McKinley, would you?' he asked.

Oh, dear Lord! Stephanie's sister and this man *had* met. But when? And where? Please, please, God, let it not be in any way connected with the Newmans' pending divorce case!

Just thinking of Jordan's reaction if he learned that she was being named as the 'other woman' in a divorce—albeit falsely—after the disgust he had shown for his own father's infidelity, was enough to make her feel ill.

'Her twin.' Jordan was the one to answer his brother—economically. 'And apparently she hates to be called Josephine,' he added.

'Do you know my sister, Mr St Claire?' Stephanie eyed Gideon warily.

'Not personally, no,' he said. 'I have heard of her, though,' he added.

And nothing good, either, if the hard glitter in those piercing dark eyes and the contemptuous curl of those sculptured lips was any indication!

Stephanie knew that Joey had earned herself something of a reputation in the courts of law these last three years, and that many of her colleagues considered her to be ruthless and uncompromising in defence of her clients. Character traits Stephanie would have thought a man like Gideon St Claire, who so obviously possessed those same traits himself, would have appreciated.

'What are you doing here, Gideon?' Jordan demanded—and thankfully saved Stephanie from having to make any sort of reply to his twin's enigmatic comment about her sister!

Instead of answering his brother, Gideon turned

those cool, dark eyes on Stephanie. 'I thought I smelt something burning when I was in the kitchen...'

'The lasagne!' Stephanie wailed as she remembered the food she had left cooking in the oven earlier. Before Jordan had begun making love to her and she had forgotten all about it! 'Excuse me.' She shot the two men a bright, meaningless smile before hurrying from the room.

It was patently obvious that Gideon wanted to talk to Jordan alone, and Stephanie was glad of an excuse to escape the intensity of emotion in being in the presence of two of the arrogantly overwhelming St Claire brothers.

'Well, you've succeeded in effectively getting Stephanie out of the room, so now you can tell me what's going on,' Jordan prompted as soon as he and Gideon were alone in the sitting room.

Gideon gazed back at him with the cynical speculation that was so characteristic of him. So typical of all three of the St Claire brothers, if he were totally honest, Jordan acknowledged ruefully; their father really did have a lot more to answer for than just hurting their mother.

Gideon gave a rueful shake of his head. 'And I've been imagining you all alone in the wilds of Gloucestershire.'

Jordan grimaced. 'I know your sarcasm usually manages to put the fear of God into most people, Gid, but I assure you I'm not one of them.' He dropped wearily back into the armchair he had only recently vacated.

'You look like hell!' his brother declared as he looked down at him with harsh disapproval.

'As complimentary as ever,' Jordan murmured, and rested his head tiredly against the chair.

He had forgotten all about the pain in his hip and leg—just as Stephanie had obviously forgotten about dinner—while the two of them were making love, but now that that rush of adrenaline had subsided Jordan once again felt the grinding and remorseless ache in his right thigh and down his leg.

Maybe he should go back to the States and see one of the specialists, as Stephanie had advised he should do?

No, damn it. He would rather live with the pain than suffer any more of those unhelpful medical examinations!

'Have they run out of razors in Gloucestershire?' Gideon raised enquiring brows.

'Just tell me what you're doing here, Gideon,' Jordan said again irritably, wondering why the hell it was that everyone was suddenly so obsessed with his appearance. What did it matter what he looked like when there was no one here to see him? Well…until Stephanie had arrived yesterday. And now Gideon, too. 'Well?' He glared at his brother.

'I certainly had no intention of interrupting your little assignation with La McKinley,' his brother retorted as he moved to fold his lean length into the chair opposite Jordan's.

'It isn't an assignation,' Jordan denied wearily.

'No?'

'Look at me, Gideon.' He sighed heavily. 'I'm just a shell of the man I used to be.'

'Stephanie doesn't seem to mind,' his brother pointed out.

Jordan's eyes narrowed warningly. 'Perhaps we should just leave Stephanie out of this.'

Gideon glanced in the direction of the kitchen. 'She doesn't seem like your usual type of woman...'

'As I just said, I'm not my usual self!' Jordan snapped back.

'Aren't you a little tired of wallowing in self-pity?' Gideon asked.

That remark was so reminiscent of the one Stephanie had made to Jordan yesterday that it totally infuriated him. In fact, if Gideon had been anyone else Jordan knew he would have given in to the urge he felt to get up and punch him on his arrogant nose! As it was, he knew that Gideon was more than capable of besting him in any fight at the moment—verbal or physical.

Not that Jordan was fooled for a moment by Gideon's seemingly hard and unsympathetic attitude; as his brother—his twin—Jordan knew how devastated Gideon had been following the accident. He also knew that his brother was a man of strong emotions—he just preferred to keep them hidden most of the time, behind a mask of cynicism.

'Just stop trying to annoy me and get on with it, Gid,' he said.

Thankfully Stephanie had managed to salvage the lasagne from the oven before it was totally ruined. A little trimming round the edges had disposed of the worst of the burnt pasta, and the potatoes were still edible too.

By the time the two St Claire men joined her in the kitchen ten minutes later she had laid three places at the table and was ready to serve the food. Whether or not Stephanie would actually be able to sit down with them and eat any of it was another matter entirely!

The ten minutes' respite from both Jordan's disturbing company and that of his coldly remote brother had at least given Stephanie a chance to regain some of her composure, although she still felt ill every time she so much as thought of making love with Jordan.

Or, more accurately, Jordan making love to her.

She wasn't a complete innocent when it came to lovemaking; she had dated and experimented a little when she was at university and found it all extremely disappointing. So much so that Stephanie had spared little time for relationships since then, and had concentrated on her career instead. Her physical response to Jordan had been far from disappointing—in fact it had been as combustible as it had been instantaneous. She had never dreamed, never imagined—not even in her wildest fantasies—the pleasure she had felt when Jordan made love to her.

Which was traumatic enough in itself, without having Jordan's coldly cynical twin—the man of whom Jordan had warned Stephanie she didn't know what arrogance was until she'd met him—as witness to that complete physical unravelling.

Not that there was any evidence of that knowledge in the remoteness of Gideon's expression now, as he entered the kitchen behind Jordan. 'I apologise once again for causing you any inconvenience, Stephanie,' he said politely as he saw the three places laid at the table.

'Not at all,' she dismissed brightly. 'After all, your family owns this estate. Now, there's more than enough food here for three— Are you all right, Jordan?' she asked with concern, as she noticed how pale he was. Worse than pale. His cheeks actually had a slightly grey cast to them. And was it her imagination or did he seem to be leaning more heavily on his cane than usual?

Was it as a result of having made love to her?

Jordan might be sarcastic and mocking, but he was also obviously still far from well—something that any excess of physical activity was sure to exacerbate. Making love could definitely be classed as excessive physical activity—especially as she'd been cuddled up on his lap!

She moved swiftly to his side. 'Perhaps you should sit down—'

'Would you stop fussing over me like some mother hen?' He turned on her savagely, eyes glittering deeply gold in warning.

Stephanie drew back sharply at his tone. 'Sorry.' She grimaced. 'I just thought—'

'Haven't I already told you that you think too damned much?' He scowled down at her.

'I trust you will excuse my brother's rudeness, Stephanie?' Gideon cut into the exchange with disapproving coldness. 'The discomfort of his injuries seems to have robbed him of his manners.'

'When I want you to apologise for me, Gid, I'll ask!' Jordan said furiously.

'When I want you to tell me what to do and when to do it, then *I'll* ask, Jord,' his brother came back with heavy sarcasm.

At any other time Stephanie would have found this challenging conversation between two obviously well-matched and determined men amusing. But as she had earlier almost made love with one of them, and been literally caught in the act by the second, Stephanie wasn't in any frame of mind at that moment to find anything either of them did in the least amusing!

Especially when Jordan already looked as if he were on the point of collapse… 'I really think you should sit down, Jordan,' she told him firmly, and she pointedly drew back one of the kitchen chairs before looking up at him expectantly.

Jordan shot her a narrow-eyed glare, more aware than ever of his own limitations when in the company of his brother's lean and healthy frame. Just as he was aware of the appraising looks Gideon was giving Stephanie as he watched her from beneath hooded lids…

Jordan slowly lowered himself down onto the wooden chair. 'Pack your bag once we've had dinner, Stephanie,' he told her tersely as he turned to place his cane conveniently against the wall behind him. 'Gideon is going to fly us all back to London in the helicopter early tomorrow morning.'

'I— What…?' Stephanie made no effort to hide her total bewilderment at Jordan's sudden announcement.

'We're all going back to London. In the morning,' Jordan repeated with ill-concealed impatience.

'But what about my car?'

'I'll arrange for someone to come and collect it,' he dismissed.

'But—why…?'

'Does it matter why?' Jordan snapped.

'Well…no, I suppose not…' Stephanie gave a slightly dazed shake of her head.

Except that Stephanie didn't *want* to be back in London; she had taken this job in Gloucestershire with Jordan St Claire for the very reason that she had wanted to get away from London and stay away—until her unwilling involvement in the Newmans' impending divorce had been effectively dealt with!

CHAPTER EIGHT

'WHAT is it, Stephanie?'

She stood hesitantly in the doorway of the study, where Jordan once again sat behind the imposing desk looking at her with enigmatic eyes. The only light in the room came from the lamp on top of the desk, reflecting down onto the papers he was working on.

As expected, as far as Stephanie was concerned, sitting down and eating dinner with the St Claire brothers had been an uncomfortable experience. She had absolutely no idea how the two men had felt about it. Conversation had been virtually non-existent as they'd both eaten in brooding silence, obviously lost in their own thoughts. Although Gideon *had* politely thanked and complimented Stephanie on the food once they had all finished eating, before excusing himself and going upstairs to bed.

Stephanie had a feeling his early departure might have had more to do with feeling that 'unwanted third' he'd mentioned than an actual need to go to bed. He had probably retired early because he thought that Jordan and Stephanie needed some privacy—if only to discuss leaving tomorrow.

If that were the case, then Gideon could have saved himself the trouble. Because Jordan had abruptly excused himself too, and disappeared off to his study only a minute or so after his brother's departure. Leaving Stephanie with far too much time on her hands to remember and cringe at her earlier behaviour...

She gave a non-committal shrug now. 'As you intend leaving with Gideon in the morning, it might be as well if we were to say goodbye now.'

Jordan straightened to narrow his speculative gaze on her. 'I'm sure I made it more than plain that I expect you to accompany us to London.'

'Yes, you did.' Stephanie stepped further into the room. 'But you've also made it clear since my arrival here that you don't want the attentions of a physiotherapist. As such, this would be the ideal opportunity for me to—'

'Have you been thinking again, Stephanie?' he taunted softly as he relaxed back against the leather chair.

'Stop it, Jordan!' She eyed him cautiously as she moved to stand in front of the desk. 'Obviously I will need to contact Lucan and let him know that as I never actually started working with you I won't be requiring any payment—'

'I'm sure that's very fair of you, Stephanie,' Jordan cut in. 'But as far as I'm aware Lucas has not yet suggested dispensing with your services.'

'No.' She sighed. 'But it's been pretty much a nonstarter from the beginning, so I assumed—'

'It never pays to make assumptions about the St Claire family, Stephanie.' Jordan shook his head even as his mouth thinned. 'When I said we're *all* going back to London in the morning, Stephanie, that's exactly what I meant.'

She frowned. 'I can't see what possible point there

would be in accompanying you when you refuse to let me do anything to help you.'

'Maybe I've reconsidered?'

Stephanie looked across at him searchingly, but found herself unable to read anything from Jordan's deliberately closed expression and the enigmatic blankness in those gold-coloured eyes. 'Jordan—'

'Stephanie, Gideon flew here to let me know that my mother has arrived in London,' Jordan announced flatly.

'Oh?'

'Yes,' he bit out curtly. 'As she rarely leaves Edinburgh, that fact is significant in itself. So much so that Lucan decided to try and find out exactly why she's in London. He's managed to discover that she has an appointment to see a cancer specialist the day after tomorrow.' Jordan spoke heavily, still having trouble accepting the reason Gideon had flown up here in person to talk to him.

The three brothers' relationship with their father had been sporadic at best after their parents' separation and divorce, with none of them in any doubt as to who was to blame for the breakdown of the marriage. But their mother—their mother had always been there for all of them. Molly loved without wanting to possess, without judging. She never pushed. She cajoled. She never forced her own views onto any of her sons but instead encouraged them to make their own decisions and choices. And if any of those choices should be the wrong ones then she was there for them. Always.

Now it was time for them to be there for her...

'I'm so sorry.' Stephanie had moved to sit down on a chair on the opposite side of the desk.

'Nothing's certain yet,' Jordan said. 'It's a preliminary examination and may amount to nothing.'

'But...'

'Exactly. *But...*' He nodded grimly. 'Strange, isn't it?' he mused. 'How learning that someone you love may be seriously ill can shake you out of what Gideon—and incidentally you too—call wallowing in self-pity!'

Stephanie's cheeks coloured hotly. 'I only said that because—'

'Because it happens to be the truth,' Jordan said honestly as he stood to pick up his cane and begin restlessly pacing the room. 'My mother was the first member of the family to arrive in LA when I had my accident. She stayed at my bedside the whole time I was in hospital, and then again at my apartment for weeks afterwards. Always encouraging. Always positive. And all the time this damned thing was eating away at her.'

'You said nothing is certain yet,' Stephanie reminded him softly as she watched him pace.

'It's enough that the possibility is there.' Jordan's expression became even grimmer. 'We're going back to London tomorrow, Stephanie, and once we know exactly what's happening with my mother you're going to help me get my full health back.'

Stephanie couldn't have been more pleased that Jordan was at last willing to consider therapy on his leg and hip—although she might have wished the circumstances for making his decision had been different—but she was no longer sure she was the person to help him do it.

She had allowed herself to become personally involved with Jordan. More than just personally involved with him on a physical level. She didn't even want to *think* about what she might feel for him on an emotional one!

Except, she realised, that she already felt something...

Later, Stephanie, she instructed herself firmly. There would be plenty of opportunity once she and Jordan had said goodbye for her to analyse her feelings for him.

'That's wonderful, Jordan,' she said with approval. 'I'm more than happy to recommend another physiotherapist to you.'

'I don't want another physiotherapist, damn it!' Jordan growled as he came to stand in front of her. 'Stephanie?' He bent down slightly to place a hand beneath her chin and tilt her face up to his. 'Look at me!' he barked as her gaze avoided meeting his.

Stephanie looked up, and then as quickly glanced away again as she found herself unable to meet the intensity of that golden gaze. She shook her head. 'You must see—understand—that I can't possibly work with you now, Jordan.' Just the touch of his fingers against her chin was enough to reawaken all that earlier arousal. She longed for his hand to be touching more than her chin...

'Are you asking for my word that what happened earlier won't happen again?' he rasped. He shook his head. 'I can't give that. Can you?'

She moistened dry lips before answering him huskily, 'No. Which is my whole point,' she continued, before Jordan could comment. 'I can't possibly work with a man I've— A man who—' Stephanie groaned. She couldn't even say the words. 'I don't get personally involved with my patients, Jordan.'

He frowned down at her, making no effort to hide his frustration with her continued stubbornness.

Having made his decision to stop wallowing and actually do something about his leg, he wasn't willing to simply let Stephanie recommend someone else and then walk away from him.

Lucan only ever employed the best person there was for any particular job—which meant that Stephanie McKinley had to be the best physiotherapist the St Claire millions could buy. If Jordan was going to get back on both his feet, then the best was what he needed.

And it was *all* that he needed from Stephanie right now...

He released her chin abruptly and stepped back. 'I don't believe we *are* personally involved.'

She blinked. 'But earlier—'

'Forget earlier,' he advised icily. 'It never happened. I've just been playing with you,' he added. 'From now on we'll concentrate on what you really came here to do.'

Forget earlier. It never happened. I've just been playing with you...

It was the last of those statements that hurt Stephanie the most. Because she knew it was the truth? Or because it was already too late for her not to be emotionally involved with him?

A lot of good it would do her if she were!

At the moment Jordan St Claire was a man who had become out of touch with his real charming self as well as the life he had led before the accident. The A-list actor Jordan Simpson wouldn't even have looked at Stephanie McKinley twice. In fact he probably wouldn't have bothered looking at her once! And when Jordan was back on two healthy legs—

'Are you going to help me or not, Stephanie?'

He wouldn't look at her again, Stephanie finished with painful honesty.

She had initially taken this job with absolutely no doubt as to her professional ability to help Lucan St Claire's brother. The fact that the brother had turned out to be Jordan Simpson had complicated things from the beginning. That Stephanie's attraction to him had allowed things between them to go as awry as they had was more than a complication.

So, was she now going to let her emotions stand in the way of giving Jordan the help he needed? Was she going to deny him that help when he had finally asked her for it?

Stephanie knew she couldn't do that. Her professional dedication simply wouldn't allow it.

'Yes, Jordan, I'm sure I can help you.' She nodded as she stood up. She only hoped it was true. Just as she hoped that she could put away her personal feelings for this man and concentrate on helping him regain full health. 'Although I'm not too sure about flying to London in a helicopter,' she added with a grimace. She found flying in a normal plane traumatic enough, so goodness knew how she would feel in a flimsy helicopter.

He chuckled softly. 'We'll be quite safe with Gideon—he flies the same way he does everything. With icy reserve,' he supplied as Stephanie gave him a curious glance.

'I thought his earlier coolness was because he disapproved of me.' After all, he'd had reason enough to disapprove after the scene he had almost walked in on!

'No.' Jordan gave a humourless smile. 'You're no

exception to the rule, Stephanie—Gideon makes a point of disapproving of everyone.'

The three St Claire men were totally different from any other men she had ever met, Stephanie mused minutes later as she made her way up the stairs to bed. Lucan was cold and arrogant. Gideon icily reserved. Jordan—

Perhaps she had better not think any more about what sort of man Jordan was!

She especially shouldn't think about his recent admission that he had just been playing with her earlier on...

Jordan was seated in the front of the helicopter beside Gideon as they took off. Instinct alone made him glance back at Stephanie, only to realise that she had a death-grip on the arms of her own seat, her short fingernails digging into the leather.

'Are you okay?' he asked with concern.

She didn't even glance at him but continued to stare straight ahead, her eyes wide in a face that was completely devoid of colour, her jaw clenched as she spoke between gritted teeth. 'Fine.'

'No, you're not,' Jordan contradicted flatly as he undid his seat-belt. 'Keep it steady, Gideon,' he warned as he began to climb into the back.

'What are you doing?' Stephanie's expression was one of complete panic as Jordan's movements redistributed the weight and made the helicopter tilt slightly from side to side.

'Coming to sit next to you,' Jordan explained patiently as he sat down and buckled himself into the seat. Then he reached out and prised the fingers closest to him from the armrest, before taking Stephanie's hand firmly into his own. 'You don't like flying.' He stated the obvious.

'Hate it!' she muttered as her fingers tightened painfully about his. 'No criticism of your capabilities intended, Gideon,' she added shakily.

'None taken, I assure you,' he drawled confidently from the front of the aircraft.

Jordan ignored his brother's insouciance and concentrated on Stephanie. 'Why the hell didn't you tell me you don't like flying?'

She flashed him a green-eyed glare before hastily resuming her death-stare towards the front of the helicopter. 'I did tell you last night that I wasn't sure about flying in a helicopter!'

'Not sure and terrified are two distinctly different things!'

'What difference would it have made if I had been more forceful about it?' she snapped.

'We could have let Gideon fly back on his own and driven down.'

Stephanie shook her head, and then obviously regretted it as even her lips seemed to go white. 'You needed to get to London as quickly as possible.' Her jaw was once again tightly clenched.

Jordan scowled. 'If it had been that urgent then we would have flown down last night. You—'

'Leave the girl alone, Jordan,' Gideon rapped out from the front of the plane. 'Can't you see she feels ill?'

Jordan could see that all too easily. He was furious with himself for not realising how nervous Stephanie was about flying—preferably before the helicopter had taken off!

His fingers tightened about hers. 'You're an idiot for not telling me.'

'Thank you so much for that, Jordan,' Stephanie snarled back. 'Comments on my mental state are just what I want to hear when I'm hanging hundreds of feet from the ground in a helicopter that looks as if a brisk wind might blow it out of the sky!'

Gideon chuckled softly in the pilot seat. 'No need to worry, Stephanie. The accident record in this type of helicopter is minimal, I assure you.'

'Minimal, maybe,' she gritted out through her teeth. 'But not non-existent.'

'I suggest you keep any more helpful information like that to yourself, Gid,' Jordan said.

'I could always turn back—'

'No!' Stephanie shuddered at the mere thought of Gideon turning the helicopter, let alone landing it on the helipad behind Mulberry Hall.

'But if this really is a problem for you, Stephanie…?' Jordan frowned, clearly not happy.

'We're in the air now,' she said tautly, her fingers curled so tightly about Jordan's that she was sure she must be cutting off the blood supply to his own fingers. 'I'll just make a mental note to myself to never, *ever* fly in a helicopter again!'

Stephanie was grateful for having Jordan's hand to hold during the rest of the flight, but even so, by the time they landed at the private airfield a few miles outside London, where the St Claire helicopter was obviously parked when not in use, she was aching from head to toe from the pure tension of just getting through the flight. Even her teeth ached as she staggered thankfully down onto the tarmac and all but fell into the chauffeur-driven car that was waiting for them to arrive.

'All right now?' Jordan prompted gently as he climbed into the back beside her, while Gideon sat in the front with the chauffeur, the glass partition raised to give them privacy.

Stephanie dropped her head back onto the leather seat beside him, some of the colour thankfully returning to her cheeks as she swallowed before answering. 'That was the most terrifying experience of my life.'

Jordan gave a mocking grin. 'You have yet to share a house with the whole of the St Claire clan.'

Stephanie had shared a house with Jordan for the past few days, and that had been traumatic enough!

Although he looked most unlike the unkempt man she had spent those two days with. When he'd appeared in the kitchen earlier this morning his long hair had been washed and brushed back from his face in silky dark waves, his jaw freshly shaven, once again revealing that fascinating—and sexy!—dimple in the centre of his chin, and he was wearing a pale brown cashmere sweater over a cream-coloured shirt and tailored brown trousers with brown shoes.

Today he looked every inch the charismatic actor Jordan Simpson—which was probably the whole point of the exercise, when he was about to see the mother the three St Claire men so obviously all adored.

Stephanie certainly felt decidedly underdressed in the company of the handsome St Claire twins, wearing her normal jeans and a white T-shirt beneath a short black jacket. Their arrival at St Claire House in Mayfair only confirmed her rapidly growing impression—after the grandeur of the Mulberry Hall estate and then flying around in a private helicopter—that she was completely out of her depth with this family. The townhouse itself was absolutely enormous: four storeys high, with a painted cream façade.

A stiffly formal butler opened the door to admit the three of them into the cavernous entrance hall.

'Mr St Claire is in his study, and Her—*Mrs* St Claire is upstairs in her suite, resting,' the grey-haired man politely answered Jordan's query.

'I'll leave Lucan to you while I go up and see Mother,' Jordan informed Gideon, and he took a firm hold on Stephanie's elbow.

'Thanks,' his twin accepted dryly. 'No doubt I'll see you later, Stephanie.' He quirked quizzical blond brows at her.

'No doubt,' she answered distractedly.

'A tray of tea things upstairs for Miss McKinley, if you please, Parker,' Jordan instructed the butler, before putting a hand beneath Stephanie's elbow and escorting her to the back of the hallway, to open the two carved oak doors there and reveal a lift. 'My grandmother had arthritis, and had it installed fifty years ago so that she could still go upstairs,' he explained as they stepped inside the spacious mirror-walled lift.

Of course she had, Stephanie accepted ruefully; obviously the St Claire family was wealthy enough to do anything it chose.

Jordan easily read the look on her face as she stood against the opposite wall of the lift. 'Don't let all the grandeur of Mulberry Hall and here fool you—normally none of us step foot in either of these houses.'

'Why on earth not?' She frowned her curiosity.

It was a curiosity Jordan had no intention of satisfying. St Claire House, like Mulberry Hall, was part of the Duke of Stourbridge's estate, and they were all only here now because their mother, still the Duchess of Stourbridge despite the divorce, always stayed at St Claire House on the rare occasions she came down to London.

'We're all too busy doing other things,' Jordan dismissed evasively as he stepped out into the thick carpeted hallway on the third floor. 'I'll make you comfortable in my suite before I go and see my mother.'

'Your...suite?' Stephanie echoed hesitantly.

'All the family have their own suite of rooms here.' Jordan gave a brief smile at she hung back uncertainly. 'Parker will bring you tea in my private sitting room. I expect the bedroom adjoining that has been prepared for your use. Is that going to be a problem?'

Stephanie had no idea—was it? It felt a little too intimate to have him next door. Entirely too close to him for comfort, in fact!

'I would be quite happy with something a little less... grand.' She frowned her discomfort.

'There isn't anything less grand,' Jordan informed her dryly as he opened a door to the left of the hallway. 'Come on, Stephanie,' he encouraged impatiently. 'I'd like to see you settled before I go and visit my mother.'

She was being ridiculous, Stephanie knew as she followed Jordan reluctantly. It just felt so very strange to be here with him and his family, in this grand house they rarely visited, but which was still run by what was no doubt an army of servants.

Who lived like this nowadays?

Only the very rich and the titled. Although not even too many titled families managed to live in such luxury nowadays, either, years of savage inheritance taxes having depleted their ranks and fortunes drastically.

The sitting-room, decorated in subtle tones of brown

and cream, and furnished with heavy dark furniture, was very much in keeping with the luxury of the rest of this London townhouse.

'There are some books over there if you feel like reading.' Jordan indicated the shelves at the back of the room. 'My bedroom and bathroom are through there.' He pointed to a door to the right. 'And your own bedroom is through there.' He pointed to another door to the left.

Far, *far* too close for comfort, she recognised with a pained wince.

'Cheer up, Stephanie,' Jordan drawled as he saw the expression on her face. 'With any luck we can both be out of here in a matter of days.'

Days?

It was the *nights* that bothered her!

How was she supposed to sleep here when she knew that Jordan's bedroom was only feet away? Knew that the two of them were cosily ensconced in the complete privacy of his suite?

'Stop looking so worried.' Jordan leant his cane against the plush brown sofa before slowly crossing the room until he stood only inches away from her. He placed a gentle hand beneath her chin and raised her face up to his. 'I'll try to ensure this is as short a stay as possible.'

It had already been too long as far as Stephanie was concerned!

Jordan grimaced. 'Wish me luck, hmm? I'm about to put on the performance of my life,' he added ruefully.

Stephanie felt slightly breathless as she looked up searchingly into that rakishly handsome face, his close proximity having once again unnerved her. 'You want your mother to believe you're already completely recovered...' she realised slowly.

'I'm going to try to convince her of that, yes.' He shrugged. 'It'll be one less thing for her to worry about.'

'You aren't going to do anything that could hinder your progress, are you?'

Jordan sighed. 'Ever the physiotherapist, Stephanie?'

'That's probably because I *am* a physiotherapist!' she defended hotly.

Although her traitorous body certainly had other ideas. Every part of her—every muscle, sinew and nerve-ending—was totally aware of Jordan as a man rather than as a patient. Of that hand still cupping her chin. Of the warmth of Jordan's body as he stood so close to her. Of the sensuality in his warm amber-coloured gaze as it moved slowly across her slightly parted lips. The soft caress of his breath against her cheeks as his head began to lower towards hers...

Stephanie stepped back abruptly as she realised Jordan intended kissing her. 'That is definitely *not* a good idea,' she stated firmly.

Only just in time too, as a faint knock sounded on the outer door, announcing the entry of the butler with the tray of tea things Jordan had requested.

'I'll probably have lunch with my mother, but I'm sure Parker will bring you something up on a tray...' Jordan looked expectantly at the butler as he straightened from placing the silver tray down on the low table in front of the sofa.

'I would be happy to do so, Miss McKinley,' the butler replied, before Stephanie even had chance to object to being waited on in this way.

She looked across at Jordan. 'That really isn't necessary...'

'Just do it, Stephanie,' Jordan said distractedly, and he left the suite, his thoughts obviously already with his mother.

Her own thoughts were in total disarray as Parker continued to treat her as if she were a guest, rather than just another employee, informing her that her bag had been safely delivered to the adjoining bedroom.

Stephanie felt totally out of place in this world of wealth and privilege that Jordan and his brothers seemed to take so much for granted. She was even less happy at being here when she remembered that she would have to telephone Joey and tell her she was now back in London if her sister needed to talk to her about the divorce case...

CHAPTER NINE

STEPHANIE felt slightly better once she had finished drinking the pot of Earl Grey tea and eaten a couple of biscuits to settle her stomach after the helicopter flight. In fact, she felt so much better that she must have dozed off for a while, because the next thing she knew Parker had returned with her lunch tray.

But the queasiness returned with a vengeance once Stephanie had eaten the delicious pasta dish and a bowl of fresh fruit and then dared to venture into the adjoining bedroom that Jordan had said was to be hers for the duration of her stay. It was a room dominated by a huge four-poster bed draped in the same gold brocade as the chair-covers and the curtains hanging at the long picture windows, which looked out onto the meticulously kept garden at the back of the house.

It was undoubtedly a beautiful room. The gold carpet was thick and luxurious, the walls papered in a pale cream silk, the light wood furniture Regency style—and no doubt, as with Mulberry Hall, all genuine antiques. The equally luxurious *en-suite* bathroom was of cream and gold-coloured marble, with gold fixtures and several thick cream towels warming on the stand beside the slightly sunken bath.

It was all very beautiful—and totally unsuitable for someone who was, after all, just an employee.

Stephanie left her bag unpacked on one of the brocade-covered chairs and hastily backed out of that luxurious bedroom. As soon as Jordan returned from visiting his mother she would have to tell him that she couldn't stay here. That if he was really serious about wanting her professional help then she would prefer to go back to her own flat and simply visit him here every day.

In the meantime, grounding herself by chatting to Joey sounded like an excellent idea...

'Has Jordan Simpson tried to seduce you into his bed yet?' Joey questioned avidly, as soon as Stephanie's call had been put through to her office.

Not into his bed, no... 'Don't be ridiculous, Joey,' she dismissed briskly.

'And I had such high hopes, too!'

'High hopes of what?' Stephanie asked.

'Of you not continuing to live the life of a nun!'

'According to Rosalind Newman, I don't.'

'She's just a vindictive woman!' The scowl could be heard in Joey's voice.

Stephanie sighed. 'How are things going with the divorce case?'

'Nothing new, I'm afraid.' Her sister became her usual businesslike self. 'Rosalind Newman is still insisting you had an affair with her husband, and Richard Newman is doing nothing to help the situation. It could get very messy, I'm afraid, Stephs,' she added regretfully.

Exactly what Stephanie was trying to avoid. 'Perhaps if we all met up and talked about it?'

'Not a good idea,' Joey advised. 'Even if all three

lawyers were there representing their clients, it would still likely end up in a slanging match.'

On a practical level Stephanie already knew that. She just didn't know what else she could do to convince Rosalind Newman that she was being delusional about Stephanie's personal involvement with her husband. It was complicated by the fact that Stephanie was convinced Richard Newman's lack of support was because he was involved in an affair with *another* woman, and he'd rather Stephanie's name was blackened than his actual mistress's.

'Just do your best to keep my name out of it, Joey,' Stephanie said heavily.

'And you try and come up with something more interesting to tell me the next time you call,' her sister encouraged teasingly.

'By "interesting" I take it you mean sexual?' Stephanie came back dryly.

'You're with *Jordan Simpson*, sis,' Joey said impatiently. 'The man you've lusted after for years!'

The man she still lusted after, Stephanie thought. 'He isn't at all like I imagined he would be.' He was so much *more* than she had expected, she admitted privately—a man who was drawing on every ounce of strength he had to get him through the worst moments of what she knew were excruciating agony.

'In what way?' Joey prompted curiously. 'Surely you aren't holding it against him because he's behaving less like a movie star and more like a man who fell off the top of a building six months ago? Because if you are, then I hate to tell you this, Stephs, but the man *did* fall off a building six months ago!'

'No, I'm not holding that against him.' Stephanie chuckled wryly; she could always rely on Joey to make her laugh. 'Joey...' She deliberately lowered her voice. 'You know those interviews he gives, where he mentions his parents' divorce as being the reason he's never married?'

'Yes...'

'Well, he's really serious about it.' She drew in a ragged breath. 'Which means—'

'He wouldn't be too happy if he were to learn that the physiotherapist his brother hired is up to her ears in another couple's divorce?' Joey finished, with her usual bluntness.

Especially considering what they'd done together yesterday evening in his study! Stephanie thought. 'Perhaps I should try talking to Richard again?'

'No, *I'll* try,' her sister insisted. 'The man is definitely hiding something—or should I say someone?—but he seems more than happy to let you take the flak.'

Yes, Stephanie believed that too. If only the man weren't so obnoxious then maybe they could have persuaded him into telling the truth. As it was...

'Just call Richard and ask him if he will speak to *me*,' Stephanie pressed.

'Will do.' Her sister rang off with her usual abruptness.

'Care to explain who Richard is?'

Stephanie drew in her breath with a sharp hiss as she turned and saw that Jordan had come quietly back into the sitting room and now stood near the door, looking across at her with icily narrowed eyes. She stood up slowly to run her damp palms down her denim-clad thighs. 'Didn't you know that it's rude to listen to other people's telephone conversations?'

'If I did then I obviously forgot,' Jordan said unapologetically as he stepped further into the room.

The hours spent convincing his mother that he was well on the road to recovery had been just as much of a strain as Jordan had thought they might be. So much so that he was now exhausted. He had come back to his suite hoping for a rest before he had to go through the whole charade all over again at dinner. He certainly didn't appreciate coming back into his suite of rooms and overhearing the end of Stephanie's telephone conversation concerning some man called Richard that she was obviously desperate to get in touch with!

He eyed Stephanie coldly. 'Well?'

'I don't see that this has anything to do with you—'

'You told me you weren't involved with anyone,' he reminded her harshly.

'I told you I wasn't married or engaged,' she corrected. 'Which I'm not.'

'But you obviously are involved with someone. Or at least you were!'

'I— Are you okay, Jordan?' Stephanie exclaimed as she saw how pale he was.

'Do I look okay?' he snapped scathingly as he swayed slightly on his feet.

'No.' She could clearly see the grey cast to his skin, and dark shadows under his eyes, deep lines grooved beside his mouth. 'You need to take some painkillers and then lie down until they start to take effect. I'll help you into your bedroom—'

'I don't need any help!' He glared across at her.

She flinched at the vehemence in Jordan's tone. 'You obviously need to go to bed—'

'Is that an invitation, Stephanie?' he cut in. 'If it is then I think I should warn you I'm really not up to making love to you right now, and I'm not exactly in the mood, either.' Those gold eyes glittered down at her with cold satisfaction as Stephanie gave a pained gasp.

'That's enough, Jordan!'

Stephanie spun sharply round to find Lucan St Claire standing in the doorway, his austerely handsome face set in disapproving lines as he looked coldly across at his youngest brother.

The fact that the critical gaze wasn't levelled at her made absolutely no difference to Stephanie; Jordan's scornful remarks had made it more than obvious that he had made love to her before today!

Tears of mortification welled in her eyes. 'If you will both excuse me?' she choked emotionally, before hurrying into the bedroom she'd as yet had no opportunity to tell Jordan she couldn't sleep in—tonight or any other night.

'Well, that was pretty nasty even for you,' Lucan said with disapproval as he closed the door behind him before striding further into the room.

'I don't remember asking for your opinion on my behaviour, Lucan,' he muttered wearily.

His brother frowned. 'It was possible to hear your raised voice all the way down the hallway.'

His mouth twisted derisively. 'How utterly shocking!'

Lucan raised dark brows. 'Exactly what *is* your relationship with Stephanie McKinley?'

'You were the one who hired her.' Jordan turned away abruptly and began walking painfully towards his bedroom.

'That wasn't what I asked.'

'It's all you're going to get!' Jordan snapped, as each step he took caused him excruciating agony.

'Have you been to bed with her?'

Jordan came to a sudden and painful halt before slowly turning back to face his eldest brother. 'Mind your own business,' he bit out with slow precision.

'I'll take that as a yes, shall I?' Lucan murmured speculatively.

Jordan glared. 'You can take it any way you please.'

'Oh, believe me, I will,' Lucan said.

'No doubt,' Jordan muttered disgustedly.

His brother gave him an arrogant look. 'That aside, I believe you owe Miss McKinley an apology—'

'Like hell I do!'

'You deliberately set out to insult her.' Lucan gave him one of his superior looks.

Jordan knew exactly what he had done. He just wasn't sure why he had done it... What difference did it make to him whether or not Stephanie was still panting after some man called Richard she had been involved with before the two of them had even met?

His eyes narrowed. 'Tell me, Lucan—when you decided to hire her, did you do your usual check into her background?'

His brother looked unconcerned by the insult in Jordan's tone. 'Stephanie McKinley graduated top of her class—'

'I meant her *personal* background,' Jordan cut in impatiently.

'I don't believe her personal life is any of my concern. Nor,' Lucan added softly, 'if your lack of interest in her is genuine, should it be any of yours.'

No, it shouldn't, Jordan acknowledged grudgingly. Except last night had made it so...

Damn it, he had thought Stephanie was different. Had hoped that she was. And all the time she had been in his arms she had been hankering for some man called Richard.

'Unless it escaped your notice, Stephanie McKinley was crying when she ran out of here.' Lucan's mouth had thinned disapprovingly.

'I noticed,' Jordan admitted. 'But we have much more important things to worry about than Stephanie's hurt feelings, remember?'

'Let's deal with one problem at a time, hmm?' Lucan insisted. 'Your first priority is to apologise to Miss McKinley—'

'For stating the truth?'

His brother looked implacable. 'I didn't hear her calling you a cruel and heartless louse, but at the moment *that* happens to be the truth, too.'

Jordan's mouth compressed into a tight line. 'Obviously Stephanie is much more restrained than I am. Now, if you wouldn't mind, Lucan?' he added pointedly. 'I need to go and lie down before I fall down.'

He didn't wait for his brother to answer, but limped the rest of the way to his bedroom and all but slammed the door behind him before collapsing on the bed with a heartfelt sigh of relief.

Hours spent putting on an act for his mother had taken much more out of Jordan than he had expected. The conversation a few minutes ago with Stephanie even more so.

Did he owe her an apology?

Her private life was her business. A few kisses— okay, so it had been more than just a few kisses—didn't entitle Jordan to know about every man she had ever slept with.

Damn it, Lucan was right; he *did* owe Stephanie an apology!

* * *

'I'm sorry.'

Stephanie turned her head abruptly on the pillow as she looked across the room to where Jordan stood stiffly in the bedroom doorway. *Swayed* in the doorway, would actually be a better description of what he was doing. He leant heavily on his cane with one hand and held on to the doorframe with the other...

She sat up with a frown. 'You should be in bed—'

'I honestly don't think I can make it back to my own bedroom,' Jordan admitted ruefully as he staggered across the room and sank down gratefully on the side of her bed. 'I'm not sure I even have enough energy left to lie down, let alone walk.'

Stephanie was pretty sure that he didn't; his cheeks were hollow, eyes dark with pain, and his mouth was set in a grimly determined line. The same determination that had enabled him to get to her bedroom and no further...

She stood up hastily to move round to Jordan's side of the bed. 'Are you going to let me help you this time?' She was hesitant about even touching him again after the way he had reacted earlier.

He gave a pained wince. 'If you don't then I'll probably just slide onto the floor before passing out.'

Stephanie shook her head even as she took away his cane and slipped off his shoes, before helping him to lie back against the pillows and carefully swing his legs up onto the brocade bedcover. 'You shouldn't have strained yourself by even attempting to come in here.'

He glanced up at her. 'Lucan seems to think I owe you an apology.'

Stephanie stilled. 'Do *you* think you owe me an apology?'

'I was out of line earlier,' Jordan murmured honestly

as he saw the way Stephanie's gaze was avoiding meeting his.

'Yes,' she agreed flatly. 'And, as I have no intention of explaining who Richard is, I think it would better for all concerned if I went back to my own flat now, and recommended someone else to take over your therapy.'

'Lucan assures me that you're the best there is,' he said.

'Even so...'

'He also told me that your private life is none of our concern.' Those gold eyes were narrowed guardedly.

'Your brother is very—opinionated,' Stephanie acknowledged dryly.

'But he's usually right,' Jordan pointed out.

'Perhaps.' Stephanie nodded, not sure whether she was relieved or disappointed that Jordan felt the same way as Lucan. If he had continued to demand to know who Richard was, then it might have meant that he was genuinely interested in her himself. As it was, he had obviously decided, on his brother's advice, that her private life was none of his business.

A complete change of subject was necessary. 'How was your mother earlier?'

'As bright and positive as she usually is.' Jordan sighed heavily. 'The two of us put on quite a show, I can tell you—my mother pretending she's only here to shop, and me pretending that everything is going well with my recovery.'

Stephanie had yet to meet Molly St Claire, but she had no doubt that she would like her; she had to be quite something for the three formidable St Claire men to adore her in the way they obviously did. She also doubted, if Molly St Claire was as close to her sons as she appeared to be, that the other woman had been any more fooled by Jordan's act of wellbeing than he had been fooled by hers...

'You shouldn't have tried to manage without your cane,' Stephanie scolded again, as Jordan gave a low groan of pain when he tried to move his leg into a more comfortable position.

'It's never been as bad as this before,' Jordan grated, a nerve pulsing in his tightly clenched jaw. 'The muscles in my leg seem to have seized up completely.'

Stephanie no longer felt hesitant as she sat down on the side of the bed and gently ran her hands over Jordan's right leg and felt the way his muscles were locked into place. Her glance flicked up to his rigidly set face. 'Perhaps some painkillers to relax the muscles—'

'No,' he told her grimly.

Stephanie chewed on her bottom lip. 'I could probably ease some of the tension by directly massaging the muscles. But it's going to be painful,' she warned regretfully.

'Can't be any worse than it already is,' Jordan muttered through gritted teeth, his fingers curled into the brocade cover at his sides.

'It will work better if we take your trousers off...'

'Are you trying to get me naked, Stephanie?' he teased, even as he concentrated on controlling the pain.

'I believe I said your trousers, not all your clothes!' Her cheeks flushed a fiery red.

'Go ahead,' Jordan invited, and he stared rigidly up at the canopy overhead, knowing that the depth of his pain was his own fault after trying to manage without his cane for a couple of hours. 'I'm certainly in no condition to stop you,' he added slightly bitterly.

Stephanie tried hard to maintain a professional façade as she unbuttoned and unzipped Jordan's trousers, before sliding them down his thighs to reveal the figure-hugging black boxers he wore beneath. Inwardly it was a different matter, however, as her fingers brushed lightly over his muscled abdomen and legs before she removed the trousers altogether and forced her gaze down to look at his legs.

His left leg was lean and muscled, covered in a dusting of dark hair and slightly tanned, but his right leg showed the white scars from the operations he had undergone these last six months, with the muscles in his thigh visibly knotted beneath the tautly stretched skin.

Stephanie winced inwardly at the thought of the pain Jordan would experience when she attempted to massage those locked muscles without the help of painkillers.

'Perhaps you should drink a couple of glasses of wine before I start—'

'Just do it, Stephanie,' Jordan encouraged gruffly, obviously guessing the reason for her hesitation.

She drew in a controlling breath as she firmly reminded herself that she was a professional. That she had to forget she had been intimate with this man and just do the job Lucan St Claire had asked her to do.

Jordan closed his eyes and clenched his teeth tightly together as he felt the first touch of Stephanie's fingers against the rigid hardness of his thigh. Keeping his eyes closed and teeth tightly clenched, he concentrated on not crying out as she began to massage and work those tense muscles. Over and over again. Until Jordan finally began to feel a slight lessening of that tension, and the rest of his body also began to relax as the pain began to ease.

'Magic,' he murmured huskily minutes later, as he finally found he could ease back onto the bedcovers.

'Training,' Stephanie dismissed briskly.

Now that the pain was easing slightly Jordan had a chance to look up at Stephanie as she continued to massage his thigh. To note how her cheeks had become flushed by her exertions. How the tip of her tongue was caught between her teeth as she concentrated. How several wisps of her fiery hair had come loose from her plait to fall unnoticed against those flushed cheeks.

'I think you can stop now.'

Stephanie gave Jordan a startled glance, having been concentrating so intensely on easing his pain that she hadn't noticed that the pain had obviously stopped and his attention had now shifted to her...

She stopped massaging his thigh to sit back abruptly. 'You should be able to sleep now.'

'I intend to,' Jordan said. 'Join me?' He held out his hand in invitation.

An invitation that Stephanie didn't take. Instead she looked down at him warily.

Jordan knew that his behaviour earlier had been completely out of line. That things had happened between the two of them so fast at Mulberry Hall, so intensely, there had been no real opportunity for either of them to talk about past or present relationships.

Maybe Stephanie *did* still have a thing for some guy she had known in the past—but it hadn't stopped her from responding to him, had it?

'Please?' he invited huskily.

Stephanie had no idea what Jordan had been thinking about during the last few minutes' silence, but after their earlier conversation it didn't take a great deal of imagination on her part to guess what it might have been!

Or for her to know that Jordan had completely the wrong idea about her relationship with Richard Newman. She wanted to tell him, but she knew that the truth would be even less acceptable to him.

'I promise I'll be good,' Jordan added cajolingly.

Stephanie gave a little laugh. 'Does this little-boy-lost act usually work?'

'On doting mothers and dedicated physiotherapists? Hopefully, yes!'

She gave a rueful shake of her head. 'You're impossible.'

'But endearing?' He held his hand out to her once again.

After the briefest of pauses Stephanie put her hand into his and allowed him to pull her down beside him on the bed, shifting slightly onto his side as he took her into his arms.

A few minutes of heaven couldn't hurt, could it? Stephanie promised herself.

Just a few minutes.

CHAPTER TEN

IT WAS already starting to get dark outside when Jordan woke up from the most refreshing sleep he'd had for months, with the still sleeping Stephanie held tightly in his arms.

Her hair had once again come loose from that confining plait, and now lay in a silky curtain of fire and gold across his chest and shoulder. Her lashes were long and dark against her creamy cheeks, and that smattering of freckles on the bridge of her nose totally enticing. Her lips were slightly parted as she breathed softly.

Jordan could feel the warmth of her hand as it lay against his chest, and the heat of her leg as it lay lightly entangled with his. A heat that seeped deep into Jordan's own body as he felt himself becoming aroused by Stephanie's proximity.

He turned carefully onto his side in an effort not to wake her, knowing that if Stephanie were awake she would probably insist that nothing of a personal nature be allowed to happen between them.

Such as Jordan running his hand slowly down her spine. Such as allowing that hand to trace her waist and hip. Such as cupping her bottom as he fitted the length of her body perfectly against his. Such as placing his mouth against her brow and temple before exploring the soft curve of her warm cheek in a direct path to the lips he longed to claim with his own...

Stephanie was sure she had to be still dreaming when she woke in the semi-darkness and found herself pressed against a hard male body. She felt warm and sure hands moving over her in exploration, the hot caress of lips against her brow, temple, cheek, and—

As Jordan's lips claimed hers Stephanie knew this was no dream. She really was lying on a bed with the semi-naked Jordan St Claire!

She pulled her mouth away from his even as her hand pushed against the hard chest pressed so firmly against her breasts. 'No, Jordan!'

'Oh, yes, Stephanie,' he murmured throatily, and he continued to hold her against him, with his hands pressed against her bottom, his lips now moving down the length of her neck and throat.

She had known sleeping with Jordan was a bad idea from the start. It was the reason she had fought so strongly against it. Because she had no defences against this man. The feelings she'd realised she had for him had stripped away all those defences and left only raw, unadulterated passion in their place.

'God, you taste good!' Jordan groaned as his lips returned to claim hers.

He tasted better than good. He was earth, and spice, and irresistible heat...

He parted the lips beneath his as he felt Stephanie curve her body into his, her hands moving up his chest and her fingers becoming entangled in his hair.

They kissed heatedly, hungrily. Lips, teeth and tongues exploring, biting, possessing, as their hunger for each other spiralled wildly, became mindless, out of all control.

It wasn't enough. Jordan wanted more.

'I need to see you—to touch you!'

Jordan quickly removed her jeans and panties before taking off her T-shirt to bare those perfect breasts, drinking his fill of her slender nakedness. Then he slowly lowered his head to claim one of those turgid nipples into the heat of his mouth, to stroking it with his tongue as his hand caressed a path down to those silky curls between her thighs.

Stephanie was beyond thought, beyond anything but the perfection of Jordan's lovemaking. Her back arched to press her breast into the heat of his mouth even as her thighs moved rhythmically against the caress of his fingers.

It wasn't enough. Stephanie wanted more.

She pulled away to sit up and roll Jordan's T-shirt up, before pulling it completely over his head to bare his torso to the exploration of her avid lips and tongue.

Kissing his heated flesh, licking him, she moved down the length of his chest to his navel, pausing there to dip her tongue into that shallow well, the heat between her own thighs intensifying as she heard Jordan's groan of pleasure.

She knelt beside him, able to see the length of his arousal pressing urgently against his boxers, and her fingers reached up for the waistband to roll them down his thighs and legs and remove them completely. Releasing the hard jut of his arousal to her heated gaze.

He was beautiful, so long and thick, and Stephanie moved to kneel between Jordan's parted legs and curled her fingers about that pulsing velvet-soft flesh, her other hand cupping him beneath.

'Dear God!' Jordan's back arched at the first lick of her hot little tongue against his engorged flesh, and he tightened the fingers of both hands in the bedcover beneath him as she slowly ran the tip of her tongue along the firm length of him, from base to tip, lingering to swirl around the sensitive head even as her hands continued to caress the length of him.

Over and over again she caressed and licked and swirled, building the tension inside Jordan to an unbearable degree. But not so unbearable that he wanted her to stop!

'Stephanie…' He gave an aching groan as she finally claimed him in her hot mouth, driving Jordan to the point of insanity. Much more of this and he knew he was going to lose control completely!

Stephanie looked slightly dazed as Jordan sat up to place his hands on her shoulders before gently pushing her away from him.

'Don't look at me like that,' he murmured, as he manoeuvred her over him, so that her knees were placed either side of his thighs. He lay back on the bed, his arousal against the moist, hot core of her. 'I want to be inside you, Stephanie,' he pleaded throatily. 'Deep inside you.' His gaze held hers as he entered her, inch by slow, pleasurable inch.

Stephanie gasped as she felt herself stretching, accommodating his size. Her flesh was pulsing as she reached down to balance herself above him with her hands on his shoulders, as she lowered down onto the width and length of him until she sheathed him completely from tip to hilt.

'That is so good…' Jordan's eyes glowed golden in the darkness as he reached out to place his hands on her hips. 'But I'm afraid you're going to have to do all the hard work now, Stephanie.'

Her cheeks were flushed, her breathing ragged as

she began to move, slowly at first, and then harder and faster. Jordan's hands cupped her breasts to capture the nipples between thumb and finger. He rolled and squeezed them, increasing those pulses of pleasure deep between her thighs to an almost unbearable degree.

She moved harder and faster still, and she felt Jordan become even harder inside her as he approached his own release. She gasped breathlessly as he moved one of his hands and his fingers found and stroked that swollen nubbin nestled in her curls, tipping her over the edge of release. At the same moment she heard him cry out, continuing to ride him as long as his hot, pulsing pleasure consumed them both.

Finally Stephanie collapsed weakly against Jordan's chest, her pulse still racing, her breathing ragged. Jordan's arms came about her and she felt him gently smoothing the fiery strands of her unconfined hair down her back. 'Thank you.'

Stephanie looked at him quizzically as she raised her head. 'Shouldn't I be the one saying that?'

He smiled. 'Surely the pleasure was mutual?'

The pleasure… Oh, God, the pleasure! Stephanie had never known anything like it before. Those few exploratory forays she had made into the physical side of sex while at university didn't even begin to compare to making love with Jordan. To the wonder of having him inside her still.

Except this should never have happened.

She was the physiotherapist Lucan St Claire had employed with the expectation that she would help Jordan regain the full mobility of his damaged leg; he certainly hadn't employed her to go to bed with his brother!

And she really *had* been to bed with him now. Had slept with him. Made love with him.

'Stop that!' Jordan instructed harshly as he saw and guessed the reason for Stephanie's suddenly pained expression.

'I can't,' she groaned.

'Stephanie—'

'I need to go to the bathroom.' Her gaze avoided his as she moved carefully upwards to release him before shifting to the side of the bed to stand up and collect her clothes from the floor. She held them in front of her protectively. 'I think it would be—be better for both of us if you've gone back to your own bedroom by the time I return.'

She could have no idea how absolutely beautiful she looked, standing there with nothing but a few scraps of clothing held in front of her to hide her nakedness. Her hair was a red-gold tangle about the slenderness of her shoulders, her eyes sultry from her release, and her lips were still swollen from the heat of the kisses they had shared.

Even so, Jordan knew from her behaviour that she regretted what had just happened between the two of them. Because of this Richard guy?

He sat up on the side of the bed, feeling only a twinge of discomfort in his leg as he did so. 'We need to talk about this, Stephanie—'

'There is no *"this"*!' Her eyes flashed deeply green. 'It shouldn't have happened, Jordan.' She held her clothes even more tightly against her.

He grimaced. 'I believe your next line is, *This was a mistake*.'

'It *was* a mistake!' She glared at him.

Jordan sighed. 'Look, I realise that you're upset—'

'Upset?' Stephanie echoed. 'I'm devastated!'

'We can talk this out—'

'No, we can't,' she said. 'I can't stay here. I have to leave. I'm sorry I won't be able to help you after all, but—'

'You *have* helped me, Stephanie,' he said gruffly. 'In ways you can't even begin to imagine.'

She became very still. 'By going to bed with you?'

He winced. 'As it happens, yes.'

She took a step back, even as she looked at him searchingly. The sudden glitter that appeared in those deep green eyes said she didn't like what she saw! 'You've had doubts since the accident about your ability to make love to a woman,' she realised incredulously.

Jordan scowled. 'I wouldn't put it quite like that—'

'I would!' She gritted her teeth. 'Well, aren't I the lucky one? I had no idea I was helping to restore the sexual confidence of the legendary lover Jordan Simpson!'

'Damn it, it was interest that I lacked—not sexual confidence!'

Obviously he hadn't expected to feel like making love to anyone immediately after the accident; he had been in so much pain at the time there hadn't been room for him to feel anything else. But once he had recovered enough to be discharged from hospital, to have friends come over to his house in Malibu, Jordan had thought he might resume his relationship with Crista. After only a few minutes spent in her company, though, he had known that he no longer wanted her. In his life or in his bed.

As the days and weeks had passed, Jordan had realised that he didn't want *any* of the beautiful women— models and actress friends—who'd come to his house and blatantly let him know they would be only too happy to fill the place Crista had once had in his life.

He hadn't wanted any of them.

Until Stephanie.

Stephanie McKinley had burst into his life like a refreshing breeze. Answering him back. Challenging him. Arousing him…

She gave an impatient shake of her head now. 'Well, I'm sure you'll be glad to know you haven't lost your touch in the slightest! Now, if you will excuse me—'

'No, I *won't* excuse you!' Jordan surged to his feet and reached out to grasp her arm and turn her forcibly back to face him. 'You're twisting this conversation deliberately because of your relationship with someone called Richard—'

'I do *not* have a relationship with someone called Richard!'

'Not any more, no,' Jordan accepted. 'I thought that was the problem,' he said. 'But don't you see that the fact you respond to *me* shows your feelings for this other guy aren't as strong as you think they are? That you wouldn't have been able to respond in the way you did just now if you were in love with someone else?'

She looked mutinous. 'I refuse to talk about this any more, Jordan.'

Jordan frowned down at her, frustrated. Half of him wanted to kiss her again, and the other half wanted to tan her obstinate little bottom. Either solution was guaranteed to make Stephanie even angrier in her present mood. 'Maybe we can talk again once you've had time to calm down?' he suggested through gritted teeth.

Those green eyes flashed in warning before she wrenched out of his grasp. 'I very much doubt that I'm going to calm down any time soon,' she said scathingly. 'Now, please *leave*!' She marched into the adjoining bathroom and slammed the door loudly behind her.

Having given Jordan a tantalising glimpse of her bare and perfectly shaped bottom!

Not his finest hour, he recognised with a pained grimace as he heard the shower being turned on as another way of Stephanie telling him she had no intention of coming out of the bathroom until after he had left.

His movements were slow as he pulled his clothes back on before using his cane to stand up and glare at that closed bathroom door. Stephanie might not want to talk to him, but she was damn well going to listen to what he had to say. And soon!

He came to an abrupt halt when he entered the adjoining sitting room to find Gideon relaxing on the sofa, idly flicking through a magazine. 'How long have you been in here?' His eyes were narrowed suspiciously.

Gideon looked across at him mockingly as he put the magazine down before standing up. 'Legendary lover?' he drawled speculatively.

'Oh, go to hell, Gid!' Jordan limped across the room into his bedroom, slamming the door just as loudly behind him as Stephanie had the bathroom door a few minutes ago.

And just as finally...

It took Stephanie only ten minutes or so to shower and dress in the bathroom, deliberately keeping her gaze firmly averted from the rumpled covers on the four-poster bed when she came back into the bedroom to collect her coat and bag.

She hurried out of the bedroom as if the devil were snapping at her heels. Or those erotic memories of herself and Jordan naked on the bed as they made love together!

'Leaving us so soon, Stephanie...?'

She turned sharply from closing the bedroom door to find Gideon St Claire leaning casually against the wall just outside the door to Jordan's suite.

Her chin rose defensively as she saw the dark speculation in Gideon's eyes. 'Obviously, with your mother here, you're all going to be kept pretty busy over the next few days, so I thought I might as well go back to my own flat.'

He gave her a straight look. 'I totally agree. Jordan can be a complete and utter ass.'

Stephanie felt warm colour bloom in her cheeks and cursed her fair skin—not for the first time. 'I don't believe I mentioned Jordan…'

'But you were thinking it,' Gideon said knowingly as he straightened. 'My mother would like to meet you.'

Stephanie's chest clenched in panic at the thought of being introduced to the matriarch of the St Claire family when she had so recently made love with her youngest son. 'I don't think that's a good idea.'

'Why not?'

'Well— Because—' She straightened her shoulders and looked him in the eye. 'I won't be coming back here again after today, Gideon.'

Blond brows rose. 'And that precludes you being introduced to my mother?'

'It makes it…an unnecessary complication.' Stephanie gave him a look, pleading with him to understand what she wasn't saying.

Gideon gave a grim smile. 'Can things between you and Jordan get any more complicated?'

Stephanie felt the colour draining from her cheeks as rapidly as it had entered. This man knew exactly what had happened in Stephanie's bedroom a short time ago.

'Obviously not.' She could no longer meet that knowing dark gaze.

'So you're just going to run away? Is that it?' Gideon asked.

Stephanie's mouth firmed. 'Lucan employed me as a physiotherapist for Jordan. Obviously that is no longer possible. There's nothing more I can do here,' she added determinedly as Gideon continued to look at her from between narrowed lids.

His mouth thinned. 'You've already done more for Jordan than anyone else has been able to do since the accident.'

'So I understand,' she said self-consciously.

Gideon gave a rueful smile. 'Actually, I wasn't referring to any personal relationship the two of you might or might not have.'

'Contrary to what you may have thought or assumed, I don't *have* a personal relationship with your brother,' Stephanie told him determinedly. 'I really do have to go now—' She broke off as Gideon reached out and lightly clasped her arm.

'Before you went to Gloucestershire Jordan had shut himself off from everyone. Had become completely reclusive. Uncommunicative.' He shook his head grimly as he slowly released her. 'It had gone on for so long that we had all begun to think he was never going to come out of it. He changed after you went there, Stephanie.' His expression softened. 'I could see the difference in him immediately after I arrived at Mulberry Hall yesterday.'

'I didn't do *anything*—'

'You didn't need to do anything but be yourself,' Gideon assured her. 'Watching the two of you together,

I've realised that it's the very nature of your personality which provokes him. Challenges him.'

'I'm not sure that saying I get on Jordan's nerves enough to provoke him into doing things is altogether flattering—'

'You're deliberately misunderstanding me,' Gideon said shrewdly.

'No, Gideon, I'm not.' She sighed, then reached out and gave his arm an apologetic squeeze, knowing that his concern for his twin was genuine. 'I'm pleased if you think I've annoyed Jordan enough that it's challenged him out of his seclusion at last, but my decision to leave is based solely on my own needs—not his. I simply can't stay on here any longer after— Well, I just can't,' she said emotionally.

'Do you think Jordan is just going to let you walk out of his life?'

Her eyes widened. 'Don't you?'

He gave her a wicked smile—the exact twin of Jordan's. 'Knowing Jordan, I somehow doubt it.'

Stephanie locked suddenly weak knees. 'I'm sure you're wrong.'

At least she hoped Gideon was wrong.

There was absolutely no future for herself and Jordan that Stephanie could see. Even if she could persuade him into believing she wasn't involved in a relationship with Richard Newman, he was still a world-famous actor while she was a mere physiotherapist. Jordan lived and worked in America; she lived and worked in England. This house, the private helicopter, the opulence of the Mulberry Hall estate—all of those things were an indication of the gulf there was between them, both socially and financially.

And, worst of all, Stephanie knew she had been

nothing more than a diversion for Jordan. A pique to his interest. Once he was back to his full health, back in LA and working again, he would forget that Stephanie McKinley even existed!

CHAPTER ELEVEN

'WHAT are you doing here, Jordan?'

Jordan scowled as Stephanie showed all too clearly, by the way she'd deliberately kept the door to her flat half-closed, that she had no intention of inviting him inside. 'Surely it's obvious why I'm here?' he bit out impatiently as he leant heavily on his cane.

He had spent the morning at the clinic with his mother, and now his hip and leg were aching from that and from the sheer effort of getting to Stephanie's apartment building—let alone discovering there was no lift when he got here, and so having to walk up two flights of stairs to her flat on the second floor.

'Not to me.' She gave a shake of her head.

Her hair was pulled back in a ponytail today, and she was dressed in a figure-hugging blue T-shirt and faded low-slung jeans. But her make-up-less face was so pale that the sprinkling of freckles across her nose showed in stark relief.

'I suggest you invite me inside, Stephanie, before you end up with an unconscious man on your doorstep,' Jordan warned her suddenly.

Stephanie kept the door half-closed as she looked at Jordan searchingly, noting the strain beside his eyes and mouth, and the slight pallor of his cheeks beneath his tan. 'How did your mother's appointment with the specialist go this morning?' She was concerned for the other woman, in spite of knowing that she wouldn't be having anything further to do with any of the St Claire family members.

Jordan had made it more than obvious from his remarks yesterday that what had happened between the two of them had meant nothing more to him than a reaffirmation of physical desire.

Just as Stephanie knew it had meant everything to her.

She had long been infatuated by Jordan Simpson. In lust with him, even, as she'd gazed at him wistfully on the big and small screen. But in the past few days she had fallen completely in love with Jordan St Claire. Quite how it had happened Stephanie had no idea, when he had been either rude or inappropriately over-familiar since the moment they'd first met. She only knew that she was in love with the man she had made love with yesterday. Totally. Irrevocably.

Unfortunately, the wealthy and privileged Jordan St Claire was as unlikely to fall in love with someone like her as Jordan Simpson was...

'Jord—' She broke off with a nervy start as the telephone began to ring in her flat.

The disturbing hang-up calls that had been part of Stephanie's reason for wanting to leave London had resumed first thing this morning. Four so far. Stephanie had answered the first two, only to have the line abruptly disconnected.

It wasn't difficult to know who was making those calls, and Stephanie had called Joey and asked her to use her legal influence with the telephone company and get her a new number as soon as possible.

Too late, Stephanie realised she should have taken the receiver off the hook while she was waiting for that new number!

Jordan quirked dark brows. 'Aren't you going to answer that?'

Stephanie gave a tense shrug. 'They'll call back if it's anything important.'

'If you let me in and answer the call then they won't need to call back,' he reasoned lightly.

Stephanie frowned her irritation. 'We have nothing to say to each other, Jordan—'

'You may not have anything to say to me,' he accepted grimly, 'but I certainly have a few things I want to say to you.' He didn't wait for Stephanie to open the door further, but instead pushed against it with his cane and walked into the flat, leaving her to close the door behind him.

At least the telephone had stopped ringing by the time she'd followed Jordan through to her sitting room. 'Well?' Stephanie prompted guardedly as she watched him drop down wearily into one of the armchairs.

His hair was as wild and windblown as ever, but he had shaved at least, and was wearing a tailored black jacket over a white shirt and faded jeans.

Jordan didn't answer her immediately, but instead looked around the sitting room. He liked the simplicity of the warm cream walls, adorned with several Turner prints of Venice. There were three colourful rugs on the polished wood floor, and the only furniture was a wide-screen television set, a low coffee table, a comfortable terracotta-coloured sofa, and two armchairs covered in numerous cushions. Despite the simplicity of the décor, Jordan found the room as warm and inviting as Stephanie was herself.

Although Jordan had to admit she didn't look very inviting at the moment, as she glared down at him!

He answered her earlier question evenly. 'Tests showed my mother's tumour to be benign.'

'That must be a relief for all of you!' Stephanie spoke with her first genuine warmth since she had opened the knock on the door and found Jordan standing outside.

'Yes.' He nodded tersely, eyes narrowed. 'Stephanie, why did you leave without saying goodbye?'

She clasped her hands tightly together so that he shouldn't see how they were shaking. 'I did what I thought was best.'

'For whom?'

'For me, actually,' she said honestly. 'For you too, of course. It would just have been awkward for everyone if I had stayed on at St Claire House after what happened between us yesterday.'

Jordan raised dark brows. 'I don't embarrass that easily.'

'Lucky you,' Stephanie said. 'When I went downstairs Lucan came out of his study to tell me my car had been delivered from Gloucestershire. I explained to him then that I didn't feel I could do anything to help you. He seemed happy with my decision to leave,' she said firmly.

'*I'm* not happy with your decision!' Jordan barked.

Her chin rose defensively. 'No? Well. You're probably just a little…irritated with me at the moment. But you'll get over it.'

'I'm upset, Stephanie, not irritated!' he corrected. 'We need to talk, and you left before we had a chance to do that.' He sat forward tensely.

'Because I have nothing else to say to you—' Stephanie broke off as the telephone began to ring again. She should definitely have taken the receiver off the hook. And she would have done so if she hadn't been waiting for the telephone company to ring her and tell her about her new number. It might even be them ringing now. But with Jordan present Stephanie didn't feel inclined to answer the call only to discover that it was Rosalind Newman making a nuisance of herself again.

Stephanie felt for the other woman, she really did, but that didn't make it any easier for her to be the fixation of the other woman's obsessive jealousy.

Jordan eyed her impatiently as she ignored the call. 'If you won't answer that, then I will!' He reached out for the receiver.

'No—' Stephanie gave up her effort to prevent him from answering the call as Jordan placed the receiver to his ear.

'Stephanie McKinley's residence.' Jordan spoke pleasantly into the receiver as he eyed Stephanie mockingly. 'Hello?' He frowned. 'Hello!' he repeated sharply, a dark frown now marring his brow. 'What the hell—?' He held the receiver away from his ear before slowly replacing it on the cradle and turning back to Stephanie, brows raised questioningly.

She moistened dry lips, knowing from Jordan's expression that this fifth call had to have ended as abruptly as the previous four. 'I—I seem to have a crank caller at the moment,' she dismissed, her gaze not quite meeting Jordan's probing one. 'The telephone company has been informed, and they're organising a new number for me.'

'Why not the police? And how long is "at the moment"?' Jordan asked slowly.

'The police are far too busy for me to worry them

about some idiot making a nuisance of themselves on the telephone,' Stephanie said hurriedly. 'It's been happening for a couple of weeks now. It's just been especially annoying this morning.' Probably because she hadn't been there to answer the calls for the past three days!

'A couple of weeks or so?' Jordan repeated incredulously as he stood up. 'Some nut has been harassing you like this for weeks, and you've only now decided to do anything about it? Your sister is a lawyer—why didn't you get her to do something about them before now?'

Because Stephanie hadn't mentioned the calls to Joey originally—had been stupid enough to hope that Rosalind would stop before either the law or the police needed to be involved!

'She's doing something about it now.'

'Not soon enough, by the state of your nerves!'

Stephanie moved away restlessly. 'They're just hang-up calls, Jordan. She— They'll get tired of it eventually and stop.'

'She?' Jordan pounced shrewdly.

'He. She.' Stephanie frowned her exasperation with his astuteness in picking up on every word she said. 'What does it matter what sex they are?'

'It doesn't,' Jordan said. 'Unless you *know* who's making the calls?'

'And why do you suppose I would know that?'

'You tell me,' Jordan said.

He had been absolutely furious last night, when he'd discovered that Stephanie had left St Claire House without so much as telling him. So furious that he had decided it would be better to delay coming here to see her until today, giving a chance for that anger to subside overnight. A few minutes in her company and he knew that twelve hours' delay had been a complete waste of his time!

'Stephanie!' he prompted harshly.

She clasped her hands even more tightly together as she scowled at him. 'It's none of your business, Jordan.'

'I'm making it my business,' he said.

Stephanie shook her head. 'You don't have the right to come here and demand to know about my private life.'

'By taking my body into yours you've given me that right,' he said outrageously.

Colour warmed her cheeks and she gasped. 'That was completely uncalled for, Jordan!'

Jordan threw his cane down on the sofa to reach out and grasp the tops of her arms. 'As your leaving yesterday without saying goodbye to me was completely uncalled for!' He glowered down at her. 'How do you think that made me feel, Stephanie?' His voice gentled. 'I know that you were upset last night, but that still doesn't excuse just walking out on me like that without any explanation.'

'The fact that I did leave should have been explanation enough,' she said exasperatedly.

Jordan released her, to take a halting step backwards, his face pale. 'It was your way of telling me you would prefer that our relationship not continue?'

'We don't *have* a relationship, Jordan,' Stephanie said emotionally. 'You said from the beginning that you were only playing with me—'

'What's your excuse?' he rasped harshly. 'Is it still this guy Richard?'

'I've told you that it isn't!' she insisted vehemently.

'Then what is it?'

'You're Jordan Simpson!' she snapped.

He eyed her warily. 'So?'

'So I've had a thing about you for *years*!'

'A thing?' Jordan repeated softly.

'A thing,' Stephanie repeated uncomfortably. 'Look at my DVD collection, Jordan.' She pointed to the cabinet next to the wide-screen television set. 'I have bought every film you've ever made. But not before I dragged my sister to the cinema to see every one of them first. My idea of an enjoyable evening at home is to put on one of your movies and sit and drool over you for a couple of hours!'

A nerve pulsed in Jordan's tightly clenched jaw. 'So this *thing* you have is only for Jordan Simpson?'

No, of course it wasn't! Stephanie's infatuation, maybe. But it was Jordan St Claire she had fallen in love with. A man as unlike the suavely charming and sophisticated screen image of Jordan Simpson as it was possible to for him to be…

Something Stephanie had no intention of ever admitting, least of all to Jordan himself!

'Yes,' she confirmed flatly. 'I'm sorry, Jordan.' She winced as she saw the way his expression had darkened ominously. 'I just—I did try not to get personally involved with you. I told you that it wasn't a good idea. But you've always been this fantasy to me, you see, and so when I found myself in bed with you yesterday—'

'You don't need to say any more,' he rasped harshly, those gold-coloured eyes as hard as the metal they resembled. He looked absolutely livid. 'I somehow never imagined you as a movie-star groupie—'

'I wouldn't go that far,' she cut in indignantly.

'I would,' he bit out frigidly. 'A pity for you that we've met when I'm obviously looking and feeling less than my best,' he added contemptuously as he bent to pick up his cane. 'I obviously didn't come even close to living up to the fantasy!'

Stephanie hated this conversation. *Hated* it!

She loved this man. Not Jordan Simpson. Not even Jordan St Claire. But the man standing in front of her right now. The man who in Gloucestershire had still been able to tease despite the fact that he was in constant pain. The man who had made love with her yesterday with a fierce heat she was never going to be able to forget. That she never wanted to forget. Just as she knew she never wanted to forget Jordan...

She wished things could be different. Wished that she could explain about Richard Newman to Jordan— that she could tell him the truth and that he would tell her he believed her. That he loved her too. But Jordan didn't love her, and he never would. After all, he had only made love with her to prove he could still desire a woman that way.

Which left Stephanie with no alternative but to try and salvage as much of her pride as she could. 'I don't have any complaints.' She shrugged.

Jordan's mouth compressed as he looked at her challengingly. 'Neither do I.'

Stephanie felt the warmth of colour in her cheeks. 'Then—' She broke off with a frown as the doorbell rang. 'That could be someone from the telephone company.'

'I don't think they usually make house-calls in order to change a number,' Jordan said.

Neither did Stephanie. Which was why she was reluctant to actually go and open the door...

Jordan found he was even more angry now than he had been the previous evening! Angry and disappointed that Stephanie was obviously as enamoured of his screen image as so many of the other women he'd met, rather than being attracted to the man he actually was.

He had dreamed of becoming a professional actor from the time he'd starred in a school play at the age of eleven. Had chosen to go to drama school rather than university. Done several years of stage work in England before being offered a film role in America ten years ago.

He enjoyed the success he had made of his career. Enjoyed the lifestyle it gave him. The celebrity status. But one of the drawbacks had always been that women were attracted to Jordan Simpson rather than Jordan St Claire, and unfortunately Stephanie was no exception...

He sighed heavily. 'It's time I was leaving—' He frowned as the doorbell rang again—longer this time, and somehow more insistent. 'Shouldn't you go and see who that is?' he asked, as Stephanie continued to ignore this second, much longer ring of the doorbell.

'I thought you said it was important that we finish our conversation?'

Jordan studied her through narrowed lids, once again noting that pallor to her cheeks and the wariness of her gaze. 'As far as I'm aware, it's finished.'

She gave him a bright, meaningless smile. 'I'm not in the mood for more visitors this morning.'

Jordan scowled at her obvious reluctance to answer the door. 'Stephanie, what the hell is going on here?'

'Nothing,' she denied hastily.

His scowl deepened. 'I don't believe you.'

Her eyes widened. 'I don't have to explain myself to you—'

'You're right, you don't,' Jordan said as he turned

to walk haltingly towards the door of the flat. 'Maybe your visitor will be a little more forthcoming?'

'No, Jordan—'

Jordan had wrenched the door open before Stephanie had fully realised his intention, frowning as he looked at the woman who stood outside in the hallway.

From Stephanie's evasive behaviour he had expected that her visitor would be a man. Perhaps this Richard he'd wanted to know about...

But the woman standing in the hallway was tall and blonde, probably aged in her mid-thirties, and the angry glitter of her blue eyes as she looked past Jordan to glare at Stephanie seemed to indicate that she was feeling less than friendly towards her!

Those blue eyes flicked scornfully over Jordan, before moving down to his cane. 'Another one, Stephanie?' the woman said insultingly.

'I—'

'Another what?' Jordan asked in a steely voice.

'Perhaps you aren't aware of it, but Stephanie makes a habit of having affairs with her patients,' the woman said. 'First my husband, and now you!'

This had to be Stephanie's worst nightmare!

Having Rosalind Newman arrive on her doorstep at all was bad enough, but having her make these awful accusations in front of Jordan was even worse.

She took a step forward. 'Rosalind, you aren't well—'

'I'm perfectly well, thank you!' the older woman snapped contemptuously.

The last few months of the emotional turmoil of her disintegrating marriage had not been kind to Rosalind; she was much too thin, and her face was much harder, older, than when Stephanie had first met her three months ago.

'Or as well as I can be after you stole my husband from me!' Rosalind spat out. 'Does Richard know about *him*?' She glared at Jordan.

Stephanie couldn't even look at Jordan to see what he was making of this conversation. She stepped around him so that she could confront Rosalind. Although he could hardly have been left in any doubt as to exactly what Rosalind was accusing her of! 'There's nothing to know, Rosalind,' she said soothingly. 'And even if there was it would be none of Richard's business. For the last time—I'm not and I never have been involved in an affair with your husband. He was my patient, yes, but that was the extent of our relationship.'

Blue eyes narrowed viciously. 'I don't believe you.'

'I know you don't.' Stephanie sighed heavily. 'And I'm really sorry that you don't. But that doesn't make it any less the truth.'

Rosalind raised her hands, her fingers curled like talons about to strike. 'You're nothing but a marriage-wrecking little—'

'I think not!' Jordan raised his cane to fend off the attack of those fingers as the woman would have reached out and raked her nails down Stephanie's face. 'Go home,' he told the other woman firmly as he stepped protectively in front of an obviously shaken Stephanie.

'I haven't finished yet—'

'Oh, yes, you have,' Jordan said. 'And if you want to know who wrecked your marriage then I suggest you try looking in a mirror,' he added bluntly.

'How dare you—?' The woman broke off abruptly as she seemed to look at him for the first time. 'Do I know you?'

'No, thank God!' Jordan said with feeling.

'You look very familiar...'

Jordan's mouth quirked. 'I get that all the time.'

The woman blinked dazedly. 'Are the two of you... involved?'

Jordan didn't even hesitate. 'Yes.'

'I—I don't understand.' She looked far less sure of herself now. 'What about Richard?' She looked frowningly at Stephanie.

'Stephanie has already told you that she isn't and never has been involved with your husband,' Jordan reiterated.

'I— But I'm divorcing him because of her!'

'I'm sorry about that.' Jordan frowned. 'But you've made a mistake concerning her involvement. Now, if you wouldn't mind...?' He carefully eased the woman back with his cane until she was once again fully outside in the hallway. 'I advise you not to come here and bother Stephanie again,' he said.

Anger seemed to have given way to confusion, as if the woman wasn't even sure how she came to be here now.

'I think you need to get some professional help before you end up actually hurting someone other than yourself,' Jordan added gently.

'I... Yes.' The woman turned away.

'Rosalind—'

'Let her go, Stephanie!' Jordan instructed swiftly as she made a move as if to follow the other woman. 'Leave her with some pride, damn it!'

Stephanie came to an abrupt halt, her breath catching in her throat as she looked up at Jordan and saw the expression in those beautiful gold-coloured eyes.

Despite his defence of her just now, both verbally

and physically, Jordan was obviously still far from convinced of her innocence in the breakdown of Rosalind Newman's marriage...

CHAPTER TWELVE

'Is SHE also the one making the telephone calls?'

Stephanie had staggered back into her flat to walk through to the kitchen and automatically go through the motions of making a pot of coffee. Certain, as she heard her flat door being closed seconds later, that Jordan had taken the opportunity to leave. Obviously she had been wrong...

She turned to face him across her red and white kitchen as he stood in the doorway, leaning heavily on his cane, the expression in those gold-coloured eyes hidden by narrowed lids. 'Yes,' she admitted wearily.

Jordan nodded. 'And having a man answer the last call was reason enough for her to decide to pay you a personal visit?'

'Probably—as the Newmans' house is only half a mile or so away.' Stephanie sighed. 'At least *Rosalind* lives only half a mile or so away,' she added. 'I believe Richard moved into an apartment of his own several weeks ago.'

'But you're not sure?'

Stephanie gritted her teeth in frustration with a situation that had already been complicated enough before Rosalind Newman's intervention! 'Look, Jordan, I know how bad this all looks and sounds—especially after what's happened between us the last few days—but—'

'I don't consider the problem you're currently experiencing with Rosalind Newman to have anything to do with what took place between us,' Jordan said.

Stephanie eyed him warily. 'You don't?'

He shrugged. 'You've already assured me that our own relationship only went as far as it did because of your long-held infatuation with Jordan Simpson,' he reminded her coldly. 'Which would seem to indicate that the two incidents have little to do with each other.'

'You were my patient too—'

'I think we can both agree that you never actually got as far as a working relationship with me,' Jordan drawled.

'I didn't have an affair with Richard Newman, either.'

He arched dark brows. 'Did I say that you did?'

'No, but Rosalind did!' Stephanie's cheeks felt warm as she thought of the accusations the other woman had made in front of Jordan.

He gave a shrug as he walked further into the kitchen to perch on the side of one of the stools at the breakfast-bar. 'I think we can safely assume the poor woman has been knocked slightly emotionally off-balance by the breakdown of her marriage.' His mouth tightened. 'So much so that she's looking for someone else to blame.'

Stephanie looked at him uncertainly. 'You really believe me when I say I didn't have an affair with Richard Newman?'

'Shouldn't I?'

Well, of course Jordan should believe her, when it was nothing less than the truth! Stephanie just hadn't expected that he would... 'I do think Rosalind is right about Richard having an affair with someone, though.'

'Just not you?'

She grimaced. 'No.'

Jordan's earlier anger had dissipated in the face of this more pressing problem for Stephanie. Much as he felt sorry for Rosalind Newman's dilemma, her behaviour earlier indicated that she was close to breaking emotionally. Dangerously close.

'Pour us both some coffee, hmm?' Jordan encouraged softly. 'And then you can tell me exactly why you think Newman is having an affair, but has no problem with letting an innocent bystander bear the brunt of his wife's anger.'

'I'm sure you don't need to be bothered with my problems—'

'Having enough of my own, presumably?' Jordan said dryly.

'I didn't mean that!'

'Just pour the coffee, Stephanie, and let me worry about what I do or don't want to be bothered with,' he rasped, and he made himself more comfortable on the bar stool.

Stephanie still looked less than certain, but she poured coffee into two mugs anyway, placing them and milk and sugar on the breakfast bar before sitting on the stool opposite Jordan's.

'What do you want to know?'

'Everything.'

It had all started out innocently enough, as far as Jordan could see. Richard Newman had been involved in a car accident which had resulted in his needing physiotherapy on a daily basis at his home, once he'd been discharged from hospital. Those treatments had lessened to three times a week and begun taking place at Stephanie's small private treatment room once he had regained most of his mobility and returned to work in the City.

'Let me guess,' Jordan commented. 'This is where the trouble started?'

Stephanie gave a heavy sigh. 'It seems that Rosalind and Richard's boss were both still under the impression he was having treatment five afternoons a week.'

'So on those other two afternoons he was meeting someone else?'

'I can only assume he must have been.' Stephanie nodded uncomfortably. 'He certainly wasn't spending them with me.'

'I've already said I believe you, Stephanie,' Jordan said.

She frowned. 'But *why* do you?'

Interesting question, Jordan acknowledged ruefully. Interesting, but totally redundant, since Stephanie had assured him that her only interest in him had been as his actor persona!

'You may have your faults, Stephanie, but I don't believe that dishonesty is one of them,' he said, and he picked up his cane to stand up suddenly. 'I hope this situation works out for you.'

She looked startled. 'You're leaving?'

Jordan gave a hard smile. 'Unless you think we have anything left to say to each other?'

No, Stephanie was pretty sure they didn't have anything left to say that would be in the least conducive to closing the ever-widening gulf that now existed between them. Certainly nothing she could say that would induce

Jordan to stay. To be as in love her as she was with him...

'No,' she said baldly.

'That's what I thought.'

It was better this way, Stephanie assured herself as she accompanied Jordan to the door. No less painful, of course, but at least she had been able to see Jordan again—however briefly. 'Thank you for listening to me,' she said ruefully as she held the door open for him. 'It helped.'

He turned to face her. 'I've made arrangements to fly back to the States tomorrow.'

Stephanie's eyes widened even as she acknowledged the sinking feeling in her chest. 'You have?'

Jordan gave a wry smile. 'I've decided to take your advice and go back to see my original specialist in LA.'

'That's wonderful news!' She smiled warmly.

Jordan's smile was humourless. 'You could try looking a little less pleased to see me go.'

As the woman who was madly in love with him, of course Stephanie wasn't pleased to know that Jordan would be leaving England tomorrow. Going back to his life in LA, to once again be with women like the beautiful Crista Moore.

But as a physiotherapist she couldn't have been more pleased by Jordan's decision to go back to America and seek the professional help she was sure he needed, and which he had totally refused to accept from her or anyone else.

'I'm only pleased because I know you're doing the right thing,' she answered evasively.

'I hope you're right,' he said enigmatically, giving

her one last searching glance before he turned and walked away.

From a professional point of view Stephanie knew she was right.

From a personal one she could feel her heart slowly breaking as she watched Jordan walk away from her for ever...

'Wine! I'm desperately in need of wine!' Joey gasped weakly as she collapsed wearily down onto Stephanie's sofa and put her booted feet up on top of the coffee table.

Stephanie eyed her twin teasingly, before going through to the kitchen to collect up the bottle of red wine and two glasses she had waiting. The two sisters usually spent one evening a week together, catching up on each other's lives. Not that Stephanie had much to tell Joey. The last two weeks had consisted of work, work, and more work. All in a futile effort to block Jordan out of her thoughts by keeping herself busy.

'Tough day?' she wanted to know as she sat down in the chair opposite Joey.

Her sister drank down half the glass of wine before answering her. She was still wearing one of the business suits she always wore to the office, brown today, with a cream silk blouse beneath, her face perfectly made up, her short red hair sleekly styled. 'Just the afternoon. *Bloody* man!' Joey muttered with feeling.

'Which man?' Stephanie couldn't help laughing at her sister's disgruntled expression.

'Gideon St Claire.' Joey glared. 'He has got to be the most pompous, arrogant—'

'*My* Gideon St Claire?' Stephanie echoed sharply as she sat forward tensely.

Joey snorted. 'Well, I wouldn't go *that* far, sis.'

'You know exactly what I mean!' Stephanie was almost beside herself with impatience. 'I didn't think Gideon ever went into a courtroom nowadays?'

'He doesn't—thank God.' Joey gave a shudder at the mere thought of that ever happening. 'He made an appointment and came to see me at my office. I have to say, Stephs, that you have some very powerful friends.' She took another obviously much-needed swig of her wine. 'Gideon St Claire is a seriously scary man. And so damned cold that I'm surprised he doesn't have icicles dripping off him! Still, he did succeed where I failed,' she added grudgingly. 'So he can't be all bad, I suppose...'

'Joey, could you possibly go back a couple of sentences?' Stephanie had finally got over the shock of Joey having met Gideon. 'For one thing, I would hardly call Gideon St Claire a friend of mine—'

'Then maybe he just lusts after you?' her sister dismissed airily. 'Whatever. He got the job done, and that's all that really—'

'Joey, *stop*!' Stephanie silenced her sister sharply, knowing that if Joey was left to her own devices she could go on like this for hours—based purely on her assumption that the person she was talking to should know exactly what she was talking about. Which Stephanie certainly didn't. 'Start from the beginning and tell me exactly *why* Gideon made an appointment and came to see you today.'

Joey took her booted feet off the table to lean forward and refill her glass with red wine. 'It's amazing—the man was only on the case a few days, and he managed to get the whole thing settled without us having to go to court. It was pretty neat, actually,' she added with grudging admiration.

'Joey, I still don't understand a word of what you're saying!' Stephanie wailed frustratedly.

'It's all over, Stephs,' her sister explained patiently. 'With the help of a private investigator, Gideon St Claire has managed to establish that Richard Newman was actually having an affair with his boss's wife. Obviously it's not good news for Rosalind—or Richard Newman, for that matter, considering that he's apparently now lost his job as well as his marriage—but it does mean that you're completely out of the picture,' Joey said warmly. 'All thanks to the arrogant Gideon St Claire.'

Stephanie was reeling with shock. Disbelief. 'But why would he do such a thing?' she finally managed to gasp.

'Because his gorgeous and sexy brother asked him to, of course,' Joey said happily.

'*Jordan* did?'

'Does he have more than one gorgeous and sexy brother?'

'He does, actually,' Stephanie acknowledged faintly, as she thought of the chillingly handsome Lucan St Claire.

'Oh.' Her sister looked nonplussed for a few seconds. But, being the irrepressible Joey, she recovered just as quickly. 'Well, this time it was Jordan Simpson who did the asking.'

Stephanie was still totally stunned. 'Did Gideon tell you that?'

'That and a lot more.' Joey nodded eagerly. 'Apparently Jordan was admitted to a private clinic in LA two weeks ago for yet another operation.'

'Was it successful?' Stephanie was unable to keep the anxiety out of her voice.

'Completely.' Joey took another swig of her wine. 'According to Gideon, the hip joint had become slightly misaligned—I'm sure you understand what that means better than I do,' she added. 'Anyway, the end result is that Jordan Simpson is back up on his two perfectly gorgeous legs. So much so that he has already got backing and is due to play the lead role in the movie of the script he's been writing the last six months.'

It was the best news Stephanie could ever have wished or hoped for. It also explained what Jordan had been doing during those hours when he had disappeared into his study while at Mulberry Hall...

What it *didn't* explain was why Jordan had asked his twin to intercede and help Stephanie in her unwilling involvement with the Newmans' messy divorce—or Gideon St Claire's uncharacteristic gregariousness in discussing his brother so candidly with Joey!

She stood up. 'I don't understand...'

'No?' Joey eyed her knowingly. 'Stephs, exactly how close did you and Jordan get during those few days together in Gloucestershire?'

Stephanie had been fighting against even allowing herself to *think* about Jordan these last couple of weeks, let alone put herself through the torture of remembering the intimacy of their lovemaking. How much she loved him. But this—Jordan asking Gideon to intercede on her behalf in the Newmans' divorce—was so totally unexpected that she no longer knew what to think.

Or to feel.

She needed to talk to Jordan. Needed to know why he had gone to the trouble of asking his brother to help her when there had been so much going on in his own life. Needed to know if Jordan had just been being kind, or if it had been something else that had prompted his actions. What if—?

Stephanie frowned as the doorbell rang.

'Expecting more company?' Joey asked interestedly.

'No,' Stephanie said. 'But at least I know it won't be Rosalind Newman, come to insult me again.'

'Maybe she's come to apologise instead?' Joey suggested ruefully.

'Poor woman.' Stephanie gave a regretful shake of her head before going to answer the door.

Only to be rendered totally speechless when she opened the door and found Jordan standing outside in the hallway. It was too much after what Joey had just told her—a complete overload to Stephanie's already raw emotions. So much so that she instantly burst into loud and choking sobs!

Not quite the reaction he had been hoping for, Jordan acknowledged with a frown as he stepped forward to take the sobbing Stephanie in his arms.

He wasn't really sure what sort of welcome he had been expecting after not seeing or speaking to her for over two weeks, but it certainly hadn't been this!

'Who is it, Stephs? What did you do to her?' An accusing redhead had appeared in the sitting room doorway, frowning darkly as she saw the sobbing Stephanie in Jordan's arms. 'Is it bad news?' She hurried to Stephanie's side. 'What's happened?' she demanded sharply, looking up at Jordan. 'Oh, my God!' Green eyes had gone wide in recognition.

Jordan gave a rueful grin. 'You must be Joey.' Her

facial similarity to Stephanie was obvious, despite the close-cropped hair and formal clothes.

She gave a slightly dazed nod of her head as she continued to stare at him. 'Would you two like to be alone?'

'No!'

'Yes! *Yes*, Stephanie,' Jordan repeated firmly, his arms tightening around her as she would have pulled away. 'It was nice meeting you,' he told Joey warmly over the top of Stephanie's head.

'The pleasure was all mine,' she murmured softly. 'Call me, Stephs.'

She couldn't seem to stop staring at Jordan, even as she gave her sister a perfunctory kiss on the cheek before quietly leaving.

Stephanie felt more than a little foolish over her reaction to seeing him again now that she was alone with him. What on earth must he think of her? Bursting into tears like that just because she had found him standing on her doorstep?

She hastily wiped the evidence of those tears from her cheeks as she straightened. 'What are you doing here, Jordan?' she asked as she pulled away from him. 'I'm not sure you should have flown to England at all when you've only recently undergone surgery,' she added worriedly.

Her breath caught in her throat as she looked at Jordan properly for the first time. His hair was shorter than she remembered, and had been cut in that casually rakish style that only an expensive professional could have achieved. And his face no longer had that grim and strained expression. The lines beside his eyes and mouth seemed to have eased, and his jaw was freshly shaven to reveal that gorgeous cleft in his chin. His eyes were a clear and searching gold as he quizzically returned her gaze. He looked fit and healthy, in a tailored charcoal-coloured jacket over a black shirt and black trousers. And he no longer carried the cane...

'The operation was a success,' Stephanie realised happily.

Jordan's smile widened. 'Yes, it was. Thanks to you,' he added huskily.

She frowned. 'I didn't do anything.'

'You repeatedly told me what a self-pitying idiot I was, and told me to go and get my leg looked at again,' he reminded her dryly. 'Are you going to invite me inside, Stephanie? Or have I made myself so unwelcome you would rather keep me standing out here in the hallway?'

'I—no, of course not.' Stephanie stepped back to allow him to walk into her apartment, her heart lifting as she saw the way Jordan walked only with a slight emphasis on his right leg now—and that was sure to disappear completely, too, after a few more weeks of full mobility.

Except she still had no idea what he was doing here!

She followed him through to the sitting room, the palms of her hands feeling damp as she faced him. 'You told me that Gideon called you a self-pitying idiot too,' she pointed out.

Jordan chuckled softly. 'It somehow had more impact coming from you.'

Stephanie eyed him quizzically. 'I can't imagine why.'

His expression became enigmatic. 'Can't you?'

'No.' God, he looked good, Stephanie acknowledged weakly. Every gorgeous, mesmerising inch of him...

'We'll get to that in a minute,' Jordan said briskly. 'I meant to arrive before Gideon had his meeting with your sister—wanted to explain exactly what was going on before he talked to Joey—but unfortunately my plane was delayed.'

'Yes, what was that all about?' Stephanie frowned. 'Don't get me wrong—it was very kind of you to ask Gideon to help extricate me from any involvement in the Newmans' divorce. I just don't understand why you did it.'

Jordan thrust his hands into his trouser pockets—he still found it a novelty to be able to do even such a simple action without falling flat on his face!—and he looked across at Stephanie through narrowed lids. 'You helped me. I wanted to help you.'

Any hopes that Stephanie might have had concerning Jordan's motives were instantly dashed. Rightly so. What had she expected? That Jordan had helped her because he actually liked her? Loved her? You're living in cloud cuckoo land, Stephanie, she admonished herself derisively.

'I do appreciate it, but you really had no need to put yourself to that trouble on my behalf.'

'I had *every* need, damn it,' Jordan rasped impatiently. 'Rosalind Newman was becoming dangerous. To other people as well as herself. Gideon has talked to her lawyer and advised that she seek medical help before she really does hurt someone.'

'Advised?' Stephanie repeated; she couldn't imagine the coldly arrogant Gideon St Claire doing anything so meek as offering *advice*.

Jordan gave a rueful grimace. 'Okay, so he made it part of the deal—you won't bring any charges against her if she seeks medical help.'

Stephanie gasped. 'But I had no intention of—'

'Could you offer me a coffee or something, Stephanie?' he cut in swiftly. 'It was a long flight, and I came straight here from the airport.'

'I—of course.' What was she thinking of, quizzing Jordan in this way over what had been a very kind act on his part? What did it matter why or how it had been achieved, so long as Stephanie no longer had the cloud of the Newmans' divorce hanging over her head? 'I have coffee already made, but Joey hasn't drunk all the wine if you would prefer that,' she added, as she looked at the half-full bottle on the table. 'I'm afraid Gideon's visit to my sister's office earlier had rather a disturbing effect on her.'

'Gideon has that effect on most people.' Jordan chuckled understandingly. 'And coffee would be great,' he added as he followed Stephanie through to the kitchen, watching her from behind guarded lids as she poured coffee into two mugs.

She looked somewhat thinner than Jordan remembered. There were slight hollows in her cheeks, shadows under those beautiful green eyes, and the stubborn set of her chin seemed more defined. That glorious red-gold hair was drawn back in its usual plait down her spine; a black T-shirt and low-slung fitted jeans outlined her slender curves.

'How have you been, Stephanie?' he asked gruffly as the two of them moved to sit at the breakfast bar.

'Good.' She nodded, her gaze on her coffee mug rather than on him. 'I have lots of work on at the moment, so I'm keeping busy. I hear you're thinking of going back to work again soon, too?' she said lightly.

Jordan wished she would look at him. Allow him to look into the 'windows of her soul' just once, so that he might have at least some idea of how she felt about him being here. 'In a couple of months, yes,' he said. 'Stephanie, I didn't come here to talk about your work or mine.'

Her lashes flickered up and she looked across at him before quickly looking away again. 'I appreciate you taking time from what is no doubt a busy family visit—'

'I came to England specifically to see *you*, Stephanie,' he interrupted. 'I—' He broke off to give an irritated shake of his head as she gave him a startled glance.

Damn it, this had seemed easier when he was sitting in his house in Malibu, just imagining seeing Stephanie again, talking to her. Now that he was actually here with her, within touching distance, Jordan didn't even know where to start!

He stood up to pace the kitchen restlessly as he tried to put into words what he wanted to say. 'Stephanie, if all you have to offer is an infatuation for me as Jordan Simpson, then for as long as it lasts I'll take it.'

Stephanie turned to stare at him in complete confusion. 'I beg your pardon?'

His mouth tightened. 'You were honest enough to tell me that your only reason for being with me, for making love with me at St Claire House, was because you've always had a thing for Jordan Simpson,' he reminded her, a nerve pulsing in his tightly clenched jaw. 'I'm here to tell you that I'm willing to continue a relationship with you on those terms.'

Stephanie's face had gone very pale. 'You want me to have an *affair* with you?'

He frowned fiercely. 'No, damn it. The last thing I want is for you to have an affair with me!'

She blinked at his vehemence. 'But you just said—'

'I just said that I would take that *if* it's all you have to offer,' Jordan corrected.

Stephanie tried to make sense of what Jordan was saying. He *did* want to have an affair with her, but he didn't. What did that mean? 'I don't understand,' she said finally, giving a confused shake of her head.

Jordan glared his frustration. 'It's really quite simple, Stephanie. If I can't have you in my life, then I don't want anyone.'

She looked taken aback. 'I— But you said—'

'I said a lot of things. As did you.' He sighed. 'One of which was a complete misunderstanding on your part. Stephanie, you *didn't* restore my sexual interest— you are the only woman that I want to make love with. Ever.'

Her eyes were wide. 'What about Crista Moore? All those beautiful leggy blondes you usually date?'

His mouth twisted. 'Just two weeks in LA, surrounded by "all those beautiful leggy blondes", was more than long enough for me to know I'm no longer attracted to any of them. The only woman who holds any attraction for me is a certain stubborn redhead who tends to argue with me most of the time.'

She looked shocked. 'You mean *me*?'

'Of *course* you, Stephanie.' He took a deep breath. 'I'm in love with you, damn it!'

'What!' She stared at him disbelievingly.

'You know, I've never said that to a woman in my life before.' Jordan gave a rueful grin. 'I somehow expected that when I did it would be received with a little more enthusiasm! I. Love. You. Stephanie McKinley,' he repeated slowly, so that there should be no further misunderstanding. 'I love you. Jordan St Claire loves you. Jordan Simpson loves you. We all love you. Is that clear enough for you?'

Stephanie was starting to feel light-headed. 'I— But you *can't* love me!'

It was so *not* the reaction that Jordan wanted. '*Why* can't I?'

'Well, because—because I'm just plain ordinary me. And you—well, you're—'

'Jordan Simpson. I know,' he accepted wearily. 'And I'm afraid it's much worse than that, actually. But that's something we can discuss in a few minutes,' he said hollowly. 'Stephanie, I love you, and I very much need to know how you would feel about having a long-term relationship with me. *Very* long-term,' he added firmly.

Stephanie swallowed hard, wondering what could be 'much worse' than him being Jordan Simpson, but too dazed at that moment to care. 'You had your operation because of the things I said about Jordan Simpson, didn't you?' she gasped as the idea suddenly occurred to her. 'Because you didn't think I wanted you as you were?'

'That wasn't the whole reason, no.' He grimaced. 'I obviously couldn't carry on in the way I was. But wanting to be fit and completely well for your sake *did* come into it, yes.'

Stephanie shook her head. 'Jordan, when I left St Claire House—when you came here—I tried to…I felt stupid because of what had happened between us.' She looked up at him emotionally. 'I said those things to you because I thought you had just used me—I was trying to salvage at least some of my pride.'

He looked at her with sudden hope. 'You mean you *aren't* infatuated with Jordan Simpson?'

'Isn't every woman?' Stephanie said as she stood up with a smile.

'Not every one, no,' Jordan retorted. 'Neither do I have any interest in what any other women might think of me.' He reached out to grasp both her hands in his. 'And "just" you isn't plain and ordinary, Stephanie. You're an exceptional woman. Beautiful. Clever. Intelligent. As well as too outspoken for your own good, of course.' He grinned affectionately at her before suddenly sobering. His expression became intense as he looked down at her. 'That time with you in Gloucestershire, and at St Claire House, was more than enough to tell me that you're everything I could ever want in a woman. Everything that I will ever want and always love,' he added fiercely as his hands tightened about hers. 'Stephanie, I don't care if it's Jordan Simpson you're infatuated with. I'll be anyone and anything you want me to be, if only you'll say— Oh, God, you're crying again!' he groaned as the tears began to fall down her cheeks.

'This time I'm crying because I'm happy!' Stephanie assured him emotionally as she looked up at him with glowing eyes. 'I'm not infatuated with Jordan Simpson any more, Jordan. He's been a wonderful object for all my secret fantasies. But it's Jordan St Claire who has occupied my fantasies these past few weeks. Jordan St Claire I fell in love with. Jordan St Claire I made love with at St Claire House.'

'You *love* me?' He looked stunned. 'But I was rude, and bad-tempered, and downright nasty to you a lot of the time. Especially after you told me it was Jordan Simpson you had "a thing" for,' he added darkly.

'I love *you*, Jordan. Whoever you are,' she assured him fervently. 'Rude and bad-tempered. Or magnetic and sexy. It's you I love. *All* of you!' She launched herself into his arms.

Jordan didn't care which of his personas Stephanie loved so long as she continued to kiss him as if she never wanted to stop. These past two weeks in LA without her had told him that he had no desire to live without Stephanie as a permanent part of his life. As the focus of his life!

'Will you marry me, Stephanie?' he asked gruffly, a long, long time later, as the two of them lay naked and replete in each other's arms.

Stephanie glowed up at the man she loved. 'With all my heart, Jordan.'

He chuckled softly. 'Our life together is never going to be dull, is it?'

Their *long* life together, Stephanie hoped, with lots of love and children. 'Are you going to tell me now what the "even worse" is you were referring to earlier?' she asked teasingly.

EPILOGUE

'DOES this mean I have to address you as Lady St Claire from now on?' Joey teased, once Jordan and Stephanie had posed in front of the cameras for the cutting of their wedding cake.

'Stephanie has always been a lady,' Jordan drawled, keeping his arm possessively about his wife's waist.

Stephanie was a very happily dazed lady at the moment!

The last six weeks had been hectic as they'd arranged the wedding in between flying backwards and forwards to LA, as Stephanie had closed down her physiotherapy practice in London and prepared to open it up again in LA when they returned from their honeymoon in a couple of weeks' time.

It had only added to the unreality of it all to learn that Jordan's 'even worse' was that he and Gideon were actually lords, and that Lucan was the Duke of Stourbridge, with Mulberry Hall being his ducal estate.

After their wedding earlier today, *she* was now officially Lady Stephanie St Claire.

Inwardly, she was still just Stephanie. As Jordan was Jordan. All the Jordans. Jordan Simpson. Jordan St Claire. Lord Jordan St Claire. And Stephanie loved every one of them to distraction!

'No, I'm still just Stephs to you,' she assured Joey ruefully, before her sister wandered off with the obvious intention of annoying Gideon as he stood talking with their parents and Molly St Claire.

Stephanie smiled as she looked around the crowded ballroom at St Claire House, where members of her own family and Jordan's mingled happily together.

She turned back to her husband. 'I love you so much, Jordan,' she said quietly to him.

His arms tightened about her. 'I'll love you for ever, Stephanie,' he vowed fiercely.

She moved up on tiptoe to whisper teasingly in his ear. 'Would you like to escape for a personal viewing of my white silk and lace underwear, Lord St Claire?'

Jordan grinned down at her. 'I thought you would never ask, Lady St Claire!'

Yes, for ever with Jordan sounded perfect, as far as Stephanie was concerned…

The Reluctant Duke

CAROLE MORTIMER

CHAPTER ONE

'HAPPY New Year, Mr St Claire!'

Lucan—the Mr St Claire referred to—stood frowning in front of the huge picture window in his executive office on the tenth floor of the St Claire Corporation building.

It was still early on this cold and frosty January morning, only eight-thirty, but Lucan had been at his desk working since six o'clock, in order to deal with some of the work needing his attention following the long Christmas and New Year break.

At least he had *told* himself he needed to come in early in order to deal with the work needing his attention. The truth was he had been only too glad to get back to normality after he and his two younger brothers had spent a traditional Christmas at his mother's home in Edinburgh, before all of them had decamped briefly—but not briefly enough for Lucan!—to Mulberry Hall, the family estate in Gloucestershire, to attend his youngest brother's wedding there on New Year's Eve.

Lucan had understood Jordan and Stephanie's reasons for wanting the wedding to be held there—it was where the two of them had met, after all—but as soon as he'd been able to do so politely, Lucan had made his excuses and gone to Klosters, skiing for three days.

He turned now, that frown still creasing his brow as he

looked at the young woman who had just stepped in from the office that adjoined his. The office belonging to his PA. Except the woman standing in the doorway *wasn't* his PA. Wasn't anyone Lucan had ever set eyes on before, in fact!

She was probably aged in her mid-twenties, very slender and a couple of inches over five feet tall. The black business suit and the snowy white blouse she wore beneath it took absolutely nothing away from the gypsy-wild effect of her long ebony hair as it cascaded riotously over her shoulders and down her back. Equally black brows were raised over eyes of a deep sparkling blue, surrounded by thick sooty lashes, and a small straight nose above sinfully and sensually full lips.

Lips that immediately—surprisingly!—stirred Lucan's body into arousal as his thoughts shifted smoothly to bedrooms, and hot and nakedly entwined bodies. Surprisingly because it was widely acknowledged that successful businessman Lucan St Claire was as ruthless emotionally in the brief relationships he had with women as he was in the boardroom.

Lucan didn't feel in the least ruthless as he stared at this dark and untamed beauty!

He scowled darkly. 'Who the hell are you?'

Lexie might almost have felt sorry for Lucan St Claire's expression of scowling bewilderment if it hadn't been for the fact that he had so obviously brought this present situation completely upon himself.

If he weren't so coldly self-absorbed, so arrogantly unable to relate to the people who worked for and with him, then perhaps his PA wouldn't have decided to walk out on him on Christmas Eve, without even bothering to tell him she was going.

Perhaps.

Lexie had a suspicion that Jessica Brown's interest in Lucan St Claire hadn't all been business-related, and that his lack of interest in return—or inability to feel any—had been the reason the other woman had finally left so abruptly...

Lexie walked over to stand in front of the imposing oak desk, aware of the ease of power that surrounded Lucan St Claire as he towered on the other side of that desk. Aware of how comfortably he wore the charcoal-grey tailored suit, and the pale grey silk shirt with a darker grey tie knotted meticulously at his throat.

This man wasn't only tall and impeccably dressed, but aristocratically handsome, too, Lexie allowed grudgingly. Although, in her opinion the dark, almost black, hair could have been worn a little longer than it was, and those powerful good looks—enigmatic black eyes, haughtily long nose, chiselled lips above a square-cut and determined chin—were stamped with a haughty arrogance she didn't find in the least appealing.

Not that there had ever been any likelihood of Lexie finding *anything* appealing about a single member of the St Claire family! Her mouth twisted derisively.

'My name is Lexie Hamilton, Mr St Claire. I'm your temporary temporary PA,' she said as he still scowled.

Those dark eyes narrowed chillingly. 'It's news to me that I'm in need of a temporary PA, let alone a temporary *temporary* one...'

Lexie's derision deepened. 'Your ex-PA called my agency on Christmas Eve to arrange for a temporary replacement until you are in a position to arrange for a permanent one. Unfortunately, the lady most qualified for the position isn't available for another three days.'

Lucan St Claire looked totally baffled by this explanation—as well he might.

Lexie had decided before coming here that even the curiosity she had always felt concerning the St Claire family should have its time limit. Three days would be quite long enough for her to confirm every bad thing she had ever thought or heard of them.

As it turned out, she had overestimated—three *minutes* in this cold and haughty man's company was quite long enough for her to know he believed himself to be arrogantly superior!

His scowl deepened. 'Exactly why and when did Jennifer make these arrangements?'

Now it was Lexie's turn to frown. 'I thought your PA's name was Jessica...?'

'Jennifer—Jessica,' Lucan St Claire dismissed irritably. 'Her name is of little relevance if, as you say, she has now left my employment.'

Lexie gave a rueful smile. 'Perhaps if you had taken the trouble to remember her name she wouldn't have felt the need to leave so abruptly...?'

Lucan's eyes narrowed to steely slits. 'When I want your opinion, Miss Hamilton, then you can be assured I will ask for it!'

'I was merely pointing out—'

'Something that I believe, as a *temporary* temporary employee, is absolutely none of your business?' Lucan rasped harshly.

'Probably not,' she conceded with a rueful grimace.

An attitude completely lacking in genuine apology, Lucan recognised with a dark frown. 'Why would Jen—Jessica,' he corrected irritably, 'leave in that unprofessional way?'

Lexie Hamilton gave a shrug. 'I believe she mentioned

to someone at the agency that the final insult came when you didn't even bother to send her so much as a Christmas card—let alone buy her a present.'

'She received a Christmas bonus in her pay cheque last month—the same as all my other employees.'

'A *personal* Christmas present,' Lexie Hamilton drawled pointedly.

'Why on earth would I do that?' Lucan was genuinely astounded by the accusation.

'I believe it's customary for one's immediate boss to— never mind,' the raven-haired beauty dismissed, as she obviously saw his impatience. 'I had no idea you were already in your office—I took a call just now that I believe is in need of your immediate attention. I wrote the details down for you.' She handed him a slip of paper.

Lucan glanced down at the neatly written message before crushing it in his hand.

John Barton, the caretaker of Mulberry Hall, was reporting some damage to the west gallery of the house, following the rapid thaw over the last two days. Damage that John believed was in need of Lucan's personal attention.

As the eldest of the three St Claire brothers, Lucan had inherited the Mulberry Hall estate on the death of their father eight years ago. But it was an estate he had rarely visited following his parents' separation and acrimonious divorce twenty-five years ago, and a place he certainly had no inclination to return to again so soon after his last visit.

The first eleven of Lucan's thirty-six years had been spent happily living at Mulberry Hall with both his parents. The three brothers had been in complete ignorance of their father's affair with a widow who lived in one of the cottages on the estate with her grown-up daughter. Or of the unhappiness that affair had caused their mother. An unhappiness that had imploded twenty-five years ago and resulted in Molly moving back to Scotland and taking her three sons with her.

Lucan had forced himself to return to Mulberry Hall for Jordan and Stephanie's wedding, almost a week ago, as no doubt had his brother Gideon, and their mother; to be asked to go back there again so soon was unacceptable.

Barton had said the damage was in the west gallery...

That was the long picture gallery, where the portrait of Lucan's father, Alexander St Claire, the previous Duke of Stourbridge, now hung in majestic state.

A portrait which revealed that Lucan, of all the three St Claire brothers, most resembled their dark-haired, dark-eyed and adulterous father!

'Mr Barton sounded as if he considered the matter urgent,' Lexie Hamilton told him now, and she looked pointedly at the message she had written out so neatly, which Lucan had crushed in his hand.

'I believe that is for me to decide, don't you?' His voice was silky soft.

'It's probably too late for me to do anything about your ten o'clock appointment.' She completely ignored his set-down. 'But I could probably cancel the rest of your appointments for the next couple of days if you were thinking of—'

'Believe me, Miss Hamilton, you really don't want to know what I'm thinking right now,' Lucan assured her harshly. 'My priority at the moment is to speak to the person in charge at your agency.'

'Why?'

Lucan raised his brows. 'I'm not accustomed to having my actions questioned.'

Lexie easily picked up on the unspoken words—least of all by a temporary, temporary employee. But the person in charge at the agency at the moment happened to be Lexie herself, since her parents, the owners of Premier Personnel, had embarked on a three-week cruise the day after Christmas, in celebration of their twenty-fifth wedding anniversary.

Her parents weren't even aware of the call that had come into the agency from Lucan St Claire's PA on Christmas Eve.

Lexie had told herself at the time that she hadn't told them because she didn't want to put any sort of cloud over her parents' excitement by so much as *mentioning* the St Claire family.

She had *told* herself that was the reason…

Initially Lexie had been so stunned by the identity of the caller that she had just taken down the details, before woodenly assuring Jessica Brown that she was not to worry, that Premier Personnel would take care of the problem.

It was only after the call had ended that Lexie had realised the possibilities that call had just opened up for her.

She was qualified for the job—just—and it was always quiet in the offices of Premier Personnel in January. Three days. Just three days, she had promised herself. Spent observing Lucan St Claire, the reputedly powerful and ruthless owner of the St Claire Corporation.

So far Lucan St Claire was proving to be everything Lexie had ever imagined he might be!

She straightened to her full height of five feet and three inches in her two-inch-high shoes. 'I assure you that I am qualified to stand in here for three days, Mr St Claire.'

Those dark eyes viewed her coldly. 'I don't believe I questioned your qualifications…'

Lexie felt irritated colour warm her cheeks. 'Nonetheless, the implication was there.'

'Really?' Lucan drawled as he moved to lean against

the side of his desk, bringing himself down onto a level with Lexie Hamilton's indignant blue eyes, and enabling him to see the perfection of her creamy skin, and the small and determined chin beneath those highly sensual—sexual—lips…

Lips like that—so moist and full, so softly pouting—could drive a man wild when applied to a certain part of his anatomy—

Lucan abruptly moved away, dismayed at the inappropriate imaginings he was having about this less-than-polite young woman, and full of self-disgust at the hardening of that certain part of his own anatomy!

'What's the name of your agency?' he bit out harshly.

'Premier Personnel,' Lexie Hamilton supplied with a frown. 'But wouldn't you like me to put through a call to Mr Barton first? He implied the matter was of some urgency—'

'I believe I'm perfectly capable of prioritising my own workload, Lexie,' Lucan rasped dismissively.

'Of course.' She nodded abruptly, a frown still between those deep blue eyes as she turned and hurried across the room, giving Lucan an unobstructed view of that long and riotous ebony-coloured hair. He could also view the provocative sway of her shapely bottom underneath the short black skirt and above slender and shapely legs.

Telling Lucan that this young woman was *just* as qualified to share his bed as she was to be his temporary, temporary PA!

'Did Jemima change the colour of her hair?'

Lucan turned slowly to look at his brother Gideon, where he stood silhouetted in the doorway leading out to the hallway. The younger man was frowning across at the closed door between the two offices with the same perplexed expression Lucan was sure had been on his own face fifteen minutes ago, when Lexie Hamilton had first made her entrance.

It gave Lucan some satisfaction to realise that Gideon had also got his PA's name wrong. His *ex*-PA, Lucan corrected irritably.

It was unbelievable that Jen—Jessica should have just walked out on him without so much as giving notice. It was even more irritating that her temporary temporary replacement should be the beautiful and totally distracting Lexie Hamilton.

Lucan gave an impatient shake of his head as he moved back behind his desk and sat down. 'Her name was Jessica.' Apparently! 'And that wasn't her,' he added stonily.

'No?' Gideon murmured with a frown as he strolled farther into the room. At thirty-four, two years Lucan's junior, Gideon was tall and blond, with piercing dark eyes set in a strikingly handsome face. 'I didn't realise you were going to replace her.'

'I wasn't,' Lucan bit out tightly, as he recalled the reasons Lexie had given him for Jessica Brown having walked out on him in that totally unprofessional way.

He somehow doubted that Lexie would ever allow her own presence to be overlooked in the same way—even for the three days she had said she intended working for him...

'No?' Gideon raised surprised brows. 'Then who was *that*?'

'A temp,' Lucan dismissed impatiently. A *temporary* temp!

'Oh.' Gideon nodded. 'She looks vaguely familiar...'

Lucan's interest sharpened. 'In what way?'

'I have no idea.' His brother gave a self-derisive grimace. 'It's a sad state of affairs, Lucan, when all the beautiful women you meet start to look alike!'

As far as Lucan was concerned Lexie didn't look or behave like any other woman he had ever met! Something he found intriguing in spite of himself.

'What can I do for you, Gideon?' He deliberately changed the subject, having no intention of discussing Lexie any further with his brother. Or of allowing Gideon to realise his instant and totally unprecedented physical response to her unusual gypsy-wild beauty.

Lucan always dated models and actresses—although 'dated' was perhaps a slight exaggeration! What he usually did was take models and actresses out to dinner, or, in the case of the latter, escort them to film premieres, and then invariably to his bed. Beautiful women, perfectly groomed and sophisticated women—women who didn't expect any serious involvement with him and were just happy to be seen with the rich and powerful Lucan St Claire.

He had certainly never been in the least interested in becoming involved with one of his employees—as proved by the fact that he hadn't even got the name of his last PA right—and it probably wouldn't be a good idea to make Lexie Hamilton the exception to that rule, either!

Gideon raised surprised blond brows. 'Don't tell me you've forgotten that you asked me to come in at nine o'clock this morning, so that we could go over the contracts together before Andrew Proctor arrives at ten?'

As the legal representative for all the St Claire Corporation's dealings, Gideon kept an office just down the hallway from this one, as well as having his own private offices in the city.

Lucan *had* forgotten Gideon was coming in this morning—a phenomenon completely unheard of until today; business had always come first, second and last with Lucan.

Gideon gave a speculative smile. 'Miss Whatever-her-name-is should sit in on the meeting—Proctor will be so distracted by the way she looks he won't have any idea what he's signing!'

'Her name is Lexie Hamilton,' Lucan supplied harshly. 'And I would prefer Andrew Proctor to know *exactly* what he's signing. I also don't think it appropriate for you to make such personal remarks about an employee, Gideon,' he added darkly.

'I didn't arrive soon enough to actually see her face, but any man with red blood still flowing in his veins couldn't help but notice that pert little bottom!' his brother assured him dryly.

A frown creased Lucan's brow as he realised he wasn't altogether sure he felt comfortable discussing his outspoken but definitely sexy temporary temp in these terms—even with Gideon. 'Perhaps she might prove too much of a distraction?'

His brother raised mocking brows. 'Too much of a distraction…?'

Once again Lucan stood up restlessly. 'Not to me personally, of course,' he bit out tersely.

'No?'

Lucan felt his irritation deepen. 'No!'

'Then there's no problem with her sitting in on the meeting later this morning, is there?' Gideon dismissed practically.

No problem at all—except that Lucan already *knew* Lexie was likely to prove as much of a distraction to him as she was to anyone else!

'I had a call from John Barton this morning, concerning some damage to Mulberry Hall that needs looking at.' Lucan firmly changed the subject. 'I don't suppose you feel like going back to Gloucestershire for a few days…?'

'I don't suppose I do,' his brother came back firmly.

Exactly what Lucan had thought Gideon might say…

* * *

Lexie was fully aware of Lucan St Claire's presence as he came through from the adjoining office fifteen minutes later, to stand looking down at her broodingly from the other side of her desk. She was so aware of him that she deliberately ignored him as she kept typing into her laptop, until she had finished writing an email to Brenda, in the office at Premier Personnel, after the other woman had emailed Lexie to tell her she had successfully managed to reassure Lucan St Claire that Lexie Hamilton was indeed a temp sent from their agency.

Lexie had panicked slightly when Lucan St Claire had told her he intended telephoning Premier Personnel himself. She'd hurried back into the adjoining office to quickly put a call through to Brenda, her assistant in her parents' absence, to explain, and also arrange to meet Brenda for coffee after work this evening, so that she could explain the situation more fully.

Although Lexie wasn't one hundred per cent certain she could completely explain this situation to *herself,* let alone a third party.

It had been pure impulse—along with a lot of curiosity!—that had prompted her into coming here in the first place. An impulse and a curiosity she already regretted...

She hadn't expected to like the powerful Lucan St Claire, and she didn't. She had already decided after their brief conversation earlier that his reputation for being cold and arrogant was well justified. But there was no denying that he was strikingly handsome, too...

His colouring—that dark hair and those piercing jet-black eyes, his sculptured features—reminded Lexie so much of his father, Alexander...

She looked up at him blandly. 'Is there a problem with the intercom, Mr St Claire...?'

Lucan's mouth thinned at her obvious sarcasm. 'I accept that we got off to something of a bad start earlier, Miss Hamilton, but let's get one thing clear, shall we?' He looked down at her coldly. 'Namely, for the moment, *I* am the employer and *you* are the employee!'

Dark brows rose over those deep, and perhaps deliberately innocent, blue eyes. 'I am?'

'For the moment, yes,' he repeated harshly—warningly.

Lexie shrugged. 'Can I take it from that remark that Premier Personnel have confirmed that my replacement will arrive in three days' time?'

'You can,' Lucan confirmed tightly. 'It would appear that we are stuck with each other until then.'

She smiled slightly. 'My sentiments exactly.'

Lucan scowled darkly. 'Tell me, Lexie, is this tendency you have to be less than respectful to your employers also the reason that you find it easier to work for an agency rather than attempting to find a permanent position?'

Two bright spots of angry colour had appeared in the delicate cream of her cheeks. 'I don't believe my reasons to be any of your concern, Mr St Claire!'

He shrugged broad and muscled shoulders beneath his tailored jacket. 'I was curious. Nothing more,' he dismissed coolly.

As Lexie had long been curious about all of the St Claire family...

'I assure you, Mr St Claire, there is nothing about my personal life that would be of the least interest to you.' She looked up at him challengingly.

He raised dark brows. 'You sound very certain of that.'

'I am,' she came back evenly.

What would this man do or say, Lexie wondered, if he

were to learn that her grandmother was none other than Sian Thomas—the widow that his own father, Alexander St Claire, had fallen in love with over twenty-five years ago? The same woman all the St Claire family had treated with such contempt for those same many years... If he were to realise that Lexie's own full name, Alexandra, had been chosen in honour of 'Grandpa Alex', as she had called *this* man's father for the first sixteen of her twenty-four years...!

CHAPTER TWO

LEXIE had been in complete ignorance for most of her childhood as to exactly who her Grandpa Alex was—apart from being her step-grandfather, of course—but once she'd reached her teens her mother had quietly and calmly sat her down and explained the situation to her.

It was then that Lexie had learned that Alexander St Claire was actually the Duke of Stourbridge, and had been virtually disowned by his three sons after his divorce from their mother, Molly St Claire.

Lexie had instantly decided that all three of the St Claire brothers had treated their father abominably—simply because he had fallen in love with her gentle and beautiful grandmother. A woman none of the brothers had even attempted to meet, let alone get to know. If they had then they might have realised how far removed Sian was from being the *femme fatale* they so obviously believed her to be. They would also have seen how much she had loved their father. How much their father had loved her in return.

As it was, despite the fact that their father was now her Grandpa Alex, Lexie hadn't so much as set eyes on any of the three St Claire brothers until Alexander had died eight years ago, when they had dutifully arranged and attended their father's funeral at the village church in Stourbridge.

Lexie had attended the funeral, too, out of sheer bloody-mindedness, after it had been made clear that her grandmother's presence would *not* be welcomed there by the St Claire family.

Out of sheer stubbornness she had decided to represent her own family that day, standing at the back of the church to mourn her Grandpa Alex. Unacknowledged and thankfully unnoticed by any of the St Claire family.

The coldly remote Lucan St Claire had been easily recognisable from the photographs Lexie had deliberately looked out for over the last few years in the business pages of newspapers and magazines. She had also known the youngest St Claire brother, the rakishly handsome actor Jordan Sinclair, which had to make the austerely attractive blond-haired man standing beside him his twin brother Gideon.

But Lexie's grandmother—the woman Alexander St Claire had loved and shared the last seventeen years of his life with—had been absent from his funeral...

For that alone Lexie would never forgive *any* of the St Claire family. The head of that family, especially. Lucan St Claire. The man who, upon his father's death, had become the fifteenth Duke of Stourbridge.

Not that Lucan St Claire ever used the title. No doubt as some further insult to the father he had all but disowned twenty-five years ago.

Lexie's eyes snapped her resentment now, as she looked up at Lucan St Claire. 'Can I help you with something else, Mr St Claire...?'

Lucan didn't believe himself to be a vain man. He recognized that he was cold, occasionally ruthless and that other than with his close family he was almost always chillingly remote. He was also aware that it was as much his considerable wealth and power that attracted all those models and actresses to him as any personal attraction he might or might not have.

That aside, Lexie Hamilton's initial attitude of dismissal, followed by this disdain, were not things Lucan had ever encountered in any other woman.

Intriguingly so...

'Are you always this disrespectful?' he rasped harshly.

She shrugged. 'My parents brought me up to believe that respect has to be earned, not just given,' she came back challengingly.

Lucan growled something unintelligible under his breath. 'I want you to sit in on my ten o'clock meeting and take notes.'

'Well, that *is* what you are paying me for,' she came back sarcastically.

Lucan's patience—what little he possessed—was fast running out where this particular woman was concerned. 'If you continue with your present attitude you will leave me with no choice but to call your agency back and explain exactly how ill-suited I believe you to be for this or any other position,' he warned her coldly.

Lexie grudgingly acknowledged that she might be allowing her inner resentment towards this man to get the better of her. After all, he *was* Lucan St Claire, world-renowned businessman, and a man who was rich as Croesus and even more powerful. The last thing Lexie wanted was for her parents to return from their cruise and discover the hard-earned reputation of Premier Personnel, which they had so painstakingly built up over the last twenty years, was in tatters after only a matter of days under Lexie's management!

'Shouldn't you at least give me a few hours to prove my efficiency before doing that?' she came back lightly.

Even when this woman was saying all the right words

she still somehow managed to sound challenging, Lucan recognised with a frown. Almost as if she had been pre-disposed to dislike him...

Simply because of the unfeeling way she believed he had behaved towards Jessica Brown?

Or was her dislike for another reason entirely?

Considering that Lexie Hamilton hadn't even known Lucan's ex-PA, the former didn't sound like an acceptable explanation for her attitude. So maybe it was something else?

Or perhaps it wasn't personal at all, and she really was just this prickly and outspoken with everyone?

If he could tolerate this woman in such close proximity to him for the next three days he was probably going to find that out.

And he still had to decide what he was going to do about John Barton's call concerning the damage to Mulberry Hall...

'Is there something wrong, Mr St Claire?' Lexie prompted lightly a couple of hours later, once Gideon St Claire had left the office to accompany Andrew Proctor and his legal representative down in the lift.

'What could possibly be wrong?' Lucan bit out tautly as he stood up impatiently, a nerve pulsing in his tightly clenched jaw. He moved around the desk, the darkness of his gaze narrowed on her icily.

Lexie gave a shake of her head. 'I had assumed you might offer to take Mr Proctor out to lunch once the con-tracts had been signed—'

'I believe Proctor would much rather have had lunch with *you* than with me.'

'Me?' Lexie repeated incredulously.

'Don't play the innocent with me, Lexie; you know

exactly what effect you had on Andrew Proctor,' he growled scathingly.

She frowned. 'I believe I laughed at several of Mr Proctor's jokes—'

'Laughed inappropriately at *all* of his jokes,' Lucan corrected disgustedly, fresh anger boiling up inside him just at the thought of the meeting that had just taken place in his office.

Andrew Proctor was a handsome man in his late forties, owner of an extensive transport business that Lucan wished to acquire for the St Claire Corporation. There had been several meetings between Gideon and Proctor's own legal adviser already, to negotiate the details of the sale, and Lucan had fully expected the meeting this morning—the signing of the contracts—to go off without a hitch.

Obviously he hadn't taken Lexie's presence into account when he'd made that assumption!

Andrew Proctor had taken one glance at Lucan's PA and the whole tenor of the meeting had changed. The man had begun to flirt with her instead of paying attention to the final discussion of the contract that had been drawn up for their signatures.

The fact that Gideon had seemed equally interested in her certainly hadn't improved the situation.

Lucan's mouth tightened. 'You all but got into bed with the man, damn it!'

Lexie's eyes widened indignantly. 'Believe me, Mr St Claire, when I get into bed with a man I *don't* do it in front of an audience!'

Lucan drew in a sharp breath at the graphic vision that remark instantly induced.

Her complexion was pure ivory, and Lucan had no doubt that the slenderness of her body would be just as palely translucent. Her skin would be soft and smooth to the touch. Her uptilted breasts would be tipped by rose or red-coloured nipples. The silky triangle of hair between her legs would be the same dark—

Good God!

Had he totally lost his mind? Christmas in Scotland, followed by the wedding at Mulberry Hall and now this call from Barton in Gloucestershire—all that had been unsettling, certainly, but surely not enough to addle Lucan's brain so much he was having these erotic thoughts about her?

Addled his brain?

It was another part of his anatomy entirely that responded to Lexie's exotic beauty.

'I have no interest in learning what you do or do not require when you go to bed with a man,' he bit out grimly—and not altogether truthfully. 'I am merely endeavouring to point out that your overtly friendly behaviour towards Andrew Proctor made a complete fiasco of what was supposed to be a business meeting.'

Lexie was uncomfortably aware that Lucan's criticism was partly merited. She had obviously been expected to just fade quietly into the background of the meeting, rather than allow Andrew Proctor to draw her into conversation. And she knew she would have done exactly that if not for the fact that she had seen exactly how annoyed Lucan had looked every time Andrew Proctor spoke to her...

She gave a self-conscious grimace now. 'I apologise if you found anything about my behaviour this morning less than professional.'

Lucan looked taken aback. '*What* did you just say...?'

Lexie shot him a frowning glance from beneath dark lashes. 'I believe I apologised,' she repeated impatiently.

Exactly what Lucan had thought she had done! Totally

unexpectedly. So much so that he wasn't quite sure what to do or say next, damn it.

Indecision wasn't something he could normally be accused of, either.

What was wrong with him this morning?

From a professional angle Lucan knew he should call this woman's agency and demand that she be replaced immediately, or he would have no choice but to contact another agency.

What he personally wanted to do was another matter entirely...

He relaxed slightly. 'It's almost one o'clock. I suggest the two of us go and get some lunch—'

'Together?' Lexie stared at him uncomprehendingly.

'Yes—together,' Lucan drawled mockingly. 'Perhaps we can come to some sort of truce while we eat?'

To say Lexie was stunned by the suggestion would be an understatement. Unless Lucan meant it as an ultimatum rather than a suggestion? An implication that the two of them either come to that truce or he would immediately go ahead with his threat to have her replaced, and in doing so damage the reputation of Premier Personnel?

Personally, Lexie would be more than happy to go. She had already done what she'd come here to do, and that was to meet Lucan St Claire and have all her preconceived ideas of him confirmed. As well as some *un*preconceived ones—namely, he was dangerously attractive...

Unfortunately, the repercussions for Premier Personnel if that were to happen were less acceptable.

Something Lexie should definitely have thought about before acting so impulsively in coming anywhere near a single member of the St Claire family!

Although, Lexie acknowledged grudgingly, she hadn't

found the blond and handsome Gideon St Claire quite so disagreeable as Lucan.

Gideon was supposed to share the same reputation for coldness and arrogance as his haughty older brother, and as such Lexie had fully expected him to ignore her altogether during this morning's meeting. Instead, Gideon had been effortlessly charming to her, and the warm interest in his gaze unmistakable…

'Does it usually take you this long to respond to an invitation to lunch?' Lucan rasped impatiently.

'No, of course not,' Lexie snapped resentfully, her cheeks heating at the taunting mockery she could see in those coal-black eyes. 'But it was hardly an invitation, was it?' she dismissed scathingly. ''More like, it's lunchtime, so let's eat!'

Lucan frowned his irritation; did this woman have to argue about everything? 'I see nothing wrong with that statement,' he bit out impatiently. 'It *is* lunchtime, and we both have to eat.'

'But not necessarily together,' she came back decisively.

Lucan's eyes narrowed to dark and dangerous slits. 'Tell me—is this dislike personal, or do you treat all your employers with the same contempt?'

Lexie stiffened warily. It was one thing for her to treat Lucan St Claire with the disdain she felt he deserved— quite another for him to become overly curious as to *why* she treated him that way. For him to ever suspect, realise, exactly who she was…

Lexie shook her head. 'It isn't personal, Mr St Claire—'
'Lucan.'
She blinked up at him. 'I beg your pardon…?'
'I invited you to call me Lucan, Lexie,' he drawled rue-

fully. 'Don't tell me you have a problem with that, too?' He frowned again as she continued to stare up at him.

Of *course* Lexie had a problem with that! The last thing she wanted—positively the last thing—was to be on a first-name basis with any of the arrogant St Claire family! 'I would prefer to keep our relationship on a completely business footing,' she said stiffly.

'And calling each other by our first names isn't doing that?' he prompted.

'You know it isn't.' She frowned. 'Any more than my having lunch with you is,' she added coolly.

Lucan scowled his impatience. 'I fail to see why not.'

Lexie eyed him frustratedly. 'That could be because you're being deliberately obtuse—' She broke off abruptly as he gave a wry chuckle.

A phenomenon that completely changed the austerity of those grimly handsome features, giving warmth to those dark, dark eyes, a softening to the hard rigidity of his cheek and jawline, and revealing an endearing cleft in his left cheek.

All things that Lexie did not want to be aware of where this particular man was concerned.

She gave him a reproving look. 'I fail to see what's so funny.'

He gave a rueful shake of his head. 'It seems that even when you try to be polite you can't help but be rude.'

She bristled. 'And you find that amusing?'

'Not really.' He gave a slow shake of his head. 'I've just never met anyone quite like you before,' he said.

Lexie wasn't sure she was altogether comfortable with the softening of his tone. Or the speculation she could see in the warmth of those dark eyes as he looked at her. It was too male an assessment. The assessment of a handsome man looking at a woman he found attractive...

No way!

Absolutely no way!

Lucan St Claire and his two brothers had all but disowned their own father after he and their mother were divorced. Had totally rejected so much as even meeting the woman their father had loved and spent the rest of his life with.

Lexie accepted that their parents' divorce must have been tough on three young boys such as Lucan and his two brothers would have been twenty-five years ago. But they *had* been only boys, and as such couldn't possibly have been aware of all the details of the situation.

Any more than Lexie, who hadn't even been born at the time, could really know...

No, she wasn't even going there.

The whole of the St Claire family had treated Grandpa Alex and her grandmother abominably as far as she was concerned. As such, they were all beneath contempt. It was better for Lexie if she continued to think that way.

Except, as she had realised this morning, Lucan St Claire was lethally and heart-poundingly handsome.

Lucan had seen some of the emotions flickering across Lexie's expressive, beautiful face. Seen them, but not understood them. Which wasn't so unusual; so far there was very little about this woman that he *did* understand.

Except that for some inexplicable reason he was attracted to her.

Her outward beauty was undeniable, but it was the things Lucan didn't know about her, the things he didn't yet understand, that intrigued him.

And that, if Lucan were completely honest with himself, was also the reason he had been so annoyed at Andrew Proctor's flirting with her earlier.

He straightened abruptly. 'I take it from your earlier remarks that you would prefer to give lunch a miss?'

She frowned. 'Not completely, no...'

'Just lunch with *me*?' Lucan guessed easily.

Her mouth tightened. 'Yes.'

It was all Lucan could do to stop himself from laughing again. No woman had ever before given him the blunt put-downs that Lexie did so effortlessly!

Put-downs he found more arousing than annoying when they were coming from between Lexie's full and sensually erotic lips...

He gave a terse nod of his head. 'I had thought you might appreciate having lunch before we leave. But we can eat later if that's what you would prefer.'

'Before we leave for where?' Lexie said slowly, suspiciously, not liking the gleam of satisfaction she could clearly see in the depths of Lucan's dark eyes.

Eyes that now met hers with mocking innocence. 'Did I forget to mention we're leaving town for a couple of days?'

Lexie very much doubted that this man ever forgot anything—after sitting in on this morning's meeting, witnessing the precision of his business acumen as he rattled off reams of facts and figures without consulting a single sheet of paper in Andrew Proctor's file, Lexie no longer believed he had forgotten his previous PA's name, either. A more logical explanation for that oversight was that the woman had simply been of such insignificance to him that he simply hadn't troubled himself to learn it.

He didn't seem to be having the same trouble where *she* was concerned.

'Yes...' Lexie confirmed warily.

He nodded tersely. 'I finally managed to return Barton's call earlier. After careful consideration I've decided that

I *should* go to Gloucestershire to deal with the problem personally after all.'

Lexie's heart gave a sickening lurch. 'And this affects me how?'

Those dark eyes glittered down at her with mocking satisfaction. 'I would have thought that was obvious, Lexie.'

'Humour me, Mr St Claire,' she bit out between gritted teeth.

He shrugged those broad shoulders beneath his tailored jacket. 'For the next three days you work for me. I need to go to Gloucestershire for the next couple of days at least, to assess the damage to the house there and to organise repairs. Obviously I expect my temporary temporary PA — namely you—to accompany me.'

Lexie felt the colour drain from her cheeks as she stared up at him in stunned disbelief.

Lucan wanted her to accompany him to Gloucestershire? To Mulberry Hall? The St Claire ducal estate in the village of Stourbridge?

The same village where Lexie's grandmother still lived…

CHAPTER THREE

LUCAN couldn't help but see the way Lexie reacted as he outlined his plans for spending the next couple of days in Gloucestershire; her eyes had become dark and haunted, her cheeks deathly pale.

Obviously Lucan had a personal aversion to going anywhere near the family estate—which was the reason he had decided to take this intriguing woman with him—but he saw no reason why she should feel the same way. Unless, of course, she had personal commitments that kept her in town—maybe a boyfriend or a live-in lover?

'Do you have a problem with that?' he rasped harshly.

Did Lexie have a problem with that?

She couldn't even begin to list the problems she had with going anywhere near the village of Stourbridge in the company of this particular man. With Lucan St Claire. The head of the despised St Claire family.

Lexie had been visiting the village of Stourbridge for years, of course, on frequent visits to her grandmother and Grandpa Alex. As a child she had gone there with her parents, and latterly on her own. Stourbridge was a delightful village, full of charming thatched cottages, and Lexie always enjoyed spending time there with her grandmother.

Which was the pertinent point, of course.

To go anywhere near Stourbridge, the village where Lexie had been known by many of the locals from the time she was a baby, with Lucan St Claire of all people, was simply asking for trouble.

Oh, what a tangled web...

And that web had just become more tangled than Lexie could ever have imagined when she had allowed curiosity to get the better of her!

Her throat moved convulsively as she swallowed hard, and her gaze avoided meeting that probing dark one as instead she looked somewhere over Lucan's left shoulder. 'I can't simply up and leave London at a moment's notice...'

'I've already checked with your agency, and part of your contract of employment states that you agree to accompany your employer in the course of his/her business,' Lucan informed her coldly.

Having worked at the agency alongside her parents for the last three years, Lexie knew exactly what the Premier Personnel contract said concerning their expectations of employees. As the daughter of the owners of the company it was also a contract *she* hadn't signed—a fact Lexie obviously couldn't share with him.

Her mouth firmed. 'Your reasons for going to Gloucestershire appear to be personal rather than business-related.'

'Correct me if I'm wrong—' his icily taunting tone implied that he already knew he wasn't '—but I believe the initials PA stand for Personal Assistant...?'

'Yes. But—'

'In which case, as you are my PA, I fully expect you to accompany me to Gloucestershire.'

'I disagree—'

'And do you believe that your opinion on the subject is of *any* relevance to me?' he cut in brutally.

Lexie looked at Lucan searchingly, easily noting the hard glitter of those dark eyes, the pulse pounding in his rigidly clenched jaw, the thin, uncompromising line of his mouth. 'No,' she finally acknowledged heavily. 'But surely this visit could wait until my replacement takes over on Thursday?' she added brightly.

'I have no intention of altering my plans to suit you, Lexie,' he bit out coldly. 'If it makes you feel any better, I shall be taking a briefcase full of work with me.'

'Oh...' She gave a pained grimace.

That ruthless mouth twisted into a humourless smile as he nodded haughtily. 'I'll expect you back here in an hour, then, with your case duly packed.'

Lexie could feel the panic rising inside her. She *couldn't* go to the St Claire estate in Gloucestershire with this man. She simply couldn't!

Her grandmother's cottage was only half a mile away from Mulberry Hall, the majestic mansion that was the St Claire ducal home. Lexie had played in the woods there when she was a child, had taken long walks in the grounds with her grandmother and Grandpa Alex, had often used the indoor swimming pool that had been built onto the back of Mulberry Hall.

Admittedly Lexie had never stayed at Mulberry Hall itself, her grandmother having always refused to live there with Alexander even after his divorce, but Lexie knew she would only have to make one slip, one remark that revealed she had been inside the house or on the estate before, for Lucan to demand an explanation. An explanation she had no intention of giving him.

This wasn't just a tangled web, it was a steel trap, waiting to snap shut behind her.

Lexie gave a firm shake of her head. 'I really would prefer not to accompany you to Gloucestershire—'

'In that case,' he interrupted grimly, 'I have no doubt that Premier Personnel will have no choice but to dispense with your services altogether. For their own sake.'

'Are you threatening me, Mr St Claire?' Lexie snapped, easily able to guess what that meant. This man had the power and influence to totally ruin Premier Personnel's reputation in the business world with only a few cutting words.

Something Lexie should definitely have thought of earlier.

'I haven't even begun to threaten you yet, Lexie,' he assured her succinctly.

There was no mistaking the hard implacability of that coal-black gaze—an indication that Lucan was determined to have his own way. What Lexie didn't understand was why. Why was he was so set on her accompanying him to Gloucestershire when she so obviously didn't want to go?

Unless that was the very reason Lucan was being so insistent?

This man was hard, cold, ruthless. A man used to people doing exactly as he wanted them to. Who insisted on it. By arguing with him Lexie had no doubt she was just making Lucan all the more determined to bend her to his indomitable will.

And Lexie, fool that she was, had placed herself—and Premier Personnel—in a position where she could do nothing to stop him.

Her eyes glittered her dislike as she glared up at him. 'An hour, I believe you said?'

Lucan felt absolutely no satisfaction in having forced Lexie to his will. Just as he had absolutely no idea what thoughts had been going through that beautiful head while Lexie deliberated as to whether or not she was going to do as he asked. But whatever those thoughts had been they didn't appear to have been particularly pleasant ones...

He couldn't read this woman at all—which was unusual in itself; most women of his acquaintance seemed intent on either sharing his bed or attempting to get him to the altar. Usually with an avaricious eye on the fortune and power he had amassed these last ten years.

Lexie Hamilton made it obvious she was unimpressed with both him and his obvious wealth, and behaved towards him accordingly. Namely, she treated him with an offhand disdain that—contrary to what she'd obviously hoped—had only succeeded in increasing his interest in her.

Enough so that he welcomed the distraction of her presence, unwilling or otherwise, during this forced second visit to Mulberry Hall in as many weeks.

'An hour,' he confirmed abruptly.

She nodded. 'Would you like me to find out the times of the trains?'

'I intend driving up,' Lucan dismissed. 'Normally we would have flown up in the company-owned helicopter, but it's being serviced at the moment.'

The St Claires really were a breed apart, Lexie decided slightly dazedly. Super-rich. Super-powerful.

How on earth her gentle and unassuming grandmother had ever dared to fall in love with the head of that rich and powerful family was a wonder in itself!

'Silly me.' Lexie grimaced.

He nodded. 'You should pack warm clothing—'

'I believe I'm intelligent enough to have worked that out for myself,' she snapped in her irritation.

'I don't think I've ever given you reason to think I believe you lacking in intelligence, Lexie,' he assured her huskily.

'So far,' she challenged.

'Ever,' Lucan corrected gruffly.

Lexie looked at him uncertainly, slightly unnerved by the throaty huskiness of his tone, and even more so by what she could see in those dark eyes as Lucan steadily returned her gaze.

Dear Lord, she was going away with this man for two days. Would be in his company for the same amount of time. Constantly in his disturbing company…!

'I'll be back within the hour,' she confirmed.

But first Lexie had to go to the office of Premier Personnel and explain the situation to Brenda.

Attempt to explain something Lexie couldn't fully explain to herself!

'Put your seat belt on,' Lucan advised as he turned on the ignition of his black Range Rover.

Lexie had looked disturbingly attractive when she'd returned to the offices of the St Claire Corporation an hour or so ago, carrying a thick calf-length woollen coat and an overnight bag, and dressed in a blue sweater the same colour as her eyes, with denims that fitted snugly over that shapely bottom and slender legs before being tucked into calf-high boots. The long length of that gloriously wild black hair was secured in a loose plait down her spine, revealing that she wore small pearls in the lobes of her ears. An oval gold locket was also visible against the blue of her sweater.

Closed in the confines of the Range Rover with her, Lucan was also aware of the subtleness of the perfume she wore, along with a softer, even more subtle smell that was provocatively feminine. In fact the small and very womanly bundle beside him was—as Lucan had hoped she would be—a distraction from the fact that their destination was Mulberry Hall.

Although Lucan knew that no one, and nothing, would ever make him feel completely relaxed about returning to the house he had lived in until he was eleven years old.

Lucan knew from attending Jordan's wedding almost a week ago that the house had changed little since he'd last spent any time there. There was no reason for it to have done. The furnishings and draperies were antiques, the floors downstairs mainly marble, the paintings on the walls originals, as were the ornamental statues, and the impressive chandeliers that hung from the high ceilings were of very old Venetian glass.

No, there was no doubting that Mulberry Hall was a beautiful house. A gracious house. A house fit for a duke. The Duke of Stourbridge. A title Lucan currently held.

Something else he had avoided thinking about for the last eight years.

As the eldest child of a broken marriage Lucan had found it all too easy to blame Mulberry Hall and the demands of holding the title of Duke of Stourbridge, as much as his father's and Sian Thomas's affair, for wrecking his parents' marriage and creating a schism in his own young life and that of his brothers. Lucan wanted to avoid all of those things. Mulberry Hall. His father. The title of Duke. Most of all, Sian Thomas—the woman Alexander had loved enough to sacrifice his whole family for...

Initially, after the divorce was over and emotions had calmed somewhat, Alexander had tried to encourage his three sons to meet and get to know Sian Thomas. An encouragement that had fallen on stony ground as they'd all refused to go anywhere near the woman they held responsible for their parents' separation and divorce.

Damn it, Lucan wouldn't be going near the place again now if John Barton, the caretaker, hadn't made it so obvious that he thought Lucan should see the damage to the house for himself.

Lucan had insisted on Lexie Hamilton coming with him because he had hoped her sharp-tongued presence would be enough of a diversion for him to repress these grim and disturbing thoughts—at least until he actually reached Gloucestershire and could no longer avoid them!

A scowling glance in her direction showed Lucan that she was, in fact, gazing out of the side window of the car as they drove out of London, obviously enjoying the winter wonderland England had become following yet another heavy snowfall two days earlier. The roads had been cleared, at least, but the countryside was still covered in a thick layer of cold and haunting beauty.

Those blue sooty-lashed eyes were bright with pleasure when Lexie turned to return his gaze. 'Everywhere looks so beautiful when it's covered in snow, doesn't it?'

Lucan's mouth twisted derisively. 'Much like papering over the cracks in life and hoping no one will notice!'

Lexie frowned slightly as she became aware of Lucan's obvious tension. 'It doesn't have to be like that.'

He gave a weary sigh. '*Please* tell me you aren't one of those people whose glass is always half-full rather than half-empty?'

Lexie felt her cheeks warm at Lucan's obvious derision. 'It's preferable to being a cynic!'

'I prefer to think of myself as a realist,' he rasped.

'Which is just a polite way of saying you're a cynic,' she dismissed.

He gave her a derisive glance. 'I don't believe that politeness is exactly your forte, Lexie!'

'Or yours!' she came back tartly.

'True,' Lucan murmured softly.

Lexie gave him a sharp glance. 'Don't tell me we actually agree on something?'

'Unusual, but the answer to that would appear to be yes,' he drawled ruefully.

'Wow!'

'Wow, indeed,' Lucan echoed dryly. 'This is going to be a long drive, Lexie, so why don't you pass some of the time away by telling me a little about yourself?' he encouraged.

Lexie stiffened warily. Lucan wanted her to tell him about herself? Such as what? Who her parents were? Her grandmother?

Every part of Lexie's life was a minefield of facts that, if revealed, would probably result in Lucan stopping the car right now and simply throwing her out into this stark and snow-covered landscape!

Which wasn't an altogether bad idea, considering the circumstances...

She moistened dry lips. 'Why don't you tell me about yourself instead?'

His mouth tightened. 'Perhaps we should just put on some music?'

Lexie slowly breathed her relief that Lucan wasn't going to insist on pursuing the subject of herself. It was also interesting to realise that Lucan was as reluctant to talk about himself as she was...

She couldn't help wondering why that was. Surely the life of Lucan St Claire, billionaire entrepreneur, was pretty much an open book? The business life of billionaire entrepreneur Lucan St Claire, maybe, but obviously there were things about his private life that Lucan preferred not to talk about.

His reticence instantly made Lexie wonder exactly what those things could be.

Perhaps a woman…?

She looked at him from beneath ebony lashes. The darkness of his hair really would look more attractive if worn a little longer, and the bleak expression in those almost black eyes as he concentrated on driving was off-putting, but neither of those things detracted from the fact that his was a magnetically handsome face. As for the leashed power of that taut and obviously toned body—

Oh, please, no…!

Lexie recoiled with inward horror. She had only wanted to meet Lucan St Claire—to see for herself how cold and ruthless he was. Becoming physically aware of him, actually finding him attractive, had *not* been part of her plan.

As much as accompanying Lucan to Mulberry Hall in Gloucestershire hadn't been part of Lexie's plan…

'What sort of music do you like?'

Lexie blinked before focusing on Lucan with effort. 'Classical, mostly.' She shrugged.

Dark brows rose over those almost black eyes as he glanced at her. 'Really?'

'Yes, really,' she confirmed sharply. 'Did you imagine I might like heavy rock or something?' she added scathingly.

'Not at all. I'm just surprised that we have the same taste in music, that's all.' He reached forward to switch on the radio, and the car was instantly filled with the soft and haunting strains of Mozart.

It would *have* to be Mozart!

Her grandmother's favourite composer.

Lexie had occasionally stayed with Nanna Sian on her own for several weeks during the school summer holidays when she was growing up and her parents had had to work.

Weeks when Mozart would invariably be playing on the CD player her grandmother kept in the kitchen.

In the kitchen of the cottage where her grandmother still lived—which was only half a mile away from Mulberry Hall...

Lexie was starting to feel ill—and it had nothing to do with travel sickness.

'Perhaps when we get there you'll find the damage to the house in Gloucestershire isn't as bad as Mr Barton thinks it is and we'll be able to return to town tomorrow?' she said hopefully.

Lucan glanced at Lexie from between narrowed lids as he heard almost a note of desperation in her voice. Because she didn't want to spend a couple of days in rural Gloucestershire with him? Or because she had a need to get back to something—someone—in London as soon as possible?

Both of those explanations were somehow unsatisfactory to Lucan.

'And perhaps I'll find it's worse than I thought and we'll have to stay for a week,' he drawled mockingly—a remark that resulted in those blue eyes widening slightly in dismay before the emotion was quickly controlled. 'Do you have personal commitments that make being away awkward for you?' Lucan asked, and scowled.

'Personal commitments?' She frowned.

'Husband? Live-in-lover? Boyfriend?'

'No, of course not,' she answered irritably.

Lucan relaxed slightly. 'And I'm sure you must have had to go away on business before with your employers?'

'Well... I— Yes. Of course.' She seemed slightly flustered. 'It's just—I'm only supposed to be working for you for a total of three days,' she reminded him tersely.

'I'm sure your agency will understand if our return

is delayed for any reason,' Lucan growled unsympathetically.

'I'm not sure that I will!' she came back pertly.

Lucan felt his irritation increasing at Lexie's continuing
arguments. Damn it, hadn't his New Year got off to enough
of a bad start already without—?

Redirected anger, Lucan recognised grimly. Not that
Lexie wasn't infuriating—she undoubtedly was. But Lucan
knew it was his own frustration and annoyance at having
to return to Mulberry Hall again so soon that was making
his mood so volatile. Otherwise Lucan knew he would have
put this woman firmly, chillingly, in her place by now.

Except Lucan wasn't completely sure what her place
was.

Stretched out naked on his bed, that glorious long dark
hair splayed behind her on the pillows as he explored every
inch of her silken body with his lips and hands, was the
place he could most easily picture her...

Lucan shifted uncomfortably in his seat as he felt himself harden just at imagining kissing every silken inch of
her naked body. 'As I believe I have already made clear—
several times,' he added grimly, 'your own requirements
in this matter are of little importance to me.'

Lexie gave a snort as she shook her head disgustedly.
'With a selfish attitude like that I have no idea why you
were in the least surprised when Jessica Brown walked out
on you without notice!'

Lucan gave a hard and humourless smile. 'What a pity
you aren't in a position to do the same...'

'Isn't it?' Lexie returned, saccharine-sweet.

Really, this man was totally obnoxious. Arrogant. Haughty.
Cold. Mocking.

And so darkly attractive he took Lexie's breath away...
Something that certainly wasn't going to help her
through the next trying couple of days...

CHAPTER FOUR

'WELL,' Lucan bit out tersely, having climbed out of the Range Rover to pull on his heavy jacket, before moving round to the passenger side of the parked vehicle to open Lexie's door for her.

Lexie's heart was beating a wild tattoo as she slowly got out of the car to look up at the mellow-stoned magnificence that was Mulberry Hall as it towered majestically over the snow-covered grounds of the Stourbridge estate.

A house and estate Lexie was more familiar with than she wanted the man at her side ever to know.

She turned to look up at him challengingly. 'Well, what?'

He raised dark and mocking brows. 'It's been my experience so far in our acquaintance that you usually have something to say about most things...'

Lexie deliberately kept her expression non-committal as she glanced back at Mulberry Hall. 'I'm betting the electricity bills are high!'

Lucan's bark of laughter was completely spontaneous. Something that seemed, surprisingly, to have occurred several times in the company of this particular woman. Rare indeed, Lucan acknowledged ruefully, for a man usually known for his grimness rather than his sense of humour.

Even rarer for Lexie not to have made some sort of

cutting remark on the obvious and exclusive grandeur that was Mulberry Hall...

'Shouldn't we go inside?' she prompted pointedly.

Lucan nodded abruptly. 'Time to assess the damage.' He took a firm hold of Lexie's arm as he glanced up at the blue tarpaulin that had been fixed temporarily over part of the roof of the west wing of the house. 'I wouldn't want you to fall over and break a leg,' he drawled mockingly when she frowned up at him.

'In case I sue you?' she taunted.

'The way this year's gone so far, it's a distinct possibility!' Lucan's other hand reached out instinctively to steady her as she would have slipped on one of the icy steps leading up to the huge front door, the movement turning her slightly and bringing her into close contact with the hardness of his chest.

Lexie stopped breathing as she felt the warmth of his body envelop her. As she became totally aware of the hardness of his chest and abdomen against her breasts, his firmly muscled legs against her much softer ones.

Even the air about them seemed to still in recognition of that awareness. There had been another fresh fall of snow the previous day, and several inches now covered the surrounding countryside, seeming to surround them in eerie silence.

Lexie slowly raised her head. And then wished she hadn't as she was immediately held captive by the intensity of Lucan's dark and fathomless eyes. The stillness of that air about them became charged, heated, as Lexie found herself unable to look away.

Close to, like this, she could see that those eyes were a deep chocolate-brown surrounded by a ring of black. Dark and compelling eyes. Eyes that Lexie knew she could drown in. Deep and fathomless eyes that seemed to turn to the deep brown of hot liquid chocolate as she continued to stare up at him.

Eyes that Lexie suddenly realised were coming closer as Lucan lowered his head and that firm and yet sensual mouth came within touching distance of her own.

Lexie reared back sharply before wrenching her arm out of Lucan's grasp. 'You really don't want to do that!' she warned.

He returned her gaze steadily. 'I don't?'

'No.' She scowled, and had to reach out instinctively to place her hand on the wall at the side of the steps as she felt herself in danger of slipping again.

Lexie might have every reason to despise Lucan St Claire, but she had absolutely no doubt that if he were to kiss her—to kiss the granddaughter of the despised Sian Thomas—Lucan would have reason to dislike himself, too.

What a bitter irony it would be, Lexie realised heavily, if he were to find himself attracted to the very last woman in the world he would ever want to feel such an interest in.

She gave a disgusted shake of her head. 'Do you think you could possibly unlock the door so that we can go inside out of the cold?' she snapped in her impatience.

Lucan drew in a rasping breath. His first for several long seconds, he realised. The whole of the length of time he had held the softness of Lexie's body moulded against the length of his, in fact...

Her breasts beneath her sweater had felt full and lush as they'd pressed against his chest, her thighs in the fitted denims soft and enticing against the hardness of his arousal. Her mouth, those deliciously provocative lips, moist and slightly parted in invitation. An invitation Lucan would have been only too happy to accept. *Would* have accepted, damn it, if Lexie hadn't pulled away so abruptly!

For a few brief moments it had been pleasant to anticipate spending the next two or three days—and nights—
dealing with the hunger Lucan seemed to have developed
for Lexie's curvaceous softness, rather than with the real
reason he was here.

Except there was really no escaping the fact that
Mulberry Hall loomed large and overpowering before
him...

'Of course.' Lucan's mouth was set grimly as he turned
away to climb the last two steps, pausing briefly to draw in
a deep and controlling breath before unlocking and pushing
open the front door.

Standing in the doorway, looking into the cavernous
marble-floored entrance hall, Lucan instantly detected a
slightly musty smell that hadn't been there a week ago. An
indication that the water damage Lucan had seen on the
outside of the building had, as John Barton had already
warned, actually entered the house.

The west wing of the house, to be exact, where that
damned portrait of his father hung so regally.

With any luck the portrait would be one of the things
to have been damaged!

'Lucan...?' Lexie prompted uncertainly as he seemed
transfixed in the doorway, apparently as reluctant as she
was to actually go inside the house.

'Sorry.' He drew himself up abruptly and stepped aside
to allow her to enter.

It felt slightly warmer as Lexie stepped inside, but not
much. 'Does anyone actually live here any more?' she
turned to ask huskily as she gave an involuntary shiver
before wrapping her long coat more tightly about her.

'Not for years.' Lucan's expression was as bleak as his
tone of voice as he followed her inside, before closing the
door behind him to shut out the icy blast of the cold wind.

'Wait for me here while I go to the back of the house
and turn up the heating.' He turned abruptly on his heel
and strode off down a hallway without waiting for her to
reply.

Not that Lexie had been going to make one. She was
as unnerved at being back at Mulberry Hall as Lucan appeared to be.

She huddled further down into her coat as she stood
looking around the familiar surroundings. She hadn't actually been inside Mulberry Hall since Grandpa Alex had
died, eight years ago, but it didn't look as if anything had
changed in that time.

The huge cut-glass Venetian chandelier still hung from
the cavernous ceiling overhead, and the two doors directly
off the entrance hall led, she knew, into a graciously furnished sitting room and a spacious dining room that would
seat at least a dozen people at its long oak table.

Another door further down the hallway opened up into
what had once been a mirrored ballroom, big enough to
hold a hundred or so guests, but which was now a gym and
games room.

Years ago Grandpa Alex had taught a nine-year-old
Lexie to play table tennis and billiards in that room, while
an indulgent Nanna Sian looked on fondly...

Lexie felt an emotional lump in her throat and an ache
in her chest as she remembered the laughter that had filled
the bleakness of this house in those days. The same love
and laughter there had always been wherever Grandpa Alex
and Nanna Sian were together.

A togetherness that Lucan St Claire and the rest of his
unforgiving family had wanted no part of.

The same Lucan St Claire who, minutes ago, had been
on the verge of kissing Lexie—the granddaughter of the
woman he and his family so despised...

Lexie gave another shiver, having absolutely no doubt as to the depth of Lucan's anger if he were ever to realise exactly who she was...

'It should warm up in here shortly,' Lucan rasped as he strode back into the entrance hall. He scowled darkly as Lexie gave an involuntary start, her deep blue eyes wary as she turned sharply to look at him. 'As far as I'm aware we don't have any family ghosts,' he said dryly, mocking her reaction.

She gave him a scathing glance. 'Very funny!'

'I don't believe I've ever been known for my sense of humour, Lexie.'

'I wonder why! Is there some tea or coffee in the kitchen so that I can at least make us a warm drink?'

Lucan arched mocking brows. 'Are you sure that making hot drinks for the two of us comes under the job description of a temporary temporary PA?'

'Probably not,' Lexie dismissed tersely. 'But I'm willing to make an exception on this occasion.'

'That's very generous of you,' Lucan drawled, and had to hold back yet another laugh.

'I thought so, too.' She nodded abruptly.

Lucan couldn't help admiring her attitude. Despite the fact that the family had spent several days here at New Years, no one had actually lived in the house for years. Consequently it wasn't very welcoming, and there were no household servants any more—just the caretaker and his wife, who occasionally came in to check that everything was okay. A lot of women—every single one of the glamorous women Lucan had dated these last ten years or so—would have declared the facilities here unsuitable, even primitive, and immediately demanded to be taken to a hotel. Lexie was obviously made of sterner stuff.

'I'm sure there will be tea and coffee, but no milk,' he told her ruefully.

'Black coffee will be fine,' Lexie assured him briskly, and turned away to walk across the entrance hall towards the back of the house. Only to come to an abrupt halt as she realised her mistake. 'Er—I take it the kitchen *is* back here?' She paused uncertainly.

'The door at the end of the hallway.' Lucan nodded before falling into step behind her.

Lexie was completely aware of Lucan as he followed her into the kitchen, to lean back against one of the oak kitchen cabinets as she prepared the coffee percolator.

And she was still completely aware of how close he had been to kissing her minutes ago. Of how, for a few brief seconds, she had wanted him to kiss her...

Admit it, Lexie, she derided herself, Lucan is like no other man you've ever met. Arrogantly confident, darkly handsome, and most of all, so effortlessly powerful. The man was a *duke,* for goodness' sake. That alone was a potent aphrodisiac without all those other...

Lexie's movements stilled self-consciously as she realised she had been so lost in thought that she hadn't noticed Lucan watching her through narrowed lids as she first filled the percolator with water, before taking ground coffee from the kitchen cabinet and pulling open the appropriate drawer to take out a teaspoon.

Because that was where the coffee and the cutlery had always been kept...

'This is going to take a couple of minutes to prepare, if you have something else you need to be doing.' Lexie sincerely hoped the adage 'offence is the best form of defence' was correct.

Lucan scowled darkly as he realised he had been enjoying watching the movement of Lexie's small and gracefully beautiful hands as she made the coffee, imagining the intensity of pleasure he would feel if those same elegant hands were trailing caressingly over every inch of his naked body...

Hell.

An apt description of the constant state of arousal he seemed to find himself in when in this particular woman's company!

Lucan straightened abruptly. 'I'll go and bring our things in from the car.' And he hoped that the icy-cold wind outside would not only dampen his arousal but also clear his head of the erotic images currently going round and round in his mind!

Lexie watched from beneath sooty lashes as Lucan strode out of the kitchen towards the front of the house, waiting until she heard the soft thud of the door closing behind him before she leant weakly back against one of the kitchen cabinets and closed her eyes.

She really wasn't very good at this. They had only been at Mulberry Hall a matter of minutes, and she had already slipped up twice by knowing where the kitchen was and everything in it.

Perhaps it was as well that she had never actually stayed here in the past; at least the bedrooms and other rooms upstairs would be a complete mystery to her!

Although, just thinking about the bedrooms upstairs was enough to remind her of how she had longed earlier to feel Lucan's mouth on and against hers...

She shouldn't be attracted to Lucan—no, not shouldn't. She *couldn't* be attracted to him!

Lucan was a St Claire. Not just *a* St Claire, but the head of the St Claire family. The same family who had hurt and rejected her beloved Nanna Sian all those years ago, and then again eight years ago, by making it obvious they didn't even want her to attend Grandpa Alex's funeral.

Lexie felt her spine straighten with fresh resolve. She disliked all of the St Claire family intensely for the way they had treated her beloved grandmother, and that included Lucan. Most especially the cold and arrogant Lucan!

Except there had been nothing cold about Lucan earlier when he looked down at her so intently. When Lexie had gazed up into those intense dark eyes and felt as if she were balancing on the edge of a volcano, knowing that the heat would intensify, burn, engulf her completely, if she allowed herself to fall into those fathomless depths...

Even now her breasts felt tight, sensitised, the nipples hard and aching against the soft material of her bra, and she felt a warmth between her thighs, a burning. What would it be like, she wondered, to have that firm and sculptured mouth closing over the tips of her breasts as Lucan suckled her deep into the moist heat of his mouth?

'Brr, it's damned cold out there— Sorry, I thought you were Lucan!' the man who had just entered through the back door of the kitchen grimaced in apology as he turned and saw Lexie.

It wasn't too difficult to guess that the tall and sandy-haired man aged in his mid-thirties was John Barton, the caretaker of Mulberry Hall—the man with a faint Scottish accent she had spoken to on the telephone earlier today.

A man Lexie didn't recognise, and so—thankfully— wouldn't recognise her, either!

'An easy mistake when we look so much alike,' she came back teasingly as she watched him place the box he was carrying on top of one of the kitchen units.

He gave a boyishly endearing grin as he straightened, his eyes a warm and friendly blue as he bundled down into the collar of his thick overcoat. 'Lucan didn't mention he was bringing someone with him...' He eyed her speculatively. 'I'm John Barton, the caretaker,' he introduced himself, and held out his hand in greeting.

Lexie briefly shook that firm and capable hand. 'Lexie,' she supplied economically. Deliberately so. The fewer people who knew that it was Lexie *Hamilton* who had accompanied Lucan to Mulberry Hall, the safer she would feel. 'I'm Mr St Claire's PA,' she said lightly. 'Temporarily,' she added firmly.

And unnecessarily.

Except Lexie somehow needed to reassure herself of that fact after the thoughts she had just been having about Lucan. After she had imagined his lips and mouth against her naked breasts—

Stop it, Lexie, she instructed herself firmly. *Stop it right now!*

She straightened abruptly. 'I'm just making some coffee, but Mr St Claire is outside getting our luggage if you want to join him?' she said dismissively. The curiosity she could see in those friendly blue eyes warned her that John Barton would rather linger in the kitchen for a while and satisfy his curiosity about her than go in search of his employer.

He smiled. 'My wife has sent over a few supplies to see you through.' He indicated the box he had placed on the worktop. 'Milk, bread and butter, cheese—stuff like that. I would have brought it over earlier, but Lucan didn't tell me what time he would be arriving,' he added.

'What a surprise!' Lexie muttered dryly as she crossed the kitchen to inspect the box of groceries. As well as the supplies John had mentioned there was also a promising-looking covered glass dish, filled with some sort of meat casserole. Her eyes glowed with pleasure as she turned back to John Barton. 'Please thank your wife—'

'Cathy,' he supplied lightly.

Lexie had been occasional friends with a girl in the village called Cathy when she was growing up. Not enough for the two of them to have remained in touch once they went off to different universities at eighteen, but enough for Lexie's grandmother to write and tell her that Cathy had married the previous year.

But there was no reason to think it was the same Cathy. No doubt John Barton's wife was as Scottish as he was…

'Do you both come from around here?' Lexie prompted conversationally as she studiously began to take the supplies from the box.

'Obviously I'm originally from Scotland.' John Barton gave a rueful smile. 'But Cathy's a local girl—from the village,' he added lightly. 'I expect she'll pop over to say hello to you both sometime tomorrow—'

'I don't think Mr St Claire is planning on staying for very long,' Lexie cut in sharply. Dear God, it probably *was* the same Cathy!

Blonde-haired, green-eyed Cathy, whom Lexie had no doubt made the amiable John Barton as wonderful a wife as he made *her* a loving husband!

'I believe I said we would probably be here for a couple of days at least, Lexie.'

She turned sharply to face Lucan as he filled the doorway into the main house, heavy lids lowered over those dark eyes as he returned her gaze challengingly. Lexie swallowed hard before speaking. 'Mr Barton has very kindly brought over some milk and other supplies.'

'Just the basics,' the other man explained as he crossed the kitchen. 'Sorry this business had to bring you back so soon, Lucan.'

'No problem, John,' Lucan lied as he shook the other man's hand warmly. 'I was thinking of taking Lexie to the

Rose and Crown for dinner this evening, so I'm hoping they still serve meals?'

'Mr Barton's wife has very kindly provided us with a casserole for this evening,' Lexie put in quickly.

The Rose and Crown pub in the village was another place she had no intention of going while she was here; Bill and Mary Collins, the landlord and his wife, were both well aware of exactly who she was, and of her connection to Sian Thomas.

One thing Lexie was now absolutely sure of: she had to go down to the village and visit her grandmother in person, before there was even a possibility of Nanna Sian hearing from anyone else that her granddaughter was currently staying at Mulberry Hall with Lucan St Claire!

CHAPTER FIVE

'I WOULDN'T have thought preparing dinner came under the heading of your duties as a PA, either?' Lucan prompted softly an hour or so later, when he returned to the kitchen after seeing John out and then returning upstairs briefly to change out of his suit. A kitchen which was now filled with the wonderful aroma of the thick and meaty casserole visibly warming through the glass door of the oven.

Blue eyes snapped with irritation as Lexie looked up from where she sat, drinking coffee at the weathered oak table. 'Technically Cathy Barton prepared it. I just put it in the oven to warm.'

'Even so...'

'Oh, stop being so pedantic, Lucan!' She stood up impatiently to pour coffee into a second mug.

'Pedantic...?' Lucan repeated softly.

'Yes, pedantic!' Lexie thrust the coffee mug into his hand. 'Milk and sugar are on the table.' She sat down in her chair to continue staring down into her own coffee mug.

Lucan looked down at that bent dark head as he sipped the black and unsweetened coffee he preferred; his absence obviously hadn't done anything to improve her mood as she didn't look at him or speak. The latter was an unusual occurrence in itself!

Lucan pulled out the chair opposite hers and sat down

to stretch his long legs out under the table. 'What would you be doing now if you were back in London...?'

Lexie eyed him from beneath her lashes, very aware that Lucan had changed out of his formal suit, shirt and tie since she'd last seen him, and now looked more comfortable— and more darkly, devastatingly attractive—in a thick black sweater and fitted black denims. 'Deciding whether to order Chinese or Indian take-out, probably.'

'You can take the girl out of the city but not the city out of the girl, hmm?' he mused softly.

She bristled. 'What's *that* supposed to mean?'

Lucan noted that several wispy strands of that glorious long black hair had come loose from the confining plait, adding a vulnerability to Lexie's heart-shaped face and the long length of her creamy throat. Except, as Lucan knew only too well, Lexie Hamilton had the vulnerability of a spitting cat!

He shrugged. 'I was just attempting to make conversation.'

She frowned. 'Did you decide on what to do about the damage upstairs?'

He nodded. 'I've arranged for a builder to come out and take a look in the morning.'

'And then we can leave?' She looked hopeful.

Lucan grimaced. 'I won't know until the builder has assessed the damage.' He frowned as she still looked disgruntled. 'I realise the facilities aren't too good here. Would you be more comfortable if I organised a couple of rooms for us tonight at the village pub?'

'*No!* I mean—that won't be necessary,' Lexie spoke more calmly when she saw the way Lucan's eyes narrowed at her unnecessary vehemence. 'The house is quite warm now, and we have Cathy Barton's casserole for dinner...'

'Yes...' Lucan acknowledged slowly.

Suspiciously?

Lexie couldn't say she would blame Lucan if he *did* feel a little suspicious when she was reacting so jumpily to almost everything he said. Although it was a little difficult for her not to be that way, when she constantly felt as if her identity as Sian Thomas's granddaughter was going to be exposed at any moment. Especially now that there was a possibility of Lucan's caretaker being married to Cathy Wilson—someone who knew exactly who Lexie was.

Maybe she should just come out with the truth now and get it over and done with?

Oh, yes—and no doubt find herself cast into the dungeon below.

Lexie had been repelled, and a little fascinated, too, when years ago Grandpa Alex had been persuaded into showing her the dungeon hidden behind the huge wine cellar in the basement of the house. A small structure, probably only six feet deep by ten feet wide, its walls, floor and ceiling were made of solid stone four feet thick. The fourth wall was a metal door with one-inch-solid metal bars that had been driven deep down into the stone floor.

She had wondered all those years ago, as she'd stood looking at that impregnable structure, what the past inhabitants of that stone and metal cell could possibly have done to merit being cast into such a lightless and virtually airless prison.

Right now Lexie couldn't help wondering if deliberately deceiving the current Duke of Stourbridge would be considered crime enough…

So, yes, she obviously had the option of coming clean—of telling Lucan exactly who she was. But it was a disclosure that would no doubt make the contempt Lexie had faced this morning—when Lucan had believed her behaviour towards Andrew Proctor to be unprofessional—seem like child's play in comparison.

Had some part of her always relished Lucan knowing who she was? Wanted to somehow spring that knowledge on him, like a magician bringing a rabbit out of a hat, and then enjoy watching Lucan squirm?

If so, then Lexie knew she didn't feel that way any longer. Just a few hours in Lucan's company had been enough to tell her she would be the one who came out worst in any springing of her relationship to Sian Thomas on him!

She stood up abruptly to cross the kitchen and stand near the warmth of the oven. As far away from Lucan as it was possible to get in the confines of what was actually a cavernous kitchen, but seemed to be getting steadily smaller and smaller by the second...

'What would *you* be doing now if you were in London? Out with a beautiful woman, dining at some exclusive restaurant, no doubt?' she prompted derisively.

Lucan studied Lexie's flushed and challenging face for several long seconds. There was something about the way her gaze refused to meet his and the husky tone of her voice that told him that wasn't what she had intended saying. That she was deliberately trying to irritate him.

'I *am* with a beautiful woman,' he pointed out softly. 'And Cathy's casserole smells better than anything I could buy in a restaurant—exclusive or otherwise,' he added ruefully, effectively cutting off the scathing comment he was sure had been about to come out of Lexie's sexy mouth at his compliment; there was nothing she could say after his last comment that wouldn't sound rude to Cathy Barton's generosity!

Instead she turned away and began busying herself getting out the plates and cutlery they would need to eat.

'The casserole is ready to serve now. I was just waiting for you.'

Lucan stood up. 'Would you like some red wine to go with it?'

'Not enough for you to have to bother going down to the cellar and—' She broke off, her eyes wide as she turned sharply to face him. 'At least, I presume that's where you keep your wine?' she added offhandedly.

'Some of it.' Lucan gave a slow inclination of his head, his narrowed gaze still fixed intently on Lexie's slightly pale face. 'But there's probably a bottle or two of red in the back of the food pantry.'

'You don't come here very often, do you?' Once again Lexie decided that offence was the best form of defence if she wanted to deflect Lucan's attention from the fact that she had made yet another slip by mentioning knowing there was a cellar at Mulberry Hall.

'Actually, I attended my brother's wedding here a week ago,' he dismissed. 'And if that was a pick up line then you didn't say it quite right...' He quirked dark and mocking brows.

As if! Only a woman who didn't mind playing with fire would even *think* of becoming involved with Lucan St Claire. Which was a strange thing for Lexie to have thought, considering she had initially thought him so icily cold...

The truth was that Lexie was having trouble continuing to see Lucan that way. How could she think of him as cold when she was still totally aware of the warmth that had emanated from him earlier? Of the feeling as if she were standing on the edge of a volcano that was threatening to erupt and engulf her in its heat?

Outwardly, there was no doubting that Lucan was a cold and arrogant man, but beneath that coldness Lexie realised there was a powerful force. A physical energy that was overwhelming in its intensity.

Much like a magnet, drawing Lexie slowly but surely towards him...

And she didn't want to be drawn to Lucan—recognised only too well the danger of such an attraction.

'I don't have a pick up line, Mr St Claire,' she assured him coldly as she took the casserole from the oven. 'And even if I did I certainly wouldn't use it on you!' she added derisively.

Instantly she realised her mistake, as instead of lessening the tension between them it suddenly seemed to become thicker, almost palpable.

Lucan's eyes had narrowed to black slits. 'Why not...?'

Lexie swallowed hard, her eyes wide as she watched Lucan cross the kitchen with the slow grace of a jungle cat. 'Why not what?' she prompted distractedly.

'Why not try a pick up line on me?'

Lucan was standing so close now Lexie could feel the warmth of his breath stirring the loose tendrils of hair at her temple as he spoke.

She flicked her tongue nervously across her lips before answering. 'Well, for one thing I make it a rule never to become involved with the people I work for or with.' She had meant the remark to be derisive, but instead she just sounded breathily expectant.

'Is that an old rule or a new one?'

'New. Very new,' Lexie assured him pointedly.

His brows rose speculatively. 'I see...'

'Do you?'

'I believe so,' Lucan murmured softly. 'And does that rule still apply if that employer is only a temporary *temporary* one?'

'Especially then.' She nodded abruptly.

Teasing Lexie had started out as a game to Lucan—a way of prodding at her outspoken and perky self-confidence. It had stopped being a game the moment she'd dismissed any interest in him so arbitrarily.

Lucan hadn't reached the age of thirty-six without knowing when a woman responded to him, and earlier this evening, outside on the steps up to the house, Lexie had been as physically aware of him as Lucan of her. Had been as receptive to his kiss as he to the idea of kissing her...

His gaze dropped to the fullness of her mouth. Those plump and sensuous lips were slightly parted, and still slightly wet from that recent nervous flick of her tongue.

Lucan's breath caught in his throat as she repeated that nervous movement. Her tongue was a moist caress across those parted lips, awakening a hunger in Lucan to do the same...

'Don't!' Lexie gasped, stepping back as she saw Lucan's intention in the raw hunger of his dark gaze. That step brought her up abruptly against one of the kitchen units. 'This is *so* not a good idea, Lucan!' She put her hands up to stop him as he followed her, those hands becoming crushed between them as Lucan leaned his body into hers so that they were now touching from breast to thigh.

Heatedly.

Achingly.

'It feels like a very good idea to me,' Lucan said softly as he moved his arms either side of her, so that his hands could grip the worktop behind her, effectively trapping her as the heat of his body fitted against her much softer curves, his arousal hard against her thighs. 'Doesn't it feel like a good idea to you, Lexie?' he prompted huskily.

Lexie couldn't breathe as she looked up, and instantly felt as if she were drowning in the warmth of those dark and mesmerizing eyes. In the longing she felt to know the touch of Lucan's mouth against her own...

Lucan St Claire's mouth!

Because that was who this man was, Lexie reminded herself desperately. Lucan St Claire. Her beloved Grandpa Alex's eldest son and heir. The same man who, with the rest of his arrogant family, had shunned Lexie's grandmother for so many years.

Ice entered Lexie's veins, and her eyes were glittering with that same cold anger as she straightened. 'Get away from me, Lucan,' she bit out icily, even as she pushed hard against his muscled chest.

Lucan frowned as he easily resisted that push, still holding her captive in the circle of his arms as his hands tightened on the worktop behind her. 'Your lips are saying one thing but your body is saying something else,' he rasped harshly, and he glanced down pointedly at the fullness of her breasts, where the nipples showed hard and aroused against the soft wool of her sweater.

'I'm cold,' she dismissed scornfully. 'Look, Lucan, I'm sure there are plenty of women who would be only too happy to share the bed of the Duke of Stourbridge—temporarily! I just don't happen to be one of them!'

Lucan's eyes narrowed, and he straightened abruptly before stepping away from her. 'I don't remember mentioning that I'm the Duke of Stourbridge.' He eyed her coldly.

She had done it again, Lexie realised sinkingly.

Because she was flustered. Because Lucan was right. Her mouth and her body weren't in agreement at all! Her brain knew that she shouldn't feel this attraction towards Lucan, of all men, but the ache in her body told her it had completely different feelings on the subject.

She breathed raggedly. 'John Barton mentioned it

earlier.' Well…he might have done, mightn't he? 'Imagine my surprise when he referred to you as "His Grace",' she added tauntingly.

'I prefer not to use the title.' Lucan bit the words out as he thrust his hands into his pockets.

'Why not?' Lexie derided. 'Just think of all the extra women you could attract into your bed if they knew you were a duke!'

His eyes narrowed at her obvious mockery. 'I said I prefer not to use it!'

'And I asked why not.'

His mouth thinned to an uncompromising line. 'It's a long story.'

'I'll be happy with the condensed version,' Lexie encouraged huskily.

His nostrils flared angrily. 'There isn't a condensed version.'

'Oh, come on, Lucan—'

'Just leave it alone, will you, Lexie?' he rasped harshly.

Lexie felt a shiver down her spine as she took in the cold glitter of his eyes, the nerve pulsing in his clenched jaw, and the uncompromising—dangerous—set of that sculpted mouth. 'I—okay, fine.' She turned away. 'Perhaps we should eat now?'

Lucan breathed deeply in an effort to control the black tide of anger that had held him in its grip at the reminder of exactly who he was and what he was doing at Mulberry Hall. Most of the time—in fact, all of the time he was in London—Lucan managed to forget completely that the Duke of Stourbridge even existed, let alone had any bearing on his own life.

Because as far as he was concerned it didn't. The title,

Mulberry Hall, the whole damned estate could all just disappear as far as he was concerned.

Damn it, he shouldn't have come back here again so soon after Jordan and Stephanie's wedding. Should have resisted John Barton's suggestion that he come up to Gloucestershire and view the damage for himself.

So why hadn't he…?

Because, Lucan realised with a frown, the idea of being alone for a few days with the beautiful and feisty Lexie Hamilton had somehow appealed to a side of his nature that he was usually at pains to control.

The sensuous side of his nature, which was so much like his father's, and which had caused so much unhappiness to Alexander's wife and sons.

He had decided long ago that no woman would ever lead him around by a certain part of his anatomy. That he would never want, desire *any* woman enough to cause the hurt and destruction that his father had brought on his own family twenty-five years ago, when he'd fallen in love with another woman.

'Lucan…?'

He scowled darkly as he looked up to find that Lexie had placed the casserole in the middle of the table, ready for serving, and was now looking across at him expectantly as she resumed her seat.

He gave a terse shake of his head. 'I don't think I'm hungry after all.'

Lexie gave a pained frown. 'As far as I'm aware, you haven't eaten anything all day…'

Lucan's expression was derisive. 'And that bothers you because…?'

'It doesn't bother me, exactly…'

'That's what I thought,' Lucan drawled ruefully.

She gave an impatient sigh. 'The Bartons didn't even

know I was going to be here, so Cathy Barton obviously prepared this meal for you.'

'Trying to guilt me into eating it, Lexie?' Lucan taunted.

Angry colour entered those ivory cheeks. 'You're being childish now!'

Lucan was usually so emotionally logical—so controlled. Too much so, perhaps? Whatever the reason, he had absolutely no way of stopping the fury that washed over him as he crossed the kitchen in two strides to reach out and pull Lexie effortlessly to her feet and into the prison of his arms. 'Does *this* feel childish to you?' he growled.

Lexie found herself unable to look away from the savagery of Lucan's expression as he loomed over her: hard and glittering dark eyes, clenched cheeks, thinned mouth, that nerve once again pulsing in the firmness of his jaw.

Pulsing with the same rhythm as the hardness of his arousal pressing into the softness of her abdomen...

Whatever she had said or done in the last few minutes, Lexie knew that part of it had somehow pushed Lucan too far—that at this moment he was beyond being reasoned with, beyond denial as his mouth came crushingly down on hers...

He kissed her fiercely, hungrily, tasting, feeding on the softness of her lips. His arms were about her as his hands cupped her bottom and he moulded the heat of her thighs into the hardness of his, lifting her slightly, accommodating her, until he found what he was looking for. Lexie groaned low in her throat as he moved that hardness rhythmically against the apex of her thighs.

She returned that kiss hungrily as she felt herself swell, moisten, felt heat course through her, her breasts becoming full, the nipples hard and aching, as Lucan moved his chest abrasively against her.

Dear Lord, she wanted this man...

Wanted Lucan. Wanted the pleasure she knew he was capable of giving her.

The pleasure he was giving her now as he pushed her sweater up to bare her breasts, before bending his head and drawing one aching nipple hungrily into the heat of his mouth.

Lexie arched her back in invitation, her hands becoming entangled in the dark thickness of Lucan's hair as he suckled her harder, deeper, and his other hand curved possessively over her other breast, to roll the aching nipple between his thumb and finger in rhythmic caress as he suckled its twin.

Lexie felt as if she was on fire. Her skin was intensely sensitised. Hot. Damp. Nothing else mattered at this moment but Lucan and the pleasure—so much pleasure!—he gave her.

She needed to touch him, too. Needed the feel of his bare flesh beneath her hands.

'Oh, God—yes...!' Lucan released Lexie's nipple to groan throatily as he felt her hands on the bareness of his back beneath his sweater. Those small, elegant, sensuous hands moved caressingly across the heat of his back, from the tensed muscles at his shoulders to the low dip of his spine, making him burn, throb, for her to touch him lower still. 'Wrap your legs around me, Lexie!' he instructed fiercely, even as his hands cupped beneath her bottom to lift her fully against his pulsing arousal, and his mouth once again captured hers as he began to thrust slowly, rhythmically, against her.

She was so tiny, so delicately beautiful, and she tasted of honey—warm, hot honey—as Lucan ran his tongue across the sensuous swell of her lips to seek, explore, the moist heat of her mouth.

Her arms were about his neck, her fingers becoming entangled in the hair at his nape as she met the fierce demand of that kiss and the hard demand of his thighs moving against and into hers.

Lucan knew he had never been so aroused. Never been this hard, this aching... Never been so aware of the need to possess, to claim as his own—

No!

Lexie groaned her hunger, her need, as Lucan wrenched his mouth away from hers, steadying her on her own feet before stepping back. That hunger faded, died, and Lexie felt her legs shaking as she looked up to see the angry glitter in the darkness of Lucan's eyes as he glared down at her with fierce intensity.

No—not just fiercely, but almost as if he *hated* her...!

CHAPTER SIX

PERHAPS he did hate her, Lexie realised painfully, as Lucan's already bleak expression turned to one of total disgust, his eyes black and hard as onyx, his top lip curled back almost in a snarl.

Lexie drew in a ragged breath. 'Lucan—'

'You were right. Kissing you was a big mistake!' he rasped scathingly.

Lexie moistened stiff lips. 'I believe what I actually said was that it wasn't a good idea.'

Lucan's mouth thinned. 'Isn't that the same thing?'

'Not at all,' Lexie rallied, as her own anger, her discomfort with the intimacies she had allowed this man, came crashing down on her. He was Lucan St Claire, for God's sake! *Lucan St Claire!* 'I only gave you a cautionary warning—but being told by the man who has just thoroughly kissed you that it was a "big mistake" is damned insulting!'

Lucan looked at Lexie and felt self-disgust begin to fade and irritated amusement take its place as he realised, by the angry sparkle in Lexie's deep blue eyes, the flush to her cheeks and the antagonistic tilt of her stubbornly pointed chin, that she really was insulted by what he had just said.

She wasn't angry because Lucan had kissed her. Or

embarrassed by the fact that her bared breast had been in the heat of his mouth. Nor was she outraged because he had worked his arousal against that swollen and sensitive place between her legs until she groaned and moved against him in her need for release.

Oh, no, it would be too much to expect the unusual, the unique Lexie Hamilton to feel any of those natural reactions to the intimacies they had just shared!

Whereas he—damn it—he was a man who was always in control. Who had always preferred the comfort of a bed when he made love to a woman.

Not with Lexie, apparently. Oh, no. With Lexie he had almost made love in the kitchen at Mulberry Hall. If he hadn't stopped when he had then they would probably have finished making love on the table or the flagstone floor.

Lucan gave a slightly bemused shake of his head as he acknowledged that Lexie was like no other woman he had ever met. Like no woman he had ever *wanted* to meet!

Her long and beautiful black hair had come loose from its plait and now fell in curling and wild disorder about her slender shoulders, and her mouth—that gloriously delicious and sensual mouth—was slightly swollen, the skin beneath slightly reddened from the passion of his kiss.

Lucan's expression darkened as he reached up to gently run the soft pad of his thumb across the mark of that abrasion on her ivory skin. 'I think I need a shave,' he murmured.

Lexie's eyes widened indignantly. This man had just kissed her until she was almost senseless, then insulted her, and all he could say now was— 'Is that it? No apology? No "it won't happen again"? Just "I think I need a shave"!'

He looked down his long, arrogant nose at her. 'I don't feel the need to apologise for something I know you enjoyed as much as I did.' His expression darkened. 'Neither do I believe in making promises I'm not sure I can keep,' he added softly.

Lexie stared at him incredulously for several long seconds before glaring up at him. 'You over-confident, pompous, unmitigated—' She broke off, too angry to be able to come up with a word bad enough to describe his attitude. *'Ass!'* she finally concluded furiously as she stepped away from him.

'Very original,' Lucan drawled dryly.

Lexie's eyes narrowed. 'I doubt you would have appreciated the word I really wanted to use!'

He gave a shake of his head, his expression bleak. 'It can't be any worse than the things I've already called myself.'

She eyed him frustratedly. 'Believe me, if there was some way I could leave here tonight then I would! As there isn't...I'm going upstairs to bed instead.' Lexie grabbed her shoulder-bag from the back of the chair. 'Do you have any preference as to which bedroom I should use? Apart from the ducal suite, of course,' she added scornfully.

'Feel free to use any of them—including the ducal suite,' he added harshly.

'Just because we shared a few kisses, it doesn't mean I'm willing to share your bed—'

'I have no intention, tonight or any other night, of going anywhere near the ducal suite,' he assured her harshly, a nerve pulsing in his tightly clenched jaw. 'With or without you in it.'

Lexie became very still. 'Why not?'

Lucan turned away, the muscles in his back tense. 'Will you stop asking so many damned questions, Lexie, and just go to bed?'

It would be the wise thing to do—the sensible thing to do, when emotions were obviously running so high.

Unfortunately Lexie's actions so far where this particular man was concerned had been neither wise nor sensible.

'You don't use your title. You obviously come here as little as possible. In fact, it's been obvious since John Barton's telephone call this morning that you didn't really want to come here today, either.'

'Is there some point to these observations?' He turned sharply to look at her, those onyx eyes glittering warningly through narrowed lids.

Lexie shrugged. 'It's such a beautiful house—'

'It's a damned mausoleum!' Lucan cut in forcefully.

'Then change it.'

'Changing the décor and the furniture won't make Mulberry Hall somewhere I ever want to live again,' he growled. 'If I could I'd raze the damned place to the ground and grass over it!'

Lexie shook her head. 'I don't understand...'

'You aren't meant to,' Lucan assured her harshly. 'Sharing a few kisses doesn't give you any rights where I'm concerned.'

Lucan never discussed his motives or emotions with anyone—not even with his two brothers. And he was closer to Gideon and Jordan than he was anyone. He certainly didn't intend confiding in Lexie and then having to listen to a lot of amateur psychobabble concerning his lack of ability to deal with his feelings of abandonment after his father left his family for another woman.

'Just go to bed, Lexie,' he advised her dully. 'I'll clear away here.'

Lexie didn't need to be told twice—knew by the bleakness of Lucan's expression that she had already stepped way over the line by probing into things he obviously had no intention of discussing with her.

Which in no way lessened her curiosity concerning Lucan's obvious aversion to Mulberry Hall and all it represented...

'I wondered where you were...'

Lexie turned sharply—guiltily?—to look at Lucan as he strode forcefully down the west gallery to where she stood, looking at the last of the portraits adorning the long gallery wall. A portrait of Alexander St Claire. The fourteenth Duke of Stourbridge.

Lucan's father. Her own beloved Grandpa Alex...

Looking from the portrait to the man who now stood at her side, Lexie could see just how much alike the two men, father and son, actually were.

The portrait of Alexander had obviously been painted when he was about the age Lucan was now. His hair was still black, rather than the iron-grey it had been during the years Lexie had known him, and the similarity of the aristocratic facial structure and dark eyes was unmistakable.

She forced a teasing smile to her lips. 'Did you think I had decided to leave this morning, after all?'

That thought *had* crossed Lucan's mind when he'd gone down to the kitchen and found there was fresh coffee keeping hot in the percolator, and signs of toast having been eaten, but no actual evidence of Lexie herself. It had been pure chance that he had come up to the west gallery, to take another look at the damage before the builder arrived.

Lexie had left her hair loose today, and it framed the delicate beauty of her face before cascading wildly over her shoulders to the middle of her back, appearing very black against the red sweater she wore with faded fitted denims. Denims that clung revealingly to the provocative swell of her bottom—

'Your father?'

Lucan's jaw clenched as he turned his gaze away from that delectable part of Lexie's anatomy to frown up at the portrait of Alexander which Lexie had been studying when he entered the gallery. Unfortunately, it had escaped damage.

'Yes,' he confirmed tightly.

She nodded slowly. 'You're very alike.'

Lucan's mouth thinned. 'Only in looks, I assure you.'

Her head tilted questioningly. 'You don't sound as if you liked your father very much.'

Lucan's eyes narrowed as he looked up again at the painting of Alexander, done forty years ago. It could almost—almost!—have been a portrait of himself.

'I didn't know him well enough to like or dislike him,' he finally bit out coldly.

'I—'

'Lexie, can we talk about something else?' Lucan deliberately turned his back on the portrait of his father and raised a mocking brow as he looked down at her. 'Did you sleep well?'

As it happened, Lexie hadn't slept well at all. Partly because she was so aware of how precarious her position here was. How, at any moment, someone she knew from the village—Cathy Barton, for example—might arrive at Mulberry Hall and recognise her for who and what she was.

But mostly she hadn't been able to sleep because of that incident with Lucan.

Incident? It had been so much more than that.

She had never, ever responded to a man in the wild and wanton way she had to Lucan last night. Never been so aroused, so lost to reason, that nothing else mattered. Not who she was. Not who Lucan was. Certainly not who her grandmother was!

That had come later, as Lexie lay awake in her bed, reliving the sensations aroused by the touch of Lucan's lips and hands. Sensations so soul-deep that she still ached. Still trembled with the memory of that dark head against the paleness of her skin as Lucan suckled and laved her breast with his lips and tongue, the warmth between her thighs. She'd almost felt again the hardness of Lucan's arousal there as he surged rhythmically, pleasurably against her.

And she'd realised that she could no longer deny her attraction to Lucan, nor the desire she felt to make love with him!

She looked now at the way the darkness of his hair fell across his wide brow, at those rock-hewn features that were normally so coldly aristocratic but which she now knew could be flushed and tense with arousal, at the thin chocolate-brown cashmere sweater moulded to the hardness of his muscled chest, the faded blue denims doing the same to powerful thighs and long legs. All of those things made Lexie tremble with remembered desire.

Desire for a man who would hate the very air she breathed if he knew she was Sian Thomas's granddaughter!

'I never sleep well the first night in a strange bed,' she dismissed abruptly.

'That must make things a little awkward for you,' he drawled mockingly.

'Not really,' she snapped, knowing exactly what Lucan was implying.

What would Lucan say, do, if she were to tell him that, apart from a few fumbling caresses with the men she had dated in the last couple of years, she had absolutely no physical experience. That the intimacies she had shared with Lucan last night had been completely unprecedented in her life.

'I'm curious as to who these four are?' She moved away to look at a painting on the wall opposite.

Lucan had been totally aware of the way Lexie had been looking at him a few seconds ago. Had seen the hunger in her eyes. The heat. Before she'd shut down both those emotions.

Sensibly.

Wisely.

Lucan accepted it was completely *un*wise on his part, and not in the least sensible, for him to be this physically attracted to Lexie Hamilton—a woman completely unlike the sophisticated women he usually bedded.

Lexie seemed to say the first thing that came into her head, uncaring whether or not it should be said. She probed and poked at emotional wounds Lucan normally discussed with no one. And her responses—those low, keening little cries of pleasure she'd given as Lucan had kissed and caressed her the previous evening—were too raw, too honest. Too addictive…

All of those things were completely dangerous to a man who had never cared enough about any woman to suffer so much as a moment's regret at the ending of one of his always brief relationships…

He wasn't about to suffer one now, over the impulsively outspoken Lexie Hamilton, either!

'The man in the centre of the painting is Hawk, the tenth Duke of Stourbridge, the other three are his siblings— Sebastian, Lucian and Arabella.' Lucan answered her question abruptly.

Her brows rose. 'Is your own name a derivative of Lucian?'

'Probably.' His tone was terse. 'Gideon is a name often used in the family, too.'

Alexander, Lexie knew, was also a St Claire family

name. As well as being Lucan's father's name, it had also been that of his great-great-grandfather.

'I believe,' Lucan continued dismissively, 'the name Gideon came into the family when the Lady Arabella called her first son by that name, in honour of the man who saved her life.'

Lexie's eyes widened. 'How did he do that?'

'I have no idea.' Lucan sounded decidedly uninterested. 'I think we should go back downstairs now; the builder should be arriving at any moment.'

'Of course.' Lexie grimaced as she fell into step beside him, slightly disappointed that Lucan felt disinclined to share the feisty-looking Lady Arabella's story with her. 'Is it okay if I go for a walk in the grounds while you're talking to the builder?' she asked casually.

Deliberately so.

Because she didn't want to alert Lucan to how important the walk was to her. Because a visit to her grand mother's cottage was first on Lexie's list of things to do this morning.

Closely followed by ensuring that Lucan would decide they could go back to London as soon he had spoken to the builder.

After their intimacy yesterday evening Lexie didn't think the two of them spending another night together at Mulberry Hall was a good idea!

'It's going to snow,' Lucan warned her with a frown.

Lexie eyed him teasingly. 'And you know that *how*?'

He looked irritated. 'I know that because I listened to the weather forecast on the radio in the kitchen a few minutes ago!'

'There's no need to get snippy!' she taunted.

'I'm not getting—' Lucan broke off abruptly to draw in a deep, controlling breath. 'You enjoy irritating me, don't you?' he realised frowningly, and easily saw the mischievous glint in Lexie's sparkling blue eyes.

'Love it,' she admitted unrepentantly.

'Because I'm an over-confident, pompous, unmitigated ass?' he came back dryly.

Colour warmed her cheeks at this reminder of the names she had called him the night before. She grimaced. 'You remember every word...'

'Well, of course I remember every word!' Lucan chuckled softly. 'Of their kind, they were unique.'

She frowned up at him. 'In what way?'

'In every way.' Lucan still smiled.

Lexie gave a self-conscious wince. 'Meaning that no one has ever spoken to you in that way before?'

'Meaning that no one has ever spoken to me in that way before,' he continued mockingly.

She grimaced. 'Oh, dear.'

Lucan found himself chuckling again. He couldn't seem to help himself when confronted with Lexie's blunt honesty. 'You could try looking a little less pleased with yourself!'

She raised dark brows. 'What would be the point, when that's exactly how I feel?'

He gave a rueful shake of his head and stood back to allow Lexie to precede him into the warmth of the kitchen. 'Do you always say the first thing that comes into your head?'

Lexie nodded. 'Usually.' But not always, she acknowledged with a frown. And she definitely needed to practise caution when in the company of this particular man.

Something she was finding she liked doing less and less...

It had been fun to tease Lucan just now, to see and hear

him laugh, to forget for a few minutes who he was and who she was.

Dear Lord—she couldn't actually be interested in a *relationship* with Lucan, could she...?

She had done some pretty stupid things in her time—deciding to stand in as Lucan's PA for three days being only one of them—but to allow this attraction she felt for him, the undeniable hunger she felt for more of Lucan's kisses and caresses to continue, would be sheer madness on her part.

A madness that wasn't going to happen!

She turned to look up at him challengingly. 'For instance, at this moment I want to say I really need to get out of this stuffy atmosphere and into the fresh air!'

Lucan's eyes narrowed as he returned the challenge in Lexie's gaze. 'Is it the house you find stuffy, or me...?'

'I'll leave that for you to decide!' she came back perkily, before grabbing her coat from the back of the chair and letting herself out, without giving Lucan the chance to reply.

Not that Lucan would have done so in any case. He had never run after a woman in his life, and he wasn't about to start now.

Even if part of him wanted to...

Lexie took a snow-covered path through the woods at the back of Mulberry Hall to her grandmother's cottage, situated on the very edge of the village. A path that in the past had been well-worn by Alexander St Claire, during the years he had visited the woman he loved.

Her grandmother's cottage looked the same as it always had as Lexie stepped out into a clearing at the back of the small white-painted building. The windows gleamed brightly, and the thatch on the roof looked new when she glanced up and saw the inviting curl of smoke drifting delicately from the chimney.

Lexie drew in a deep breath as she hesitated outside the red-painted front door of the cottage, knowing she would have some explaining to do once she was inside.

And also knowing that what had happened last night between herself and Lucan, this attraction for him that Lexie was trying so desperately to fight, wouldn't be a part of the conversation...!

CHAPTER SEVEN

'WHERE the hell have you been?' Lucan demanded furiously.

Lexie had paused in the kitchen doorway to brush the snow from her hair and coat. She glanced across the kitchen as a chair scraped on the flagstones and he stood up from his seat at the oak table, his expression grim.

'Sorry...?' she said lightly as she carefully closed the kitchen door behind her.

Lucan wasn't fooled for a moment by the innocence of her expression. 'You gave me the impression you were only going for a stroll in the grounds, and you've been gone for over two hours!' he bit out coldly.

She raised dark brows. 'Did you have some work you wanted me to do?'

'Obviously not, when I've been talking to the builder.'

'Then I don't understand the problem...?'

'The problem is that it began to snow not long after you left the house,' he said, with a pointed glance at the dampness caused by the snow melting in Lexie's hair.

'Surely you weren't *worried* about me, Lucan?' she taunted dryly.

As it happened, yes, Lucan *had* been concerned by Lexie's prolonged absence. Not only was it freezing cold outside, but the predicted snow had started to fall heavily almost as soon as Lexie had stepped out of the house, and was now a couple of inches deep on the ground.

'It isn't a question of being worried, Lexie,' he dismissed impatiently. 'You aren't familiar with the area,' he continued tautly. 'You could have fallen through the ice on the lake and drowned, for all I knew.'

'You aren't thinking positively, Lucan. At least that way I wouldn't be here annoying you any more,' she said ruefully as she slipped her damp coat down her arms to drape it across the back of one of the chairs to dry.

Lucan felt an icy chill down his spine as he immediately had an image of Lexie's dead body floating beneath the layer of ice that presently covered the lake behind Mulberry Hall.

'Damn it, this isn't funny, Lexie!'

'It wasn't meant to be.' She snapped her own impatience with the conversation. 'And I'm no more used to answering to anyone for my actions than *you* are,' she added pointedly.

'While you're staying here with me you had better get used to it!' Lucan grated harshly.

She became very still. 'I think not,' she returned evenly, the angry glitter of her eyes a complete contradiction to that vocal calmness.

It was a warning Lucan had no intention of heeding.

He hadn't been too worried when it first began to snow—had believed those icy flakes would bring Lexie back to the house sooner rather than later. When the minutes had ticked past, passing an hour, he had put on his own coat in order to go outside and look for her.

Unfortunately, the grounds of Mulberry Hall were vast—too much for Lucan to be able to search them properly. He hadn't even been able to find any footprints in the snow to tell him which direction Lexie might have taken

on her walk. After twenty minutes of futile searching he
had returned to the kitchen to sit and wait for her.

His temper rising by the minute.

Which—considering Lucan hadn't even realised he *had*
a temper until he'd met Lexie Hamilton—didn't bode well
for the outcome of their present conversation.

'I think *yes*,' he ground out harshly.

Her mouth firmed. 'You can think what you damn well
please, Lucan, but that isn't going to make it happen.'

'Where were you for the last two hours?' Lucan's voice
was hard as he reverted to his original question.

A question Lexie had no intention of answering
honestly.

Because she couldn't.

Her grandmother had been surprised but overjoyed to
see Lexie again so soon after spending the Christmas holi-
day in London with all the family. Less pleased once she'd
realised how and why Lexie was here...

It hadn't been a comfortable conversation. Her grandmother was totally disapproving of Lexie's subterfuge in
going to work for Lucan in the first place. And deeply
concerned at the way it had backfired on Lexie so that
she'd had no choice but to accompany Lucan to Mulberry
Hall yesterday.

Her grandmother had given dire warning as to Lucan's
reaction if he should discover the truth.

A totally unnecessary warning; Lexie already knew how
angry Lucan was going to be if he ever learnt she was Sian
Thomas's granddaughter. How much he was going to hate
himself—and her—for having kissed her...

Her gaze avoided meeting his probing dark one. 'I told
you—I was walking.'

'Walking where?' Lucan studied her through narrowed
lids, having noted that evasion and wondering at the reason

for it. As far as he was aware Lexie had never been to Gloucestershire before, didn't know anyone in the area—so what was her problem with telling him where she had been?

'Here and there.' She kept her tone light as she moved to pour herself a mug of coffee. 'Want some?' She held up the coffee pot invitingly.

'No.' Lucan was still far from satisfied with her answer. 'What I want is to know where you've been all this time.'

'For God's sake, Lucan. I'm a grown woman, not a child!' She slammed the coffee pot back down on the percolator before turning to glare at him.

Lucan's mouth firmed as he strode forcefully across the kitchen until he stood directly in front of Lexie, effectively blocking her exit if she should try to make one. 'Neither you nor your coat appear to be particularly wet, so you obviously took shelter somewhere—'

'And you obviously missed your vocation as a nosy busybody!' she cut in mockingly.

Lucan drew in a harshly controlling breath, hands clenched at his sides as he glared down at her. 'You are the most infuriating, impossible, stubborn woman I have ever had the misfortune to meet.'

She grimaced. 'Which makes me more than a match for an over-confident, pompous ass, wouldn't you say?'

She had done it again, Lucan realised as he felt his anger begin to evaporate and amusement take its place. The tension began to ease from his shoulders as he gave a derisive smile. 'You really *are* impossible, you know.'

'I *do* know, actually.' She nodded ruefully. 'From all accounts I used to drive my parents to distraction when I was younger. It's probably the reason I'm an only child!'

Lucan realised it was the first real piece of personal

information she had given him. 'What's that like? I grew up with two brothers only two years younger than I am, so I can't imagine what it must be like to be an only child.'

'It could be a little lonely on occasion,' Lexie admitted cautiously, having no intention of telling him any more details about herself. 'But obviously I survived the hardship,' she dismissed brightly as she straightened. 'So, what are we going to do for the rest of the day? Do you want to do some of the work you brought with you? Or should we try to drive back to London now, before the snow gets any deeper?' she added, with a frown looking out of the kitchen window at the steadily falling snow.

She certainly didn't want to get snowed in at Mulberry Hall for several days—and nights—with Lucan!

'Just think, Lucan,' she added encouragingly. 'I could be out of your hair in just a matter of hours!'

It *would* be a good idea to try and get back to London today, Lucan inwardly acknowledged as he frowned. And not only because of the snow!

Staying on here for another day or so with Lexie—a woman who succeeded in making him laugh when it was the last thing he wanted to do—could be a mistake on his part. A big mistake.

And yet...

Therein lay the problem.

After years of avoiding coming anywhere near the Mulberry Hall estate, and all it represented, a part of Lucan was now reluctant to leave. Not because he wanted to be at Mulberry Hall itself, but because he was pretty sure that Lexie, once back in London, would make sure the agency she worked for immediately replaced her as his PA.

But wasn't that what Lucan had decided he wanted last night, after Lexie had left the kitchen to go to bed? To put her out of his life? To never see or hear from her again? To once again put himself behind that barrier of cold aloofness that he allowed no one to penetrate?

That was exactly what he had decided!

And yet…

'You seem to be taking an awful long time to decide, Lucan.' Lexie broke teasingly into his thoughts.

He looked down into her upturned face. 'Much as I might want to return to London, I'm not willing to do it at the risk of either your safety or my own. That being the case, we'll give it a couple of hours and see if the snow stops.'

One dark brow quirked. 'And if it gets worse instead…?'

He shrugged. 'Then I guess we're stuck with each other for another night.'

Which was exactly what Lexie *didn't* want.

What she had assured her grandmother wouldn't happen!

Nanna Sian had been as concerned for Lexie as she was for Lucan St Claire. Her grandmother knew only too well how much the St Claire family hated her, and consequently anyone connected to her. The only thing that had soothed her grandmother's anxiety was Lexie giving her word that she would put an end to this situation as soon as she and Lucan returned to London.

Unfortunately, when Lexie had made that promise she hadn't taken into account the possibility of being snowed in here with Lucan for several days!

She gave a firm shake of her head. 'I think we should leave now.'

Lucan eyed Lexie mockingly as he took in the wilful sparkle in her eyes and the stubborn set to her mouth. 'In case you haven't realised it yet, Lexie, this is a dictatorship, not a democracy! And, as the driver of the only vehicle at our disposal, I have decided that the conditions aren't safe for us to leave yet.'

A frown appeared between those dark brows. 'Isn't it just for conditions like this that you *have* a four-wheel drive vehicle, for goodness' sake!'

He shrugged. 'I'm still not willing to take the risk. That being the case, what's for lunch?' he added tauntingly.

She frowned up at him. 'As you're obviously the dictator, and I'm only the poor, oppressed peasant, I suggest *you* decide. And once you've decided I suggest that you also prepare it. I am going upstairs to pack my bag, ready for when we can leave!' She turned on her heel and marched out of the kitchen.

Lucan gave a wolfish grin as he stood and enjoyed watching the provocative sway of Lexie's denim-clad hips and perfectly rounded bottom until she had left the room and slammed the kitchen door behind her.

Lexie Hamilton might be infuriating and impossible, and stubborn as a mule, but she was also the sexiest bundle of femininity Lucan had ever met.

Dangerously so...

'Well?'

Lucan relaxed back in his chair to look across at Lexie as she appeared in the kitchen doorway. 'Well, what?'

Lexie eyed him frustratedly as he continued to sit calmly at the kitchen table, eating toast. 'In case you haven't noticed, it's stopped snowing.' There was only a couple of inches of snow on the ground outside, which certainly wasn't enough to hamper the progress of the monster vehicle parked outside in the driveway.

'I noticed.'

'Well?'

'W—'

'If you say "well, what?" again I may be provoked into hitting you!' Lexie warned between gritted teeth, breathing hard in the face of Lucan's unruffled calm when she was so agitated she really could have hit something. Or someone!

The visit to her grandmother earlier had only emphasised how vulnerable Lexie was—how at any minute she could be exposed as the granddaughter of Sian Thomas.

And if that happened then not only would Lucan make Lexie personally suffer for that exposure, but probably Premier Personnel, too...

Lucan raised dark brows. 'I was actually going to ask what's in London for you to rush back to?'

'Civilisation?' she came back scathingly.

Once again Lucan found himself laughing at one of Lexie's remarks. At the way she didn't even attempt to stop herself from saying the first thing that came into her head. It was totally refreshing to a man who always thought long and hard before speaking. Mainly because millions of pounds and thousands of people's jobs very often depended upon what Lucan did or didn't say, but also because that was just the way he was. The way he had deliberately schooled himself to be.

He gave a rueful shake of his head. 'It will still be there tomorrow.'

'I want to go back *today*!'

Lucan shrugged. '"I want" doesn't always get.'

'You're being ridiculous again—'

'No, Lexie, I think at the moment *you* have the monopoly on that,' he said harshly.

'I'm not the one who's being so difficult about leaving.'

'John mentioned before he left yesterday that there are

some things he needs to discuss with me before I go back to London.' Lucan frowned down at her.

Lexie stilled. 'Estate business?'

'I believe so, yes.' Lucan gave a slow inclination of his head.

'Oh.' Lexie felt like a deflated balloon at the realisation that Lucan wasn't just being bloody-minded, after all. He had a perfectly valid reason for staying on awhile longer.

Why had Lucan had to laugh again in that totally unself-conscious way?

It changed his whole appearance—gave warmth to the darkness of his eyes, revealed laughter lines beside that sculpted mouth, as well as that cleft in his left cheek. A very sexy cleft. A sexy cleft that made Lexie want to move closer and lick it, taste it with her tongue—

Oh, good Lord!

Why did just being anywhere near this man now make her think about sex?

About having sex.

No, not sex. Making love. Sex for sex's sake had never appealed to Lexie. Which was probably why she was still a virgin at twenty-four!

Even so, Lexie had absolutely no doubt that the person she wanted to make love to and with was definitely Lucan. *Only* Lucan.

Was this the same emotional and physical trap that her grandmother had fallen into all those years ago when she'd first met Alexander? Did Lucan, as far as Lexie was concerned, possess the same magnetic hold over her that his father had held over Sian? The sort of magnetic hold that could reduce a woman who was usually sensible, logical, into forgetting everything else but him?

If he did, then Lexie wanted no part of it!

'If it's estate business…' She nodded abruptly, very conscious of how close Lucan was standing to her.

'That's very understanding of you,' he murmured huskily.

'I think so.' Lexie couldn't look away from those mesmerising dark eyes. Could feel the heat emanating from her own body now as well as Lucan's. A heat that doubled, tripled, when Lucan raised one of his hands and curved it over the warm contours of her cheek. 'What are you doing?' she breathed unevenly.

He gave a half-smile. 'You're looking a little… flushed.'

Lexie was more than a little flushed—and not just outwardly. She felt that familiar fire once again burning between her thighs.

Lucan raised one dark brow. 'You aren't coming down with something, are you?'

Lucanitis, probably!

Lexie had to say something, do something—anything to break this magnetic pull that just made her want to move closer to the warmth of this man's body. 'Do you always wear your hair so short…?'

He frowned slightly and raised his other hand to run it through that dark hair. 'You don't approve?' His voice was gravelly and low.

Lexie looked up at him consideringly. 'It makes you look…'

'Older?' he suggested harshly.

'I was going to say severe,' she corrected dryly.

He gave a mocking half smile. 'But I *am* severe, Lexie.'

Not all the time. Most definitely not all the time!

In fact, standing this close to him, with the heat from their bodies mingling, matching, Lexie was finding it harder and harder to think of him as the arrogant and aloof Lucan St Claire!

Which wasn't surprising when what she most wanted to do at that moment was rip those faded denims and that brown sweater from the muscled leanness of Lucan's body and caress and taste every inch of him!

Help…!

Lexie definitely needed help. Something to give her the strength, the will, to fight this growing attraction she felt for Lucan.

Where was a lightning bolt when she most needed one?

Lucan was totally aware of the tension that permeated the room. A sexual, sensual tension that swirled around the two of them like an ever-deepening, sense-drugging transparent mist.

He looked down into the deep, dark blue of Lexie's eyes before moving his gaze lower, to the soft pout of her lips. Plump and enticing lips, which parted slightly even as he looked at them. As if knowing, waiting for his kiss.

The skin of Lexie's cheek felt like velvet against the palm of his hand, reminding him all too forcefully of how her bared breasts had felt as velvety soft as he'd cupped them the previous evening, before caressing and savouring them with his hands and mouth. Inciting a need deep inside him to touch and taste her like that again…

'Lexie—' He broke off as a knock sounded briefly on the outside door before it was pushed open and John Barton stood framed in the doorway.

The caretaker shivered in the icy wind blowing outside and stepped quickly into the room to close the door behind him. Coming to an abrupt halt, he glanced across the kitchen to where Lucan and Lexie stood so close together they were almost touching…

CHAPTER EIGHT

'I'M NOT interrupting anything, am I?' John Barton continued to hesitate near the door.

Not interrupting anything...!

Lexie didn't even want to think about what John Barton had so nearly interrupted as she shifted sideways and then stepped completely away from the heat and seduction of Lucan's body so close to her own.

Once across the kitchen she was at least able to breathe more easily—even managing to give a strained smile to the obviously uncomfortable, but also slightly curious, John Barton.

'Has it started snowing again...?' She gave a dismayed frown as she saw the droplets of moisture on his sandy-coloured hair.

'I'm afraid so.' He shrugged, with another awkward glance in Lucan's direction.

Lucan straightened abruptly, only the glittering black onyx of his eyes revealing—to Lexie, at least—his displeasure at the other man's untimely interruption.

Or perhaps that displeasure was levelled at Lexie?

His firmly clenched jaw and those cold dark eyes, as he turned to look directly at her, certainly didn't give the impression that she had escaped Lucan's displeasure. A fact that instantly raised Lexie's hackles.

Damn it, *she* wasn't the one who had initiated the intimacy between them. The one who had tried to seduce her with a touch. Who would have kissed her—probably more than kissed her—if John Barton hadn't interrupted them!

'I suggest we go to my study and talk, John,' Lucan stated coldly as he saw the angry sparkle building in Lexie's expressive eyes. 'Lexie informs me she wants to get back to London as soon as possible,' he added, having noted the look of dismay on Lexie's face when she had realised it was snowing again, and the possibility of delaying their departure. Something she obviously wasn't too happy about.

Lucan couldn't say he was exactly happy at the thought of staying on here with Lexie any longer, either.

He had thought when he'd insisted on bringing her here that she would be a diversion—a way for him to be at Mulberry Hall without his usual feelings of aversion. Instead, Lexie had made him forget all caution, all those barriers Lucan had so carefully placed about his emotions over the years. To the point where all he could think about now was touching her again, kissing her, making love to her.

If John hadn't arrived when he had—

'I merely commented that if we didn't want to get snowed in then we should probably leave sometime today.' She looked across at him challengingly.

Lucan glanced out of the window. He could see that the snow was falling heavily again. 'I think it may already be too late for that...'

Lexie glanced out of the kitchen window, too, her heart sinking as she saw the huge flakes of snow falling delicately past the window. Her eyes narrowed accusingly as she turned back to Lucan. 'If we had left when I first suggested it—'

'Then we would be out in the middle of it right now,' Lucan reasoned impatiently. 'I have no doubt that the motorways will have been kept clear, but I very much doubt the small country roads we'd have to travel on first will have received the same treatment.'

He was right, of course, Lexie acknowledged heavily. As usual.

She straightened. 'I'll leave the two of you to have your talk—'

'You need to eat some lunch first,' Lucan cut in firmly.

Lexie's cheeks warmed at having John Barton witness this exchange. 'I'm really not hungry—'

'You need to stay here and eat,' Lucan insisted.

What Lexie needed and what she wanted were two entirely different things.

She might possibly need to eat something, but what she wanted was to get as far away from Lucan as it was possible for her to be. But, as Lucan had already pointed out to her once today, 'I want' didn't always get...

'Fine,' she managed tautly, hoping that Lucan had picked up on her tone, and the warning in the glance she gave him. Otherwise—John Barton's presence or not—she was going to be forced into saying something they might all regret.

The younger man gave her a rueful smile. 'Cathy's longing to come over and say hello.'

'Oh?' Lexie felt flustered at the mere idea of John's wife coming to the house. It might not be the Cathy she knew, but chances were—the way Lexie's luck was going—that she was.

John nodded. 'But I didn't think it was a good idea for her to come over today, in this weather. She's expecting our first baby in three months' time,' he explained happily.

'Congratulations! Maybe next time.' Lexie managed to

gather herself enough to speak, knowing there wouldn't be a 'next time' at Mulberry Hall for her. Not if she had any say in the matter. And she did.

Lucan gave her one last questioning glance through narrowed lids before he and John went out into the hallway.

Alerting Lexie to the fact that she hadn't quite managed to hide the panic she'd felt when John had told her Cathy wanted to come over and say hello...

'So what's your problem with meeting Cathy Barton?' Lucan prompted as soon as he rejoined Lexie in the kitchen once John had left.

'Sorry?' Lexie raised innocent brows as she turned from staring accusingly out of the window at the falling snow.

To Lucan's sharp gaze Lexie's expression looked a little too innocent to be true. 'You seemed...unsettled earlier by the idea of meeting Cathy Barton.'

'Don't be silly, Lucan,' she dismissed lightly. 'If I appeared concerned then it was probably at the thought of a heavily pregnant woman even thinking of venturing outside in this weather.'

Except Lucan knew that John hadn't mentioned that his wife was pregnant until *after* Lexie had responded so alarmingly to his statement that Cathy wanted to meet Lexie...

'Your concern is admirable,' he drawled dryly. 'So you don't have any objections to meeting her?'

'I've just said that I don't,' Lexie answered slowly, warily, not at all happy with the challenge she sensed in Lucan's attitude.

He nodded. 'In that case there's no problem with my having accepted the Bartons' invitation for both of us to join them for dinner this evening.'

Lexie's only outward show of emotion at that statement

was the curling of her hands into fists at her sides. Hands that clenched so tightly her nails were digging painfully into her palms.

Have dinner with the Bartons? With Cathy Barton—a woman Lexie was becoming more and more convinced was the Cathy Wilson she had known and been friends with all those years ago.

She swallowed hard. 'Is it a good idea for us to go out in this weather?'

Lucan gave a rueful shrug. 'I think we're going to have to if we want to eat something other than toast.' He gave a pointed glance at the empty plate in front of Lexie, with several toast crumbs still on its surface.

'We still have Cathy's casserole from last night,' Lexie reminded him.

He grimaced. 'I doubt that's going to be very appetising when it's already been warmed up once and left.'

Lexie was starting to feel more and more as if she were standing in quicksand rather than snow.

'We could always go to the pub in the village, I suppose,' Lucan continued lightly. 'Although that might be a little insulting when I've already accepted John's invitation.' He quirked dark questioning brows.

'Why don't *you* go?' Lexie encouraged, her voice brittle. 'I'm not really hungry after eating toast, and I'm feeling a little tired, too, after my walk this morning. I'll probably just read for a bit and then have an early night.'

'An early night sounds good.'

It also, Lexie thought warily, sounded slightly threatening when Lucan said it in that sensually husky voice.

She looked at him searchingly, sure she saw a glint of laughter lurking in the darkness of his eyes before it was quickly masked. Could he possibly be playing with her? If he was, then he had chosen the wrong woman to play with!

'You *have* to go to the Bartons, Lucan,' she insisted. 'It would look rude if neither of us showed up after you've accepted the invitation.'

He shrugged. 'I've never had a problem in the past with people thinking I'm rude.'

'I can personally vouch for that,' Lexie muttered disgustedly.

'And it isn't a problem for me now, either,' Lucan continued dryly. 'But if it bothers you…'

'It doesn't,' she assured him quickly.

'Then I'll telephone and make our excuses.'

She gave an impatient shake of her head. 'That isn't very fair, when Cathy has probably already started cooking for you.'

'For *us*,' he corrected pointedly.

'You're the one that's important,' Lexie reasoned derisively. 'After all, I'm just an insignificant PA—a temporary one at that. Whereas you're the local celebrity. The illustrious Duke of Stourbridge,' she added tauntingly.

He gave a rueful shake of his head. 'Temporary PA or otherwise, there's nothing in the least insignificant about *you*, Lexie,' he said dryly.

'You know exactly what I meant!' she snapped impatiently.

Yes, Lucan knew exactly what Lexie was up to…

'Neither is there anything in the least illustrious about the title of Duke of Stourbridge!' he added bitterly.

'Oh?'

'*Oh*,' he echoed unhelpfully, having no intention of satisfying her obvious curiosity by opening up that particular can of worms. 'As I've already told you, the title doesn't interest me.'

'Whether you choose to use the title or not, that's obviously how the people of Stourbridge think of you,' she came back dismissively.

Lucan's eyes narrowed. 'And how would *you* know how the people of Stourbridge think of me...?'

Yet another slip, Lexie realised with a self-disgusted wince. She really wasn't very good at this.

Damn it—it was a little late for her to realise that she should have just refused to come here and invited Lucan to do his worst where Premier Personnel was concerned!

'It's pretty obvious that John Barton is slightly in awe of you.' She shrugged. 'Besides, all small villages function on gossip, don't they?'

'Do they?'

'Oh, stop being difficult, Lucan! If you had bothered to consult me before accepting John's invitation then you would have known that I'm not in the mood to play lowly servant to your arrogant duke in public!'

Lucan's eyes narrowed on Lexie as he drew in a long, slow, calming breath, knowing that by referring to his title again she was deliberately trying to annoy him. He had no intention of giving her that satisfaction.

He knew that something was slightly off about Lexie's behaviour. Something he couldn't quite put his finger on but nevertheless could sense was there.

Perhaps it was her avoidance of telling him where she had gone on her walk this morning? Or her reluctance to go to the Bartons' for dinner? Or perhaps the fact that she'd seemed just as reluctant to eat at the pub in the village, both last night and again today?

At the moment, all Lucan was sure of was that there had been something different about Lexie's behaviour, something guarded, since they'd arrived at Mulberry Hall yesterday...

He regarded her consideringly. 'What *are* you in the mood for?'

Lexie gave a start even as she eyed him warily. 'I told you—an early night.'

Lucan shrugged. 'And I've already agreed that sounds like a good idea.'

As far as Lexie could tell Lucan hadn't moved from his stance near the cooker, and yet she still found herself taking a defensive step backwards. Away from him. Away from the danger Lucan suddenly represented. The physical danger...

Her tongue moved nervously, moistly, across her suddenly dry lips. 'I have no idea what your usual arrangement is with your PA, Lucan, but I can assure you—'

'Oh, I think my "usual arrangement" with my PA has been made more than obvious by the fact that the last one walked out on me before Christmas, without giving notice, and that I didn't even get her name right yesterday,' Lucan drawled. 'Don't you?' he added challengingly.

Yes, Lexie was more convinced than ever that part of the reason—the *main* reason—Jessica Brown had left her employment at the St Claire Corporation was because she hadn't succeeded in tempting Lucan into a personal relationship with her.

So why did Lexie suddenly feel that without even trying the opposite was true where she was concerned? That if she gave Lucan the slightest encouragement she would be in his arms. In his bed.

Maybe it was the heat she could now see in Lucan's coal-black eyes as they swept over her slowly from her toes to the top of her head? Or the sensual softening of that sculpted mouth? Or perhaps it was the fact that he was once again standing much too close to her, the heat in his dark gaze intensifying as it shifted to her mouth...

How could she not have noticed, been aware of the soft, panther-like tread that had brought Lucan across the kitchen so that once again he stood only inches away from her?

This time Lexie had nowhere to go. She was already backed up against one of the kitchen cabinets. Her eyes wcre wide as she looked up at Lucan, her throat moving convulsively as she swallowed before speaking. 'Look, I realise this is the warmest room in the house, but even so I don't think that gives you the right to try and make love to me every time we're alone in here together.'

'*Try* and make love to you, Lexie?' he drawled softly.

Her cheeks felt warm. 'Don't you have some sort of unwritten policy concerning not getting personally involved with your employees?'

He gave a derisive smile. 'I think it's a little late to worry about that in our particular case, don't you?'

Because this man had already kissed Lexie, caressed her, touched her more intimately than any other man ever had in all of her twenty-four years!

'Besides,' Lucan continued dryly, 'you and I both know that you have no intention of still being my employee once we get back to London.'

'Do we?'

His smile widened, revealing even white teeth against those sensually carved lips. 'Oh, yes,' he acknowledged softly. 'Which means there's absolutely no reason why we can't…pursue a relationship now.'

'Pursue a relationship…?' Lexie repeated inanely. And was that high-pitched squeak *really* her voice? She sounded like Minnie Mouse on helium!

Lucan frowned his impatience with what he was sure was Lexie being deliberately obtuse. She knew—couldn't help but know—of the physical awareness between the two of them. Of the way the very air seemed to sizzle with that awareness whenever the two of them were alone together.

Having decided last night, and again earlier, that he couldn't allow Lexie into his life, Lucan had then spent the hour in the study with John Barton thinking of her rather than listening to anything the other man said. Most of all of how his body hardened in arousal every time he was anywhere near her...

The sensible thing to do would be to continue fighting that attraction until they were back in London and Lexie had gone out of his life.

The fact that he hadn't heard a single word John had said to him during that hour told Lucan that it was already too late for that. He needed to get Lexie out of his system now. And the only way he could think of to do that was to take their relationship to the next level.

Invariably once the chase was over and he'd had sex with a woman—any woman—Lucan completely lost interest. Lexie wasn't—couldn't be—any different. Besides, he had never been a man who ran away from his problems. And Lexie was becoming more and more of a problem with every minute spent with her.

'Oh, come on, Lexie,' he chided huskily. 'We're both adults. We know exactly what's going on here—'

'*Nothing* is going on here!' she cut in determinedly. 'Now, would you please step away from me?' Her hands rose to push against his chest.

Lucan immediately felt the warmth of those hands through his thin cashmere sweater. Such tiny, elegant hands. Hands that he wanted to feel on every inch of his flesh. Every aroused inch!

His gaze easily held hers as his hands moved up and over hers, pressing their warmth against him, making Lexie totally aware of the beating of his heart as it throbbed in rhythm with his pulsing arousal. That same heat had caused Lexie's eyes to brighten feverishly and her cheeks to flush.

'Do you still think nothing is going on here, Lexie?' Lucan prompted huskily.

Of *course* Lexie knew that something was going on between the two of them; she might be physically inexperienced, but she wasn't stupid. She knew that there had been something between the two of them from the moment they'd first met. The problem was Lexie had thought it was dislike, when in reality it was the opposite. At least definitely desire...

The look of determination in Lucan's eyes told her that he wanted to take that *something* a step further.

She gave a shake of her head. 'I'm not into having casual affairs with my boss.'

'It doesn't have to be that casual,' he assured her huskily.

'What?' Lexie's heart was beating so fast, so loudly, that she was sure Lucan couldn't help but be aware of it. Or of the heat, the scent of her arousal emanating from her body in heady waves...

Lucan shrugged. 'Instead of going back to London, maybe meeting up there occasionally, we could stay on here for several more days and see the whole thing through.'

Lexie eyed him disbelievingly. 'To its bitter end, no doubt?'

His smile was rueful as he shook his head. 'It doesn't have to be that way.'

'Believe me, between us it would be.' Lexie had good reason for knowing it would.

'You don't know that—'

'How long do your affairs usually last, Lucan? A couple

of weeks? A month? And then what? A nice piece of expensive and ostentatious jewellery as payment for services rendered? A costly gesture to ensure there are no hurt feelings?' Her mouth twisted scornfully.

Lucan's jaw tightened. 'My women don't usually leave with hurt feelings.'

'No, they leave with that expensive piece of jewellery!' Lexie gave an inelegant snort. 'I very much doubt that I'm your usual type of woman, Lucan!'

No, she wasn't, Lucan acknowledged impatiently. Which was why he had decided the best thing to do was to stay on here and get this inexplicable desire he felt for her out of his system.

He should have known it wouldn't be that easy. This was Lexie, for goodness' sake. The most frustrating woman—on so many levels—that he had ever had the misfortune to meet.

A woman whose only pieces of jewellery were pearl earrings and that simple gold locket she habitually wore about her slender neck…

Lucan's eyes narrowed on that gold oval where it nestled against her breasts. 'Whose picture do you have in the locket, Lexie?'

'What…?' She looked panicked as Lucan moved one of his hands up to cradle the gold locket in his palm. 'Don't touch that!' She slapped at that hand.

Lucan's fingers instantly closed about the locket, his eyes glittering darkly as he saw that the colour had drained from Lexie's face, leaving her cheeks pale and her eyes dark and haunted. 'Who is it, Lexie?' he repeated harshly. 'Some long lost lover you still pine for? Or someone you have in your life now? Someone whose picture you carry around next to your heart?' he added.

'And what if it is?' Lexie tried unsuccessfully to release

the locket from his closed fingers. 'I said let *go,* Lucan,' she grated between clenched teeth.

'Make me,' he challenged softly.

Lexie tried, but Lucan's fingers were closed about the locket like a steel trap, just as impenetrable. So much so that after several seconds of struggle the chain on the locket suddenly broke.

Lexie stared down disbelievingly at the broken chain as it dangled loosely over those lean but powerful fingers.

The antique gold locket and chain had been a sixteenth birthday gift from Nanna Sian and Grandpa Alex—the last they had ever given her together. Grandpa Alex had died only weeks later. And inside, together for ever, were smiling photographs of them both.

CHAPTER NINE

'No!' LEXIE choked. 'What have you *done*?'

What the hell had he been thinking? Lucan questioned self-disgustedly as he saw tears balancing on Lexie's lashes as she stared down, disbelieving, at the broken chain, at the locket still firmly clasped in the palm of Lucan's hand.

The simple truth was he hadn't been thinking at all—only reacting. In a way he could never remember reacting before as he'd become lost in a rising black tide of—

Of what?

Lucan felt stunned by his actions and shied away from answering that question.

'I'm sorry, Lexie—'

'Sorry?' she repeated, her voice high. 'Sorry?' she repeated disbelievingly. 'You behave like a complete Neanderthal a few minutes ago, succeeding in breaking my necklace in the process, and all you can do is say you're sorry?' She gave an emotional shake of her head. 'Give that to me!' She snatched the locket out of Lucan's hand the moment he relaxed his grip on it.

'I'll buy you a new chain as soon as—'

'I don't want a new chain!' Her eyes flashed in warning as she glared up at him.

'Then I'll have that one repaired—'

'I'll get it repaired myself, thank you very much,' she ground out icily.

Lucan hadn't missed the way Lexie's own fingers had tightened about the locket now. Protectively? Lovingly...? 'I'm responsible for breaking it, so I should—'

'You've already done enough, Lucan,' she assured him flatly. 'Now, I am going upstairs to my room, to read for a while before I go to bed, and you—you can do what the hell you please!'

Those tears on Lexie's lashes were in complete contrast to the aggression of her words. Not that Lucan didn't fully deserve her anger. He had behaved like an idiot a few minutes ago. An unthinking, mindless—what? Lexie had called him a Neanderthal, but what had he *really* been thinking, feeling, when he'd demanded to know whose photograph she carried in her locket?

Damn it—no wonder Lucan hadn't immediately recognised the emotion for what it was! How could he, when it was an emotion he had never experienced before?

Jealousy.

Pure, unadulterated, green-eyed, monstrous jealousy.

An emotion Lucan had always considered completely irrational. Certainly not one he had ever felt over any woman before.

And yet he was aware that he still felt it. Those tears glistening on Lexie's lashes seemed to confirm that the locket did indeed contain a photograph of someone she'd loved. Was possibly still in love with.

So what? Why should it bother him when it was *him* Lexie responded to so passionately? Passion and desire were the only two emotions Lucan was prepared to accept. Love, he had decided long ago, was for fools, male and female, who allowed that emotion to rule their lives.

Including his brother Jordan and Stephanie?

Did Lucan feel *pity* for the two of them because they loved and were in love with each other?

No, of course he didn't. But that was different. Jordan was different from Lucan—didn't seem to remember the complete destruction of their family that had resulted when Alexander had fallen in love with another woman.

If that was what love did to you, the fool it made of you, then Lucan didn't want any part of it.

He stepped back abruptly now. 'Fine.' He nodded grimly. 'I'll make your excuses to the Bartons.'

'Do that,' Lexie rasped, still shaken by the scene that had just occurred. A fraught and emotional scene that had culminated in the chain on her precious necklace being broken.

Almost as if Lucan had known who had given her the locket and had wanted to destroy it and all it represented...

Except there was no way that Lucan could know his father and her grandmother had given her the locket on her sixteenth birthday.

Then why had he been so angry? So *un*-Lucan-like?

What had they been talking about immediately before he'd grabbed at her necklace?

'Can I take it that all discussion of the possibility of the two of us "pursuing a relationship" is now at an end?' she taunted bitterly.

'I don't believe it ever really started.' Lucan looked down at her coldly.

'No.' Lexie's mouth twisted ruefully; Lucan couldn't possibly want to forget that conversation any more strongly than she did!

No doubt some women would have felt flattered by Lucan's suggestion that the two of them stay on here for a few days and pursue an affair—and, no matter what word

Lucan might have chosen to describe it, that was exactly what it would have been. Lexie just felt insulted.

And maybe just a little flattered…?

Maybe just a little.

She might have only known Lucan for two days—was it *really* only two days since she had first met this forcefully arrogant and lethally attractive man?—but she already knew that he was a man who admitted to few, if any, weaknesses. Acknowledging desire for her was definitely a weakness coming from a man whose air of complete detachment proclaimed he didn't need anyone or anything, and never had.

He didn't need her, either, Lexie told herself ruefully; Lucan wanted her, desired her, wanted to go to bed with her, but he didn't *need* her.

Her chin rose as she looked up at him defiantly. 'Isn't it time you were going to the Bartons?'

His mouth tightened at her obvious dismissal. 'They aren't expecting us for another hour.'

'So you thought you might be able to fit in a quickie before you left?' she scorned.

Lucan's eyes narrowed dangerously. 'Someone should have washed your mouth out with soap when you were younger!' he rasped. 'And, just for the record, Lexie—if I ever take you to bed, then it won't be for a quickie!'

The implication of it being the opposite made Lexie's cheeks burn, her breasts tingle and that unfamiliar warmth build between her thighs. 'Luckily for both of us that was always a very big if,' she came back scathingly.

'Luckily, yes.' He nodded abruptly.

They were going nowhere with this conversation, Lexie realised heavily. 'I'm going upstairs to put this away and then to read.' She cradled her broken necklace tightly to her chest. 'I expect you'll have gone if I come back down-stairs.'

Lucan deeply regretted that he had ever suggested the two of them do anything about the desire that seemed to flare between them more and more often the longer they were together.

All he had to do now was convince his still raging arousal of how stupid that suggestion had been!

'I expect I will,' he agreed harshly. 'If you change your mind about allowing me to have your necklace repaired—'

'I won't,' she assured him quickly.

The way her fingers tightened instinctively about the piece of jewellery, almost as if she expected Lucan to try to wrench it out of her hand again at any moment, only served to convince him that the locket did have emotional significance to her. To the extent that Lexie didn't even like the thought of Lucan touching it again, let alone allowing him to take it out of her possession...

His jaw tightened. 'My business here is finished, and so, weather permitting, I'm sure you'll be pleased to know we'll be able to leave first thing in the morning.'

'Ecstatically pleased,' she acknowledged tautly.

There was nothing more to be said, Lucan realised. Certainly nothing more he should do.

The fact that he had admitted his desire for Lexie to the extent that he had suggested they stay on here together for a few days and pursue that desire was already much more than he had ever intended to do where this woman was concerned...

Apart from the light that had been left on in the kitchen, the house was in complete darkness when Lucan returned after spending a couple of hours at the Bartons' cottage, assuring him that Lexie had gone to bed in his absence—as she had said she would.

Before or after she had eaten?

Why should it matter to Lucan whether or not Lexie had eaten any supper? She was a grown woman and quite capable of taking care of herself.

He wasn't responsible for Lexie having refused the Bartons' dinner invitation. She had already done that before the conversation that had so angered her and resulted in him accidentally breaking the necklace that obviously meant so much to her.

Nevertheless, Lucan found himself striding past the bedroom he had opted to use for the duration of his stay to Lexie's bedroom, farther down the darkened hallway, where he could see a shaft of light showing beneath the door. She was obviously still awake. But doing what? Reading, as she had suggested she might? Or perhaps sitting there plotting a way she could leave?

Lucan frowned as he heard the sound of movement inside the bedroom. A door closed softly—possibly the one to the adjoining bathroom—and then there was the soft pad of bare feet walking across the carpeted floor.

Was it just Lexie's feet that were bare? Or had she just taken a bath or shower prior to going to bed and was now completely naked on the other side of this door?

Lucan's hands clenched at his sides as he was instantly beset with an image of Lexie's lithely compact body, completely naked, proud up-tilting breasts tipped with those rosy aureoles above a flat and toned stomach, the gentle slope of her hips above a silky triangle of curls nestling between her thighs, slender and graceful legs.

Dear God…!

Lucan shook his head to try and clear it of that erotically seductive image, hoping—needing—to stop the arousal that had instantly gripped his own body. Knowing he had failed as his erection stirred and lengthened, pressing against the restraint of his denims, its hard throb becoming a burning ache.

He should go back to his own bedroom. Now. Away from the temptation of knowing that Lexie was just on the other side of this closed door. Possibly naked...

Lexie looked up with a start as a knock sounded briefly on her bedroom door only a second or so before it was opened, to reveal Lucan silhouetted in the darkness of the hallway outside.

Of course it was Lucan. How could it be anyone else when there were only the two of them in the house?

Besides, who else did Lexie know arrogant enough to walk into someone else's bedroom as if he owned it?

He *did* own it, a little voice inside her head reminded her; Lucan owned the whole of Mulberry Hall!

Oh, shut up, Lexie told that mocking voice. The only thing that mattered was that Lucan had walked into her bedroom without being invited.

She straightened abruptly from where she had been packing the clothes she had worn today into her already full overnight bag, determined that Lucan wouldn't know how vulnerable she felt, wearing only the white vest-top and loose-fitting grey pyjama bottoms that were her usual night attire. Not that she thought Lucan would be in the least disturbed by what she was wearing—no doubt the women who shared his bed usually wore silk and lace, and not much of it at that.

'What do you want, Lucan?' She deliberately held his gaze as she crossed the bedroom to sit on top of the gold brocade cover of the bed—she might be feeling vulnerable talking to him when only wearing her nightclothes, but she wasn't about to dive under the bedcovers as if she were a frightened virgin!

She could see in the softness of the lamplight that Lucan was still wearing the faded denims and grey sweater he'd changed into earlier to go to the Bartons. There was a dark frown between his eyes.

'Lexie, do you think we could just stop the hostilities?'

Every part of Lexie, every alert—alarmed?—nerve, muscle and sinew of her body, told her that she and Lucan were incapable of talking politely to each other. That perhaps they always had been.

'And why would we want to do that?' she prompted warily.

'Because, Lexie, I made a mistake earlier—for which I apologise.' He spoke gruffly.

'And that makes everything OK, does it?'

He breathed out exasperatedly. 'I don't know what else you want from me!'

What *did* Lexie want from Lucan? Something she knew she couldn't have. Ever. Not only because Lucan had already shown himself to be a man who wouldn't allow himself to feel deep emotion for anyone, but also because he was Lucan St Claire. And she was Lexie Hamilton. Granddaughter of the despised Sian Thomas...

She grimaced. 'Which mistake are you apologising for, Lucan?' she asked. 'The suggestion we have an affair? Or the breaking of my necklace when I refused?' Her voice hardened as she remembered the feel of the necklace snapping against her throat, and the shock of seeing it lying broken in Lucan's hand.

His face darkened. 'I didn't— Damn it, you *can't* believe I did that deliberately!'

'No,' she accepted heavily. 'But the fact that it happened

is still…still indicative of how—how *destructive* this attraction between the two of us is.' She shook her head.

'Destructive…?' he repeated slowly.

She nodded. 'We hurt each other, Lucan. Sometimes deliberately, sometimes not, but one way or another we've been doing it since we first met.'

It was because Lucan had wanted to put things right between them that he had knocked on her bedroom door just now. Well…not the only reason, he admitted. But it had certainly entered into the equation. The rift that now existed between himself and Lexie had been at the back of his mind the whole of the time he had been at the Bartons' cottage this evening.

'Please just leave, Lucan,' Lexie advised him wearily now. 'Go back to your own bedroom and leave me alone in mine. That way we can both leave here tomorrow with there being no regrets on either side.'

Lucan's jaw clenched impatiently. He could never remember feeling this frustrated in his life before—so incapable of putting a situation right.

It wasn't helping that Lexie looked so delicately delectable, even edible, as she sat cross-legged on top of the bedclothes, bathed in the golden glow given out by the bedside lamp, the wild darkness of her hair loose about her pale, make-up-less face and the bareness of her slender shoulders. The soft, enticing swell of her breasts, with their deep rose tips, was clearly visible beneath the soft material of her white vest top.

His gaze rose to meet and hold hers as he took a step farther into the bedroom. Followed by another when she didn't object. Then another. Until Lucan stood beside the bed looking down at her.

'Do you really want me to leave, Lexie?' he prompted huskily.

Did she? Did she want Lucan to turn around and leave her alone here? Alone and aching?

No, of course Lexie didn't want Lucan to leave. She just knew that he should. For both their sakes.

The house had seemed strangely empty after Lucan had left earlier this evening. Giving Lexie time to think—time to realise how attracted she was to him. How she wanted more from Lucan than he was willing to give. Than he was capable of giving. Not just to her, she had realised, but to any woman.

Whatever the reason—possibly a love affair that had gone wrong in his youth, or maybe simply his parents' broken marriage—she was sure that at some time in the past Lucan had made a conscious decision to shut himself off from emotion.

Except Lexie had seen him laugh several times during the last two days. Usually *at* something she had said or done rather than with her, admittedly, but nevertheless those moments of humour had enabled Lexie to see another side of Lucan. A boyish, softer side it was all too easy to find attractive, even irresistible.

And Lexie didn't want to be attracted to Lucan. Didn't want to find him irresistible. What she wanted was to continue thinking of him as the cold and ruthless man she had believed him to be before she'd met him.

And she could no longer do that...

Every time she tried to slot Lucan back into that unlikeable role another memory would come along to destroy it. Lucan teasing her. Lucan laughing huskily. Lucan with pain in those dark eyes earlier today, rather than the contempt she would have expected, as he'd stood in the west gallery looking up at the portrait of his father.

Most of all Lexie couldn't erase the memory of Lucan almost making love to her...

Lucan might be a lot of the things she had previously thought him to be—arrogant, bossy and remote being only three of them!—but she only had to think of the passion that had flared so unexpectedly between the two of them the previous evening, and again several times today, to know that he wasn't *only* cold and ruthless.

To know also that her own heated, out-of-control response to Lucan was totally off the scale of any of her previous lukewarm relationships.

'You're taking a long time to answer, Lexie,' he said huskily now.

Because Lexie knew that what she *should* do was repeat her request for Lucan to go. That he should leave her bedroom now, before she made the biggest mistake of her life.

She couldn't do it!

Just as she could no longer bear even the thought of going back to London tomorrow and never seeing Lucan again...

Her throat moved convulsively as she swallowed. 'Did you have a pleasant evening with John and Cathy?'

Lucan frowned at this abrupt change of subject. 'Very pleasant.' He nodded. 'They were sorry you were unable to be there because you had gone to bed with a headache,' he added dryly.

Lexie gave a rueful smile. 'Was that the excuse you gave them for my absence?'

Lucan grimaced. 'Well, I could hardly tell them the truth, could I? That you had gone to bed because I had been so damned obnoxious you couldn't bear the thought of spending the evening in my company.'

'That isn't true!' Lexie protested breathlessly.

'Isn't it?' Lucan moved to sit on the side of the bed, before reaching out to curve his hand against the softness of Lexie's cheek as he gazed deeply into her wide blue eyes. 'Something about you makes me do things, say things—cruel things—that I wouldn't normally do or say.' He gave a self-disgusted shake of his head.

'The fact that I'm infuriating, impossible and stubborn, perhaps?' she suggested huskily.

Lucan wished those were the *only* things he thought of this woman! Unfortunately, Lexie's actions also showed her to be loyal—he knew it was loyalty to Premier Personnel that had made her agree to come to Mulberry Hall with him in the first place, courageous in the face of Lucan's displeasure, which had been known to make grown men quake in their shoes. Lexie was also intelligent, witty, feisty and so beautiful that just looking at her now intensified his arousal to almost painful levels.

'No.' He gave a rueful shake of his head and raised both his hands to place them gently against her temples and smooth back the silky dark hair from her face. 'It's because I want to make love to you so much I can't think straight,' he admitted huskily.

She moistened her lips with the tip of her delicate pink tongue. 'You do…?'

Lucan nodded, unable to break his gaze away from those parted lips. 'Lexie, I want—need—to make love to you so badly at this moment that I can't think of anything else!'

Lexie's heart leapt, thundering in her chest at the admission, and her skin was suddenly warm and ultra-sensitive as she felt the touch, the heat, of Lucan's hands as they threaded lightly in her hair. As she saw the raw hunger burning in his eyes, in the tense, raw angles of his face.

A hunger that was echoed deep inside Lexie.

Even more deeply than the knowledge that making love with Lucan, to Lucan, having him make love with and to her, was exactly what she shouldn't allow to happen…

CHAPTER TEN

'SAY SOMETHING, Lexie...!' he groaned achingly.

'Shh,' she soothed huskily, as one of her hands moved up to cup the side of his face.

A hot, quivering awareness coursed the length of her arm and down her spine as she stared up into the heat of Lucan's eyes.

Her breasts were tingling in anticipation as she imagined Lucan's hands, his mouth, on her there, the nipples hardening to a burning, sensual ache, and there was a low throbbing between her thighs as she felt herself swell there as those delicate tissues became damp, wet in invitation.

She wanted Lucan to make love to her. Wanted to make love to him. Just once wanted to touch, to caress, to taste every single beautiful inch of him...!

Her gaze continued to hold his as she moved up onto her knees and slowly raised her hands to touch his chest, so close now she was able to feel his hard warmth and the rapid beat of his heart through the thin wool of his sweater.

It wasn't close enough. Lexie wanted to touch the bareness of Lucan's skin. To feel the quivering response of his flesh against her fingertips and palms, her lips and tongue.

Her gaze continued to hold his as her hands moved down

to the bottom of his sweater to slowly, oh-so-slowly, pull the woollen garment up and above the flatness of his defined stomach to his muscled chest.

'Lexie?' Lucan questioned again gruffly.

'Please don't talk, Lucan.' She placed gentle fingertips against his firm lips. 'It always ends up in an argument and one of us always says the wrong thing.' She turned her attention to the light dusting of dark chest hair ending in a V at the base of his stomach before disappearing beneath the waistband of his denims.

His skin was so hard and muscled beneath the touch of her fingers—testament to the fact that Lucan didn't spend all of his time in a boardroom! Lexie was drawn, tempted to touch the tight buds hidden amongst that dusting of silky dark hair.

She glanced up at Lucan when he drew in a raggedly sharp breath as her fingertips grazed across them. 'You like that…?'

'Oh, yes…!' he encouraged achingly, cheeks flushed, a nerve pulsing in the rigidness of his jaw, hunger burning in the depths of those dark, dark eyes as he continued to look at her from beneath lowered lids.

Her head slowly lowered so she could taste Lucan there, and his hand moved up instinctively to cup her head, his back arching, lids closing, as her lips skimmed across his chest. The air was cool, arousing, as it brushed against the residue of moisture left on the surface of his skin from those caressing lips and tongue.

Lucan released her only long enough to pull his sweater up and over his head, before tossing it down onto the carpeted floor, his body on fire as Lexie's arms now moved about his waist, her hands a fiery caress against his shoulders and down the length of his back as she continued to kiss and caress his chest with her lips and tongue.

Lucan wanted—needed—to touch her, too…

Lexie gasped hoarsely as one of Lucan's hands cupped beneath her breast, over her vest top, and the soft pad of his thumb lightly caressed that aching tip, sending rivulets of pleasure down her body to pool, burn, between her aching and needy thighs.

Lucan was breathing raggedly as he pulled back slightly. 'Lexie, let me look at you,' he said hotly.

Lexie's hands shook slightly as she sat back on her heels to pull the vest top over her head and discard it, her cheeks becoming hot as Lucan looked down at her semi-nakedness with dark and hungry eyes.

Her breasts seemed to swell under the intensity of that gaze, the already puckered nipples hardening to ripe berries against her otherwise pale skin. Asking, begging to be in the heat of Lucan's mouth!

'You're so beautiful, Lexie.' Lucan's breath was a warm caress against those aroused nipples, and his hands cupped beneath both her breasts to hold them up in sacrifice to his tongue as he paid homage to first one sensitive peak and then the other.

Lexie could only cling mindlessly to his muscled shoulders as sensation surged through her and down her, to clench in hot, sweet pleasure between her thighs. As Lucan sucked one of her nipples strongly, deeply into the heat of his mouth, that pleasure became a burning ache as she felt the need to have Lucan inside her.

'Lucan…!' Lexie groaned that need as her fingers became entangled in the dark thickness of his hair, holding him to her as her back arched, lifting her breasts and tilting her nipple deeper into the heat of his hungry mouth.

Lucan drew on her hungrily and allowed his hands to move to her waist. Lexie's skin was like silken velvet beneath his touch as he pushed the waistband of those loose-fitting pyjama bottoms lower down her thighs, exposing her pelvic bone and then a silky triangle of curls before he sought the tiny centre of pleasure between her legs.

Lucan stroked it, again and again, and Lexie's breath caught in her throat in small needy groans as each stroke brought her closer to release, but never quite close enough.

Her body tensed as she trembled in anticipation. 'Lucan, please!' Lexie's hands tightened in his hair as she shifted slightly, legs parting wider, her hips arching into him in a more urgent plea.

His mouth left her breast, trailing heated kisses upwards along that silken slope, and he was able to feel her trembling response as his tongue rasped against the sensitive cord in her throat and then up to her mouth. His other hand tangled in the heavy thickness of her hair, holding her as his mouth claimed hers, his tongue surging hotly into her mouth, capturing Lexie's keening cry of pleasure as she found her release.

She had barely recovered when his fingers surged inside her. Her muscles clenched, holding him there as they thrust into her slowly, rhythmically, giving and at the same time taking all she had to give. His mouth left hers and returned to claim the ripe berry of her nipple in that same dancing rhythm, once again sending her over that plateau of sensual pleasure.

'Oh, God—oh, God—oh, God…!' Lexie's head dropped forward onto Lucan's chest minutes later, her fingers clinging, digging into his muscled shoulders, as the pleasurable ripples of release continued to shake her body.

Lucan's lips were a sensual caress along the line of her jaw as he gently eased his fingers from inside her, teeth gently biting the softness of her lobe before his tongue stroked the shell-like shape of her ear and his fingers once more circled that throb between her thighs.

Lexie trembled, her back tensing, as she felt a quiver of response deep inside her. 'I can't,' she groaned weakly. 'Lucan, I really can't...'

'You can,' he encouraged softly, and moved back slightly so that he could help her to lie down on top of the bed-clothes, remaining up on his knees as he lightly gripped the waistband of her pyjama bottoms and began to slide them down her thighs, over her knees, before pulling them fully from her body and dropping them beside the bed.

Naked now, bathed in the golden glow of the bedside lamp, Lexie felt as well as saw the way Lucan's dark and devouring gaze moved slowly, hungrily, over every inch of her naked body—her breasts, the flatness of her stomach, curvaceous hips and thighs.

He looked every inch a pagan god as he knelt above her, his hair falling wildly across his brow, eyes dark and stormy, his face all harsh and yet sensual angles, his chest and shoulders hard and with rippling muscle.

'Take off your denims, Lucan,' she encouraged huskily.

His eyes glowed warmly in challenge. 'You take them off for me,' he invited gruffly.

Lexie swallowed hard as she slowly moved up onto her haunches, unable to look away from that dark and com-pelling gaze. She reached out for the button fastening at his waist, feeling the quivering response of his stomach muscles as she inadvertently touched bare flesh before managing to slowly slide down the zipper, realising as she did so that there was no way she was going to get the body-hugging denims down over his hips and muscled thighs without help from Lucan.

But maybe she didn't need to take them off completely just yet...

She caught her bottom lip between her teeth as her gaze lowered to the black boxers revealed by parting the two sides of the zip, the soft cotton clinging lovingly to the hard bulge beneath. Its hardness pulsed and surged upwards as Lexie cupped Lucan there, before her fingers stroked that hard length with slow circular caresses that made Lucan harder still, allowing Lexie to feel that pumping surge of his blood against her fingertips.

'Touch me, Lexie!' Lucan's voice was a harsh growl. 'I need to feel your hands on my skin!'

'Lie back,' she encouraged softly, moving to kneel beside him once he had lain back against the pillows. He allowed Lexie to peel the two garments slowly down his body before she moved back between Lucan's thighs and looked down at him admiringly from beneath lowered lashes.

Beautiful.

There was no other word to describe the hard and muscled contours of Lucan's completely naked body.

Beautiful like a Greek statue come to life—every part of him in proportion: his shoulders and chest wide, waist tapered, his arousal long and hard as it jutted out from a nest of dark curls, his legs long and perfect.

Lexie's hungry gaze returned to his thrusting arousal, her tongue moving moistly across her lips as that long and silken hardness instantly responded to her interest. She was able to see the blood surging beneath the surface as it pulsed, lifting up towards her in invitation.

An invitation she couldn't resist...

He'd died and gone to heaven.

Where else could Lucan be when his imaginings on that

first day he had met Lexie, of having the mind-shattering heat and pleasure of Lexie's mouth against his pulsing shaft, the lap of her tongue along his throbbing length, had come true?

Maybe he wasn't in heaven, after all. Maybe he had just lost his mind…

If this was insanity then Lucan knew he would be happy to remain out of his mind for the rest of his life!

Lexie's hands grasped him firmly as the rasp of her tongue moved slowly—excruciatingly slowly—along the length of his shaft from base to tip. Lucan groaned as it dipped and tasted the delicacy of the tip.

'You like that, too…?'

Lucan could barely focus on Lexie, he liked it so much! 'Does *more* answer your question?' he groaned huskily.

'Oh, yes.' Lexie chuckled softly, her fingers curled lightly about that pulsing shaft as she sat back and caressed him, her eyes a deep navy blue as she watched his responses from beneath dark, silky lashes, her cheeks flushed and her lips—God, those plump and pouting lips!—once again driving him insane.

Lucan's fingers clenched into the bedcovers beneath him as he watched the expression on Lexie's face even as she watched him, watched his responses to her caresses. She was obviously enjoying pleasuring him as much as Lucan was enjoying being pleasured.

'I want to be inside you when I come, Lexie,' he told her gruffly when she gave him a slightly reproachful look as he sat up to lift her gently but firmly away from him, before moving to take her into his arms.

Lucan wanted to be inside her…

The sexual haze faded from Lexie's head. Not because she didn't want all of Lucan's silken hardness inside her—

Lexie ached for that. No, her sudden wariness was for another reason entirely.

She was an avid reader, enjoyed nothing more than a good love story, and in every book she had ever read where the hero realised the heroine's lack of experience only as he pierced her virginity the man reacted in one of two ways: accusing, because he suspected entrapment, or emotional at being the heroine's first lover because he was deeply in love with her.

Lexie knew that Lucan wasn't in love with her—which left only accusations...

'Lexie?'

She moistened dry lips, a pained frown creasing her brow as she met his concerned gaze. 'I think I ought to ask how you feel about being a woman's first lover.'

Lucan stared at her blankly for several tense seconds. '*Your* first lover?' he finally realised.

She grimaced. 'Yes.'

How did Lucan feel about being Lexie's first lover? How would *any* man feel at the thought of being this beautiful woman's first lover?

Probably exactly the way Lucan did—privileged. And a little surprised.

'I had no idea,' he murmured softly. 'You're so outspoken, so self-confident, it never occurred to me there hadn't been another man in your bed.'

'Yes... Well...' A delicate blush heightened her cheeks. 'Technically speaking, this isn't my bed, either.'

'For the moment it is.'

She nodded. 'I just thought I ought to mention the thing to you before—well, before we go any further. Every woman has to start somewhere, right?' She brightened. 'So it might just as well be with a man who knows what he's doing.'

'Just as well,' Lucan echoed gruffly, not sure that he wasn't going to smile at this typically Lexie comment, at the realisation that no other man had ever made love to this lovely woman in the way that he had. In the way that he was going to.

And Lexie had never touched another man in the intimate way she had him just now. Just the thought of that possibility was enough to increase the aching throb between his thighs.

'And I can really do without you getting either angry or sentimental over it,' she warned him firmly.

'Angry or sentimental…?' Lucan repeated dryly.

'Well—okay. It's unlikely, you being you, that you're going to feel the second of those emotions.' She gave a rueful shrug. 'But I don't want to take any chances.'

Lucan looked down at her quizzically. 'Me being me?'

'You know, Lucan, this conversation would go along much quicker if you just stopped repeating everything I say!' She glared at him reprovingly.

It was no good. Lucan couldn't hold back his smile, his laughter, any longer.

He should be annoyed at that crack—'you being you'—but the truth of the matter was he was too damned bemused by this woman to feel annoyed about anything she said.

In the past, lovemaking had always seemed rather a serious business to Lucan. Something to be mutually enjoyed, certainly, but ultimately lacking in any emotion except the need to satisfy the lust he and his partner felt for each other. Only Lexie, a woman like no other woman Lucan had ever met, could bring him to task, make him want to laugh, in the middle of lovemaking.

'I'm not sure I want to be laughed at, either!' She gave him a reproving frown.

'I'm not laughing *at* you, Lexie,' Lucan assured as he took her gently in his arms and held her. 'I'm laughing *with* you!'

That would certainly be a change, Lexie acknowledged ruefully. A very pleasant one now that Lucan knew she was a virgin.

'You're an extraordinary woman, Lexie Hamilton,' he murmured into the thickness of her hair.

'Something else we agree on!' she came back sassily as her self-confidence returned.

'No, you were right the first time: we *do* end up arguing every time we talk!' Lucan gave her a wry smile. 'And to answer your question,' he continued huskily, 'I would very much enjoy being your first lover.'

Her eyes widened. 'You would...?'

He nodded. 'Very much.'

It suddenly struck Lexie as being very funny that she was sitting there stark naked, with a man equally naked— with *Lucan* gorgeously, wonderfully naked—engaging in a conversation as to whether or not they should continue making love together. How ridiculous was that?

'Lexie...?' Lucan prompted indulgently as she let out a sudden burst of laughter.

'Sorry. I just— It's—' She broke off as she was consumed with another bout of laughter.

Out of sheer relief, probably, Lexie recognised ruefully, at Lucan's unexpected but very welcome reaction to her revelation of still being a virgin. Whatever the reason, she couldn't seem to stop laughing—and seconds later she felt the reverberation of Lucan's chest against her as he also began to chuckle.

CHAPTER ELEVEN

'How do you feel about going downstairs for a late-night snack?' Lucan lay back on the bed, Lexie's head on his shoulder, her arm across his abdomen. He held her curved tightly against his side, their laughter having finally subsided.

Cathy Barton had prepared a delicious meal earlier this evening, but Lucan really hadn't been hungry enough to do Cathy's cooking justice following his argument with Lexie. He had a feeling that Lexie hadn't eaten anything this evening, either.

Besides, he would like to savour the thought of being Lexie's first lover a little longer…

'What?' A slightly bemused Lexie raised her head to look up at him.

'Did you eat anything after I left earlier this evening?' Lucan prompted softly.

'Well…no. But wouldn't you like to—? I mean, I know *I* did—several times—but you certainly didn't, and—'

Lucan shifted slightly so that Lexie was the one who now lay back on the pillows, with him looking down at her. 'Lexie, if you're trying, in your own inimitable style, to say that you had multiple orgasms earlier, and I haven't had any yet, then—'

'Lucan!' She buried her flushed face against his chest in obvious embarrassment.

Endearingly so, Lucan recognised indulgently. 'Well, are you?' he prompted teasingly, and was rewarded by a muttered 'yes' against his chest. The warmth of Lexie's breath was a warm and sensual caress on his bare flesh. 'There's no rush, Lexie. After all, we have all night,' he assured her huskily.

She looked up at him with wide blue eyes. 'All night...?'

'*Now* who's repeating everything I say?' he teased.

'Well, yes—but... *All night,* Lucan?' Her tone was a mixture of awe and anticipation.

'I don't see why not—as long as you feed me the occasional morsel of food to keep my strength up,' he drawled softly.

'Let's go and eat!' She moved out of his arms to sit up.

The sight of Lexie's pouting and naked breasts instantly caused Lucan to review his decision concerning a need for food right now. They could easily delay eating for another fifteen minutes—possibly half an hour...an hour...

An option he had realised too late, as Lexie stood up to modestly turn her back towards him and pull a robe on over her nakedness. Her uncharacteristic shyness instantly reminded Lucan that for all her outspoken self-confidence, Lexie really wasn't one of the sophisticated women who usually shared his bed.

And they really did have all night...

Lexie was amazed ten minutes later at how relaxed she felt, sitting in the warmth of the kitchen with Lucan, snacking on the cheese and biscuits Cathy Barton had included in the box of food yesterday, and drinking strong coffee.

It made Lucan seem less like the powerhouse of energy she had first met, and more like the man who was about to become her first lover...

Possibly helped by the darkness of his hair still falling rakishly across his brow rather than being brushed back in the severe style he usually favoured. Or it might have been the casual denims and jumper he had pulled back on before coming downstairs. Or the comfortable way they had set about preparing the food and coffee together a few minutes ago. Or the warmth of the smile that curved the corners of Lucan's sculpted mouth every time he glanced across the table at her.

Whatever the reason, Lexie felt at ease in his company. 'This is nice.'

'Yes.' He nodded. 'Yes, it is.'

'There's no need to seem so surprised!' Lexie laughed softly.

Lucan *was* surprised at how pleasant it was just to sit there and eat a snack with Lexie. At how pleasant it was to just sit there and do anything with Lexie.

He felt completely relaxed—a rare commodity in a life that was usually hectic in the extreme, with no time for just sitting back and 'smelling the roses', as his mother had put it the last time she'd lectured him concerning his need to relax more and work less.

Considering the tension between them from the beginning of their acquaintance, Lexie Hamilton was the last person Lucan would ever have thought he could relax with. And in the kitchen at Mulberry Hall, of all places!

'It's very good, Lexie,' he assured her huskily.

She returned his gaze quizzically. 'But you *are* surprised?'

'You're always surprising me, Lexie,' he stated truthfully.

Which was probably part of her attraction, Lucan recognised consideringly; he never knew what Lexie was going to say or do next!

'In what way?' she prompted curiously.

'In every way!'

'So.' She looked over at him from beneath dark lashes. 'Will I be your first virgin?'

Lucan's laugh was completely spontaneous as he stared across the table at her incredulously. 'Will you be—?' He gave a slightly dazed shake of his head. 'I really haven't met anyone quite like you before, Lexie.'

'But that's good, isn't it?'

Lucan wasn't sure that 'good' was exactly the way he would have described this experience. It was certainly novel to talk in this frank and open way with a woman he had every intention of making love to—several times—before the night was over. Tomorrow, too, if he could persuade Lexie into reconsidering their decision to leave in the morning.

'It's certainly different,' he finally conceded dryly.

'Good or bad different?'

'Good. I think,' he added with a frown.

Her eyes glowed with laughter. 'But you aren't sure?'

'I don't think I've been really sure of anything since the moment I first met you,' he acknowledged ruefully. 'You obviously weren't present when they were handing out the reserve gene!'

'Oh, I was probably just hiding behind a door,' she dismissed unconcernedly.

'Right.' Lucan straightened in his chair. 'Then, yes, Lexie, you will be my first virgin.'

She tilted her head. 'And how do you feel about that?'

'Nervous.'

'What?' She sat back to eye him disbelievingly, absolutely astounded that Lucan had admitted to feeling nervous about anything.

The very first thing Lexie had noticed about him had been the air of power that he wore like an invisible cloak. An inborn self-confidence that said he knew who and what he was, and dared anyone to challenge that knowledge.

He gave a derisive smile. 'Try looking at it from my point of view, Lexie. You're—what…? Twenty-something?'

'Four.'

'Hmm. And no doubt in those twenty-four years you've read books and seen films that depict lovemaking as being a wild and wonderful experience?'

A delicate blush warmed her cheeks. 'No doubt.'

Lucan nodded. 'What if the reality doesn't measure up to the things they write in books and show in the movies?'

'It has so far!'

He smiled. 'You're doing wonders for my ego, Lexie.'

She eyed him teasingly. 'Your ego doesn't need any more stroking!'

He gave a lazy smile. 'You sound very sure of that.'

Well, of course Lexie was sure of that. She only had to look at him as he sat across the table from her, so relaxed and sure of himself, just like a big, sleepy cat. The untamed variety, of course. Lucan St Claire was a law unto himself and always would be—a man who indulged in sensual relationships without ever becoming emotionally involved.

Which suited Lexie perfectly. She only had this one night with Lucan, and would never see him again—could never see him again—once the two of them returned to London tomorrow.

'Have any of your other women ever had cause to complain?' she teased.

He frowned. 'Lexie—'

'Don't tell me—it simply isn't done to talk about the other women you've been to bed with?'

He looked slightly bemused. 'Believe me, nothing that's happened with you has ever happened to me before.'

'Really…?' She caught her bottom lip between her teeth and stood up to move slowly round the table to where Lucan sat, pushing her robe back over her hips and placing her hands on his shoulders for support as she settled herself across his muscled thighs.

'That isn't my ego you're stroking, Lexie,' Lucan drawled huskily as she moved slowly, oh-so-slowly, against the rigid hardness of the arousal pressing against his denims.

'No?' She gave him a warm and sensuous smile as she continued that rocking movement.

His eyes darkened almost to black as he parted the top folds of her robe to bare the pertness of her breasts. 'You really are very beautiful here, Lexie,' he murmured softly, and he lowered his head to lightly kiss each aroused nipple in turn, before concentrating his attentions on just one.

Lexie's breath caught in her throat. 'I need you to make love to me, Lucan,' she groaned achingly, her fingers becoming entangled in the darkness of his hair as she held him to her.

'Here?'

'Anywhere!'

Lucan truly had never met a woman like Lexie. So open. So totally honest. About herself and her needs.

The same needs were raging within him—and had been, he now acknowledged, since the moment he'd first met her.

Needs they both became totally lost in as they kissed and touched. Heatedly. Wildly. Lips and hands seeking and finding every pleasure point. Every touch, every caress, driving their passion higher and then higher still as desire spiralled out of control. As their need raged totally out of control.

Lucan's hands cupped beneath Lexie's bottom as he surged to his feet, her hands clinging to his shoulders, her legs wrapped tightly about his waist as he strode from the kitchen and carried her back up the stairs to her bedroom, to lay her gently down on the bed.

Lexie cast aside her robe and watched as Lucan threw off his own clothes before joining her on the bed, nudging her legs gently apart before kneeling between her thighs to part her dark curls and bare her to his dark and searing gaze.

'God, you're beautiful, Lexie…' he groaned, his hands moving lightly across her burning flesh as his head began to lower. 'So damned beautiful,' he said achingly, his breath a warm caress against her sensitivity.

Lexie gasped at the first touch of Lucan's mouth against her heat. He laved her with his tongue, and the sensation, the pleasure, was unlike anything she had ever experienced before. Deeper, even stronger than during their earlier lovemaking.

Her head fell back against the pillows as she felt the onset of orgasm surging through her, burning her, as pleasure ripped through her, seeming never-ending as Lucan drank, lapped up every last vestige of that release before moving up to position himself between her thighs.

'Take me inside you, Lexie,' he encouraged gruffly. 'Take me before I lose my mind!'

Lexie needed no further encouragement, and she curled her fingers about him and began to guide him inside her, inch by beautiful inch. Her delicate folds widened, stretching to accommodate the width and length of him, until he reached the barrier of her virginity.

Lucan was breathing hard, determined to maintain control, to ensure that Lexie enjoyed her first experience of lovemaking.

That control didn't come easy. Lucan was raging inside as his shaft surged, pulsed with the need to take what was already his!

He leant his weight on his elbows as he looked down at her. 'I don't want to hurt you!' he groaned.

'You won't.' There was complete trust in her eyes as she gazed up at him.

He rested the dampness of his forehead against hers, breathing deeply through his nose. 'I might—'

'You won't,' she repeated with certainty.

Lucan's chest swelled at her complete faith in his ability not to hurt her. 'Hold on to my shoulders,' he encouraged huskily, and he drew his thighs back slightly before thrusting those last few inches, breaching the barrier of her virginity as she took him fully inside her.

Lucan heard Lexie gasp, felt her body tensing as her fingernails dug briefly into his flesh before she relaxed again, allowing the softness of her inner folds to wrap around him. Hot, so very hot, and velvet-soft. He grasped her hips, his mouth capturing hers as he began to thrust slowly, rhythmically inside her.

Pleasure engulfed him as his thrusts deepened, hardened, drowning Lucan in pleasure, in ecstasy unlike anything he had ever known before. He felt his release building, higher and higher, and Lexie's keening cries told him that she was fast approaching her own climax.

Her legs wrapped about his waist as she tensed beneath him, tightening around him as her orgasm ripped through her, those clenching spasms taking Lucan with her. And he felt the heat of his own release surge down the length of his shaft and burst inside her in hot and never-ending pleasure.

'Wow...' Lexie breathed weakly long minutes later, when she finally found enough breath to be able to talk at all. Her hands moved in a long, slow caress across and down the broad width of Lucan's back as he lay still, above and inside her.

Lucan chuckled huskily. 'That was—'

'Please don't burst my happy bubble by telling me I was rubbish at it!' she groaned.

'—incredible!' he finished softly as he moved up on his elbows to look down at her. 'You're incredible, Lexie,' he assured her gruffly, his expression serious as his hands moved to cradle either side of her face. 'Did I hurt you?'

'No.' Lexie had felt only a small pinch of pain, brief and quickly forgotten as she became caught up in the pleasure of having Lucan deeply inside her.

Lucan didn't look reassured. 'You're probably a little sore?'

Lexie still felt full, completely filled by Lucan, and it certainly wasn't a painful feeling. The opposite, in fact, as her sensitive inner muscles continued to spasm and clench pleasurably about him.

'Not at all.' She reached up to gently smooth the dark hair from Lucan's brow. 'In fact, as soon as you're able, I would like to do it all over again!'

'Greedy little baggage,' he murmured admiringly.

'Mmm.' Her legs tightened about his waist. 'I intend keeping you exactly where you are for the rest of the night!' She wasn't about to waste a single minute, a second, of the one night she would have with Lucan.

He gave a rueful shake of his head. 'Your honesty is overwhelming.'

Lexie stilled. Her honesty...?

She had been completely honest about her enjoyment of their lovemaking, but about everything else...?

Lexie hadn't been honest with Lucan about any other part of her life!

She didn't work as a temp for Premier Personnel— she helped to run it with her parents. It wasn't true that there was no other temp available to send to the St Claire Corporation—Lexie had deliberately decided to go and work there herself for three days, in order to settle her long-held curiosity concerning the St Claire family itself. Most especially about the head of that family, Lucan St Claire.

Well, she had done a lot more than settle her curiosity about Lucan. A lot, lot more.

'Lexie...?' There was a dark frown between Lucan's eyes as Lexie slid her legs down the backs of his thighs to rest her feet on the bed. Her hand fell limply back to her side. 'Are you having regrets, after all?'

Not the sort Lucan obviously meant—but, yes, Lexie *was* having regrets.

Lots of them. Mainly she was regretting that she had ever begun this dangerous subterfuge. Because if Lucan ever found out exactly who she was, her connection to Sian Thomas, then he really was going to hate her.

Lexie didn't want Lucan to hate her. And she didn't still hate him...

How could she ever have thought she could make love with Lucan—physically take what he had to give—the pleasure she had already glimpsed so fleetingly on those other occasions when he had held her in his arms and kissed her—and then just walk away without there being any repercussions to herself?

How could she have been so naive?

How could she have been so stupid not to have realised she was already in love with him…?

CHAPTER TWELVE

'LEXIE, what's wrong?' Lucan frowned when she could only stare up at him in shock. 'Talk to me, damn it!' He grasped her shoulders and shook her as she didn't respond.

Talk to him? Lexie wasn't sure she would ever be able to talk to Lucan again, let alone coherently. She was in love with him! Had fallen in love with Lucan St Claire—the man she had always hated. The one man who believed he had every reason to despise all her family.

Lexie had heard it said that there was a very thin line between love and hate...

How could this have happened? *Why* had it happened? What mad and vengeful god—goddess—could have wished this upon her?

'Lucan—could you move?' Lexie pleaded desperately as the food she had eaten earlier rose like bile in the back of her throat. The feeling grew worse as she was totally over-whelmed by Lucan's close proximity. By the fact that his body was still intimately joined with hers. 'Now, Lucan!' she begged. 'I—I think I'm going to be sick!'

Lucan barely had time to disengage and roll to the side before Lexie stood up to dash madly—nakedly—to the adjoining bathroom. The door slammed shut behind her, followed seconds later by the sound of forceful retching.

Lucan fell heavily back against the pillows to stare

sightlessly up at the ceiling, feeling slightly nauseous himself at the possibility that it had been their lovemaking that had made Lexie ill.

Had he hurt her, after all?

Was she in so much pain it had actually made her physically sick?

Or was it something else? Possibly the realisation of what had just happened between the two of them had affected her so dramatically?

Lucan sat up, only to come to an abrupt halt and feel a painful wrenching in his gut as he saw the smear of blood on the sheet beside him in evidence of Lexie's innocence.

Lucan's expression was grim as he stood up to pull his denims on over his nakedness, before padding across the room barefoot to knock softly on the bathroom door. He turned the handle. 'Lexie...'

'Don't come in here!' Lexie cried desperately as she realised Lucan's intention. Wasn't it enough that Lucan must know she was in here throwing up the food and drink she'd had earlier, without the added humiliation of having Lucan see her actually bent naked over the toilet? 'Go away, Lucan,' she instructed him crossly. She glared across to where she could see Lucan—as he must surely be able to see her!—where he stood on the other side of the partially opened bathroom door.

'Do you need any help—?'

'To be sick?' she scorned. 'I don't think so, thank you very much! Just go away and leave me alone,' she repeated impatiently.

'I can't do that—'

'Of course you can.' Lexie turned to grab a towel from the rack and wrap it about herself before standing up. 'It's easy, Lucan. You just close the damned door and turn around and walk away!'

'No.'

'What do you mean, no?' Lexie flushed the toilet before marching across the bathroom to wrench the door open and glare up at Lucan. At Lucan so sexily attractive dressed only in faded denims that Lexie's knees went weak just looking at him!

His chest was so broad and muscled, his stomach so flat and toned, and those denims rested on narrow hips above long and muscled legs. Shifting her gaze quickly back to Lucan's face wasn't really any help either, when his hair was still slightly mussed and falling sexily across his forehead. His eyes were dark and full of concern, and that firm mouth was just asking to be kissed.

Well…asking to be kissed if Lexie's own mouth hadn't felt so unpleasant after she'd been so thoroughly sick!

She turned back into the bathroom and crossed over to the sink to brush her teeth.

'I mean no, Lexie,' Lucan repeated firmly behind her. 'We need to talk.'

'We don't need to do anything of the sort!' She rinsed her mouth with water before turning to look at him. 'I've obviously eaten something that disagreed with me—'

'Cheese and biscuits?' Lucan drawled sceptically.

Lexie glared up at him. 'Something!' She pushed past him to cross the bedroom and pick up her robe from where it had been thrown onto the carpet earlier.

Lucan leant against the bathroom doorway and watched her through narrowed lids. The dark wildness of Lexie's hair just added to the deathly pallor of her cheeks, but neither of those things detracted in the least from how sexy she looked, wearing only a very inadequate bath towel, with the swell of her breasts visible above and her legs bare and shapely beneath.

His thighs stirred in renewed arousal as she turned away to slip her arms into the robe, before pulling the towel off and tying the belt firmly at her slender waist. Her breasts were outlined against the silk material as she turned to face him.

Lucan pushed away from the doorframe, eyes narrowed grimly at the inappropriateness of his arousal. 'What just happened, Lexie?'

Her chin rose. 'I told you—'

'You don't get food poisoning from eating fresh cheese and biscuits,' he dismissed firmly.

Lexie wished that Lucan would put some more clothes on; it was very disconcerting trying to have a conversation with a man who looked as sexy as Lucan did right now. With a man whose arousal was unmistakably outlined against those close-fitting denims.

With a man Lexie had realised only minutes ago she was in love with...

She thrust trembling hands into the pockets of her robe. 'I do,' she answered firmly. 'Obviously.'

He gave a slow shake of his head. 'It wasn't the cheese and biscuits that made you sick.'

'Then what did, Dr St Claire?' She eyed him scathingly.

His mouth thinned at the taunt. 'I was hoping you could tell me that.'

'Oh, no.' Lexie shook her head scornfully. 'You're the one who seems to think he has all the answers!'

Lucan breathed deeply through his nose, having no intention of allowing Lexie to goad him into losing his temper. As she seemed so set on doing... 'Maybe you regret what just happened?'

She frowned. 'I already said I didn't.'

'Before you were violently ill!' Lucan bit out harshly, positive that Lexie was lying to him—that the honesty he had remarked upon earlier was completely lacking at this moment. He just had no idea why that was.

'Obviously eating cheese at midnight doesn't agree with me.'

'I have already discounted that as the cause, Lexie.'

'But I haven't!' Those blue eyes flashed angrily. 'Would you just *go*, Lucan?' She grimaced. 'I'm feeling pretty awful and I'd like to go to bed.'

'Alone?'

'Well, of course alone! Unless you're feeling a perverted desire to make love to a sick woman?'

Lucan's desire for Lexie's wasn't in the least perverted— just continuous, it seemed. A never-ending ache that hadn't been in the least assuaged by their lovemaking earlier. It would perhaps never be completely satisfied, no matter how deeply or how often he made love with and to this particular woman...

His jaw tightened. 'Perhaps I should sleep in here, in case you're ill again in the night.'

'Haven't I just made it obvious how much I hate having an audience when I'm ill?' she snapped.

Lucan gave an abrupt inclination of his head. 'You made it just as obvious earlier that you couldn't wait for us to make love again.'

Lexie drew in a sharp breath. She had said that, hadn't she? Before she had realised her feelings for this man. Before she had realised she was in love with Lucan St Claire, fifteenth Duke of Stourbridge, a man she had always considered her bitterest enemy. As she and the whole of her family were his...

'Post-coital euphoria,' she dismissed tersely, before turning away. Just looking at Lucan was enough to make her long for pre-coital, coital and post-coital pleasure all over again! 'You know—a little like enjoying a delicious slice of gooey chocolate cake and anticipating having another slice but just knowing that it really wouldn't be good for you.'

Lucan gave a humourless smile. 'Interesting euphemism.'

Lexie returned that smile with a bright, meaningless one of her own. 'I thought so.'

'Did you know that chocolate can be addictive?'

'Only in its true form,' Lexie came back pertly.

Lucan's mouth tightened. 'Lexie, we just made love together, and it was really good, so why are we arguing?'

It *had* been really good, Lexie acknowledged heavily. More than good for her. It had been magical—so much more than anything Lexie could ever have imagined. Until she had realised that the reason it had been so magical, so wonderful, was because she was in love with Lucan...

'I told you earlier—we always argue when we bother to talk to each other. This time let's just put it down to the fact that I'm a grouch when I've been ill.' She shrugged.

Lucan studied her for long, tense seconds. Seconds when Lexie's defiant gaze didn't so much as waver from his. 'I don't accept that as an excuse.'

'Newsflash, Lucan—I really don't give a damn what you do or don't accept,' she told him wearily. 'I'm not denying we both had a good time earlier. The point is that we aren't now. That being the case, would you please just accept that I want you to go?'

Lucan eyed her frustratedly, knowing by the defiant way she continued to meet his gaze that they really weren't going to solve anything tonight by continuing their present conversation.

'Okay, I'll go,' he agreed abruptly. 'We'll talk again in the morning.'

'In the morning I'm out of here. With or without you!' she stated firmly.

Lucan's impatience intensified. 'I'm the one with the car, Lexie, and I'm no longer sure I'll be ready to leave in the morning.' He had no intention of going anywhere until he and Lexie had stopped arguing enough to make some sense out of what had just happened.

'Then I'll get a train home.'

'And if there aren't any?'

'There are,' she assured him with satisfaction.

Lucan's eyes narrowed. 'And you know this how...?'

Too late Lexie realised she had once again fallen into the trap of revealing too much. Of saying too much. Of knowing too much. 'I checked on the running of the trains before coming here.' Her chin rose as she told the lie. Visiting her grandmother, as she did regularly, Lexie had been conversant with the running times of the trains to Stourbridge for several years now. 'Just in case I decided to leave,' she added.

Lucan gave a humourless smile as he shook his head. 'You really are something else!'

Lexie was starting to feel ill again. 'Goodnight, Lucan,' she said firmly.

His nostrils flared as he breathed out his frustration. 'I'm really not that easily dismissed!'

Lexie felt a shiver down her spine at the warning she heard in his tone. 'As we aren't likely to meet again after tomorrow, there's really no need for me to know that, is there?'

He shrugged those broad and magnificently bare shoulders. 'As I said, I'm not that easily dismissed.'

'You just were!'

He gave a tight smile. 'Goodnight, Lexie.' He grabbed his jumper from the floor before strolling unhurriedly to the door. 'We will talk again in the morning,' he repeated firmly.

'Maybe I won't be here in the morning.'

Lucan turned at the door. 'Then I'll hunt you down when I get back to London,' he informed her calmly.

Too calmly. And with too much of a sense of purpose for Lexie's comfort… 'The arrogant and elusive Lucan St Claire, chasing after a woman?' she taunted. 'Whatever next?'

His eyes narrowed to glittering onyx slits. 'Believe me, Lexie, if you put me to the trouble of coming after then you won't like what happens next.'

Her eyes widened. 'Are you threatening me?'

'Just stating a fact.'

She gave an impatient sigh. 'Can't we just leave things the way they are?'

His jaw tightened. 'No.'

She grimaced. 'I had a feeling you were going to say that.'

'Then you weren't disappointed, were you?' Lucan drawled unsympathetically. 'Sweet dreams, Lexie,' he added huskily, before closing the door softly behind him.

Lexie's fingernails dug painfully into the palms of her hands where they clenched in the pockets of her robe as painful resistance to the urge she felt to run after him. To ask Lucan to stay. To beg him to hold her and never let her go…

But how ridiculous was it to expect that Lucan, a man who had never wanted to stay with any woman, let alone the granddaughter of Sian Thomas, would ever want to do that?

Almost as ridiculous as Lexie having allowed herself to fall in love with him...

'It's midday, sleepyhead. Time to wake up.'

Lexie kept her eyes firmly closed. She'd guessed from the nearness of Lucan's voice that he was standing beside the bed, where she lay with her face partly buried in the pillows.

She didn't care what time it was. She didn't want Lucan to know she was awake. Didn't want to look at him again. Didn't want to start last night's argument with him all over again.

She hadn't been able to sleep at all after Lucan had left her bedroom the night before—too upset, too emotionally raw to be able to turn off her thoughts and relax into sleep. How could she possibly relax when she had been stupid enough to fall in love with Lucan?

Just thinking about it now was enough to make her feel ill all over again!

Lucan stared down at Lexie frustratedly. He was pretty sure that she was awake and choosing to ignore him. And after the virtually sleepless night he'd had he wasn't in the mood to humour her. Instead he strode over to the window and pulled the curtains back, instantly letting in the bright sunlight.

'Ooh! Ow! That is *so* mean!' Lexie sat up abruptly, her eyes screwed up against the brightness, her hair standing up in tangled tufts. She looked so much like an indignant hedgehog that Lucan had trouble holding back a smile. 'That had better be coffee you have in that mug, otherwise you're a dead man!' she warned him fiercely.

'It's coffee, with milk and two sugars, just the way you like it,' Lucan confirmed mockingly as he strode back to the bedside and handed her the steaming mug of coffee he had brought with him as a peace offering. 'Not a morning person, I see?'

'Don't start on me, Lucan!' She scowled as she pushed some of that dark hair away from her face. 'And according to you it isn't still morning.' She had both hands wrapped about the warmth of the mug as she took a reviving sip.

A *cute* indignant hedgehog, Lucan revised. Even with her hair tangled, her face bare of make-up and little creases in one of her cheeks from where she had been in deep sleep on the pillow, Lexie still managed to arouse him. Damn it!

He crossed his arms in front of his chest. 'Do you want to go to the bathroom first, or shall we finish our conversation now?'

She looked up at him from beneath lowered brows. 'Persistent, aren't you!'

Lucan shrugged. 'I prefer to think of it as single-minded.'

'Hmm...'

'Was that, *Yes, Lucan, I would like to use the bathroom first,* or was it, *Okay, we can talk now...*?'

'Neither.' Lexie shook her head. 'It was please go away until I've woken up properly!'

'That isn't very polite when I've brought you coffee,' Lucan admonished.

She looked more disgruntled than ever. 'How long have you been up?'

'Five hours or so.' He shrugged. 'I managed to get a lot of the work that I brought with me done while you slept the morning away.' Working had also succeeded in keeping Lucan occupied while he waited for Lexie to get up. Until he had finally got tired of waiting and decided to wake her himself.

'That's good.' She nodded unconcernedly. 'I'm really

pleased for you. Now, would you just go away and leave me to enjoy my coffee in peace?'

Lucan had no idea—when this woman irritated him, annoyed him, frustrated him—why it was that she could still manage to make him laugh, too.

'Don't tell me.' Lexie looked up at Lucan wearily as she heard him chuckle. The few hours' sleep she had managed had not been in the least restful when she'd known she still had to face Lucan again this morning. 'People don't talk to you in this disrespectful way.'

'No, they don't.' He still smiled. 'But I could probably get used to it...' he added enigmatically.

Lexie straightened, more unnerved by having Lucan standing beside her bed than she wanted him to realize. Her pulse was racing, every part of her completely aware of how dark and powerful he looked in another black sweater and black denims. 'Luckily for you, you don't have to.'

'No?'

'No—*Damn!*' Lexie swore irritably as, having turned to place her empty mug on the bedside table, she heard something fall onto the carpeted floor. 'What—?'

She froze as she bent over the side of the bed and looked down at exactly what had fallen to the floor.

Everything stopped for Lexie in that moment. Movement. Breathing. Even her heart felt as if it had stopped beating as she stared down at the broken chain and the locket, where they had fallen onto the green carpet.

'Don't!' she protested when Lucan instantly went down on his haunches to retrieve them.

'What the hell *is* it with you and this damned locket?' Lucan rasped. He scooped the locket and chain up in his hand, taking a step back out of Lexie's reach as he straightened. 'Maybe you really *do* keep a photograph of a secret lover in here?' He frowned darkly. 'Maybe I should take a look...'

'*No!*' Even as she protested Lexie desperately threw back the bedclothes and tried to stand up.

Too late.

Far, far too late!

Lucan had already flicked the clasp open and was looking down at the two photographs inside the locket, a perplexed frown darkening his brow.

Long seconds, a minute passed, with no other sound in the room but the two of them breathing. Lexie's was laboured; Lucan barely breathed at all.

Finally he looked up. His face was deathly pale, his cheekbones raw beneath the tautness of his skin. His mouth was a thin, uncompromising line. A pulse pounded in his tightly clenched jaw. And eyes that had been dark and teasing a few minutes ago were now as cold and hard as the onyx they resembled.

Those black eyes narrowed dangerously. 'Who the hell *are* you?'

CHAPTER THIRTEEN

'GIVE me the locket, Lucan,' Lexie demanded shakily as she held out her hand.

Instead of complying, Lucan tightened his fingers instinctively about the piece of jewellery, uncaring of the open clasp digging painfully into his palm. The contents of the locket were firmly branded—seared—into his brain as he took a step away from that questing hand.

There were two photographs inside the locket. One of a grey-haired man, obviously in his sixties, although his face was still handsome as he smiled warmly at the person taking the photograph. A hard and aristocratic face that Lucan had instantly recognised as belonging to his father, Alexander.

The second photograph was of a woman. Only the streaks of grey in her shoulder-length black hair betrayed her age. Her face was youthfully unlined as she, too, laughed happily towards the camera.

It was a beautiful face: creamy brow, wide blue eyes, a pert nose and a wide and smiling mouth. Facial features too reminiscent of the woman now standing in front of Lucan for the two of them not to be related.

'I asked who you are…' Lucan repeated, icily soft.

Lexie swallowed hard, her breathing still shallow, and

she felt slightly light-headed as she looked at the pale and arrogant stranger who now stood before her.

Lucan the lover had gone.

The teasing Lucan had also disappeared. And in his place was a man who exuded such cold and remorseless fury Lexie felt as if she could almost reach out and touch it.

She shook her head. 'I can explain, Lucan—'

'Then I advise you to do it! *Now,*' he added harshly. 'A good place to start would be the name of the woman in the photograph.'

Lexie staggered back from the relentless force of Lucan's anger, sitting down on the edge of the bed before she fell down.

She had only intended working at the St Claire Corporation for three days—satisfying her curiosity about the St Claire family and then just walking away, hopefully with that curiosity satisfied. Since coming to know Lucan she had realised exactly how dangerous it would be for him ever to know she was the granddaughter of Sian Thomas.

As dangerous as Lexie falling in love with Lucan…

Lucan who now looked at her with such dislike, such cold contempt, that it sent an icy shiver down the length of her spine.

'Tell me, damn it!' he ordered savagely.

Lexie moistened lips that had gone dry. 'Her name is Sian Thomas…'

'Louder, Lexie,' Lucan bit out coldly.

Her chin rose. 'Her name is Sian Thomas. She's my grandmother,' she added softly as hot tears burned the backs of her eyes.

Lucan drew in a harshly hissing breath. He had known, of course—had guessed that the woman in the locket could only be one woman. The woman his father had loved. The same woman who had been responsible for the destruction of Lucan's family twenty-five years ago.

Sian Thomas.

Unbelievably, Lexie's grandmother!

He had known that Sian Thomas was a widow when his father had met her all those years ago, and that she'd had a nineteen-year-old daughter. He had just never thought of that daughter as having married and possibly having had children—a daughter of her own.

Lucan turned and strode forcefully over to stand in front of the window with his back to the room. He fought for control, not even attempting to look out onto the grounds but instead opening his hand so that he could once again look down at the locket in the palm of his hand.

Dear God, these photographs of his distinguished grey-haired father and Lexie's gracefully beautiful grandmother could have been of himself and Lexie in thirty years' time. Their similarity to the two was so marked!

'Lucan—'

'Don't say anything for the moment, Lexie,' he warned between gritted teeth.

'Alexandra.'

Lucan turned sharply. 'What?'

Lexie drew in a shaky breath as she saw the hard set of Lucan's face and the hands clenched at his sides. 'My full name is Alexandra Claire Hamilton. I was named for my step-grandfather,' she added unnecessarily.

Those dark eyes narrowed icily. 'As far as I'm aware my father never married your grandmother.'

'No,' she conceded, aware that Lucan had meant the remark to be insulting. 'But my mother still called him Papa Alex, and I called him Grandpa Alex.'

Lucan's nostrils flared sneeringly. 'My father was the Duke of Stourbridge!'

Her breath caught in her throat. 'You're implying *that* was the reason the two of them never married?'

'Why else?' he scorned. 'It would never have done, would it? The illustrious Duke of Stourbridge married to a—'

'Don't you *dare* say anything insulting about my grandmother!' Lexie said emotionally. 'Don't you dare, Lucan!' Her eyes flashed. 'Whether or not he was married to my grandmother, your father *was* my Grandpa Alex.' She raised her chin defiantly.

He nodded. 'And when did you intend sharing that little fact with me?'

Lexie gave a shiver of apprehension as she felt the full blast of Lucan's icy fury. 'I didn't,' she assured him shakily.

'I don't believe you,' he snapped.

She shook her head from side to side. 'I didn't plan any of this, Lucan. I—It just happened.'

Lucan's top lip turned back scornfully. 'You can't really expect me to believe that you had no idea who I was the day you came to work for me?'

'I didn't say that.' Impatience edged her tone. 'Of course I knew who you were. I just—I had no intention of ever telling you of my relationship to—to Sian Thomas…' she added lamely. 'I was curious, okay?' she continued defensively when Lucan just continued to look down his arrogant nose at her—as if she were a particularly unpleasant species of insect that had wandered into his line of vision. 'I didn't even know you existed until I was fourteen, when my mother explained…explained the situation to me.'

'No doubt your mother's version of what happened

twenty-five years ago differs greatly from my own,' Lucan bit out contemptuously.

Lexie stood up abruptly. 'You were only eleven when it happened, Lucan.'

'And you were told at fourteen. Do you seriously think those few extra years—fifteen years after the event—make you any better equipped to know, to comment on what did or didn't happen?' he scorned.

No, of course she didn't. In fact, Lexie had become aware over the past few days of just how sketchy her knowledge was concerning the whys and hows of her grandmother's relationship with Alexander St Claire twenty-five years ago...

She had only been fourteen years old, for goodness' sake, teetering on the brink of womanhood. Her grandmother and Grandpa Alex's love story had seemed so romantic to her. A Greek tragedy with a happy ending.

Except Lexie had realised since coming to Mulberry Hall with Lucan, witnessing firsthand his bitterness, his underlying sadness when he looked at that portrait of his father in the west gallery, that there had been no happy ending for Lucan and the rest of his family...

'Maybe you should talk to my grandmother—'

'Are you *insane*?' Lucan burst out incredulously.

Lexie bristled. 'She's the only one still alive who can tell you what really happened.'

'I was there, Lexie. I know what "really" happened!' he assured coldly.

She shook her head. 'I don't think you do. I *know* my grandmother, Lucan,' she defended as he gave a scathing snort. 'She's not the sort of woman who would ever deliberately hurt anyone.'

'You're predisposed to think that, Lexie.' He looked at

her pityingly. 'You obviously love her, and as such she can do no wrong in your eyes,' he added with hard dismissal.

'You must have loved your father once, and yet you've seemed quite willing to believe the worst of him all these years!' she came back defensively.

Lucan became very still. He *had* loved his father once—had looked up to him, believed him to be omnipotent, a man who could do no wrong. What a complete fallacy that had turned out to be!

'I have no intention of discussing my feelings for my father with you, Lexie,' he grated. 'At this moment I'm far more interested in knowing exactly what you thought you were doing—what you expected, when you went to bed with me,' he said softly.

'What I *expected*...?' she gasped.

'Yes,' Lucan snapped tersely. 'You said earlier that you came to work for me because you were curious. Curious about what, exactly?'

'You. Your family.' Lexie tried to explain. 'I was there the day of Grandpa Alex's funeral. I stood at the back of the church, watching the three of you—Gideon, Jordan and Lucan St Claire—as you sat in the front pew, publicly mourning the man you had privately shunned for twenty-five years.' She gave a shake of her head, her voice hardening. 'While my grandmother—the woman who had loved him and been loved by him for those same twenty-five years—had to sit at home in her cottage and mourn him. For that alone I've always hated you!'

'Me?'

'Yes, you!' She glared accusingly. 'The high and mighty fifteenth Duke of Stourbridge.'

'I have already told you that I don't use the title!' A nerve pulsed in Lucan's tightly clenched jaw.

'I'm sure you used it when you ensured that my

grandmother didn't attend your father's funeral,' Lexie scorned.

He shook his head. 'I have absolutely no idea what you're talking about.'

'Please don't lie to me, Lucan.' She sighed. 'At least let there be truth between us now.'

'Truth?' he repeated incredulously. 'You dare to talk to me of truth when from the moment we first met every word out of your mouth has been a lie?' He gave a disgusted shake of his head. 'God knows how you managed to manoeuvre things with Premier Personnel so that you came to work for me in the first place—'

'My parents own the company.'

'Your—!'

'They're away on a cruise at the moment, and left me in charge,' she said miserably.

Lucan gave a disbelieving shake of his head. 'And poor misguided Jessica gave you exactly the opening you needed!'

Lexie groaned. 'I'll admit what I did was wrong—'

'Because you got caught out? Or because you don't truly believe that this is none of your business?' Lucan was still having trouble believing, accepting that Lexie was the granddaughter of Sian Thomas, of all women. Except he still held the undeniable proof in his hand. And, of course, had Lexie's own confession…

'None of my business?' she repeated quietly, indignantly. 'Tell me, Lucan, did you know that my grandmother still lives in the same cottage in the village that she's owned for the past twenty-five years?'

He frowned darkly. 'In Stourbridge?'

'In Stourbridge,' she confirmed stonily.

'Owned?' he sneered. 'Or was she given it by my father,

so that he could have his mistress close at hand while he continued to live out a lie here, with his wife and sons?'

'You know, Lucan, I would feel sorry for you if you weren't so damned arrogant.' Lexie looked at him pityingly. 'For your information, my grandmother didn't come to live in Stourbridge until *after* your mother and father were divorced.'

Lucan sighed his impatience. 'I don't really see what this has to do with anything—'

'Because you aren't listening!' Lexie gave an exasperated shake of her head. 'Not that it's your business, but my grandmother bought her cottage with money left to her by my real grandfather when he died. But that isn't what's important. Do you have any idea why she still lives in Stourbridge, Lucan? Why she continues to stay on in the village alone? In spite of the gossip that still circulates about her and your father? Despite my parents' repeated entreaties for her to move to London and live with them?'

'No doubt you're about to enlighten me,' Lucan scorned uninterestedly.

'She stays here out of *love,* Lucan,' Lexie told him proudly. 'She can't bear to leave the place where she and Grandpa Alex were so happy together. Where he's buried.' Her voice broke emotionally. 'It's been eight years, Lucan, and yet she still visits his grave several times a week. Can any of your family say the same?'

'We live in London—'

'So do I. But I always go and place fresh flowers on Grandpa Alex's grave whenever I come to visit my grandmother, which is usually every couple of months. We went there together yesterday morning,' she added softly.

Lucan's eyes widened. 'That's why you were gone for over two hours...?'

'Yes,' she sighed.

Lucan eyed her coldly. 'How does your grandmother feel about your being here with me?'

Lexie bit her top lip. 'She was naturally...concerned once she knew that you had no idea who I was.'

'And does who you are have anything to do with your not wanting to go to the Bartons' for dinner yesterday evening? John didn't recognise you, but perhaps Cathy would have done...?'

Lexie nodded. 'I think she may be someone I knew in the village when I was younger.'

He gave a humourless laugh. 'And I was stupid enough to think it was because I had upset you!'

'You *did* upset me—'

'Not enough, obviously!'

Her chin rose stubbornly. 'You might be interested to know that my grandmother talked to Grandpa Alex about you yesterday morning—told him that you were staying at Mulberry Hall. She also told him how successful you are. How proud he would be. Of *all* his sons.'

Lucan mouth twisted derisively. 'I'm sure this is all very touching, Lexie—'

'Don't you dare say anything insulting about the love my grandmother and Grandpa Alex felt for each other!' she warned him heatedly. 'Don't you dare!'

He sighed heavily. 'Okay, Lexie, I won't do that. I'll leave you with your perfect little dream world intact.'

'I'm not naïve, Lucan. I know people were hurt because the two of them fell in love—'

'Hurt?' he echoed coldly. 'My family was destroyed because of it. As for my mother—! It's been twenty-five years, Lexie. Twenty-five years! My mother was only thirty-two at the time, and very beautiful, but she's never remarried. Never even let another man into her life, as far as I'm aware. She's still beautiful, and young enough to have another life with someone else, but because of what *he* did to her—his betrayal of their marriage with your grandmother—'

'You have to *stop,* Lucan!' Lexie choked. 'So much bitterness…! Can't you see how destructive it all is? Hasn't enough damage been done without letting it affect your own life in this way?'

Lucan looked at her coldly. 'You don't think it was bitter and destructive to go to bed with me out of some sort of misguided need for revenge?'

'Revenge?' Lexie repeated, absolutely astounded. Was he insane? 'What sort of revenge could I possibly hope to achieve by going to bed with you?'

'How the hell should I know?' he rasped. 'Perhaps you were hoping that I would fall in love with you, and then you could laugh in my face when I told you how I felt…?'

Lexie did laugh—but not in Lucan's face. She laughed out of self-derision; she was the one who had fallen in love with Lucan, not the other way round! 'Five minutes in your company—a minute!—would be enough to tell any woman that you don't know the meaning of the word love, let alone how to feel the emotion!'

'Really?' Lucan became very still, deathly calm again—the sort of cold, remorseless calm that anyone with any sense of self-preservation would know to back away from.

Lexie might have behaved recklessly by going anywhere near Lucan, might have committed the ultimate in stupidity by falling in love with him, but she wasn't totally bereft of a sense of self-preservation. 'I think it's time I left, Lucan.'

'To go back to London?'

She shook her head. 'To my grandmother's cottage. I need to see her before I leave—assure her that all is well.' Even if it wasn't! 'I'll get a train back to London later today.'

'Being completely conversant with the train times, as you said.'

'Yes.'

Lucan nodded abruptly. 'I trust you'll forgive me if I don't stand on the platform and wave you a fond farewell…?'

Did hearts really break? Until that moment Lexie hadn't thought that they did. But if they didn't, then what was the wrenching pain in her chest just at the thought of never seeing Lucan again after today? Of knowing that he was somewhere in the world, hating her…?

She gave a shaky smile. 'I'll forgive you, Lucan.'

'I won't forgive *you*,' he came back gratingly.

Yes, hearts really did break, Lexie accepted desolately. In fact they shattered. 'Goodbye, Lucan.'

He stared at her with those cold, analytical eyes for several long seconds more, before turning on his heel and striding purposefully from the bedroom.

Lexie moved to once again sit down shakily on the side of the bed, burying her face in her hands as she at last let hot, scalding tears cascade down her cheeks.

It wasn't until much later—after Lexie had visited her grandmother and was sitting on the train taking her back to London—that she realised Lucan hadn't returned her locket and chain to her…

CHAPTER FOURTEEN

'LEXIE, I know it's late, but there's someone here to see you...'

'It's okay—Brenda, isn't it? I told you I can see myself in,' drawled a familiar—achingly familiar—voice, before Lexie had a chance to look up from the paperwork on her desk, which she had been trying to finish before leaving work for the evening.

But her head snapped up now, the colour draining from her face as she saw Lucan looming tall and dark behind Brenda where she stood protectively in the doorway. Devastatingly handsome Lucan, dressed in one of those dark tailored suits he favoured, with a snowy-white shirt beneath and a black wool overcoat that reached almost down to his ankles.

It had been five days since the two of them parted so ignominiously in Gloucestershire. Five long and painful days when Lexie had see-sawed between aching to see Lucan again and the certainty that seeing him would only make the heartache she was suffering even harder to bear.

Her gaze quickly returned to his face, searching those austerely handsome features for some sign of why Lucan was here now. That sculpted mouth was unsmiling, and those dark eyes returned her gaze unblinkingly, almost challengingly...

Lexie's eyes veered away from those penetrating depths and she smiled at her assistant instead. 'You get along home, Brenda,' she encouraged the other woman as she slowly stood up. 'Mr St Claire is probably here to discuss his account.' Although Lexie very much doubted that 'account' really described the invoice she had sent to the St Claire Corporation two days ago, on behalf of Premier Personnel.

She moved to stand in front of her desk once Brenda had left, after shooting her a sympathetic grimace, relieved that she looked businesslike today, in a black suit with a pale blue blouse beneath the jacket, her hair pulled back from her face and secured with a black clasp at her crown.

'Do you have a query on your account, Mr St Claire?' she prompted lightly.

Lucan strolled farther into the office. Lexie's nervousness increased as he softly closed the door behind him before turning slowly, his expression still totally unreadable. 'Unless I'm mistaken, the invoice submitted from Premier Personnel was for zero?'

Lexie leant back against her desk. 'That's correct.'

Even *thinking* of sending Lucan a bill for the two days she had supposedly worked for him had smacked of demanding payment for services rendered; Lexie felt bad enough already, without that. She certainly hadn't expected that the invoice would bring Lucan here in person. Had she…?

'Was there something else, Mr St Claire?'

Lucan walked towards her, once again reminding Lexie of that jungle cat stalking its prey. His steps were measured and somehow menacing, his dark and predatory gaze holding her captive. 'Why no charge, Lexie? You did work for me for two days, after all.'

'Not really.' She shook her head, her hands moving to

rest on the desk either side of her. She gripped the edge tightly, so that Lucan shouldn't see how badly her hands were shaking just at being near him again. 'I—I just thought it best.'

'For whom?'

'For all concerned.' Lexie grimaced.

'Hmm.' Lucan nodded slowly. 'Would you like to go out to dinner?'

Lexie's head snapped back as she eyed him warily. 'Go out to dinner…?' She moistened her lips nervously.

He gave a humourless smile. 'Let's not start repeating each other's words again, hmm?'

Lexie was too stunned by the invitation to be able to think of any coherent words of her own. It was traumatic enough that Lucan was here at all, without the complete shock of having him invite her to dinner. She swallowed hard. 'I'm not sure I understand.'

Lucan had known by Lexie's shocked expression when she first saw him, and the wariness in her eyes now, that his dinner invitation was the last thing she had been expecting. After the way they had parted five days ago, and his response to discovering she was Sian Thomas's granddaughter, it was probably a natural reaction.

Lexie looked very professional today, in a black suit, with the wild ebony of her hair pulled back from the paleness of her face. Very un-Lexie-like!

'I believe there are still some things the two of us need to discuss,' he bit out grimly.

Lexie watched him guardedly as he stood only inches away from her. 'And I thought we had agreed to disagree on the subject of my grandmother and your father?'

Lucan thrust his hands into the pockets of his overcoat to stop himself from giving in to the impulse he felt to remove the clip from Lexie's hair and so allow it to cascade wildly about her shoulders as it usually did. His fingers instead came into contact with the rectangular box at the bottom of the right-hand pocket. He removed the velvet-covered box, glancing down at it before holding it out to Lexie.

'You forgot this when you left...'

Her expression became even more wary, and she eyed the box as if it were a snake about to strike her a lethal blow.

'It's only your locket, Lexie,' Lucan drawled.

'Oh,' she breathed softly, and was very careful that her fingers shouldn't come into contact with his hand as she took the box from him to flip up the lid and look inside. 'You've had it repaired...' She looked up at him almost accusingly.

Lucan's mouth tightened. 'There seemed little point in not doing so once I knew of its contents.'

Little point at all, Lexie accepted as she gently ran a finger over the surface of her locket. The gold chain looped through it was now intact.

'Unless there was some other reason you didn't want me to have it repaired...?'

Her gaze flicked back up at Lucan. She was very aware of his close proximity. Of the tangy smell of his aftershave. The warmth of his body...

'I—No—no other reason,' she assured him huskily.

He nodded abruptly. 'According to my mother, the locket and necklace once belonged to my father's grandmother—a lady he was very fond of.'

Lexie bristled. 'If you're trying to say this is some sort of family heirloom and you want it returned—'

'I'm not,' Lucan dismissed impatiently. 'Why do you always assume the worst of me, Lexie?'

Lexie chose not to answer that particular question in

favour of asking a more pressing—shocking—one. 'You've shown my locket to your *mother*?'

He gave another inclination of his head. 'She believes my father must have loved you very much to have given you something that meant so much to him.'

Lexie had absolutely no doubt as to how much her Grandpa Alex had loved her. How much he had loved *all* his beloved Sian's family. 'You showed my locket to your mother?' she said again, incredulously.

Lucan gave a rueful smile. 'You're starting to repeat yourself now, Lexie. Or would you prefer I call you Alexandra?' He quirked dark brows.

'No, I would *not* prefer that you call me Alexandra!' she snapped, and moved determinedly away from the sensuous lethargy, the heated reaction Lucan's closeness was starting to have on her senses after she had felt cold for so long.

'Because it's what your family call you?'

Lexie dropped the closed velvet jewellery box into her handbag behind the desk before straightening to answer him suspiciously. 'How do you know what my family call me?'

Lucan shrugged. 'That's one of the things I would like to discuss with you over dinner.'

Lexie moved her head from side to side. 'I don't want to have dinner.'

'With me? Or at all?'

'At all!' She'd had absolutely no appetite since returning from Gloucestershire five days ago. In fact, the mere thought of food made her feel ill—to a degree that she had lost several pounds in weight over the past few days! 'I can't believe you took my necklace and showed it to your mother!' she muttered again.

'You seem a bit hung up on that fact.'

'Of course I'm "hung up" on it!' Lexie snapped. 'You

had no right to do that, Lucan,' she told him emotionally. 'No right at all.'

He gave a rueful grimace. 'Lexie, I took your advice after you left Mulberry Hall five days ago.'

'*My* advice?' she repeated incredulously. 'I'm pretty sure I didn't say anything that day about taking my locket and showing it to your mother!' All Lexie remembered about that day was her complete devastation at the realisation that she had fallen in love with this man.

Seeing Lucan again, being near him again, only served to show her how deeply she loved him. How much she wished that things could be different between them. That the two of them were free to have a relationship, even if it only lasted a matter of days or weeks.

Instead, Lexie had fallen in love with the one man who would never love her...

'No,' Lucan conceded dryly. 'But you did suggest that I talk to your grandmother,' he added softly.

Lexie's eyes widened as she stared across the desk at him. 'I— You—'

'I think perhaps you should sit down, Lexie—before you fall down!' Lucan drawled derisively.

Yes, she should perhaps sit down. No, not perhaps—she *had* to sit down, Lexie acknowledged as her legs began to tremble. She dropped weakly down into the chair behind the desk.

'You've spoken to my grandmother...?'

'At length,' Lucan confirmed softly. 'Want to change your mind about coming out to dinner with me...?' He lifted a mocking brow.

'This was a much better idea than going out and eating dinner in a restaurant,' Lucan approved huskily an hour or so later, as he and Lexie sat opposite each other at the breakfast bar in the kitchen of her apartment.

Their conversation had been put on hold while Lucan drove them there from the offices of Premier Personnel, stopping briefly to buy a selection of cheeses and fruits from a local delicatessen, along with a bottle of red wine, which Lucan had acquired from the off-licence next door.

In fact, the whole scenario of sitting in the kitchen, food spread out before them on the breakfast bar, reminded Lucan strongly of their last evening together at Mulberry Hall, when he and Lexie had eaten cheese and biscuits together before making love…

Especially so as Lexie looked more like herself now. She had disappeared to her bedroom as soon as they'd arrived, emerging ten minutes later having changed into a fitted cream woollen jumper and figure-hugging denims, and with her hair released in disarray about her shoulders.

She grimaced now. 'I'm sure you're no more eager than I am to make a scene in public.'

'A scene?' he repeated slowly. 'I'm hoping it won't come to that!'

'No doubt that's a case of hope springing eternal!' She took a sip of the red wine.

'Possibly,' Lucan allowed dryly. 'You need to eat something, Lexie, You're looking very pale.'

Her eyes flashed deeply blue as she glared across the breakfast bar at him. 'We've been very busy at the office.'

He frowned. 'I wasn't implying anything else…'

Lexie drew in a ragged breath, knowing she had over-reacted to a perfectly innocent observation; she *was* very pale, and she *did* need to eat. Except, more than ever, she had a feeling that food would choke her!

It wasn't helping her already frayed nerves that Lucan had taken off his overcoat and jacket while she was in her bedroom changing out of her work clothes. His tie had also been removed, and the top button of his shirt undone, revealing a tantalising glimpse of the dark hair on his muscle-rippling chest...

'Sorry.' Lexie gave another grimace. 'Things have just been a bit hectic the past few days, with both my parents away.' Despite her self-assurances to the contrary, when she had disappeared out of the office the previous week... 'I suppose that at least shows me you haven't felt compelled to damage the reputation of Premier Personnel after last week...' she added lamely.

Lucan's brows lowered over narrowed dark eyes. 'What happened between us is personal, Lexie, not business-related.'

'It's—good of you to say so.'

'But unexpected?' he guessed dryly.

'Maybe,' she answered guardedly.

'It really pains you to have to admit that I'm capable of doing anything decent, doesn't it?'

'Not at all,' Lexie protested. 'You have every right to want to make trouble for Premier Personnel after the way I behaved.'

Lucan regarded her quizzically. 'I seem to remember that you said Premier Personnel belongs to your parents, and I have absolutely no reason to wish them harm.'

Just her, Lexie accepted heavily.

She had behaved badly the previous week. Worse than badly. She had been totally stupid in going anywhere near the St Claire family. All Lexie had done was rake up a past that would have been better left alone.

'Thank you,' she said softly.

Lucan leant back on his bar chair to look across at her.

'You know, Lexie, I'm not sure I know what to do with all this self-flagellation!' He gave a rueful shake of his head. 'Where's the woman who told me she doesn't give a damn about anything I do or say? The woman who felt no hesitation in telling me exactly what she thought of me?'

Lexie gave a humourless smile. 'She grew up.'

'Pity,' he drawled.

Her eyes widened. 'You would rather I went back to being rude and outspoken?'

'Hell, yes,' Lucan assured her unhesitatingly. 'At least then I'd have an excuse to kiss you into silence.'

Lexie stared across at him, her lips frozen on a silent *oh* of surprise. Shock, actually. Was Lucan saying he *wanted* an excuse to kiss her...?

Her mouth had gone as dry as her lips felt. 'Do you need an excuse?'

'Not really,' he drawled. 'But it might be handy to use in my defence when you turn on me like a wildcat afterwards!'

Lexie gave a slow shake of her head. 'I don't understand...'

Lucan grimaced, knowing he had a lot of things he needed to tell Lexie before they could even begin to talk about a relationship—the possibility of a relationship—between the two of them. He was here now because he owed Lexie the truth. He had no reason to believe that Lexie would want anything else from him once he had given her that.

'No, I don't suppose you do.' He sighed, taking a sip of his own wine before continuing. 'From what I said to you earlier, you will have gathered that I've seen and talked with both your grandmother and my mother since we last spoke together.'

'Yes.' Lexie still eyed him warily.

Lucan nodded. 'What I haven't explained is that they have also seen and spoken to each other.'

She gasped. 'Nanna Sian and your mother?' Her hand shook slightly as she carefully replaced her wine glass on the breakfast bar.

Lucan smiled. 'My mother flew from Edinburgh to Gloucestershire with me yesterday.'

'In the family-owned helicopter?' she guessed.

'As it happens, yes.'

'Which you flew?'

'Again, yes... Is there a problem with that?' He frowned.

'Not at all,' Lexie assured him wryly; it only served as a reminder of the social and financial differences between the two of them, as well as the emotional ones. 'So, your mother is in Gloucestershire talking to my Nanna Sian now,' she said pointedly, still totally stunned at the idea of such a thing happening.

'*With* your Nanna Sian, not *to* her,' Lucan corrected.

'But why?' Lexie stood up again restlessly. 'What can the two of them possibly have to talk about after all these years?'

He shrugged. 'I only brought them together, Lexie. I think it's for the two of them to work out what they want to talk about.'

'But why would you do such a thing?' She groaned disbelievingly. 'You all *hate* my poor Nanna!' Her eyes flashed as she became angry. 'If your mother says or does one single thing to hurt her—'

'That's better,' Lucan said with satisfaction. He also stood up, instantly dwarfing Lexie's kitchen—and her. 'What else can I do or say that's going to anger or annoy you?'

'I'm already angry enough—*oof!*' Lexie's breath left

her in a whoosh as Lucan pulled her into his arms and her chest came into hard contact with his. 'Lucan, you—'

Any further protest was cut off as his head lowered and his mouth claimed hers.

Fiercely.

Hungrily.

Lucan continued to hold her, to kiss her, until Lexie stopped being so stunned, and then her arms moved slowly about his waist and she began to return those kisses with a hunger of her own. Deep, searing kisses that plundered the very heart of her.

Finally Lucan pulled back slightly to rest his forehead against hers. 'It isn't my intention, or my mother's, to hurt your Nanna Sian, Lexie,' he assured her gruffly. 'What I did—what I'm trying to do—is put things right after all these years. Sort the situation out enough so that some of the hurt, at least, goes away.'

'But why…?' she asked in a hushed voice.

Good question, Lucan acknowledged self-derisively. And not one that he felt he could answer just yet…

He reached up to grasp Lexie's arms and put her firmly away from him. 'We still have a few things of our own to sort out, Lexie. Firstly, I did not, as you seem to think, stop your grandmother from attending my father's funeral.'

'But—'

'It was your grandmother's decision, Lexie. Not mine. Made, she assures me, because she didn't want to cause any more hurt to my mother and the rest of Alexander's family.'

'But your mother wasn't at the funeral—'

'No, she wasn't. But your grandmother didn't know that,' he pointed out gently. 'It was also because she felt there had already been enough hurt caused because she and

Alexander loved each other that she consistently refused to marry my father when he asked her.'

'What?'

'It's true, Lexie,' he assured her softly. 'If you don't believe me, once we've finished talking you can telephone your grandmother and I'm sure she will confirm everything I'm going to say—okay?'

Lexie was starting to feel as if she were standing on a surface that kept moving beneath her feet. As if every preconceived idea she had ever had was being slowly, determinedly stripped away.

Could any of what Lucan was saying be true? He insisted that it was, knowing that Lexie could indeed telephone her grandmother at any time during this conversation...

'Okay.' Lexie nodded abruptly.

'Let's sit down and drink some more of our wine, Lexie,' Lucan suggested huskily as he pulled back the bar stool for her. 'I still have quite a bit more to say, and we might as well be comfortable,' he added when she paused uncertainly.

Her mouth felt slightly swollen from the force of Lucan's kisses, and her head was buzzing with the things he had already told her. 'Fine.' She sat back on the stool and watched him warily as he moved around the breakfast bar to sit opposite her. 'My grandmother refused to marry your father...?'

Lucan smiled slightly. 'Many, many times.'

'She told you that...?'

'Yes.'

'And you believe her?'

'Yes.'

Lexie picked up her wine glass and took a sip before speaking again. 'I'm more confused than ever...'

'Why she refused? Or why I believe her?' Lucan prompted.

'Both!'

His smile widened. 'Yep, she's still in there!'

She gave him a confused glance. 'Who's still in where?'

Lucan gave a slow shake of his head. 'We haven't got to that part of our conversation yet.'

Lexie scowled at him. 'You can be incredibly annoying at times, Lucan!'

'True,' he accepted with an unapologetic grin. 'Your grandmother told me a lot of other things that I never knew.' He sat forward. 'For instance, did you know that she and my father had known each other for years, loved each other for years, before he even met my mother?'

'That can't be true.' Lexie slowly shook her head. 'Nanna Sian had been married and was widowed. She had a daughter—my mother...'.

'The two of them knew each other before Sian married your natural grandfather, Lexie.'

Her eyes were wide. 'I—But how?'

Lucan grimaced. 'They grew up together on the Mulberry Hall estate. Alexander was the son and heir, your grandmother was the daughter of the cook. Needless to say, my own grandfather, the then Duke of Stourbridge, did not look favourably upon the relationship. To such a degree that he set about deliberately separating the two of them,' he added grimly.

Lexie had a terrible feeling she knew exactly where this was going...

'Alexander duly went off to university at Oxford, and within days of his leaving his father had the cook and her daughter relocated to a friend's estate in Norfolk,' Lucan continued darkly. 'Sian and Alexander had agreed that he would write to her as soon as he had a mailing address, and that the two of them would continue to write to each other until he came home at Christmas, when they would try once again to persuade his father into seeing how much in love they were.' Lucan gave a disgusted shake of his head. 'I believe you can guess what happened next?'

Lexie gave a pained frown. 'Alexander's letters to Sian were intercepted by the Duke as soon as they arrived at Mulberry Hall?'

A nerve pulsed in Lucan's clenched jaw. 'Intercepted and destroyed, rather than sent on to where Sian lived in Norfolk,' he confirmed harshly. 'As Sian's letters to Alexander, also care of Mulberry Hall, were duly intercepted and destroyed.'

'Resulting in Sian believing that Alexander had forgotten about her as soon as he was away at university,' Lexie realised heavily.

'Unbelievable, isn't it?' Lucan stood up again restlessly, his expression grim.

Lexie shook her head. 'We didn't have the same technology fifty years ago that we have today. No mobile phones. No email. Sian and Alexander's only means of communication were those letters.'

Lucan nodded tersely. 'Which neither of them received because of my grandfather's intervention. When Alexander came home for the Christmas holidays his father told him that the cook and her daughter had simply handed in their notice and left. That he had no idea where they had gone. That Alexander should just accept that as far as Sian was concerned the relationship was obviously over, and he should just forget about her and get on with his life.'

'It's all so unbelievable it can only be true!' Lexie said achingly.

'Yes.' Lucan drew in a harsh breath. 'Sian eventually married a local boy in Norfolk and had your mother, and my father finished university just in time to take over the running of the estate when his father died suddenly of a heart attack. Knowing what I do now, I'm not sure the old guy even had a heart to *be* attacked!' he added disgustedly as he began to restlessly pace the small confines of the kitchen.

'What he did was wicked and cruel.' Lexie nodded. 'But perhaps he thought he was acting for the best—'

'Your grandmother made the same excuse for him,' Lucan cut in wearily. 'When in reality it *was* just wicked and cruel, as well as totally dishonest,' he insisted firmly. 'But for his interference my father and Sian would have married each other—could have been together for years before they eventually were!'

'And then neither you, nor your two brothers, nor I, would ever have been born.'

The things Lucan had told her—even more of a Greek tragedy than Lexie could have imagined—were incredible. Incredible and so very sad. But, loving Lucan as she did, it was impossible for Lexie to imagine—selfishly—a world without the two of them in it...

'My grandfather deliberately ruined two young people's lives with his machinations.' He gave a disgusted shake of his head. 'Your grandmother has assured me that she was happy with your grandfather, and that she loved him. Not in the way she loved Alexander, but nevertheless she did love him. My father, on the other hand, threw all his energies into running the estate. He only married at all in the end because he needed to provide an heir for that estate. He was almost thirty and my mother only nineteen when they met and married each other. I've spoken to my mother about this, and she assures me it was always a fragile relationship at best—and one that was completely blown apart the moment my father saw Sian again at a weekend house party given by a mutual friend they hadn't even known they had.'

'They never had an affair, Lucan,' Lexie insisted firmly. 'Admittedly, the two of them realising they were still in love with each other all those years later was wrong, so very wrong, when Alexander was married. But I know that they weren't together again until after your father and mother were divorced.'

'I know that, too.'

She raised dark brows. 'Again from my grandmother?'

'Yes.'

She smiled. 'I'm sure you must have been something of a surprise to her! You look so much like Grandpa Alex,' she explained huskily when Lucan looked at her questioningly.

He nodded, his gaze suddenly darkly intense. 'Just as you look like your grandmother...'

Lexie felt the colour warm her cheeks. 'Strange, isn't it?'

'Not strange at all.' Lucan gave a slow shake of his head.

Lexie lowered her gaze, not sure what to say or do next now that Lucan had told her all these things. 'I still don't understand why, Lucan...'

'Why what?'

She frowned. 'Why you went to the trouble of speaking to my grandmother and your mother...'

Lucan looked at her quizzically. 'Do you believe in fate, Lexie?'

'In what context?' she prompted warily.

He gave a rueful smile. 'In the context that almost fifty

years after Alexander fell in love with Sian, against all the odds, against his better judgement, his eldest son has met and fallen in love with Sian's granddaughter...!'

CHAPTER FIFTEEN

LUCAN had no idea what he had expected—hoped—Lexie's reaction would be to his declaration of being in love with her.

Her complete and utter silence certainly wasn't it!

She stared up at him with those huge blue eyes, her expression one of shock more than anything else.

Lucan thrust his hands into his trouser pockets. 'Don't look so worried, Lexie,' he said wryly. 'I'm not expecting some grand announcement of your having fallen in love with me, too. I just… Because of my parents' divorce I didn't want to even believe in love—was determined never to feel the emotion for any woman. And then I met you.' His expression softened. 'From that very first morning I knew you were different.'

'You didn't like me…'

'Oh, I liked you,' he assured her huskily. 'I spent most of that morning imagining making love with you. On the desk. On the floor. Up against the wall.' He gave a shake of his head. 'It was totally out of character! And I was so damned jealous of the easy way you and Andrew Proctor laughed and joked together!' he recalled grimly.

'Really?' Lexie breathed softly.

'Oh, yes,' Lucan confirmed self-derisively. 'Gideon found it most amusing, watching me squirm!'

'Your brother *knew* you felt that way?'

'He guessed, yes. You challenged me, Lexie—drew me to you in a way I had never known before.' He grimaced. 'I knew, feeling that intensity of desire for you, that taking you to Mulberry Hall with me was a bad idea. I just couldn't seem to help myself. Being alone there with you was torturous. But at the same time I felt alive, experienced more emotions than I had ever allowed myself to feel before.'

'And you don't hate your father any more?'

'I'm not sure I ever hated him.' He sighed. 'I was disappointed in him. Felt hurt that he had left us. But, damn it, if he loved his Sian as much as I love you, then I can only feel sorry for the pain and misery he must have felt when he lost her! The joy he must have known when he found her again and they both realised what had happened in the past, that they still loved each other!' he added huskily. 'You asked why I had spoken to your grandmother, been to see my mother, why the two of them are at Mulberry Hall at this very moment coming to some sort of truce?'

Lexie swallowed hard before moistening stiff, barely moving lips. 'And why are they...?'

Lucan's smile was self-derisive. 'Because I didn't want there to be any barriers standing between the two of us while I attempt to persuade you into falling in love with me. Because I want to marry you. To that end, I'm going to haunt you, Lexie,' he told her intensely. 'I'm going to make sure there's no room for any misunderstandings between the two of us. Going to make such a nuisance of myself that you won't be able to turn around and not find me there!'

Lexie could never imagine Lucan's love being a nuisance to *any* woman. Certainly never to her!

Lucan loved her.

Lucan wanted to marry her.

'I don't— You—' Now she sounded like a gibbering

idiot. Probably because she felt like a gibbering idiot! Her heart had felt as if it were breaking these past five days, and now Lucan was offering her paradise.

Lucan's expression was concerned as he reached out and took both her hands in his. 'I *do* love you, Lexie. To distraction. But I don't want that to scare you—'

'I'm not scared, Lucan.' Her fingers tightened about his. 'I'm stunned. In awe. But I'm not scared,' she assured him emotionally.

'In awe?' he repeated uncertainly.

It was an uncertainty that Lexie couldn't bear a moment longer; the Lucan she loved was arrogant, self-assured, never uncertain!

'I already love you, Lucan,' she told him joyfully. 'I fell in love with you while we were at Mulberry Hall, too. Against all the odds. Against my better judgement.' She deliberately quoted his own words back at him. 'I *love* you, Lucan!' She glowed up at him.

Lucan felt as if he'd had all the breath knocked out of his lungs. As if he couldn't form a coherent thought in his head. All he could do was stare at Lexie in wonder. In total, absolute wonder that this beautiful woman, the woman he loved and adored, had just said that she loved him, too.

She smiled up at him teasingly. 'I never thought I would see the day!'

'What day?' Lucan managed to breathe shakily.

'When I would succeed in rendering the arrogantly self-assured Lucan St Claire speechless!' she came back cheekily. 'Tell me—is this going to happen every time I tell you I love you?'

She was back. The outspoken little minx that Lucan had fallen head over heels in love with was most definitely back!

'No,' he growled huskily as he took her firmly in his

arms. '*This* is what's going to happen every time you tell me you love me!'

He lowered his head and his mouth captured hers as he proceeded to show Lexie exactly how much he loved her. How much he would *always* love her.

One month later

'Why are you smiling in that cat-that-got-the-cream way?' Lexie prompted Lucan suspiciously as he chuckled softly.

It was their wedding day. A day when both of their families had gathered together at Mulberry Hall to celebrate their love for each other. A day Lexie had been longing for since the moment Lucan had told her he loved her as much as she loved him.

Lucan grinned down at her as the two of them danced together at their wedding reception in the ballroom at Mulberry Hall. He was so much more relaxed now than the cold and unemotional man Lexie had met five weeks ago. The love he felt for her shone unabashedly in the dark glow of his eyes.

He shook his head. 'Gideon has been secretly laughing at me for the last five weeks because of how much I love you, and I was just savouring the moment—because, looking at his face, I believe he has just learned the joke's now on him!'

Lexie glanced across to where her new brother-in-law stood in the corner of the room, glowering accusingly at Lucan. 'What have you done, Lucan?' She looked up at her husband reprovingly.

'Never mind what I've done.' Lucan tapped her playfully on the nose. 'Just concentrate on what the two of us are going to be doing later.' He grinned down at her wolfishly.

Lexie felt herself melt inside at the heat of desire she could clearly see glowing in his eyes. 'You've become a very wicked man, Lucan St Claire,' she murmured indulgently.

'My Duchess has had a very bad influence on me,' he came back throatily.

His Duchess.

Lexie was now, incredibly, the Duchess of Stourbridge.

But most important of all, she was the woman Lucan loved to distraction.

And he was the man Lexie loved with all her heart.

It was a deep love for each other that she had absolutely no doubt would endure and last for a lifetime.

Taming the Last St Claire

CAROLE MORTIMER

CHAPTER ONE

'SO, ARE you going to stand there all morning looking down your superior nose at me, or are you going to do something useful and offer to carry one of these boxes up in the lift for me?'

Gideon closed his eyes. Counted to ten. Slowly. Breathed in. And then out again. Even more slowly. Before once again opening his eyes.

No, Joey McKinley was still there. In fact she had straightened from bending over the boot of her car, parked two bays down from Gideon's own in this private underground car park, and was now peremptorily tapping the sole of one three-inch stiletto-heeled shoe against the concrete floor. He knew this woman would become the bane of his existence for the next four weeks, if this situation was allowed to continue.

Joey McKinley. Twenty-eight years old, five foot four inches tall, with short, silky red hair that somehow wisped up and away from the heart-shaped beauty of her face, challenging jade-green eyes, and a creamily smooth complexion with a soft sprinkling of freckles across the bridge of her tiny nose, her lips full and sensual. The leanness of her obviously physically fit body was shown to advantage in a smart black tailored business suit and a silk blouse the same jade-green colour as her eyes.

'Well?' his own personal nemesis challenged, that impatient tapping of her shoe against the concrete floor increasing as she looked across at him with auburn brows arched over those mocking green eyes.

Gideon drew in another deep and steadying breath as he considered the numerous ways in which he might cause his older brother Lucan pain for having placed him in this untenable position in the first place. Not enough to do any serious damage, of course. But a *little* pain? Gideon felt no qualms whatsoever about that. Lucan obviously felt a similar lack of concern about Gideon's welfare, having inflicted this woman on him without a second's consideration.

It was something Gideon had been contemplating for the last thirty-six hours, in fact. Ever since Lucan had informed him, at his wedding reception on Saturday evening, that when Gideon took over as temporary chairman of the St Claire Corporation for the month that he and Lexie were away on their honeymoon, he had arranged for Joey McKinley to take Gideon's place as the company's legal representative.

Gideon's assurances that he was perfectly capable of fulfilling both roles had made absolutely no impact on his older brother. He'd also ignored Gideon when he'd confessed he had his doubts that he and Joey McKinley could work together.

Gideon respected the woman as a lawyer, having heard only positive comments from other colleagues concerning her ability in a courtroom, but on every other level she succeeded in making his hackles rise.

That red hair was like a shining beacon in any room she happened to be in, and she had a husky and sensual laugh that, when released, had every male head in the vicinity turning in her direction. She had been wearing a dress the last two times Gideon had met her—firstly, an ankle-length sheath of a maid of honour gown in a deep jade colour at her sister Stephanie and his brother Jordan's wedding, almost two months ago, and a red knee-length dress at Lucan and Lexie's wedding on Saturday. The latter should have clashed with the bright copper cap of her hair, but instead it had just seemed to emphasise the natural gold and cinnamon highlights running through those strands.

The black business suit she was wearing today should have looked crisp and professional, but somehow…didn't. The jacket was short and figure-hugging, and the top three buttons left unfastened on the green silk blouse she wore beneath enabled him to see the tops of full and creamy breasts. The fitted knee-length skirt showed off an expanse of her shapely legs.

In other words, Joey McKinley was—

'You know, I've seen paint dry quicker than you appear to be able to make up your mind!' she called out.

—a veritable thorn in his side!

He drew in another controlling breath in an effort to force the tension from his body. 'Do you always have to be this abrasive?' Silly question; he knew her well enough by now to know that she always said exactly what happened to be on her mind at the time. Something that Gideon, a man who always measured his words carefully before speaking, found disturbing to say the least.

Her next comment was a prime example of that bluntness. 'Maybe I wouldn't feel the need if you occasionally took that I'm-so-superior stick out of your backside and joined the rest of us mortals in the real world.'

Gideon winced. The two of them had met—what?—four times in total. Most recently two days ago, at Lucan and Lexie's wedding, and before that nine weeks ago, when he'd first met her in her office at Pickard, Pickard and Wright, after he had gone to inform her he had managed to extricate her twin sister Stephanie from an awkward legal situation. Two weeks after that he'd met her at the wedding rehearsal of his twin brother Jordan and Stephanie, and then he'd seen her again at their wedding a week later.

Gideon frowned now as he remembered his absolute astonishment during Jordan and Stephanie's marriage ceremony. Everything had gone so smoothly in the lead-up to the wedding, and Gideon, as his brother's best man, had ensured that he and Jordan arrived at the church in plenty of time. Gideon had even felt a lump of emotion in his own throat, on his twin's behalf, when the two of them had turned to see how beautiful Stephanie looked as she walked down the aisle. Until, that was, Gideon had caught the look of derision in Joey's gaze as she'd glanced at him from where she followed just behind her twin.

Not that this was anything unusual; the two of them seemed to have taken an instant dislike to each other the very first time they'd met. No, the reason for Gideon's astonishment had come later in the ceremony, when everyone had sat down while Jordan and Stephanie and their two witnesses signed the register, and he'd heard an angel singing.

A single, unaccompanied voice had soared majestically to the heavens, filling the church to the rafters, as sweet and clear as the perfect, melodic chiming of a bell.

He had never before heard anything so beautiful as that voice—so clear and plaintive it had been almost magical as it claimed his emotions. He had felt so dazed, his senses so completely captivated by the pure and haunting beauty of that voice, that it had taken him a minute or so to realise that all the wedding guests were looking towards the right side of the church—which was when Gideon had realised that the singing 'angel' was none other than Joey McKinley!

* * *

Joey had no idea why it was that Gideon St Claire brought
out the very worst in her—to the extent that she enjoyed
nothing more than deliberately baiting him out of what
she considered his arrogant complacency. Maybe it really
was that superior attitude of his that bugged her. Or the
fact that, with his icy reserve firmly clamped in place, he
was always so emotionally unresponsive. Everything about
him was restrained, from the short style of his wonderful
gold-coloured hair, the tailored dark suits he wore—always
over a white shirt and matched with a discreetly subdued
silk tie—to the expensive but unremarkable metallic-grey
saloon car he drove. If Joey had been as rich as the St Claire
family was reputed to be then she would have driven a
sporty red Ferrari at the very least!

Or her resentment *could* just stem from the fact that a
couple of months ago Gideon St Claire had stepped in, with
his highly polished size eleven handmade leather shoes,
and sorted out a delicate and personal legal matter for her
sister, which Joey had been trying—unsuccessfully—to
settle for weeks.

It certainly couldn't have anything to do with the fact
that, putting the icy reserve apart, the man was as handsome as sin but gave every impression he hadn't so much
as noticed Joey was a female, let alone a passably attractive
one!

His hair—cut too short for her liking—was the colour
and texture of spun gold, and styled over his ears and brow.
His eyes were a dark and piercing brown, set in a ruggedly
handsome face, and as if that wasn't enough, nature had
bestowed upon him high cheekbones, sensually chiselled
lips, and an arrogantly square jaw.

Having studied him from beneath lowered lashes at
their second meeting—she had been too overwhelmed by
both his legal reputation and his considerable arrogance

the first time they met in her office!—Joey had no doubt, just from the predatory way that he moved, that the body beneath those dark tailored suits and white silk shirts was powerfully lean and muscled.

Wheat-gold hair, chocolate-brown eyes, broodingly sensual features that any male model would kill for, and a body that was all hard masculine contours meant that Gideon St Claire was seriously hot—with a capital H. A description that, if he were to hear it, would no doubt offend all his icily reserved sensibilities!

Taking all that smouldering sensuality into consideration, Joey had been intrigued by the fact that he hadn't brought a woman with him to the weddings of his brothers. That coupled with the fact that Gideon didn't even seem to register her as a female, had eventually made Joey ask her sister whether Gideon maybe preferred men to women. She had assumed Stephanie's answer to be a resounding *no* after it had taken her sister almost five minutes to stop laughing hysterically.

So, Mr Arrogantly Reserved and Broodingly Sensual obviously liked women—just not Joey!

Well, that was fine with her—Gideon St Claire might be one of the most disturbingly attractive men Joey had ever met, but the lack of interest he always showed in her only succeeded in making her feel defensive, and more often than not she deliberately set out to shock him.

'Are you suffering from laryngitis, or are you just not a morning person?' The bright cheerfulness with which Joey spoke showed neither of those two things applied to her.

'Perhaps if you were to stop talking long enough to allow me to answer you?' He spoke tersely, yet even the low and gravelly tenor of his voice was sexy, she thought with a mental sigh. He made no move to close the short distance between their two parked cars. 'Miss McKinley—'

'Joey.'

His nostrils flared with obvious distaste. 'Would you object if I were to call you Josephine?'

'Not at all—as long as you don't mind me reacting the same way I did the last time someone tried to do that,' she came back breezily. 'He ended up with a black eye,' she supplied with a smile as Gideon raised questioning blond brows.

One of those brows remained raised. 'You don't like the name Josephine?'

'Obviously not.'

This was not going well, Gideon accepted heavily. He had come to the conclusion, during the hours since Lucan had spoken to him on Saturday evening, that the only solution to this problem was for him to talk to Joey and calmly and logically explain why he didn't feel they could work together, before waving her a cheery goodbye and getting on with his role of acting chairman of the St Claire Corporation. For heaven's sake, she must be as aware as he was of their different approaches to—well, *everything*!

A reasonable and well thought out plan, he had believed at the time. Until he had actually been faced with the abrasively outspoken woman in person. Just these few minutes of conversation with her was enough to show him that his conclusion had been entirely correct. However, he'd also swiftly realised that any suggestion on his part that she might care to rethink agreeing to work with him for a month would probably only result in the contrary Joey McKinley doing the exact opposite.

For once in Gideon's well-ordered life he had no idea what to do or say to best achieve his objective. He just knew he couldn't tolerate working in close proximity with this forthright young woman for four weeks and stay sane!

Even if she did have the singing voice of an angel…

The fact that Lucan had announced he was taking a whole month off for his honeymoon, during which he intended to be completely incommunicado except for absolute emergencies, was extraordinary in itself.

Not that Gideon should have been surprised—both his brothers had been behaving in a completely unpredictable manner since they had met and as quickly married the two women they had fallen in love with. It wasn't that he didn't like both Stephanie and Lexie—he did. It was the change in his two brothers that he found…unsettling.

Jordan, an A-list actor who had enjoyed any number of relationships with beautiful actresses and models during the past ten years, had surprisingly fallen in love with his physiotherapist two months ago, and showed every appearance of continuing to be totally besotted with Stephanie now the two of them were married. To the extent that the filming of his current movie was completely scheduled around the hours Stephanie worked at the clinic she had opened since moving to LA.

And until Lucan had met and fallen in love with Lexie he had never taken more than a few days away from the company he had built up into one of the most diverse and successful in the world. In fact, *driven* was the word Gideon would most have associated with his older brother until the advent of Lexie into his life only a few short weeks ago.

It was a word that could have been associated with all three of the St Claire brothers since they'd reached adulthood and entered their chosen professions: Gideon in law, Jordan in acting, Lucan in the world of business.

All of that had changed in the past two months, and as a man who preferred order and continuity Gideon was still trying to come to terms with it. Something he wasn't likely to do with the annoying Joey McKinley haunting his every working moment!

'Very well, then. Joey it is.' He gave an almost imperceptible sigh. 'I'm sure that Pickard, Pickard and Wright—Jason Pickard, in particular—was sorry to see you go.'

'See me go where, exactly?'

Gideon eyed her impatiently. Really, nothing he had heard about this woman had ever given him reason to question her intelligence. '*Here*, of course.'

Joey looked taken aback. 'I'm sorry, but you'll have to explain what you mean. Especially the "Jason Pickard, in particular" remark,' she added coolly.

Gideon wasn't enjoying having this personal conversation in the middle of a private car park, of all places, where any of the other company employees might arrive at any moment. Admittedly it was only a little after eight o'clock in the morning, and most St Claire Corporation employees didn't arrive until nearly nine o'clock, but it would be most unprofessional for anyone to arrive early and see the acting chairman at loggerheads with an unknown woman in the car park.

Gideon closed the distance between them in three long strides, to stand only feet away from Joey, and instantly became uncomfortably aware of the light but heady perfume she wore. The choice of perfume was a surprise; Gideon would have thought, with her forceful personality, that she would wear one of those I'm-here-notice-me perfumes. The type of perfume that tended to give Gideon a headache the moment he inhaled. Instead, it was a delicate, subtly sensuous scent that made him react in an immediate way he intended to ignore.

His mouth thinned. 'I was merely trying to express my sympathy at how unreasonable it was of Lucan to ask you to give up your place at Pickard, Pickard and Wright in order to work here for only four weeks.'

Joey found herself momentarily distracted as she watched Gideon move, with the lean and predatory grace of a jungle cat.

Once again she considered it a perfect waste of a gorgeous man that he was as tightly buttoned down as the points on the collar of his pristine white shirt. A little effort on Gideon's part—and fewer disapproving looks!—and the man wouldn't only be arrogantly handsome but also totally devastating to any female with a pulse and a heartbeat.

If he would just grow his hair a little longer he would look younger, and also rakishly sexy. Ditto as regards those conservative tailored suits he always wore. Put him in a pair of faded jeans and a figure-hugging black T-shirt, to show off his muscled chest and arms, and any woman with red blood in her veins was likely to have an orgasm just looking at him!

Joey smiled wickedly to herself, imagining the look of horror that would no doubt come over his arrogantly handsome face if he were even to *guess* at the inappropriateness of the thoughts she was having about him.

'Do you find something amusing?'

It *was* amusing to imagine a more relaxed and sexy Gideon St Claire, as he attempted to fend off the attentions of all those panting women! But it was not so funny that Joey was actually aware of how much more dangerously attractive this man could be if he would just lighten up a little…

She gave herself a mental shake as she looked up into that darkly disapproving face; this man really wasn't her type. She preferred men with the daring and energy to try anything new; Gideon gave the impression that the last new thing he had tried was wearing black socks instead of grey!

She drew in a deep breath. 'Oh, but I haven't given up my place at Pickard, Pickard and Wright; the senior partners were only too happy to give me a month's leave of absence so I can help Lucan out.'

Something, Gideon realised with rising impatience, that must have taken some time to arrange. 'Exactly *when* did Lucan make all these arrangements?'

'Three weeks ago—' Joey broke off to look up at him with narrowed, assessing eyes. 'When did Lucan break the bad news to *you*?'

Gideon stiffened. 'I don't remember saying I regard it as bad news.'

'You implied it,' she dismissed shortly. 'So—when?'

His jaw tightened. 'I really don't see—'

'He only told you at the wedding on Saturday, didn't he?' she realised slowly.

Gideon had absolutely no idea why it was he always felt less in control of the situation around this particular woman. During his years in a courtroom he knew he'd acquired a reputation for being formidable. Now, as a corporate lawyer for Lucan's vast companies worldwide, he knew he was regarded as being no less ruthless than his older brother. And yet just having a conversation with the unpredictable Joey McKinley was enough to set his teeth on edge. To set the *whole* of him on edge, in fact...

'He did, didn't he?' Joey said with satisfaction, those green eyes now openly laughing at him. 'It probably totally ruined the rest of your weekend, too!'

Gideon's fingers tightened about the handle of his black briefcase. 'My weekend was perfectly enjoyable, thank you,' he lied stiffly. 'In fact I had lunch with Stephanie and Jordan yesterday, as they are flying back to LA early today.'

'And I had breakfast with them this morning, before driving them to the airport, and neither of them mentioned you'd asked for my telephone number. Which I'd have thought you *would* have done if you had wanted to have this conversation with me earlier.' Joey McKinley gave a taunting shake of her head.

It *had* crossed Gideon's mind, in fact, to ask Stephanie for her sister's private telephone number, but on consideration he had decided not to involve either of their families in what was, after all, a private clash of personalities.

'Or maybe you just didn't want either of them to jump to the wrong conclusions?'

He scowled his displeasure. 'I beg your pardon?'

'By you asking for my home telephone number. I'm sure you wouldn't have wanted to give Steph and Jordan the impression that you have a personal interest in me,' she answered mockingly.

Gideon drew in yet another deep, controlling breath—a futile exercise, he thought wryly. He couldn't remember feeling as rattled as this in a long time. 'I believe that's very unlikely.'

'You do?'

Was it his imagination, or was Joey suddenly standing closer than she had been a few seconds ago? So close that Gideon could actually see the full swell of her breasts and the top of the lacy cup of her bra, and the pulse beating smoothly, enticingly, at the base of her throat.

Dear Lord…

His gaze turned to ice. 'Surely you recognise just from this conversation that we can't possibly work together?'

She was suddenly all business again as she straightened. 'My arrangement is with Lucan, Gideon—not you. And I make a point of never letting people down once I've agreed to do something. A character trait I believe you share?'

It appeared that Joey was as aware of parts of Gideon's nature as he was of hers! 'I'm sure that Pickard, Pickard and Wright are more in need of your professional skills than I am,' he pointed out smoothly.

'On the contrary, they were only too happy to accommodate Lucan's request,' she assured him.

Of course they were, he thought derisively. No doubt Pickard, Pickard and Wright were perfectly aware of the prestige of allowing one of their associates to work at the St Claire Corporation for a month. Being asked for personally by a man of Lucan St Claire's standing in the business world wouldn't do Joey McKinley's career any harm, either.

'So, Gideon, Lucan's happy with the arrangement, Pickard, Pickard and Wright are happy with the arrangement and I'm happy with the arrangement—it appears *you're* the only one who isn't.' She looked him straight in the eye—an obvious challenge.

Gideon coldly returned that gaze. 'I don't recall saying I was unhappy with it.'

'No?'

'No.'

'Then that little problem appears to have been settled to everyone's satisfaction, doesn't it,' she dismissed lightly.

Like hell it was! As far as Gideon was concerned, having Joey in the St Claire building for the next four weeks was totally unacceptable.

She cut into his dire thoughts with another equally unwelcome sally. 'Perhaps now you would care to explain exactly what you meant when you commented that "Jason Pickard, in particular" would have been sorry to see me go?'

Gideon realised she wasn't being deliberately provocative

any more. Her emotions were now much more subtle. On the surface she sounded pleasantly interested, but he recognised the anger burning beneath that supposedly calm surface; it was there in the sparkling green of her eyes and the flush to those creamy cheeks. Although why she should feel that way Gideon had no idea; everyone in the close-knit law community knew that she had been involved with the junior Pickard for the past six months.

He shrugged broad shoulders. 'It's public knowledge that the two of you are friends.'

'That's exactly what we are—*friends*,' she stated evenly. 'Nothing more, nothing less.'

'I apologise if I've stepped on your personal toes.'

'I've just told you that you haven't,' she said.

Gideon's mouth thinned. 'I'm not prepared to get into an argument with you over a perfectly innocent remark which I have already apologised for.'

'Does anyone ever dare to argue with you, Gideon?' Joey McKinley eyed him with obvious frustration.

'Obviously,' he drawled, looking at her pointedly.

'This isn't an argument, Gideon, it's a dialogue,' she snapped.

He shook his head. 'I really don't have time for this, so if you wouldn't mind—'

'But I *do* mind, Gideon.' She was suddenly standing much too close to him again as she interrupted him ruthlessly. So close that he could feel the warmth of her breath against his jaw as the three-inch stiletto heels on her shoes brought the top of her head to his eye level.

Gideon dearly wished he had never started this conversation. That he had just picked up one of the boxes from the boot of this woman's bright red Mini and travelled up in the lift with her, before shutting himself away for the day in Lucan's office.

He was thirty-four years old, successful in his chosen career, and the brief and businesslike affairs he occasionally indulged in rarely even registered on the scale of his emotions. Other than the affection Gideon felt for his two brothers and his mother, he preferred to keep a physical and emotional distance from the rest of humanity.

It was difficult to do that around the forceful Joey McKinley. Especially when she was now so close to him that he could smell the lemon of her shampoo, and see the auburn, gold and cinnamon highlights in that glossy red hair. An unusual colour that Gideon knew didn't come out of a bottle, because her twin sister had hair with exactly the same beautiful autumn shades.

What would that hair feel like to touch? As soft and silky as it looked? Or as brittle and defensive as the woman herself—

Gideon took an abrupt step back, shutting down his thoughts as he realised what he was doing, his jaw tight as he looked down the length of his nose at her. 'Joey, I appreciate the fact that your sister being married to my brother puts us in the position of being almost related.' *Almost* being the operative word! 'But let me state here and now that I have absolutely no interest in knowing anything about your sex life.'

Joey's eyed widened at the vehemence she heard in Gideon's tone. She had no doubt that he genuinely respected and liked her sister, and that he approved of Stephanie's marriage to his brother. So why had he decided he disliked Joey from their very first meeting?

Maybe he had disliked and disapproved of her *before* that first meeting, if his assumptions about her friendship with Jason Pickard were any indication, she mused. She was well aware of the rumours that had circulated about her and the junior partner at Pickard, Pickard and Wright for the past six months. Erroneous rumours, as it happened.

Oh, Jason was incredibly handsome, and the two of them went out to dinner at least once a week. Joey always enjoyed herself on those evenings as she found Jason good company. But their friendship wasn't based on either sexual attraction or love.

In actual fact their friendship had become more in the nature of a smokescreen, because Jason was really in love with a man he had met at university and had shared an apartment with for the past ten years. Unfortunately his parents, Pickard Senior and Gloria, had no idea that their son's relationship with the other man was anything more than friendship, and would have vehemently disapproved if they did.

Joey had been thrilled the first time Jason had asked her out—after all, he was the second Pickard in Pickard, Pickard and Wright. But it hadn't taken her long to realise that Jason wasn't in the least sexually interested in her. With her usual straightforwardness she had asked a couple of blunt questions, and eventually received a couple of straight answers. The revelation about Jason's sexuality hadn't changed anything as far as Joey was concerned; she liked him and enjoyed his company. Enough to agree to go out to dinner with him often—and why not, when there was very little happening in her own love life at the moment! And so the myth of their having a relationship had been born, a myth, it seemed, that even the coldly aloof Gideon St Claire was aware of...

Joey gave him a cool smile. 'Then why are we still standing here discussing my sex life?'

'You—' Gideon broke off in obvious frustration, choosing instead to exercise rigid self-control. 'Shall we just take your things upstairs and get to work?' He moved to pick up one of the boxes from the boot of her car before walking stiffly over to the private lift.

Joey picked up the other box and then closed the boot and locked her car, a smile of satisfaction curving her lips as she followed him.

The next four weeks—if they entailed shaking Gideon St Claire out of his aloof complacency—promised to be a lot of fun. For her, if not for himself...

CHAPTER TWO

'WHERE are you going?' Gideon questioned sharply as he turned and saw that, instead of following him down the hallway to his own office, Joey had stopped outside the office usually reserved for Lucan's PA. It wasn't currently occupied, because Lexie had become Lucan's PA three weeks ago, and the two of them were now happily honeymooning together on a private Caribbean island for a month.

Mocking green eyes met his. 'I believe it was an attempt at diplomacy on Lucan's part when he suggested I might like to use Lexie's vacant office rather than your own.'

After the bombshell Lucan had dropped on Gideon at the wedding reception on Saturday evening, he didn't have too much faith in his older brother's 'diplomacy'!

'And how did you *know* that particular office was Lexie's?'

'You mean apart from the fact her name is printed on the door?'

Gideon scowled darkly at Joey's obvious sarcasm. 'Apart from that, yes,' he gritted out.

She shrugged slender shoulders. 'I came over on Thursday afternoon, so that Lucan could explain exactly what it is he wants me to do while he and Lexie are away.'

Thursday afternoon. The one afternoon in the week

when Gideon didn't work at the St Claire Corporation but instead went to the small office he kept across town and dealt with private legal matters needing his attention. A fact that Lucan would have been well aware of, damn him.

Maybe Gideon had been overly generous concerning that 'little' amount of pain he had considered inflicting on his older brother the next time he saw him!

'And exactly what *is* it he wants you to do here while he and Lexie are away?' Besides be a damned nuisance to him, of course!

Joey shrugged. 'Well, Lucan seemed to have a pretty good idea that you aren't going to release too much of the legal side of things to me.' Those jade-green eyes danced knowingly. 'But obviously I'll be only too happy to take up the slack. There's also the fact that with Lexie away too you're without a PA.'

'My own secretary—'

'Is now *my* secretary,' she reminded him pertly.

Damn it, this situation was just getting worse—made even more so by the fact that he suspected Lucan and Lexie were sitting on their private Caribbean island right now having a really good laugh at his expense. Falling in love hadn't just made his older brother unpredictable; it had also brought out a distinctly warped sense of humour in him!

'If you would prefer, I can use your office rather than this one,' Joey said as she once again tapped the toe of one stiletto-heeled shoe to mark her impatience. 'Could you make your mind up soon, Gideon; this box is getting heavy!'

His mouth pursed with frustration. He had always thought of the office down the hallway as being his own personal space: all wood-panelled walls, floor to ceiling bookshelves containing his reference books on English and foreign law, all in alphabetical order. And the top of his mahogany desk was always completely cleared at the end of each working day, with none of the personal clutter that so many people seemed to surround themselves with during working hours.

The two bursting boxes they had carried upstairs seemed to imply Joey intended surrounding herself with exactly that sort of reprehensible clutter for the next four weeks, he mused. No, he *didn't* relish the idea of having his office personalised by this woman. But knowing that Joey McKinley's disturbing presence was in the office next door to the one he intended using would be just as unacceptable—

'Too late,' Joey announced decisively, and she lowered the door handle to Lexie's office with her elbow before breezing inside. 'Very nice,' she could be heard murmuring appreciatively.

Gideon reluctantly followed her into the office Lucan had decorated before Lexie became his permanent PA three weeks ago, seeing again that the desk of mellow pine, the cream walls and gold-coloured carpet were all a perfect foil for Lexie's long black hair.

But he couldn't help noticing against his will that they were equally complementary to Joey's rich auburn-gold-cinnamon-red hair and jade green eyes...

'What on earth do you have in here—rocks?' Gideon muttered bad-temperedly as he crossed the room to drop the box he was carrying down onto the desktop beside Joey's own.

Not a happy bunny, she recognised ruefully as she saw his dark scowl. Not a bunny at all, actually. No, as Gideon began to prowl restlessly about the office he looked more like the predator Joey had likened him to earlier...

'Not quite,' she answered, as she flipped up the lid of one

of the boxes to start taking out the objects and unwrapping them from protective newspaper.

The usual predictable clutter, Gideon recognised. Her law degree. A couple of framed photographs—one of her parents, the other of Stephanie and Jordan at their wedding. A paperweight with a perfect yellow rose inside. A golden dragon.

Hold on a minute—*a golden dragon*?

'Yes?' Joey continued to hold the small golden ornament almost defensively in the palm of her hand as she turned to look at him.

It was Gideon's first indication that he had actually made an exclamation out loud. But, damn it, a *dragon*! Even one as romantically beautiful as this—with the creature's scaled body beautifully etched in gold, its wings extended as if it were about to take flight, and two small yellow sapphires set in the fierceness of its face for eyes—didn't quite fit in with the abrasive image he had formed of this woman.

Any more than that angelic singing voice, he suddenly recalled.

Joey looked across at him and frowned; really, you would think from his disgusted expression that she had just produced a semi-automatic rifle and intended mounting it on the wall!

'Stephanie had this made for me when I got my law degree.'

Her twin had always known that the dragon meant something to Joey. A golden dragon had been a feature in Joey's dreams since she was seven years old. Whenever she'd had a problem—difficulties at school, or with friends—and when she and Stephanie were ten and had been involved in the car accident that had left her twin unable to walk for two years, Joey had dreamt of her golden dragon and instantly felt reassured that everything would work out.

Consequently, where she went, this dragon went too.

She placed it firmly in the centre of the empty desk. 'It has great sentimental value.'

'If Stephanie gave it to you, then I'm sure it does.' Gideon acknowledged softly.

Joey looked up at him, looking for this man's usual cold distance whenever he spoke to her. Instead she sensed almost an affinity... 'Do you miss Jordan?'

Gideon looked taken aback by the question. 'There's hardly been time for that when he only left this morning.'

'I meant before that, of course,' Joey said impatiently. 'He's been in LA how long now?'

He frowned. 'Ten years.'

Stephanie had only been gone for two months, but Joey was still deeply aware of the void her twin had left in her own life. 'Did you miss him when he first left?'

'You're still missing Stephanie?'

'There's no need to sound so surprised, Gideon,' she said ruefully.

Gideon *was* surprised, and yet he knew he shouldn't have been. Just because Joey appeared to enjoy mocking him at every opportunity, there was absolutely no reason for him to assume she didn't have the same deep emotional connection to her own twin that he had with Jordan.

'Yes, I missed Jordan very much when he first went to LA,' he acknowledged gruffly. 'It does get easier,' he added.

The two of them stared across the office at each other for several long minutes. As if each recognised something in the other that they hadn't been aware of before. A softness. A chink in their armour. A vulnerability...

Whilst Gideon found this insight into Joey's emotions faintly disturbing, he found it even more so in himself;

revealing vulnerability of any kind was not something Gideon did. *Ever.*

'The dragon is very beautiful,' he said, in a swift change of subject. 'But personally I prefer to believe in the things I can see and touch,' he added.

'Maybe that's your problem,' Joey said as she turned away to continue unpacking the contents of the box.

Gideon's jaw tightened. 'I wasn't aware that I *had* a problem.'

Joey raised auburn brows as she sat on the edge of the desk behind her, her pencil-slim skirt hitching up slightly as she did so, exposing more of her shapely legs. 'You don't see the fact that you have absolutely no imagination as being a problem?'

Gideon ignored that bare expanse of skin and kept his gaze firmly fixed on her beautiful heart-shaped face. 'I have always found basing my opinions on cold, hard reality to be the better option.'

'Don't you mean the boring, unimaginative option?' she taunted.

'I believe I know myself well enough to know exactly what I mean, Joey.' He glared down at her.

Joey had regretted telling him how much she still missed Stephanie almost as soon as she had started the conversation. But she had been surprised when Gideon admitted missing his own twin just as much.

He gave every impression of being self-contained. A cold and unsentimental man. To imagine him feeling the same ache of loneliness for his own twin as she felt for Stephanie suddenly made him seem all too human.

But perhaps he felt the same about her? The thought suddenly seemed much too intimate. 'There's no need to get your boxers in a twist, Gideon,' she murmured, being deliberately provocative to hide her uneasiness.

'My boxers?' Gideon's nostrils flared in distaste.

'That's always supposing you *wear* boxers, of course,' Joey continued outrageously. 'Yet I somehow can't see you going commando—'

'I would prefer that we not discuss my underwear, or lack of it, if you don't mind,' he bit out with an incredulous shake of his head. 'You really are the most irritating woman I have ever met.'

'Really?' Joey smiled appreciatively.

Gideon eyed her in exasperation. 'It wasn't meant as a compliment!'

'I didn't think for one moment that it was,' she said dryly. 'But can I help it if I feel honoured that the coolly aloof Gideon St Claire has lowered his aristocratic brown eyes far enough to even notice my existence, let alone to actually form an opinion about me?'

Gideon realised it was this woman's impulsiveness that made him feel so uneasy in her company. So unsure and definitely wary of what she was going to do or say next. It wasn't a comfortable admission from a man who usually maintained a tight control over his own emotions. Not comfortable at all…

His mouth compressed into a hard line. 'Now who's being insulting?'

'Was I?' she came back airily. 'But you *do* have brown eyes. And you *are* an aristocrat. Lord Gideon St Claire, to be exact,' she added, as though he'd forgotten.

Neither he, nor his two brothers ever used their titles. In fact most people were completely unaware that Lucan was the current Duke of Stourbridge, or that his younger twin brothers were both lords. A fact that Joey was well aware of.

Instead of answering her, Gideon glanced down at the plain gold watch on his wrist. 'I'm afraid I don't have any more time to waste on this. I have an appointment at nine o'clock.'

She smiled unabashedly. 'Does that mean the welcome speech—you know...the usual *glad to have you with us, don't hesitate to ask if you need anything, blah, blah, blah*—is now over?'

Gideon drew in a harsh breath. Both of them knew there had been no welcome speech from him at all—not even a brief, unenthusiastic one. Which was obviously the whole point of her remark.

'I'm sure you're fully aware by now that I would be happier not to have you working here at all,' he said honestly.

'Life can be cruel that way, can't it?' she said, her smile undimmed.

Gideon gave her one last frustrated frown, before turning on his heel and going into the adjoining office and all but slamming the door closed behind him.

Joey's breath left her lungs in a relieved whoosh once she was alone in Lexie's office. That last conversation about Gideon's underwear had no doubt completely restored the opinion he'd obviously held of her *before* her earlier lapse in admitting that she deeply missed Stephanie.

Joey was well aware of what people thought of her lawyer persona—aggressive, forceful, too outspoken. She was a shark circling her prey when she defended her client in a courtroom—and it was a reputation she had deliberately nurtured.

Not too many people were ever allowed to see past that veneer of professional toughness to the real Joey beneath, as Gideon had when she'd talked of missing her twin...

Joey had deliberately donned her professional toughness a couple of years ago, after one too many slights, because she was a woman in the male-dominated career she had chosen to enter. And after one too many men, less capable than she believed herself to be, had been given jobs because of their gender rather than their ability. The third time Joey had been passed over in that way was when she had decided that if she couldn't beat them then she was going to join them and beat them at their own game.

Consequently, before she went for her interview at Pickard, Pickard and Wright two years ago, Joey had gone out and bought herself half a dozen of what she considered to be power suits, had had her hair styled unfemininely short, and adopted an abrasive and aggressive personality to match. The changes had proved to be successful, and she had managed to land the job with that prestigious firm of lawyers.

Once she had been given the job Joey had softened her attitude and appearance slightly, recognising that in some circumstances femininity—showing a little cleavage and wearing stiletto-heeled shoes for example—could be just as effective as abrasive aggression.

But she couldn't say she was altogether comfortable with the fact that her highly professional persona had slipped slightly when she had been talking with Gideon St Claire.

'I'm taking a break now, and going to the coffee shop down the street to get a hot chocolate. Do you want anything while I'm there?'

Gideon scowled his irritation as he looked up from the figures he had been studying on his computer screen to where Joey stood in the now open doorway between their two offices. A door she had opened without even the courtesy of knocking first.

'Surely there's a coffee-making machine in Lexie's office?'

'I don't drink coffee.'

'There are drinks machines on each floor, and a company restaurant on the eighth floor.' Gideon should have known that the past hour and a half of relative peace and quiet wasn't going to last with Joey McKinley in the building! 'I'm sure you can get hot chocolate there.'

'But not with whipped cream on top, or served by a buff twenty-year-old male with shoulder-length blond hair, I bet.'

Gideon's frown deepened as he thought of the three slightly plump, kindly middle-aged women who usually worked in the restaurant two floors below. 'Well...no.'

'There you go, then.'

'I take it this "buff" vision of manhood *does* work in the coffee shop down the road?'

'Oh, yes.' She smiled at him. 'So, do you want anything? Something to drink? Muffin? Pastry?'

'No, thank you,' he answered, with a barely repressed shudder.

'No to just the drink, or no to all of it?'

Gideon gritted his teeth at her persistence. 'All of it.'

'They do a really great lemon muffin—'

'I said no and I meant *no!*' Gideon was growing more and more irritated. If he wanted coffee he had his own pot, already made on the percolator, and if he wanted something to eat then he would send his secretary—Lucan's secretary, now that Joey McKinley had commandeered his own—down to the restaurant to get it for him.

Joey lingered in the doorway, seemingly unperturbed by his irritability. 'Tell me, Gideon, have you ever been into a coffee shop?'

'No,' he bit out tersely.

'How about a burger place?'

'If by that you are referring to a fast food restaurant, then the answer is no. Neither have I ever been roller skating, hang-gliding or scuba-diving—and I feel no more inclination to do any of them than I do to go to the coffee shop down the street!'

'Nix to the scuba-diving—I've never been too sure what's lurking down there in the depths,' Joey said with a contrived little shudder. 'But I've been roller skating and hang-gliding and loved both of them. As for fast food places and the coffee shop—you have no idea what you're missing!'

'In the case of the coffee shop, apparently a twenty-year-old male with shoulder-length blond hair.' His mouth twisted. 'Who obviously isn't my type. And isn't he a little on the young side for *you*?' he added with disdain.

'Younger men are all the rage at the moment.' Joey McKinley was completely undaunted as she wiggled suggestive auburn brows at him. 'Probably has something to do with the fact that they have more stamina in bed than older guys.'

Gideon stiffened. Who on *earth* had conversations like this one? Joey McKinley, apparently! Personally, he never discussed any of his own brief physical relationships with a third party, and he wasn't enjoying these insights into Joey's private life, either. Especially when she included slights to older men in her blunt commentary. He couldn't help wondering—and he was severely annoyed with himself for doing so—whether she meant men of his own age!

He leant back in his chair to look across at her from between narrowed lids. 'I would have thought experience would win over stamina every time.'

Joey almost shouted her *yes*! out loud, at having actually managed to engage the aloof Gideon St Claire in this slightly risqué conversation. His whole I-am-an-island thing was like a red rag to a bull as far as she was concerned;

she wanted to say outrageous things purely to shock him out of it!

With the weak February sun shining through the huge window behind him Gideon's hair was the colour of pure gold. It looked as if it would be soft and silky to the touch. His eyes were dark and enigmatic between those narrowed lids, and there was a slight smile curving the sensuous line of his lips—as if he were enjoying the conversation in spite of himself.

Joey's hands clenched at her sides as she resisted the urge she felt to cross the office and see if his hair really *would* be soft and silky to the touch. This was Gideon St Claire, she reminded herself impatiently. The man she had believed—*until earlier this morning*, a little voice reminded her—to be completely immune to all emotional feeling.

'Don't knock the stamina until you've tried it,' she said wickedly.

That sensuous mouth thinned immediately. 'Which you obviously have.'

As it happened, no...

Oh, Joey knew she gave off an image of eating up men of all ages for breakfast, and that most people assumed she lived alone and was unmarried through choice. But the truth of the matter was she had been too busy, too single-minded in attaining her law degree during her late teens and early twenties, to have much time left over for relationships. In fact, she'd had no time for them at all. There had been the occasional date, of course—the one with Jason Pickard six months ago being the most recent. And look how successfully *that* had turned out! But she had never been in the sort of long-term and loving relationship she felt necessary, and longed for. Her parents had been happily married for over thirty years, and Joey had decided at a young age that she wasn't going to settle for anything less.

Unfortunately, the downside of the tough, uncaring image she had deliberately adopted was that it tended to completely overwhelm weak men, and the strong ones just felt threatened by her. Which was probably why, at the age of twenty-eight, abrasive, driven Joey McKinley hadn't yet managed to find a man she could love completely and who loved her in the same way.

And the same reason she was still a virgin…

Something she was sure the cynical Gideon St Claire would find very hard to believe.

'Not yet—but I'll be happy to let you know when I have,' she came back provocatively.

Gideon winced as he sat forward to lean his elbows stiffly on the desktop in front of him. 'Do I take it that there's some sexual connection between the whipped cream and the buff twenty-year-old?'

Those green eyes widened, and for an instant Gideon could have sworn he saw a slight blush to those creamy cheeks. As if the outspoken Joey McKinley was actually *embarrassed* by his comment. He was intrigued at the thought…

'Whew—I think I'm having a hot flush, just thinking about it!' She waved a hand in front of her face.

Gideon sighed. 'If you've quite finished interrupting my morning, I have a business meeting to go to in a few minutes, followed by a luncheon appointment,' he told her.

The provocative smile instantly disappeared, to be replaced by professional interest. 'Do you need me to come with you to either of them?'

Did he need to spend any more time today with this irritating, outspoken and highly disturbing woman? 'No,' he assured her firmly. 'The business meeting isn't going to last long, and the luncheon appointment is personal.'

'Okaaay...' She eyed him speculatively.

'As in none of your business,' he said grimly.

'Fine.' She gave an unconcerned shrug. 'Well, you know where to find me if you need me.'

'Either in the office next door, or at the coffee shop down the road having fantasies about whipped cream and attractive young men, apparently,' Gideon drawled with cool derision.

'Hey, I think you're finally starting to enjoy my sense of humour!' Joey murmured appreciatively.

'Lord, I hope not,' he muttered with feeling.

She gave a husky laugh, before turning to go back into her own office and closing the door softly behind her.

Gideon drew in a sharp breath. Three weeks, four days, six and a half hours—and counting.

Until Joey McKinley was out of the St Claire Corporation building.

Out of the office next door.

Out of Gideon's life altogether...

CHAPTER THREE

JOEY was still so unsettled by the manner in which Gideon had neatly turned the tables on her with his remark about whipped cream that she completely forgot to ask for any on her hot chocolate—and didn't even notice that it was a young girl serving today, rather than the golden-haired god!

Maybe Gideon really wasn't as uptight as she had always thought him to be if he could make sexual references like that? After all, Stephanie hadn't been able to stop laughing when Joey had asked her if Gideon was gay. Just because Joey had never seen him with a woman it didn't mean Gideon didn't have one in his life—perhaps there was. Just not someone he wanted to take to a family wedding.

To her intense discomfort, just imagining lying naked on a bed with white silk sheets and having the heat of Gideon's tongue lapping whipped cream from her bare breasts was enough to make Joey's nipples go hard inside her bra.

This was *so* not a good idea—

'Get you anything else…?'

Joey looked up blankly at the young girl behind the counter, a blush darkening her cheeks as she realised her hot chocolate was sitting there, ready for her to collect, and there was a queue of people behind her still waiting to be served.

'No. That's fine. Thank you,' she muttered awkwardly as she grabbed up the hot chocolate and made a quick about face, instantly bumping into the bearded man standing directly behind her in the queue. 'Sorry.' She grimaced awkwardly.

'No problem,' he replied.

Joey hurried out of the coffee shop before she did anything else to embarrass herself, breathing deeply once she was outside on the pavement and grateful for the cold February wind to cool her hot and flushed cheeks. She was aware that her hands were trembling slightly as her fingers curled tightly about the warmth of the cup containing the hot chocolate.

What the hell was *wrong* with her? Well…she knew very well what was wrong—she'd been aroused by a sexual fantasy about Gideon St Claire and whipped cream in the middle of a coffee shop! He was the very *last* man Joey should ever think of in that way—especially as they were going to be working closely together for the next four weeks.

Gideon didn't even *like* her, and certainly didn't approve of her, so what on earth—?

'Are you feeling okay?'

Joey looked up to see that the bearded man from the coffee shop had collected his order and was now standing beside her on the pavement. *Was* she feeling okay? Well, she didn't know about that—she was hot, bothered and aroused! Something she hadn't felt for a long time—if ever.

'You're looking a little feverish,' the man continued. 'Perhaps you're coming down with a cold? There's a lot of it about. It's the weather, of course. One day it's cold and the next it's sunny.'

'Yes, probably,' Joey answered awkwardly, looking up at the man for the first time.

He looked to be aged in his late thirties, and was quite handsome from what she could tell through the dark beard that hid most of his lower face. His eyes were a deep and pleasant blue. He also looked vaguely familiar...

'Do I know you?' she asked politely.

'I'm sure I would have remembered you if we had met before.' He gave her a brief, noncommittal smile.

Joey accepted the compliment. 'Sorry to have held you up in there. I was miles away.' On a bed with silk sheets, with Gideon... *No*! She had to stop thinking about that!

'As I said, no problem,' the man assured her lightly. 'Do you work around here?'

Joey frowned slightly; it was one thing to apologise to this man for holding him up, but she wasn't about to tell a complete stranger where she worked. A stranger who still looked vaguely familiar, despite his denial...

'Yes. And it's time I was getting back.' She smiled again, to take the sting out of her dismissal, as she turned to walk away.

'Enjoy your hot chocolate,' he called after her.

'Thanks.' Joey was a little disconcerted to realise that the man must have been aware of her enough earlier to have noticed she had ordered hot chocolate to go. And she was sure she felt his blue eyes following her as she walked back down the street.

Paranoid.

She was becoming paranoid. The man was just being polite to show that he wasn't annoyed at being delayed, for goodness' sake. She was probably just feeling oversensitive after indulging in that steamy fantasy.

Probably? She was *definitely* feeling oversensitive. And in all the wrong places too.

* * *

'Good lunch?'

Gideon had only just arrived back in the office, and he drew in a sharp breath as he turned and saw Joey, once again standing in the connecting doorway between their two offices.

'I think we need to lay down a few ground rules, Joey,' he rasped as he removed his jacket and hung it in the closet before moving to sit behind Lucan's imposing desk. 'The first one being that in future I would prefer you to knock before you come barging into my office.'

'Why?'

He clenched his teeth. 'Because I would *prefer* it,' he repeated evenly.

She twinkled at him. 'Are you going to be doing something...*private* in here that you don't want me to walk in on?'

Three weeks, six days, two hours—and counting!

Gideon felt a nerve pulsing in his tightly clenched jaw. 'I just don't like you coming in here unannounced.'

Joey had decided, during the three hours since she had last seen Gideon, that the best way to deal with her earlier lapse into fantasyland was to face it head on. To face *him* head-on.

Looking at him now, as he sat behind Lucan's desk, golden hair slightly ruffled from the cool breeze outside, his jacket removed and the width of his shoulders and muscled chest clearly visible beneath that white silk shirt, suddenly she wasn't so sure...

Oh, get a grip, Joey, she instructed herself impatiently. So she'd had a sexual fantasy about the man? So what? Yes, Gideon was as handsome as sin, but he had just been out for a minimum two-hour lunch with another woman. No doubt a woman only too happy to cater to his sexual preferences, whatever they were...

'My mother sends her regards, by the way.'

Joey blinked. 'Your mother?'

Gideon gave a mocking smile—almost as if he had known exactly what she was thinking. 'I had lunch with her before she caught the afternoon train back to Edinburgh.'

The still beautiful and very gracious Molly St Claire. Dowager Duchess of Stourbridge now, following Lucan's marriage to Lexie on Saturday. And apparently the woman Gideon had just had a two-hour lunch with...

Was that *relief* Joey was feeling? If it was, then it was totally inappropriate. Ridiculous, even, when he had already made it perfectly obvious she was the last woman he would ever be attracted to.

And was she attracted to him?

Well, she was a woman with a pulse and a heartbeat, wasn't she?

Maybe she was—but she wasn't a *stupid* woman with a pulse and a heartbeat! Being attracted to Gideon—a man who showed no interest in her, and no emotion whatsoever for anyone other than those he considered his close family—would be the height of stupidity on her part.

She might choose to present an outer shell of sophistication, but inside Joey knew herself to be as soft as marshmallow—as emotional and vulnerable, in fact, as her outwardly softer twin. She really wasn't about to get her heart broken by falling for the coldly unattainable Gideon St Claire.

'What an attentive son you are, to be sure,' she commented.

Gideon visibly stiffened. 'Maybe you aren't aware of it, but the wedding on Saturday was a difficult time for my mother.'

Joey instantly felt guilty at this reminder that Lucan and Lexie's wedding must have been something of an ordeal for Molly St Claire; Lexie was the granddaughter of Sian Thomas—the woman Molly's husband, Alexander St Claire, the previous Duke of Stourbridge, had left Molly for twenty-five years ago.

Some sort of truce on the past had been called between the two older women before Lucan and Lexie's wedding on Saturday, but even so it couldn't have been an easy time for Gideon's mother.

'I am aware of it.' Joey grimaced in acknowledgement of her faux pas. 'Sorry.'

Gideon continued to eye her coldly for several seconds, before giving an abrupt nod. 'Let's move on, shall we? What did you want to see me about?'

What *did* she want to see Gideon about? Oh, yes. 'Jordan rang while you were out; he and Steph have arrived safely back in LA.'

Gideon nodded. 'He left a message on my voicemail.

It still felt slightly odd to him that he and this woman were connected by the marriage of their twin siblings. Not that he and Jordan were identical twins. But Joey and Stephanie were—even if they chose to be completely different in appearance. Gideon had always thought Stephanie to be warm and charming, while her sister had all the softness of a porcupine. An impression that had been shaken earlier that morning, when he'd heard the aching loneliness in Joey's voice as she'd admitted how much she missed her twin...

Gideon had actually found himself thinking of Joey during lunch, as he and his mother ate dessert. Well, it had been his mother's dessert that had actually triggered the memory—fresh strawberries covered in whipped cream. To his horror and intense discomfort he had found himself

imagining Joey lying back on red satin sheets—they would
have to be red; he already knew how beautiful her exotic-
coloured hair looked against red—while he sensuously
licked cream from every inch of her naked body.

The image had been so startlingly vivid that Gideon had
felt himself harden, his erection hot and aching beneath
the table where he and his mother sat eating together! He'd
had to discreetly drape his napkin across his thighs in case
anyone noticed that throbbing bulge in his trousers.

'How did your visit to the coffee shop go earlier?' His
tone was all the harsher because of his unprecedented reaction to just imagining Joey naked.

There was no way she could have prevented the blush
that warmed her cheeks as she was instantly reminded of
her drift off into fantasyland earlier. Her breasts became
fuller, the nipples hard and sensitive as they chafed against
the black lace of her bra.

She moistened dry lips. 'It was—good, thanks.'

Gideon gave her a tight smile. 'Any luck with the buff
young god?'

Joey wasn't sure she would have noticed him earlier,
even if he *had* been on duty today. Not when her thoughts
had been so vividly fixed on Gideon.

Those images of the two of them in bed suddenly flashed
into her brain again, so that she couldn't even look him in
the face as she answered. 'I'm still working on it.'

Gideon stood up as Joey turned to leave the office, crossing the distance between them in long, purposeful strides.
She turned round to face him as he spoke.

'Thank you for passing on the message that Jordan and
Stephanie arrived back in LA safely.' His voice was now
huskily soft.

'A superfluous message, as it happens,' she commented,

very much aware of how close Gideon was now standing to her.

'But you didn't know that,' he said. 'And, despite my earlier comments, I appreciate you coming to tell me as soon as I returned from lunch.'

Joey smiled. 'Even if I did come *barging* into your office?'

'Even so,' Gideon allowed ruefully, realising how tiny she was as he stood only inches away from her; her manner was always so mocking, so forcefully independent, that she had somehow always seemed...more fiercely substantial to him.

Her admission earlier of missing Stephanie had given Gideon a different insight into her—had hinted at that forceful independence being a defensive veneer rather than an intrinsic part of her nature. Perhaps a defence mechanism that came into play to hide the vulnerability that lay beneath her surface bravado—the same vulnerability that had enabled Joey to sing with such beauty and depth of emotion at Jordan and Stephanie's wedding, maybe?

Joey was shorter than Gideon had thought too. The top of her head only reached up to his chin—no, that couldn't be right. This morning, in the underground car park, he distinctly remembered that her eyes had been level with his mouth as they'd talked.

Gideon stood back slightly to look down at her feet. 'You aren't wearing any shoes...'

Even Joey's feet were beautiful—her ankles shapely, her toes gracefully slender, with pearly pink nails at their tips.

'I have a habit of taking them off whenever I sit down,' Joey admitted.

'It's a little...unorthodox when you're at work.' It also,

Gideon realised with a frown, gave an intimacy to this situation that he would rather didn't exist.

She tossed her head. 'Haven't you noticed? I *am* unorthodox!'

Gideon had noticed far too many things about this woman today! Such as the softness of her hair. The creaminess of her skin. The fullness of her breasts beneath the silk of her blouse. The delicious curves of her hips and bottom. The slight vulnerability to those sensuously full lips when she wasn't being smart-mouthed…

Joey was very aware of the sudden tension that surrounded herself and Gideon. She was also aware, so close to him like this, that his chest appeared as hard and muscled as she had imagined it would be, and her senses were being bombarded equally with the heat of his body and his smell: an elusive spicy aftershave mixed with hot and heady male.

She was almost afraid to breathe, and she resisted the impulse she had to step closer to him, to put her arms about his waist and feel the ripple of muscles beneath his shirt as her palms rested against his back. She was certain that he would feel good to touch. Hot and hard. Like steel encased in velvet.

It was a dangerous impulse—especially after the erotic thoughts Joey had had about him earlier on today. And yet she couldn't move away. Could feel the mesmerising pull of his seductive heat. Couldn't take her gaze from those hard and chiselled features. Except they didn't look quite so hard any more. Gideon's mouth was more relaxed than Joey had ever seen it—lips slightly parted, his breath a warm caress against her brow—and his eyes…oh, God, his eyes…

They were no longer just that dark and brooding bitter chocolate brown, but now had shards of gold fanning out from the pupil. That gold deepened, increased as his gaze shifted from her eyes to her parted lips. As if he too were imagining what it would feel like if they were to kiss—

A knock sounded softly on the outer door before it was immediately opened.

'Gideon, I—Oh!'

Lucan's secretary, May Randall, came to an awkward halt in the doorway, her eyes wide as she stared across the room and saw the two of them standing so close together.

'I—I'll come back later!' Her cheeks were bright red as she turned away and shut the door behind her.

May's unexpected interruption had the same effect as a cold shower on Gideon, bringing him instantly to a sense of exactly what he was doing—and what he had been about to do.

Damn it, he had been about to kiss Joey McKinley. *Joey McKinley*, for heaven's sake!

She was everything Gideon disliked in a woman.

The women who briefly held a place in his life were chosen for having the same qualities as his favourite white wine: cool and crisp, with just a hint of seduction to tantalise the senses. Joey had all the explosive qualities of a rich and ruby-red wine: deep and fruity to the palate, with a headiness that attacked rather than tantalised the senses.

Joey only had to take one brief glance up into Gideon's expressive face to know that he regretted even this much of a lapse in the previous antagonism that had existed between them. It was there in the way he breathed deeply through his nose, in his eyes, now a dark glitter, his stiff shoulders, hands tightly clenched at his sides.

Whereas *she* was still reeling from the very real and heart-pounding desire that had ripped through to her very core as she'd become mesmerised by the intensity of emotion burning in the deep gold of his eyes.

Eyes that had suddenly been the same colour as the beloved dragon sitting on her desktop…

CHAPTER FOUR

'AND how do you suggest we explain *that* touching little scene to May?' Gideon barked.

Coldly. Harshly. Disapprovingly. Typically!

The warmth Joey had thought she'd seen as she looked up into the depths of Gideon's gold-coloured eyes had to have been an illusion, she inwardly derided herself as she saw those eyes were now a deep and scathing brown.

'What's to explain?' she dismissed flippantly. 'We were only talking.'

'We were obviously standing much too close to be discussing business contracts.'

Gideon realised with self-disgust that after only a single morning of working with Joey he was already starting to lose his mind. What other explanation could there possibly be for even *thinking* about kissing her? Thinking? He hadn't been thinking at all as he gazed down at her soft and moistly parted lips!

'Personally, I think we're better off just forgetting about it,' Joey said with a shrug. 'It's been my experience that people will carry on thinking what they want about you, no matter what you might have to say on the subject, so it's better not even to bother to offering explanations in the first place.'

Gideon frowned slightly as he heard the underlying

thread of cynicism in her voice. Was it because most people—including him—tended to judge her on that let-people-think-of-me-what-they-will attitude? It was an opinion Gideon knew he was guilty of harbouring towards her, and it had already been made something of a nonsense of earlier that morning. And yet it was an opinion he had to continue to maintain if he were to have any defences against the attraction he obviously now felt for her—perhaps always had?

'Maybe you don't care what people think about you, Joey, but I do,' he said coldly. 'Especially people I have to work with on a daily basis.'

Bright wings of angry colour heightened her previously pale cheeks. 'You're working with *me* on a daily basis at the moment, Gideon—perhaps you would be interested to know what *I* think of *you*?'

No, he really didn't care to hear what Joey's opinion of him was!

She had made it obvious from their very first meeting in her office two months ago that she didn't like his high-handed attitude, or him—that in fact, she resented his interference in solving the problem of Stephanie having been wrongly accused of being 'the other woman' in the divorce of Richard Newman, one of her male ex-patients. An accusation Newman, for reasons of his own, had been happy to allow to continue.

Gideon had only stepped in at Jordan's behest, when his brother had become worried about the mental stability of Richard Newman's wife Rosalind, who had come dangerously close to causing Stephanie physical harm in her distress over the divorce. Maybe Gideon *could* have been a little more tactful in the way he had resolved the situation. Maybe he *should* have consulted Joey, who at the time had been acting on Stephanie's behalf, before instructing a private investigator to follow Richard Newman and ascertain who the man was really having an affair with. That it had turned out to be his boss's wife explained the man's reluctance to clear Stephanie of blame!

Gideon hadn't hesitated in using that knowledge to extract Stephanie from all involvement in the divorce, and he hadn't felt any guilt when Richard Newman had deservedly lost his job, as well as his wife and family.

Yes, Gideon accepted that he might have handled the situation more tactfully than he had, by including Joey in what he was doing, but he liked and respected Stephanie, knew how much Jordan loved her, and at the time hadn't thought of how Joey might interpret his behavior. He had only been concerned with extricating her sister from what had rapidly been becoming a dangerous situation.

He realised now—although Joey had obviously been relieved to have her sister removed from that tangled web— she had every reason to resent the arrogance of Gideon's abrupt intervention. The resentment had been there in Joey's manner towards him every time the two of them had spoken since...

He owed this woman an apology, Gideon acknowledged. An apology he daren't even *think* of offering at this moment, when emotions had been so heightened between them a few minutes ago.

'Only if I can return the favour and tell you what I think of you too,' he said.

Perhaps not, Joey acknowledged. Earlier fantasies of being held in Gideon's arms aside, they obviously just didn't like each other.

'I'll pass, thanks,' she replied in a bored voice.

'Then perhaps we should both just get back to work?' He raised dark brows in mute query.

No, they didn't like each other at all!

'Yes, sir!' She gave a mocking salute before turning to go back to her own office.

'Joey?'

She looked back at him with guarded eyes. 'Yes?'

'Put some shoes on, hmm? It sets a bad example for the troops!'

Joey's husky laugh was completely spontaneous, and the shake of her head rueful as she sobered. 'Be careful, Gideon—you might start to develop that sense of humour, after all!'

His mouth twisted wryly. 'I doubt it, when I have that I'm-so-superior stick up my backside.'

She looked ashamed. 'I shouldn't have said that to you.'

Gideon shrugged. 'Why not? If it's what you really think.'

Joey was no longer sure *what* she thought of him. Maybe there were reasons why Gideon was always so emotionally shut-off? An impression that had been severely dented earlier, when he'd admitted that he missed his own twin as much as Joey missed hers, she had to acknowledge.

The break-up of his parents' marriage when Gideon was only ten years old couldn't have been a pleasant experience. Stephanie had confided in her that Alexander St Claire's abandonment of his wife and three sons twenty-five years ago had definitely affected Jordan's opinion of long-term relationships. Perhaps Gideon had similar issues? Maybe that was the reason—

Good Lord—she couldn't actually be making *excuses* for this man's coldness, could she?

'Would you please leave, Joey, and allow me to get on with some work?' he growled, and at the same time pointedly moved to sit behind his desk.

No, Joey answered her own question. She certainly

wasn't about to make excuses for Gideon; he *was* cold and arrogant and superior, and every other uncomplimentary name she had ever called him—to his face or otherwise!

Gideon watched through narrowed lids as Joey finally left his office, waiting until the door had clicked firmly closed behind her before leaning against the back of his chair to let out a deep sigh.

He was acutely aware that the reason he had moved so quickly to sit behind Lucan's desk was because he was once again aroused by thoughts of passionately kissing Joey McKinley—and he wanted to do more to her than just kiss her, damn it!

Three weeks, six days, and one hour and thirty minutes of this torture left to get through...

'Need any help?'

Joey closed her eyes and wished herself anywhere but down on her knees in the underground car park of the St Claire Corporation, with Gideon looming over her as she attempted to replace the tyre that had gone flat since she'd left her car parked there that morning.

She had left her office a little before six o'clock, convinced by the silence in the adjoining office that Gideon had already left for the day—until she'd arrived in the underground car park and seen their cars were the only two still parked there. Even so, she had still hoped to get away before Gideon came down in the lift.

It was a hope that had been dashed once she had approached her car and found that the front tyre on the driver's side was completely flat. Which was why, after trying to pump the thing up again with no success, Joey was now down on her knees on the blanket she had spread on the oil-spattered concrete, attempting to replace the wheel with the spare from the boot of her car. She'd heard the lift descending and then Gideon walking over to her.

'It's nothing I can't handle,' she assured him as she continued to struggle with that last nut.

'Would you like me to—?'

'No!'

Gideon bit back a smile at Joey's vehemence, well aware of the reason for it, and knowing that she didn't like appearing at a disadvantage any more than he did. 'Perhaps I could—?'

'Perhaps you could just get into your damned car, drive away and let me get on with this!' she grated as she turned to glare up at him.

Maybe he would have done just that if he'd thought she was ever going to be able to get that wheel off and replace it with the spare. Although perhaps not: one thing Molly St Claire had drummed into her three sons when they were growing up was that a gentleman always helped a lady in distress. And, whether Joey liked it or not, she was definitely in distress.

Besides which, he had no intention of driving away and leaving a woman alone in a deserted car park at almost six-thirty on a dark winter's evening.

'Give that to me,' he instructed firmly as he moved to kneel beside her on the blanket and took the wrench out of her hand. Or at least attempted to take it, because her fingers instantly tightened about the metal tool, refusing to relinquish it.

'Joey, stop being so damned childish and give me the spanner!' Gideon glared down at her.

Jade green eyes glared right back at him. 'I'm not being childish. I just resent being treated like the helpless little woman to your big strong man!'

Gideon growled in his throat. 'Would it help you to know that I consider you as helpless as a Sherman tank?'

Joey's lips twitched at the description coming so soon after his comment earlier about 'the troops'. 'We aren't in a war zone, you know, Gideon.'

'No?' He arched blond brows.

'No.'

'Then stop being so stubbornly independent and give me the spanner.' He met her gaze challengingly.

Joey slowly released the metal tool into his hand, and sat back on her heels to watch as he easily undid that last traitorous nut before sliding the wheel off completely. He stood up to place it in the boot of her car, and then briskly rolled over the spare.

'Don't you just hate it when that happens?' she muttered irritably as she straightened up.

Gideon smiled at her patent annoyance. 'It's no reflection on your capabilities that the last nut was slightly rusted.'

Maybe it wasn't, but Joey *hated* appearing less than capable of dealing with her own problems.

'There didn't seem to be a problem with the tyre this morning...' She strolled over to the boot of her car to inspect it, but couldn't see any visible reason for the puncture. 'Never mind. I'll go and get a replacement at lunchtime tomorrow.' She turned to look over to where Gideon had finished putting on the spare and was now tidying the tools back into the box before folding the blanket.

His tailored suit and white silk shirt were as pristine as always, but there was a small smudge of oil just to the left of his mouth, which meant he probably had oil on his hands, too.

'Here you go.' He placed the toolkit and the folded blanket back in the boot, beside the punctured tyre.

Joey swallowed. 'I—thanks for your help.'

'No problem.'

'Nevertheless, it was kind of you.'

His mouth twisted wryly. 'Considering how ungracious you were when I first offered?'

Joey frowned slightly. 'I don't remember you offering. As usual, you just took over.'

'The way I took over in the Newman case a couple of months ago?'

Joey looked up sharply at the gentleness—and the un-expectedness—of Gideon's query.

'Yes,' she finally answered slowly. 'Exactly the way you took over in the Newman case.'

'I owe you an explanation and an apology for that.'

Joey's uncertainty deepened. Her resentment towards Gideon's arrogant intervention two months ago was the basis upon which she had placed all her future dealings with him. If he now explained and apologised she would have no defences against this rapidly growing attraction she felt towards him. Towards a man who so clearly showed that he only tolerated her at best...

'Joey...?'

Her startled gaze moved up to meet shrewd brown eyes, and there was a hint of a blush in her cheeks. 'I'm sure you had your reasons for doing it.'

He nodded. 'Because I liked Stephanie from the first, and Jordan asked me to see what I could do to help her. But I realise now that I should have considered your feelings before I acted.'

Much as Joey appreciated knowing that Gideon liked her twin enough to want to help her, she really wasn't sure she could cope right now with his apology. It had been such a strange day already. Not least because she had real-ised her deepening attraction towards Gideon had already severely battered the defences she usually kept about her emotions.

'You have a smudge of oil beside your mouth,' she said, deliberately changing the subject.

'I do?' Gideon instantly raised a hand and wiped the wrong cheek.

Why did people invariably do that? Joey wondered ruefully. 'Wrong cheek.'

He quirked one brow. 'Maybe you should just do it for me?'

Joey winced inwardly at the thought of touching him so intimately when she was already so completely aware of him. Maybe it would have been better if she hadn't mentioned that smudge of oil at all!

'I have some wipes in my handbag.' She hurried to open the car door, and bent down to get the wipes from where she had placed her handbag on the passenger seat before attempting to change the wheel, sincerely hoping that the visible warmth in her cheeks would fade by the time she straightened.

'Here.' She held the wipe out to him.

'It really would be easier if you did it for me,' he insisted.

Not for Joey!

'You're a big boy now, Gideon, and perfectly capable of cleaning your own face,' she muttered irritably, her nerves already frayed enough without the added possibility of touching him accidentally. 'Use one of the side mirrors on my car,' she suggested when he didn't move.

Gideon could see Joey's reflection in the mirror as she stood just behind him, and was very aware that not only had she refused to discuss the Newman case with him, but she had also dismissed his attempt at an apology.

Which didn't bode well for them having to continue to work together for the next four weeks...

Gideon's mouth tightened determinedly as he balled the damp wipe into his hand before turning back to face her. 'Look, Joey, we seem to have got off to something of a shaky start—' he began.

'We did that a couple of months ago.'

'And I have just tried to apologise for that,' Gideon reminded her gently. 'Why don't we go somewhere and have a glass of wine together and discuss it further?'

Much as he might have thought he was acting for the best at the time, he knew that if the situations had been reversed he would have felt exactly the same resentment she did.

Joey didn't want to 'go somewhere' and have *anything* with Gideon St Claire! Not if it meant she would be in danger of the physical attraction that had been growing between them throughout the day deepening even further.

Something had changed, she realised—shifted in their opinions of each other. And it was a shift Joey wasn't altogether comfortable with. Verbally sparring with Gideon was one thing, feeling anything else for a man who totally rejected having any of the softer emotions in his life was something else completely.

Besides which, she wasn't one hundred per cent sure his offer wasn't because he felt sorry for her after her admission earlier of missing Stephanie.

'I have plenty of friends I can share a glass of wine with if I feel in need of company, thank you, Gideon. In fact—' she gave a pointed glance at her wristwatch '—I have a date this evening, so I really need to get going if I want to make it on time.'

Gideon's mouth thinned. 'With Jason Pickard?'

'As it happens, yes. Do you have a problem with that?' She met the darkness of his gaze head-on.

'Not in the least,' Gideon denied, obviously regretting whatever impulse had made him make the offer in the first place. 'I hope the two of you have a nice evening.'

'Oh, I'm sure that we will,' Joey taunted. 'Jason is wonderful company.'

When he wasn't in a fluster, that was, because he and Trevor had had yet another argument—usually over the fact that Jason still hadn't told his parents about the two of them!

'No doubt,' Gideon drawled, with a marked lack of interest. 'You probably shouldn't wait until lunchtime to get your tyre replaced tomorrow, so I'll understand it if you're a little late in the morning.'

'Is that a suggestion or an order?' Joey raised mocking brows.

His eyes narrowed. 'I believe it's I'll understand if you're a few minutes late coming in tomorrow morning. You might have to wait until the garage opens so you can get your tyre replaced.'

Strange how Gideon's so-called 'understanding' sounded just like an order...

Or maybe Joey really was just over-sensitive where this particular man was concerned? If anyone else had made the same offer she would have believed they were being kind. Kindness just wasn't an emotion Joey associated with the icily reserved Gideon St Claire.

However, he *had* admitted that it was his liking of Stephanie and his love for Jordan that had prompted his arrogant interference in the Newman case. And he had also demonstrated today that he had a sense of humour, after all. Just as the way his eyes had changed from dark brown to gold earlier had been demonstrative of another emotion. Joey just wasn't sure quite what that emotion had been...

'In that case I'll do as you suggest. Thank you,' she added gruffly.

'You're welcome,' Gideon said, aware of how much that 'thank you' had cost her.

Perhaps it was as well Joey had refused his invitation; spending part of his evening in a verbal slanging match with her as he futilely tried to explain the reasons for his interference two months ago was *not* what Gideon would consider a pleasant way of spending his precious spare time.

He had no idea what his plans were for the evening. Being with his family over the weekend—his twin, especially—had left Gideon feeling restless now they had all returned to their respective homes.

Maybe he would just spend a quiet evening at home in his apartment? Or perhaps he should give Valerie Temple a call; she had seemed receptive to a dinner invitation from him when they had met at an art exhibition a couple of weeks ago.

Whatever he decided to do, Gideon couldn't help but take note of the fact that Joey had refused his invitation because she had a date with the man she had earlier told him she wasn't romantically involved with, and he was infuriated with his own interest in the matter.

'Enjoy your evening,' he muttered as he turned away.

'You too,' Joey murmured distractedly as she watched Gideon walk over to his own car.

Surely that wasn't *disappointment* she was feeling because he hadn't insisted that surely she had time to join him for one glass of wine, at least, before her date with Jason?

It couldn't be!

Could it...?

CHAPTER FIVE

'WOULD you happen to know anything about the air being let out of two of the tyres on my car?'

Joey looked up in amazement as Gideon burst unannounced into her office late on Wednesday evening, a coldly accusing expression on his face as he spat the question at her.

The last couple of days working at the St Claire Corporation had passed in much the same way as the first one had. Well, without Joey meeting Gideon first thing in the morning in the car park. Or any conversation about the buff young man in the coffee shop. Or the verbal sparring. Oh, and without Gideon inviting her to join him for a glass of wine after work because he wanted to explain and apologise to her for his behaviour two months ago...

Apart from those things, Tuesday and Wednesday had been pretty much like Monday!

In actual fact, Joey had hardly seen Gideon these past forty-eight hours. His car was already parked in his spot in the car park when she arrived in the mornings, and any work he had for her had either arrived mysteriously on her desk by the time she came in, or was delivered by May Randall later in the morning.

The connecting door between their two offices had remained firmly closed. Gideon obviously felt no necessity to talk to her, and Joey was experiencing an uncharacteristic reluctance to engage in another bout of verbal sparring with him.

Now this…

'What do you mean?' she asked incredulously.

'Stop playing the innocent, Joey.' Gideon began to pace the office restlessly. 'I should have guessed this past two days of relative peace and quiet were just the calm before the storm. You've just been biding your time, haven't you?' He gave Joey no opportunity to reply before continuing. 'Lulling me into a false sense of security before hitting out!'

'I have absolutely no idea what you're talking about, Gideon,' Joey informed him stiltedly as she stood up slowly. So much for the peace and quiet! 'Why on earth would you assume that *I* had let down the tyres on your car?'

'Who the hell knows how your mind works?' he asked, throwing his hands up into the air. 'Maybe because I openly showed my aversion to allowing you to work here in the first place—'

'Let's get one thing clear, Gideon—*you* didn't *allow* me to do anything,' Joey cut in forcefully, her eyes flashing a warning. 'As I've already told you, my arrangement is with Lucan—and has absolutely nothing to do with you. Your own feelings in the matter are of absolutely no interest to me,' she added scathingly.

'I advise you *make* them of interest,' he advised coldly.

'I don't care to,' Joey snapped.

'Oh, but you *do* care,' Gideon said silkily. 'You obviously care very much.'

Joey blinked, a shutter coming down over her emotions as she wondered if she could in some way have revealed her growing physical attraction to this man. Although how and when she could have done that, considering she hadn't even seen Gideon for the past two days, she had no idea!

'Care about *you*? I don't think so!' she scorned.

'Of course not about me personally.' Gideon dismissed the idea impatiently, making her breathe an inward sigh of relief. 'But no matter how you may have dismissed the idea on Monday I believe you care very much about the fact that I should have consulted with you over the Newman case. And you also feel that once I became aware of what Newman was up to I should have informed you and left you to handle the problem, rather than stepping in and dealing with it myself.'

Joey gave a terse inclination of her head. 'Of course I care about that. If for no other reason than that you should have done both those things out of professional courtesy, if nothing else!'

'I tried to explain and apologise on Monday—'

'Two months later!' Her voice rose. She was very aware that it was the sexual tension that had been slowly building inside her over the past two days that was responsible for her shrewishness now, as much as anything else. 'The fact that you didn't so much as consider my feelings at the time is indicative of how your own inability to feel emotion makes you blind to how another person is feeling.'

'What exactly do you mean by that?' he asked, dangerously calm.

'Oh, come on, Gideon,' Joey said with a short laugh. 'We both know that if your ability to show emotion was compared to that of an iceberg, the iceberg would win every time!'

Gideon looked at Joey from between lowered lids, noting the softness of her red hair. The blouse she was wearing today was of a shimmering red that brought out the blonde and cinnamon highlights in those short tresses and her breasts were a full and tantalising swell beneath that silky material. As for the way her black knee-length skirt moulded to the curve of her hips and perfect bottom… Well, what would she have to say about his lack of emotion if she were to realise how many times just thinking about her these past few days had caused his body to harden and throb?

Just as he was hard and throbbing now…

His eyes narrowed to golden slits as he slowly walked towards her. 'That's really what you think of me? That I'm incapable of feeling emotion?'

Joey took several steps back as Gideon suddenly became the stalking predator once again—with her as the prey. And she realised—too late—that it was his rigid control over his emotions that made him appear cold, rather than any lack of them. He was no longer making any effort to hide his emotions now, as the focus of his anger and desire became centred on her.

She came to an abrupt halt as she felt the window behind her and realised she had backed as far as she could go. She was now trapped between the coldness of the window and the heat of Gideon's body as he came to a halt mere inches away from her.

Joey licked her lips nervously. 'Maybe I was being a little hasty when I made such a sweeping statement—'

'Maybe?' he drawled softly, that golden gaze holding hers captive as he took that last step which brought his body flush up against hers.

Oh, dear Lord!

Her breath caught in her throat as the heat of Gideon's muscled chest against her breasts caused her nipples to swell to a hot and throbbing ache. Her eyes widened as that throb was echoed between her thighs as he slowly and deliberately pressed the pulsing length of his arousal into her welcoming warmth.

'Still think I lack emotion?' Gideon asked huskily, enjoying flaunting the evidence of his own desire and watching her eyes widen even further.

He captured both of her hands in one of his before raising them above her head and pressing them against the window. At the same time his other hand moved to the buttons on her blouse.

'I— What are you doing?' Joey cursed the mouse-like squeak that was her own voice at the same time as congratulating herself on being able to speak at all. Gideon was unfastening the buttons on her blouse, one slow button at a time, until it was completely undone and he could push the two sides of the material aside to reveal her breasts cupped in black lace.

'I would have thought that was obvious,' Gideon mocked softly, and he deliberately held Joey's startled gaze with his own before that gaze lowered to the swell of her breasts, the dusky-rose of her hardened nipples easily discernible beneath the fine black lace of her bra.

'I— Well— Yes— But—'

'No buts, Joey,' he said gruffly, and he finally lowered his head to taste the creamy length of her throat with his lips, his tongue lingering on the pulsing heat of the blood thrumming just beneath the surface of her creamy skin.

Joey couldn't think when Gideon's body was pressed so intimately against hers—when she could feel the hard pulsing of his considerable erection pressing against the throbbing nubbin nestled between her own thighs.

She groaned low in her throat as his mouth travelled down to the swell of her breasts. The warmth of his hand was moving beneath her loosened blouse to rest against the bareness of her back as he pulled her against him. His tongue stroked a caress against her flesh in a trail across the flimsy black lace to first encircle and then draw one swollen nipple deep into the heat of his mouth.

Joey's knees buckled at the intensity of the pleasure that claimed her as Gideon continued to draw rhythmically on that highly sensitive peak. His tongue swept moistly over that aching nipple again and again, and the place between her thighs pulsed in that same aching rhythm.

Joey desperately sought relief for that ache, parting her legs and allowing herself to press the aroused nubbin between her thighs against the iron-hardness of Gideon's arousal. Her breath was coming in panting sobs as she felt a climax building, growing deep inside her, clamouring for release.

Gideon had only intended to show Joey how wrong she was when she'd accused him of lacking in emotion. But his demonstration had quickly turned to something else— something more basic, primal—and Gideon knew that he wanted this pleasure to continue. *Needed*, to see Joey as she came apart in his arms as orgasm claimed her.

And where did they go from here? a tiny voice of reason mocked deep inside his head. What happened *after* Joey had climaxed? Did he then strip away all their clothes— first from her body and then his own—before draping her over the desk and burying himself to the hilt between her thighs?

Much as might want to do that, Gideon knew that he couldn't. He had already allowed this to go so much further than he had intended. He was more aroused, his body positively aching for release, just from kissing and caressing Joey than when fully making love to another woman. Somehow she stripped away all of his defences and left him feeling vulnerable in a way he had never felt before.

And he certainly didn't want to feel it with Joey McKinley!

Joey felt disorientated, bereft, when Gideon suddenly pulled away from her, leaving desire still coursing hotly through her body. That desire turned swiftly to dismay, and then humiliation, as Gideon looked down at her briefly with dark, enigmatic eyes before turning abruptly on his heel and walking away from her, crossing to the other side of the office to stand with his back towards her.

The other side of Lexie St Claire's office, Joey acknowledged, her embarrassment total as she realised what she had just allowed to happen. How much more could have happened in this public place if Gideon hadn't called a halt to their lovemaking…?

She quickly grasped the two sides of her blouse together over her semi-nakedness, her cheeks blazing with humiliation as she began to refasten the buttons with fingers that trembled and fumbled over the simple task.

Joey knew exactly why Gideon had behaved in the way he had, of course: he had wanted to teach her a lesson for what he had taken as a slight on his emotions. But how could she have let things go as far as they had? *Why* had she? With Gideon St Claire, of all people!

'Point proved, I believe?'

Joey looked up sharply at Gideon's comment, relieved that at least her blouse was once again fastened when she saw that he had turned back to face her, his dark gaze now sweeping over her with what looked like mockery. The fact that she deserved it after responding to him in such an uninhibited way brought the bile rising to the back of Joey's throat—so much so that she had to swallow before answering.

'We've established that you're capable of a physical reaction, at least—if that's what you mean?' She silently congratulated herself for managing to meet the challenge in that dark gaze.

Gideon couldn't help but admire Joey's quick recovery from what had been a dangerous situation for both of them. A danger he was still fully aware of as he looked at the flushed beauty of her face and recalled how much he had enjoyed the taste of her in his mouth.

His mouth tightened as he fought against those memories. 'And so, obviously, are you.'

Colour blazed once again in Joey's cheeks. 'I don't think *my* emotions were ever in question!'

'Well, not any more, no,' Gideon drawled, accepting he was behaving badly, but aware that he needed to re-establish distance between them. Fast! 'Unfortunately none of that provides us with any answers as to how two of the tyres on my car appear to have gone flat at the same time,' he reminded her.

Jade green eyes glittered with anger once again. 'I've already told you I don't know anything about that.'

Yes—and Gideon believed her. Hell, he had believed her the first time she'd denied it, and had no idea what he'd been doing in the first place, even suggesting that Joey might have done it.

Just being around her on a day-to-day basis was totally screwing with his normal ability for rational thinking, Gideon acknowledged heavily. Even when he avoided her—as he had been trying to do for the past two days—he was still totally aware of her. So much so that it had been all too easy, when he'd left the office and arrived down in the car park to find two of the tyres on his car flat, to apportion the blame to Joey. Impulsively. Irrationally. Gideon was acting completely out of character, and he knew it. He had to pull himself together!

He nodded. 'I'm inclined to believe you—'

'How kind of you,' she shot back sarcastically.

Gideon ignored her. 'I'm also wondering,' he continued, 'whether this and the flat tyre on your own car on Monday night aren't somehow connected.'

Joey stilled. Initially she had been relieved to have the subject changed to something other than the embarrassment of the intimacies she had allowed Gideon, but with the mention of her own problem with her car, her attention became fully engaged on the subject.

'What exactly are you suggesting?'

Gideon shrugged. 'Could you try very hard not to take it as yet another character defect on my part when I tell you that I don't believe in coincidences?'

Neither did Joey. And what were the chances of two people who worked in the same building and parked their car in the same car park finding both their cars had flat tyres within a couple of days of each other?

'Has anyone else working here had a similar problem?'

'Not that I'm aware of—and I can do without any comment from you on how unlikely it is, with the superior stick-up-my-backside attitude you say I have, that any of St Claire's employees would bother to inform me if they *did* have a problem,' Gideon warned as he saw the sceptical look that had entered those jade-green eyes at his first comment.

He was aware that she had become popular with the other members of the staff over the past three days. His own secretary was full of praise for her, as was May Randall. It seemed that he was the only one who had a problem being around her on a daily basis.

'Just accept that I would have heard if there was anything to hear.'

'Okay.' She shrugged. 'Maybe it is just a coincidence, after all?'

'I doubt it.' Gideon grimaced. 'Did the people at the garage give a reason for why your own tyre went flat when you took it in to be repaired yesterday morning?'

'They didn't bother to look,' Joey revealed reluctantly. 'I had all four tyres replaced after the mechanic took one look at them and decided that they wouldn't pass a safety check—I've been busy, okay?' she defended herself when Gideon raised disapproving brows. Could she help it if she was one of those drivers who knew absolutely nothing about the mechanics of her car and only required that it start when she turned the key in the ignition? 'I doubt that there's any way we can check, either. By now all four tyres have probably been consigned to a tyre graveyard.'

'No doubt,' Gideon agreed.

Joey gave a puzzled shake of her head. 'Why just sabotage the two of us, do you think?'

'It's only supposition so far—'

'This isn't a court of law, Gideon,' she jeered gently. 'I promise not to write down anything you say and use it in evidence against you!'

'Very funny,' he drawled dryly.

Not really. But Joey was most comfortable around this man when she was mocking him for one reason or another—she certainly didn't want to think any more just now about the way he had unbuttoned her blouse a few minutes ago and kissed her breasts with a skill and passion that had blown her away.

'There's plenty more where that came from,' she murmured.

'I'm sure there is.' Gideon sighed. 'But it isn't exactly helping us to solve this puzzle, is it?'

'Maybe it was just vandals.' Joey shrugged. 'Kids who are bored and looking for mischief?'

'Maybe,' he said, not looking particularly convinced. 'But I think it should be looked into further before we totally dismiss it as such.'

'And how do you suggest we do that?'

Gideon's gaze sharpened. 'I wasn't suggesting *we* do it at all.'

Joey's eyes widened. 'I hope this isn't going to be another case of the big strong man protecting the helpless little woman?'

'Flattered as I am that you should even *think* of me as a "big strong man", Joey,' Gideon said, noting the wings of colour that appeared in her cheeks at his teasing, 'your own role as helpless little woman is, as usual, seriously in question!'

'Good,' Joey muttered with vehemence—at the same time knowing that helpless was precisely how she had felt a few minutes ago, with her hands raised above her head, her blouse unbuttoned and her breasts being plundered by Gideon's marauding lips and tongue. And she'd loved every second of it!

Looking at him now, every inch his usual cold and aloof self, Joey found it extremely difficult to imagine those intimacies had ever taken place...

'So, how do you suggest *we* proceed?' she pressed on.

'I don't want you involved, Joey,' he insisted.

'Isn't it a little late for that?'

'Involved any further than you already are,' Gideon amended. 'The most sensible thing for you to do is to go home and leave me here to investigate further,' he added grimly.

He had no idea what the hell was going on, and until he did he would feel happier if Joey was safely at home.

She quirked auburn brows. 'No date tonight?'

No date for some time, as it happened. 'No,' he admitted. 'You?'

'No.'

'I hope your agreement to work here for a month isn't in any way affecting your...*friendship* with Jason Pickard?'

As it happened, Jason had finally told his parents the truth about himself and Trevor. The senior Pickards hadn't been overjoyed at the news—especially as they'd realised it meant they would probably never have any grandchildren— but according to Jason they were slowly getting used to the idea.

Which, of course, meant there was no longer any reason for Joey to go out to dinner with Jason...

'Wouldn't it be more sensible if I hung around for a while and helped you to investigate?' Joey said brightly. 'That way I could give you a lift home once we've finished.'

'Not necessary,' Gideon said. 'I've already telephoned my garage, and they're driving over a replacement car and will take mine away to fix it,' he added firmly as Joey would have interrupted again.

Must be nice, Joey acknowledged ruefully; the most the garage who serviced *her* car ever gave her was a bill! Not that they were even open at six-thirty on a Wednesday evening. There were obviously benefits to being Gideon St Claire—*Lord* Gideon St Claire! 'I could still stay and help—'

'Joey, I may have suggested that you're far from being helpless,' he rasped, 'but that doesn't mean I don't still intend to protect you. From yourself, if necessary.'

'You really are a male chauvinist, aren't you?' Joey accused.

He smiled slightly. 'Didn't you miss *pig* out of that statement?'

'Oink!' she muttered, with feeling.

Gideon had to bite back another smile. At the same time he wondered how it was that Joey could so easily turn his mood to amusement as well as anger. Along with several other emotions he would rather not think about right now. Such as an uneasy jealousy of any *friendship* she might have with a certain Jason Pickard...

'Just go home, hmm, Joey,' he said, suddenly deadly serious again.

Her chin rose in direct challenge. 'And what exactly are you going to be doing to investigate after I've gone?'

He gave a noncommittal shrug. 'Checking into a few things.'

'Such as?'

'How about I discuss that with you in the morning?'

Joey eyed him warily, not sure she altogether trusted him to do that, and yet not seeing any hint of evasion in the steadiness of his darkened gaze as it so easily met hers.

Those same eyes had turned the colour of molten gold when he'd looked down at her semi-naked breasts only minutes ago. Well, at least she now had the answer to *that* particular question; Gideon's eyes blazed that beautiful colour when he was aroused—to passion as well as to anger!

Something Joey would probably be better off not thinking about just now...

'Okay.' She gave a stiff nod of her head. 'But I'll expect a full report from you first thing in the morning,' she warned.

'Yes, ma'am!' Gideon echoed her mocking salute of two days ago.

It was somehow an intimately shared gesture that made Joey feel uneasy as she turned away quickly to collect her coat from the back of her chair, keeping her back turned firmly towards Gideon as she thrust her arms into the sleeves of her jacket before straightening her blouse over the collar.

She had accused him of lacking in emotion, but at the same time she knew she had never felt this seesawing of her own emotions until she'd met him. Aroused one minute. Amused the next. With both those emotions usually followed by anger. This uneasiness was new, though...

Her expression was deliberately bland when she turned back to face him. 'I'll wish you goodnight, then.'

''Night.'

Joey gave him one last frowning glance, before picking up her bag and turning to leave, anxious to get away now. Away from the memories of being in his arms...

'And, Joey...?'

She tensed warily, schooling her features into mild curiosity as she looked back over her shoulder at him. 'Yes?'

His face was harsh: eyes glacial, cheekbones defined, jaw clenched. 'I apologise for what happened earlier.'

This wasn't happening. It really *wasn't* happening!

Wasn't it humiliating enough that they both still had the memories of those shared intimacies without Gideon actually apologising for them? That she had to try and work in the office where it had happened for the next three and a half weeks? With the added knowledge that Gideon was in the office next door?

He shook his head. 'It was ridiculous of me to accuse you of vandalising my car.'

Joey's breath left her in a controlled—relieved!—sigh; he wasn't apologising for kissing and caressing her, after all...

'Forget it, Gideon,' she said pertly. 'After all, you can't help being a bigoted idiot!'

Gideon found himself chuckling in spite of himself. No

one—absolutely no one—spoke to him with the same irreverence Joey did. 'You know, one day you might actually say something nice about me,' he said wryly.

'You think?'

'I can dream, can't I?'

'I shouldn't hold your breath if I were you!'

Those green eyes openly laughed at him for several seconds, beguiling him into sharing her amusement, before she turned and left the office, flashing him one last triumphant smile on the way out.

Gideon moved to sit on the side of the desk, an amused smile still curving his lips. Joey McKinley was every bit as impossible as he had always thought her to be.

She was also every bit as desirable as he had imagined she might be.

Gideon's smiled faded as he thought of those few intensely pleasurable minutes of making love to Joey. It had been like holding a living flame in his arms. Sensuously seductive. Fiercely hot. With the real possibility of that flame bursting dangerously out of control and consuming him.

Joey herself was every bit as unpredictable, as volatile, as that flame. In fact, he thought uncomfortably, she was every uncertain, unpredictable emotion that he had been at such pains to banish from his own well-ordered life for the past twenty-five years...

CHAPTER SIX

'GIDEON?' To say that Joey was surprised to answer
the door of her apartment at almost nine o'clock that
evening and find Gideon standing outside had to be an
understatement!

It was a less formal Gideon than she was used to seeing,
in a thin black cashmere sweater that moulded to his muscled chest and the flatness of his stomach, over a pair of
tailored black trousers. The gold of his hair contrasted
dramatically with the black clothing, giving him the appearance of a devastatingly handsome fallen angel, and
his appearance rendered Joey completely speechless for
several seconds.

He shouldn't have come here, Gideon realised when
he saw the shocked wariness on Joey's face, before that
emotion was quickly replaced by frowning confusion.

'What are you doing here?' Joey prompted, fingers
tightly gripping the edge of the door.

As if she were prepared to slam that door in his face if
his answer wasn't one that she liked!

No, he really shouldn't have come here, Gideon acknowledged as he saw the wariness return once again to
those expressive jade-green eyes. Eyes the same colour
as the fitted sweater Joey wore over figure-hugging, low-
riding blue jeans. Her face was bare of the make-up she

wore during the day, making her look much younger than twenty-eight.

Gideon's mouth twisted. 'Obviously visiting you.'

She chewed briefly on her top lip before answering him. 'How did you even know where I live?'

He shrugged. 'I looked it up in your file.'

Joey's brows rose. 'I have a *file*?'

'Every employee at St Claire's has a file,' he answered dryly. 'Even the ones only employed by us for four weeks.'

'Oh.'

'You don't have any shoes on again…' He looked down at those graceful bare feet, poking out from beneath the bottoms of her jeans.

She shrugged. 'I prefer not to wear them whenever possible.'

He nodded.

'Gideon, why are you here?' she asked again.

Gideon grimaced. 'This was a bad idea, wasn't it?'

Her tongue flicked nervously over her bottom lip. 'That depends…'

His eyes narrowed. 'On what?'

'On what you came here for,' Joey said slowly; it was one thing to deliberately provoke and argue with Gideon in the office, where they were on neutral ground, and something else entirely for him to come to her home like this. Especially after the intimacies they had shared earlier.

If Gideon had come here expecting to carry on where they'd left off, though, he was going to be disappointed. Haunted as Joey might be by those memories, she had no intention of reliving them. No matter how much just seeing him again made her ache to do just that.

It was all too easy for Gideon to see what direction Joey's thoughts had taken. To guess from the sudden warm flush that appeared in her cheeks, followed by the glitter of determination in her eyes, that she was thinking of how he had kissed her and touched her.

Those same thoughts had kept Gideon in a state of increasingly aching arousal for the past three hours!

Was it that which was the real driving force behind his decision to come to Joey's apartment this evening? Oh, he had told himself that his only reason for coming here was so that they could discuss privately whatever was going on with the vandalism to both their cars—he was more convinced than ever that the two incidences were connected. But seeing Joey again now, and becoming increasingly aware of the jealousy he felt just thinking of her friendship with Jason Pickard, he wasn't so sure any more that his motives had been that innocent...

He straightened determinedly. 'I'm here to discuss the fact that the mechanics who came to pick up my car checked the punctures before loading the car onto the trailer, and found that a knife, or something similarly sharp, had been used to slash the inside of the tyres.'

Joey's eyes widened in alarm. 'It was deliberate, then?'

Gideon's expression was grim. 'Undoubtedly.'

She gave another moistening sweep of her tongue across her lips. 'And my own car?'

'The same, probably. After you left earlier I decided to look at the security camera film from the underground car park for today. I couldn't see anything unusual, so I had Security make copies onto disks, and thought we could save some time if we looked through them this evening. You might spot something—or someone—that I missed.' Gideon held up the disks he had brought with him. 'You said earlier that you weren't going out this evening, so I thought—' He stopped and shook his head. 'I shouldn't have come here. This can wait.'

'No! No, it's fine. Come in. Please.' Joey opened the door wider, knowing she was behaving like a nervous virgin by keeping him standing on the doorstep in this way.

Well…she *was* a nervous virgin. But that didn't mean she had to behave like one—especially in front of the obviously experienced Gideon St Claire!

'I was only watching a boring detective programme on TV, anyway.' Joey closed the door behind Gideon to follow him through to the sitting room, switching the television off before turning back to face him. 'Can I get you tea or coffee before we start—er—before we look at the disks?' Damn it—now she was blushing like a nervous virgin, too!

Gideon arched curious brows. 'I thought you didn't drink coffee?'

Joey gave a graceful shrug. 'I don't, but that doesn't mean I don't have some to give to my guests.' She could also do with a few minutes on her own while she made that coffee—if only to allow time for the blush to fade from her cheeks! 'Have you eaten, or can I get you something…?'

'You can cook too?'

'Not really.' She grinned unapologetically. 'Stephanie is the cook in our family. I was really only offering to get you some toast, or something simple like that, if you hadn't eaten dinner yet.'

Gideon gave a rueful smile. 'Just coffee would be great, thanks.'

He lowered his lids guardedly as he watched Joey go through to the kitchen, enjoying looking at the way her gently rounded bottom swayed from side to side in unknowing provocation, before he turned to look at the sitting room in which he stood.

He had somehow expected her apartment to be as crisp and modern as the woman was herself, with art and furniture that tended to be fashionable rather than comfortable. Instead Gideon found himself in a room predominantly in warm autumnal colours: yellow-painted walls, sofa and chairs in a reddish terracotta, with scatter cushions in a mixture of yellows and oranges, and rugs of equally bright colours on the polished wooden floor. The prints on the walls were also unexpected—poppy fields, and ladies in long floaty dresses wandering around abundantly floral gardens.

Could it be that the abrasive and prickly Joey McKinley was secretly a closet romantic?

Joey wasn't sure she liked the look of thoughtful speculation on Gideon's face when she returned from the kitchen, carrying a tray with the coffee and teapots and two cups, a jug of milk and another of cream, and a bowl of sugar.

'You can sit down, you know,' she invited as she placed the tray down on a low coffee table, before sitting down in the middle of the three-seater sofa—a definite hint to Gideon that she expected him to sit in one of the two armchairs.

The few minutes she had spent in the kitchen making coffee and tea hadn't succeeded in dampening her complete physical awareness of him, but she did at least have it under control enough not to give in to the temptation he represented. She hoped!

Gideon hesitated. 'Are you sure I'm not inconveniencing you?'

'Even if you are, you're going to drink this coffee now that I've made it,' she came back tartly as she poured the aromatic brew into one of the cups.

The apartment might be something of a surprise to

Gideon, but it was reassuring to know that Joey's manner could be just as acerbic here as it was at the office!

'Black, thanks,' he accepted, and he took the cup of coffee from her before sitting down in the armchair beside the warm gas fire. 'Have you lived here long?'

She shrugged as she sat back on the sofa to drink her tea. 'A couple of years.'

'Have you always lived in London?'

'Steph and I shared a small flat here when we were both at university.'

'Where you studied law?'

'Obviously.'

'Has your singing voice been professionally trained?' Gideon at last voiced the question that had been intriguing him ever since he had heard her sing so angelically at Stephanie and Jordan's wedding.

'Yes.' The answer almost seemed to be forced out of her.

'I had no idea you had such a fantastic voice until I heard you sing at the wedding.'

'That was a special occasion,' she dismissed stiffly.

'Did you never think of—?'

'Gideon, did you come here to ask me a lot of personal questions, or so that we could view the disks?' Joey cut in sharply.

Gideon eyed her quizzically as he sipped his coffee. 'I was merely curious as to why you didn't pursue a professional singing career.'

'Maybe my voice isn't good enough,' she suggested dryly.

'We both know that it is.'

'It's personal, okay?' Joey said curtly.

'You don't like to talk about yourself, do you?'

'Said the pot to the kettle!'

Gideon smiled. 'You already know that I have a twin, and another brother two years older. My mother lives in Edinburgh—'

'None of those things are just about *you*—they are equally true of Jordan,' Joey pointed out.

'True.' Gideon nodded. 'This is good coffee, by the way.' He took another sip of the strong brew.

'It's also a good diversionary tactic from talking about yourself.' Joey eyed him mockingly.

'Said the kettle to the pot?' he returned, with a definite glint in his eye.

Joey shrugged. 'I guess we both value our privacy.'

Gideon frowned slightly. 'And I've invaded yours by coming here unexpectedly this evening, haven't I?'

'Stop worrying about it, Gideon. I can always check your own file for your home address and reciprocate one evening!'

Gideon immediately found himself wondering what Joey would make of his own apartment, which, for all it was expensively furnished and decorated, was of a modern and clinical style rather than being casually comfortable. He knew instinctively that she would absolutely hate it.

Which was of absolutely no relevance when he had no intention of ever allowing her to visit him there; his apartment was his personal space, and he only ever invited his close family.

'Perhaps you're right. We should look at the disks now,' he suggested as he leant forward to place his empty cup back on the tray.

'Fine,' Joey answered lightly, easily able to tell that she had unknowingly touched upon a sensitive subject.

Not that she had ever intended visiting him at his place uninvited, but Gideon's adverse reaction was intriguing, nonetheless. Perhaps because he wasn't always alone there, and an unexpected visit from her might prove embarrassing for all of them?

Or it could just be because Gideon valued his privacy even more than she did?

Whatever the reason, his reluctance to have her anywhere near his apartment was more than obvious! As obvious as her own aversion to discussing why, when she acknowledged her voice had been trained, she hadn't pursued a professional singing career...

'Hand me the disks.' Joey stood up to take them from him, crossing the room to where her DVD player was and kneeling down to switch it and the television back on before loading the first disk.

'The cameras are movement-activated, so it isn't as bad as it looks,' Gideon told her after they had watched the first disk showing many of the St Claire employees arriving to park their cars in the morning.

'Perhaps that's as well!' Joey eyed the three discs left to play.

It took almost two hours, and the emptying of both the coffee and the tea pot, before they had viewed all four disks. Like Gideon earlier, Joey had seen nothing unusual on any of them.

Even though she had only worked at St Claire's for three days, she already recognised many of the employees arriving and leaving the building. All very interesting— not!—and not in the least helpful in terms of discovering if anyone had actually tampered with Gideon's car.

'Nothing?' he prompted as the last disk came to an end.

'I'm afraid not.' Joey sighed as she handed all four disks back to him.

'It was a bit of a long shot, anyway,' he acknowledged.

Joey stood up. 'Would you like some fresh coffee?'

'It's getting late. Don't you want to get to bed—' Gideon broke off abruptly as he saw the telling blush that had entered Joey's cheeks, and the way her gaze suddenly avoided meeting his.

The more time he spent in her company the more he realised what an enigma Joey was—one minute the sophisticate, the next blushing like a schoolgirl over a perfectly innocent remark.

A remark that no longer seemed quite so innocent…

'Joey?'

Her gaze settled in the vicinity of the middle of his chest. 'You're right. It is late—and we both have work in the morning—'

'Look at me, Joey,' Gideon cut in firmly.

Joey was looking at him. And liking—far too much— what she saw! She had always thought Gideon would be lean and muscled beneath those formal suits and silk shirts he always wore, and had been increasingly aware throughout the evening of just how attractive he looked in that fitted black cashmere sweater and tailored black trousers.

To her dismay, she could once again feel the revealing hardening of her nipples as they rubbed against the soft wool of her own sweater, and the less visually obvious aching arousal between her thighs. Joey didn't dare so much as look at Gideon's face now, knowing that if she saw awareness in his own expression she would be well and truly lost.

She flicked her tongue nervously across her lips. 'I'm sorry I wasn't of any help with—Gideon…!' Her gasp was breathily panicked as she was suddenly pulled into his arms, her gaze alarmed as she finally looked up at him.

Oh, help…

His eyes were that pure molten gold as he looked down searchingly into her face. There was a telling, aroused flush along those high, aristocratic cheekbones, and his lips—those sensually sculptured, perfectly delicious lips—were slightly parted, as if he were about to kiss her!

Gideon would be lying to himself as well as to Joey if he were to claim that he hadn't known from the moment he'd arrived at her apartment that this was going to happen. The whole time the disks had been playing he had been watching her from beneath lowered lids, rather than the television screen. Watching. And waiting. The hardness of his arousal becoming a pulsing ache as the minutes slowly ticked by.

He wanted Joey McKinley.

Damn it, he didn't just want her. His desire for her had reached a point where he *had* to have her!

There were too many complications, he reminded himself cautiously. His twin brother was married to her twin sister. Their two families were connected by that marriage. An affair between the two of them would be a problem—especially when it ended. Whether the affair ended amicably or badly, Gideon knew the memory of it would linger for both of them, making it uncomfortable for them to attend family occasions together.

Unfortunately none of those things mattered a damn now, when Gideon burned to take her to bed and make love to her in every way possible.

And Joey's response earlier had already shown him that she returned that desire, at least...

Maybe desire was the real basis for their dislike of each other? Maybe if they made love together it would ease that tension rather than heighten it—?

Who the hell was he trying to kid? At this moment he couldn't care less what happened after he and Joey had made love, as long as they *did*!

He held her gaze with his. 'In a few moments I'm going

to strip every article of clothing from your body, and then have you do the same to me, before carrying you into your bedroom and making love to you. If that isn't what you want too, then you had better say so now.'

Joey looked up at Gideon searchingly, knowing by the complete lack of embellishment to his words that it was a statement of intent rather than a declaration of feelings. Oh, there was desire, of course—Joey now knew exactly what emotion the glittering gold of Gideon's eyes signified! But that was all this was. A desire to make love to her.

Was it the same desire she felt for Gideon?

Maybe. No—not maybe. She *did* desire him. More than she had ever wanted or desired any other man, if her response earlier was any indication. But Joey had always believed that when she made love for the first time it would be with a man who loved her and whom she loved in return. She wanted that even more now that she had seen the happiness her twin had found in loving Jordan and having that love reciprocated. Their commitment to each other was absolute.

She and Gideon didn't have any of that.

What they did have—would always have—was a family connection from Stephanie and Jordan's marriage. As well as a commitment from Joey to work at St Claire's for the next three and a half weeks, of course!

She pulled back slightly to look up at Gideon with guarded eyes. 'Does this blunt, no-nonsense approach usually work for you?'

Gideon scowled darkly. 'I have always believed in honesty in my personal relationships, yes.'

Joey shrugged. 'There's honesty,' she said, 'and then there's cold, hard logic. I'm sure in other circumstances the first is commendable,' she said dryly. 'But I have to tell you that cold, hard logic coming from a potential lover isn't in the least appealing.'

Gideon's jaw tensed. 'Damn it, Joey, I can see how much you want me!' He looked down to where her nipples stood out revealingly against her sweater.

Her chin rose and her gaze steadily met the burning gold of those stunning eyes. 'Wanting something doesn't always mean it's wise to take it.' She twisted out of his arms to step away from him. 'Believe me, Gideon, when you wake up alone in your own bed tomorrow morning, you'll thank me for saying no tonight.'

Somehow he doubted that very much! He also doubted this constant state of arousal whenever he was in her company—damn it, even when he was *out* of it too—was going to go away any time soon.

But perhaps, for all the reasons he had already told himself, Joey was right to shy away from any deeper involvement between the two of them... *Damn it!*

He thrust his hands into his trouser pockets. 'You're right, of course,' he admitted distantly.

'I am?' She tried teasing. 'That must be a first for me where you're concerned. I should make a note of it in my diary—'

'Don't push it, hmm, Joey?' Gideon said.

Joey was so relieved to have the tension eased between them, and in a way that hadn't caused too much embarrassment to either of them, that she could only grin up at him. 'Do you want that coffee, or do you have to go now?'

Derision sparked in his eyes. 'What do you think?'

'I think I'll see you in morning.'

'Actually, you won't.' He shook his head. 'That was another reason I decided to come here tonight. I had forgotten I'm driving to Oxford in the morning, for a ten o'clock appointment with the owner of a family-run hotel there that Lucan is considering taking into our existing chain.'

'Oh.' Joey nodded. It was the most knowledge concerning St Claire's that Gideon had confided to her in the past three days; the man gave a whole new meaning to playing things close to his chest. 'Do you need me to come with you?'

'Not at this stage, no.'

'I'll see you later in the day, then?'

Again Gideon shook his head. 'I don't work at St Claire's on Thursday afternoons.'

'You don't?'

'It's a long-standing agreement with Lucan.'

Joey eyed him speculatively. 'What *do* you do on Thursday afternoons? Or shouldn't I ask?'

Gideon's gaze was just as direct as her question. 'You shouldn't ask.'

Joey had meant the remark teasingly, but obviously Gideon had taken it literally. Now she was curious—what did he do on Thursday afternoons that was so secret?

Joey was so intrigued by the puzzle that, long after he'd left, she tried to guess what possible incentive could take him away from St Claire's each week.

With any other man Joey would have said it was a woman, perhaps a married one, he could only see on a Thursday afternoon when her husband was away or at work. But as the man was Gideon, she somehow didn't think that was the right explanation.

For one thing he was something of a workaholic, with his own life and emotions taking second place to that dedication. Taking an afternoon off from that work in order to spend time in bed with his married mistress would, Joey felt sure, be complete anathema to a man like him. Or perhaps she just hoped that it would?

More to the point, Gideon's own parents' marriage had broken down because of his father's relationship with another woman, and it had succeeded in emotionally scarring all three of the St Claire brothers. Even if Gideon found himself attracted to a married woman, Joey somehow couldn't see him ever giving in to that attraction.

She was so intrigued by the mystery of what he did on a Thursday afternoon, that it wasn't until after she had gone to bed and fallen asleep that the possible answer to that other, more pressing puzzle of who might have vandalised their two cars, literally came to her in a dream...

CHAPTER SEVEN

JOEY was literally jumping up and down in frustrated excitement by the time Gideon arrived at St Claire's at eight-thirty on Friday morning. Looking his usual cool and aloof self, in a charcoal-grey suit, white shirt and pale grey silk tie, rather than like a man who had might possibly have spent yesterday afternoon in bed with his married mistress—whatever that might look like!

Was that a sense of relief Joey was feeling?

If it was, then it was entirely inappropriate. She'd had her chance on Wednesday evening if she'd wanted to go to bed with Gideon, making any feelings of jealousy on her part over where he went on Thursday afternoons completely ridiculous.

Which wasn't to say that she hadn't casually tried to find out if May knew what Gideon did every Thursday afternoon...

Either the woman didn't know the answer to that question, or she simply wasn't willing to share the information; whichever it was, despite casually mentioning the subject to both secretaries, by Friday morning Joey was still none the wiser as to where he went!

Gideon came to a halt in the doorway as soon as he saw Joey, standing beside the desk in Lucan's office. 'I thought your office was next door?'

She gave an impatient squeak which made him raise an amused blond brow in query. 'I needed to talk to you as soon as you got in.'

Gideon strolled farther into the room to place his brief-case beside the desk before turning to look at her. 'What could possibly be so urgent that you felt the need to ambush me as soon as I walked in the door?' He leant back on the front of the desk; yesterday had been a long and tiring day—not least because of the need to try and banish from his mind the unsatisfactory ending to the evening before, regarding the unlooked-for and unwanted desire he felt for Joey.

A desire that had, unfortunately, leapt into being the moment Gideon set eyes on her again just now...

Joey was looking especially attractive today, in a red business suit and snowy white silk blouse. Her legs were long and silky beneath a pert short skirt, and she wore matching red high-heeled shoes—the latter still surprisingly on her feet, at the moment.

Why *this* woman? Gideon asked himself for what had to be the hundredth time. Why was it that just looking at Joey McKinley instantly took his thoughts to long, naked bodies stretched out invitingly on red satin sheets? Whatever it was, Gideon had every intention of mastering it rather than allowing it to master him.

Joey's jade-green eyes glowed with repressed excitement. 'I think I know who vandalised our cars. Well...I don't know his name or anything. But I do know what he looks like. I think...' She frowned in brief uncertainty before once again brightening. 'Well, I asked around the building, and no one seemed to know who I was talking about, and then I managed to walk casually onto every floor myself to see if I could see him working in any of the offices, but I couldn't, so—'

'Joey, could you take a couple of deep breaths and start again? From the beginning, if possible?' Gideon said, finally managing to interrupt her flow of words. 'You really aren't making a lot of sense at the moment,' he added, as she looked at him with frowning irritation.

She *had* been babbling, Joey acknowledged, taking a deep breath and willing herself to just calm down; she never babbled—and certainly not in front of Gideon St Claire! Besides, she only thought she *might* have solved the riddle of who had deliberately punctured the tyres on both her own car and Gideon's.

Speaking of which... 'Did you get your car back yet?'

Gideon nodded. 'Yesterday evening.'

'That's good. And the security disks we looked at the other evening? Do you have those with you now?'

Joey had gone down to Security herself and asked to look at the disks again, but the supervisor there had been unwilling to let her do that without Gideon's permission. It was understandable, but it would have made her enquiries so much easier if she could have had a printed photograph to show around and see if anyone recognised the person caught on camera.

Gideon's expression darkened. 'They're still in my briefcase. Why?'

'Because I think I might know—' Joey broke off, determined not to start babbling again.

The beginning, Joey, she instructed herself firmly. Start at the beginning. Calmly. Logically. That last one should be something that Gideon recognised, at least!

'As you know, I went to the coffee shop on Monday morning—'

'To see the buff and golden-haired young god—yes, I remember.' Gideon eyed her mockingly.

Joey shot him a glare. 'Will you just forget about him?'

'*I'm* not the one who's obsessed with him!'

Neither was she, really; at the time it had just been another way of teasing Gideon for being so uptight. A teasing that seemed to have backfired on her, if he was going to keep bringing it into every conversation...

'Forget him, okay?' she instructed irritably. 'It's the other man I met on Monday that I want to talk about—'

'Good God, Joey, how many men are involved in this balancing act you call your social life?' Gideon stood up abruptly and went to sit behind the desk, his eyes narrowed as he looked up at her. 'You already regularly date Jason Pickard, and lust after the golden-haired youth with stamina who serves you with your hot chocolate.' He gave a disgusted shake of his head. 'Apparently there's now another man to add to that list.'

And all of them could just as easily be dismissed—because she wasn't romantically involved with any of them.

'I believe you missed yourself off the list,' she retorted a little snidely.

'Perhaps that's as well,' he bit out.

'No doubt,' Joey said. 'The thing is, I remember seeing this particular man on one of those security disks we looked at on Wednesday evening. Around lunchtime, entering the car park on foot,' she added as Gideon opened his briefcase to look for the discs. 'Now, it could all be perfectly innocent,' she said cautiously, 'but when he spoke to me I remember thinking that he seemed slightly familiar—which again might just mean I've seen him here somewhere.'

'This man actually spoke to you?' Gideon closed his briefcase with a decisive snap, eyes dark with disapproval.

She grimaced. 'I spoke to him first, when I apologised for holding him up in the queue.'

'No doubt you were distracted at the time, drooling over the—'

'Gideon, I swear, if you mention the buff twenty-year-old *one more time*, I'm afraid I will really have to become violent!' Joey was very aware that it had been *Gideon*, the seriously buff thirty-four-year-old, who had been responsible for her distraction on Monday morning, rather than someone barely out of adolescence!

His expression was derisive. 'I'll forget about him if you will.'

'Consider him forgotten!' she said through gritted teeth. 'So, I apologised to this man for delaying him and then left, but I was still standing on the pavement outside when he came out, which was when he talked to me—'

'Understandably,' Gideon interjected. 'You had given him an opening earlier, and you're a very beautiful woman.' He shrugged when Joey gave him a questioning look. 'Well, you are,' he mocked lightly as her glance became quelling.

Joey eyed him uncertainly. 'You didn't always seem to think so.'

His jaw tensed. 'I've never denied that you're a beautiful woman, Joey.'

'Just not one any sane man should ever be attracted to, hmm?'

He scowled. 'If that's the case, then it would seem I've joined the ranks of the insane.'

And Joey, having changed her opinion of Gideon being a cold and stuck-up aristocrat, also had to be out of her mind!

'Maybe we should just forget about that too?' she suggested.

He arched blond brows. 'For the moment? Or indefinitely?'

'Gideon, are you being deliberately awkward, or am I just imagining it?' She glared at him in frustration.

No, he conceded ruefully, she wasn't imagining anything. He had just been thrown slightly by the strength of his protective reaction on hearing that some strange man had obviously tried to pick her up.

It was because she was Stephanie's sister, he told himself. That connection made Joey 'family', and as such under the protection of the St Claires. It had absolutely nothing to do with his own illogical attraction to her. Nothing at all...

'Sorry,' he said, aware she was still waiting for a reply. 'So this man spoke to you?'

'It seemed perfectly natural at the time,' she said, obviously accepting his apology. 'How the changeable weather was causing colds, et cetera. But he also asked me if I worked locally—'

'You didn't tell him, did you?' he barked.

'Gideon, will you give me credit for having *some* intelligence?' She gave him a fierce frown.

'Sorry,' he muttered again.

'Of course I didn't tell him where I worked,' Joey continued calmly. 'But I do remember at the time making a conscious effort not to do so. Almost as if I somehow knew that I shouldn't.' She frowned. 'I excused myself as quickly as possible, but I remember feeling as if he was watching me as I walked away— What now?' she asked, when she saw Gideon's knowing expression.

He shook his head. 'I'm just surprised you would find that behaviour strange. Any red-blooded man would feel the same temptation to watch you as you walk away in those sexy high-heeled shoes.' He eyed her as he leant back in the chair. 'And do you have any idea how much like my mother you sound when you talk in that scolding tone of voice?'

'That's probably because—no doubt, *exactly* like your mother—I'm tempted to smack you every time you do or say something aggravating!'

Gideon smiled. 'My mother didn't believe in smacking any of her sons.'

'That probably explains why you, at least, have grown into such an annoying adult.'

Gideon found himself chuckling softly as he answered her. 'What's *your* excuse?'

'Oh, my ability to aggravate and annoy just comes naturally,' she assured him dryly.

Gideon laughed outright this time. Something he seemed to do quite a lot of around Joey, he found himself thinking.

'Well, at least I know when I'm being annoying,' Joey defended.

'Unlike some people?'

'Exactly!'

'In your case, you do it regardless,' Gideon accused.

She grinned. 'Of course.'

'Especially where I'm concerned.'

'Oh, especially then.' She nodded unabashedly. 'It's just too irresistible when you're so easy to tease.'

He looked rueful. 'Most people would know better than to even attempt it.'

Joey shrugged. 'I've already told you—I'm not most people.'

No, she certainly wasn't. Joey McKinley was unlike anyone else—certainly any other woman—Gideon had ever met.

'Perhaps we should just look at the disk for lunchtime?'

He took out his laptop to place it on top of the desk and turn it on.

Joey was thrown slightly by the sudden change of conversation. Although why she should be, she had no idea; Gideon had proved, time and time again, how adept he was at avoiding subjects he didn't wish to talk about.

Talking of which...

'Did you do anything nice on your afternoon off yesterday?' She deliberately kept her tone lightly enquiring, having no intention of letting him see how consumed with curiosity she really was regarding his whereabouts.

He glanced at her over the top of his laptop, his expression inscrutable as he answered. 'I did what I usually do on a Thursday afternoon.'

'Which is?' Joey definitely had a problem imagining a workaholic like Gideon actually taking an afternoon off work to visit a mistress—or maybe that was just wishful thinking on her part? An aversion to even imagining him spending the afternoon in bed with another woman?

Which was pretty stupid when she could have gone to bed with him herself on Wednesday night. Something that still sent quivers of awareness down the length of her spine...

'Why the interest?' Gideon asked directly.

Joey shrugged. 'It just seems...out of character for you, and that intrigues me.'

'Really?' Gideon drawled.

'Okay—fine.' Joey held up her hands in surrender. 'If you want me to continue to think you spend Thursday afternoons in bed with your married mistress—'

'If I want you to carry on thinking *what*?' Gideon spluttered incredulously.

Joey's cheeks warmed as she saw the disbelief in his expression. Proof, if she had needed it, that she was way off the mark with the mistress remark. 'It was just a thought...'

'I'm not sure whether I should feel insulted or flattered,' Gideon grated. 'Maybe, as a precaution against allowing your imagination to run even wilder than it already has, I should tell you I deal with...other legal matters on Thursday afternoons.'

Joey blinked. That certainly hadn't been in her list of possibilities when she'd been considering Gideon's Thursday afternoon activities!

'I didn't know you still had a private practice.'

Gideon looked as if he wished he had never started this conversation, his jaw tense. 'I don't.'

'Then I don't understand.'

He sighed heavily. 'Do you really *need* to understand?'

'I think so, yes.'

Gideon continued to look at her for several long seconds before giving in. 'Purely in the interest of keeping you quiet, I'll tell you. I've helped to run a free legal advice clinic here in the city for the last couple of years.' He shrugged casually. 'See—no big secret. And no mistress—married or otherwise!'

'Oh.' It was so *not* what Joey had been expecting that she couldn't think of anything else to say.

'Yes—*oh*,' Gideon echoed dryly. 'Now, could we stop wasting time and just look at the appropriate disk?'

In other words, end of subject. Joey understood that as she moved around the desk to stand beside him. But it didn't stop her thinking. From realising that she had once again misjudged him...

She was so close to him now that she could take in tantalising breaths of clean male overlaid with an elusive tangy aftershave. Close enough to become uncomfortably aware of the heat of his body. Of how one of them only had to move slightly in order for them to be touching…

Stop it, Joey, she instructed herself firmly, even as she moved as far away from Gideon as it was possible for her to be and still be able to see the screen of his laptop. What was wrong with her? She and Gideon had absolutely nothing in common. Well…that wasn't quite true, was it? They were both twins. Both valued their family. Liked their independence. Were both focused on their work—to the extent that Gideon actually helped run a free legal clinic, which she deeply admired.

Just those four things alone were more than some couples who had been married for years had in common!

'Joey, are you paying attention?'

She gave a guilty start as she realised that Gideon had been playing the disk while her thoughts wandered.

'Of course I'm paying attention,' Joey said mendaciously. 'I'll tell you when we get to the relevant part—*there*!' she shouted excitedly as the image came onto the screen. Her hands moved instinctively to grip Gideon's shoulder. And as quickly she removed them again once she realised what she had done. 'Sorry,' she muttered awkwardly.

Gideon glanced up at her curiously, surprised to see the slight flush to her cheeks, and the way her downcast gaze avoided meeting his own. Almost as if…

'Joey, if you would like to rethink your decision of Wednesday evening—and despite the wildness of your earlier imaginings—I'm still open to the idea.' He swivelled his chair so that she now stood between his parted legs.

Joey raised startled eyes, a frown creasing her creamy brow, her breasts rapidly rising and falling beneath the white silk of her blouse. 'I thought we had agreed it isn't a good idea for us to become involved?'

They had. And it wasn't. Not two days ago. Not now.

Except Gideon had only needed to take one look at Joey again this morning for all the pent-up desire of the past few days to once again attack every one of his senses. Damn it, he would only be trying to deceive himself if he didn't admit he had spent every one of the past thirty-six hours aching to make love to her.

He held her gaze with his as his arms moved about her waist, to slowly pull her towards him until the warm dip of her thighs rested against his erection, Joey's breasts beneath the silk blouse warm and soft against the hardness of his shirted chest, her lips only inches away from his.

'I want to take you right here and right now,' he rasped harshly.

Joey moistened suddenly dry lips, her hands once again resting on his shoulders, this time in a feeble effort to try and keep her distance. 'You do?' she whispered.

'Oh, yes,' Gideon admitted throatily.

She still wanted him too—needed him to assuage this constant burning ache inside her. Yet… 'I seem to remember we were interrupted the last time we tried this here,' she protested.

'I'll lock the doors,' he murmured.

'There's still the window…'

'The window?' Gideon's gaze moved past her incredulously, to the huge picture window.

Joey nodded. They might be ten floors up, but the building across the street was nine floors high, and had a roof garden that Joey had seen several of the employees there step out onto over the past few days, whenever they wanted a cigarette. As if to prove her point, right at that moment a couple of men appeared on the roof opposite.

Gideon frowned his irritation. 'Then we'll go into the adjoining bathroom and lock the damned door!'

Joey's cheeks burned. 'Wouldn't that look…a little strange, if May should come in here?'

Gideon's eyes glittered a deep burnished gold as he stood up. 'Who the hell cares how it looks?' He retained a tight grip on Joey's wrist as he led the way into a huge private bathroom she hadn't even realised was through this door from Lucan's office.

And it truly *was* a bathroom, Joey noted slightly dazedly as she looked around them. With a huge smoky-glass-sided shower in one corner, a marble bench seat beside it, and two sinks against the mirrored wall opposite. The walls and floor were also covered in mellow terracotta and cream marble, and the fittings were all in gold, with huge brown bath towels draped over a warm towel rail.

Gideon shut and locked the door behind them, before turning to press Joey back against the marble wall, his whole body tense as he lowered his head and his mouth captured hers for the first time.

Not roughly or demandingly, as Joey would have expected, but with a raw, absorbing sensuality that she had no will or desire to resist.

His mouth sipped from hers time and time again, his tongue a soft caress between her lips, before venturing deeper, claiming the heat of her mouth, and then retreating, only to claim her again. And again. Igniting a hunger inside her…a need for more.

Joey was too lost in those arousing kisses to protest as Gideon moved her slightly away from the wall to push her jacket down her arms, before discarding it completely. Her blouse quickly followed and Gideon broke the kiss long enough to gaze his fill of her breasts, cupped in a cream lacy bra, the nipples dusky-pink rosettes beneath that lace. He ran the soft pad of his thumb across their engorged tips.

'I want you naked, Joey,' he breathed huskily, and turned

her so that she stood with her back towards him, facing the mirrored wall, his hands lightly cupping her breasts as he looked over her shoulder at their reflection.

Joey stared at that reflection too, her arousal deepening as she felt the warmth of Gideon's breath on her shoulder, the press of his arousal against the curve of her bottom where he stood so goldenly handsome behind her, his hands dark against her bra and much paler skin.

Gideon continued to hold her gaze with his as he lowered his head to move his mouth lightly against her throat, sipping, tasting. Joey's back arched invitingly as his hands tightened about her breasts, pushing them up so that they swelled temptingly over the cream lace.

'Unfasten your bra for me, Joey,' he encouraged huskily.

Joey continued to stare at their reflection in the mirror as she slowly reached behind her to unfasten the hooks of her bra, too mesmerised to be shocked at her behaviour, barely able to breathe as the hooks came loose. Only Gideon's cupping hands and the thin satin straps on her shoulders were keeping her bra in place now.

He didn't touch her in any other way as he kissed first one shoulder and then the other, nudging those thin straps down her arms and allowing the bra to fall away and bare her breasts completely.

His breath caught in his throat as he stared at Joey's reflection. Her breasts were full and tipped with temptingly beautiful dusky rose nipples, which became even harder, more swollen, as Gideon continued to look at them in the mirror.

'You're beautiful,' he breathed, stepping out from behind her to move her, so that she now sat on the marble bench seat, and pushing her skirt up her thighs so that he could kneel between her legs. He was able to feel the heat of her arousal as he cupped her breasts before bending to find first one dusky rose nipple and then the other with his mouth.

She tasted wonderful, her nipples swelling as Gideon drew on them hungrily, stroking with his tongue at the same time, all the while feeling Joey's trembling response as he allowed his teeth to gently scrape across those sensitive tips.

Joey was too lost in the vortex of pleasure to question why it was she was responding so totally to Gideon, of all men.

'Aren't you…a little overdressed still…?' she prompted restlessly, desperate now to touch him in the same way he was touching her.

'A little.' He gave a rueful smile as he straightened, slipping out of his jacket and pulling off his tie before dropping them down on the floor with Joey's discarded clothes.

'Let me.' Joey gently pushed his hands away as he would have unbuttoned his shirt himself, and her gaze easily held his as she slowly unfastened each of those buttons. She only lowered it to look at him as she took off his shirt completely, to bare his tanned chest.

His shoulders were so wide, his muscled chest so clearly defined, with a light dusting of golden hair that dipped lower, to taper down beneath his trousers. Joey touched him lingeringly, running her fingers lightly over that tanned flesh. Gideon's nipples were hard little buds beneath her fingertips where they nestled amongst those golden curls.

Would kissing one give Gideon the same pleasure he had just given her? she wondered. She satisfied that curiosity, knowing by his sharply indrawn breath as he cupped the back of her head and held her against him that the answer to that question was a definite yes.

Emboldened, she turned to give the second hard bud the

same treatment. His skin felt hot to the touch, and Joey was able to feel the rapid beating of Gideon's heart beneath her fingertips. Her hands moved lower, feeling the leap of his hard shaft as her fingers swept against him tentatively.

'God, yes, Joey…' Gideon groaned achingly, his hips pushing against her hands. Her caresses instantly became bolder at his encouragement, and she started to stroke the pulsing length of his erection harder and faster.

Gideon unbuttoned and unzipped his trousers himself, pushing them and his boxers down to his hips and instantly feeling relief as his arousal sprang free. He growled softly in his throat as he felt her hands taking possession of his bared flesh, instinctively thrusting into those caressing hands, knowing he was on the brink of release, and need-ing–oh, God—needing it so badly.

'Change places with me, Gideon,' Joey encouraged ur-gently, and she released him long enough for him to take her place on the marble seat. Now she knelt in front of him, stroking her tongue lightly across his sensitive tip, licking and tasting as her hand continued to stroke him firmly.

Gideon's vision became slightly blurred as he looked down and saw Joey taking him into her mouth, her slender fingers still curled about him, her tongue continuing that rasping, rhythmic swirl.

'I'm going to come if you don't stop!'

In complete contradiction of that warning Gideon moved one of his hands to the back of Joey's head, and his fingers became entangled in the glossy red of her hair, holding her to him as he instinctively began to thrust deeper. At the same time his other hand cupped and caressed one of her uptilting breasts, teasing, squeezing, before rolling the engorged nipple between finger and thumb.

Joey moaned in pleasure even as she felt the responsive warmth flood between her thighs.

She had never been this intimate with any man before. Never *wanted* to be this intimate with any man before Gideon. Had never felt this heady exhilaration at the giving and receiving of pleasure. Her caresses were purely instinctive...

'Yes, Joey...' Gideon's eyes glowed like molten gold between narrowed lids. 'Oh, God,' he groaned.

'Gideon?' A knock sounded on the bathroom door. 'Are you unwell, Gideon?' Concern could be clearly heard in May Randall's voice as she obviously stood on the other side of the locked bathroom door.

Joey froze, totally stricken, shocked at her complete lack of inhibition!

CHAPTER EIGHT

'OKAY, so you were proved right. Attempting to make love in a bathroom *wasn't* the most sensible thing I've ever thought of doing!'

Gideon paced Joey's office impatiently fifteen minutes later as she sat looking at him guardedly from behind her desk. Both of them were now fully dressed, and the pallor of her cheeks told him exactly how upset she still was.

Was is embarrassment at the depth of the intimacy they had shared earlier? Or disappointment because that intimacy had been interrupted? Gideon wasn't sure...

He did know that they had both reacted like guilty teenagers when May Randall knocked on the bathroom door. Joey's face had been stricken as she'd stood up to turn her back on him, quickly dressing in her cream lace bra and silk blouse. Gideon hadn't been much better as he'd forced his still aching erection back inside his boxers and zipped up his trousers. Tersely, he had assured May that he was fine, and would join her in her office in a few minutes, before pulling his shirt on and fastening the buttons with hands that had shaken slightly.

No, it certainly hadn't been Gideon's finest hour...

As he had just told Joey it hadn't been his most sensible one, either. Sadly, his usual cool sensibility had gone out of the window the moment she had come to work in the adjoining office!

'Will you please say something, Joey?' he pleaded now, at her continued uncomfortable silence.

Maybe she would break her silence if she could think of something to say. If she wasn't still so totally shocked by her own behaviour...

Ideally she needed to say something dismissive and sophisticated. But, as she didn't feel in the least dismissive *or* sophisticated at the moment, she had no idea what she could say without sounding ridiculously gauche and inexperienced.

Just looking at Gideon now, remembering the depth of the intimacy between them earlier, was enough to make her want to crawl away somewhere and hide. At least until she stopped feeling as if she might die from embarrassment every time she so much as looked at him. Which would be never...

Maybe the best thing was to just avoid the subject altogether. 'Have you had chance yet to look at that security disk?'

Gideon stopped his pacing to stare across the desk at her incredulously. 'Is that the best you can do?'

'I can see no benefit to either of us in talking about what just happened.' Especially as she was still in shock because of it!

Neither did he. Until, that was, Joey expressed her own reluctance to talk about it...

Just being near this woman made him behave recklessly, impulsively, illogically. Something he never, ever did—in any situation. Hearing her dismiss that behaviour as if it were of absolutely no consequence was enough to make him want to shake her!

He glowered down at her from the other side of the desk.

'How about we discuss a time when we can finish what we started?'

Green eyes met his briefly before Joey looked quickly away again. 'That would be extremely stupid of us.'

'No more stupid than me walking about with a constant erection and you on the brink of orgasm!' he retorted.

Two bright wings of colour appeared in the pallor of her cheeks. 'You're being deliberately crude—'

'I'm being honest,' Gideon corrected.

'Then perhaps you ought to consider being less honest and a little more circumspect!' She glared up at him.

Gideon gave a humourless laugh. 'Until you came along, *circumspect* used to be my middle name. It seems to have abandoned me.'

'Then I suggest you find it again!'

She briskly shifted some papers on top of her desk, drawing Gideon's attention to the golden dragon sitting majestically at the front. Those glittering yellow eyes seemed to glower at him malevolently.

'Your good luck charm doesn't appear to be working at the moment,' he murmured ruefully.

'My good luck charm is working just fine.' Joey reached out to touch the dragon defensively. 'It's the two of *us* who are behaving irrationally.'

Gideon looked slightly self-conscious. 'I have no more idea than you do what's going on between us.' He scowled his frustration. 'But something obviously is,' he added less forcefully as he gentled his expression. 'And we obviously can't keep doing this.'

Her fingers curled about the golden dragon. 'Doing what?'

'Going a little further each time we make love and then stopping.' He frowned darkly. 'Besides being frustrating as hell, it's totally disruptive!'

Joey smiled tightly. 'How typical that you should look at this from the point of view of how it affects your work—'

'Totally disruptive for both of us in regard to just living our lives,' he corrected her. 'Damn it, Joey, you're like a constant itch I can't scratch.'

'I believe that's the first time a man has compared me to having the irritation of a rash! How complimentary!' she said sarcastically.

'I don't recall using the word irritating.'

She shrugged. 'Nevertheless, it was there in your tone of voice.'

Gideon growled his impatience. 'You don't know me well enough yet to say *what's* in my tone of voice.'

'And I have no wish to know you well enough, either,' Joey stated firmly. 'Gideon, I can't stress strongly enough how much of a mistake I consider our earlier behaviour to be.' She met his gaze unflinchingly. 'Especially when you consider how much we dislike and disapprove of each other.'

Gideon became very still, his expression guarded, as he considered whether that statement was still true. In regard to himself, at least. He certainly hadn't liked or approved of Joey before she'd come to work with him. Right now he wasn't sure what he felt towards her...

'You're right, of course,' Gideon said calmly.

Joey looked up at him searchingly, unsure about his sudden capitulation. Gideon's expression was back to being cold and aloof, and revealed none of his real emotions.

Perhaps that was as well, considering how badly shaken she still was at the way they hadn't been able to keep their hands off each other the moment they saw each other again.

'And the answer to your earlier question is no—I haven't

had a chance to look at the security disk yet,' he admitted. 'I thought—obviously mistakenly!—that it was more important for me come in here and offer you reassurance over what just happened rather than look at it.'

The inexperienced Joey would have welcomed his reassurance fifteen minutes ago—after May had first interrupted them. Now she just wanted to forget the whole embarrassing incident.

She gave a haughty inclination of her head. 'Obviously you *were* mistaken.'

Gideon dragged in a harsh breath and resisted the impulse he had to reach across the desk, grab hold of Joey's shoulders, and shake her until her teeth rattled—a move guaranteed, as it involved touching her, into tempting him into pulling her back into his arms. Which would take them God only knew where!

His jaw clenched as he ground his teeth together. 'Let's go and look at the damned thing now, if that's what you want.'

He turned on his heel and strode forcefully into the adjoining office without waiting to see if Joey followed him. At that moment he didn't particularly care whether she did or not.

Gideon had known from the first that having her working here was going to cause unwanted complications—he just hadn't realised what direction those complications would take.

He always chose his bed partners with care—invariably because those women were able to regard physical relationships with the same detachment Gideon did. Yet just the smell of Joey's perfume, combining sexily aroused woman with a lightly floral scent, as she once again came to stand beside him as he brought up the image on his computer screen, was enough to cause a resurgence of his earlier arousal. So much for detachment, he thought frustratedly...

'I know him.' Gideon bent down for a closer look as the image she had frozen earlier, of a bearded man, reappeared on his computer screen. 'Where the hell do I know him from?'

'Maybe he works here after all?' Joey suggested helpfully.

'No, that isn't it.' Gideon continued to study the image. 'Maybe if we took away the beard? Put a little weight on him? Possibly a shirt and tie—'

'And you'd have Richard Newman,' Joey said slowly.

Gideon glanced at her briefly, before turning his attention back to the man on the screen. 'We have Richard Newman,' he agreed.

The same Richard Newman who had been only too happy to let Joey's sister Stephanie be named as the other woman in his divorce a couple of months ago, in order to protect the woman he was really having an affair with— namely his boss's wife. Richard Newman who had subsequently lost his wife and custody of his children, his home and his mistress, and his job, when the truth finally came out.

A truth that Gideon and Joey, between them, had discovered and revealed...

Well...mainly Gideon, to be perfectly honest. But Joey had certainly been working towards proving her twin's innocence, too.

Which was perhaps why Newman had now chosen to target both of them with malicious sabotage?

Gideon turned to look at Joey, frowning slightly as he saw that she had stepped away from the desk and now stood with her back towards him in front of the window, her arms wrapped almost protectively about her waist.

'Joey?'

She didn't answer, but her shoulders began to tremble.

Gideon pushed his chair back to stand up slowly. 'Joey, are you okay?'

'Am I *okay*?' she repeated sharply as she turned, those jade-green eyes glittering brightly. 'We almost made love in the damned bathroom, and now—'

'Let's just concentrate on Richard Newman,' Gideon muttered grimly.

She shook her head. 'They warned me about this when I took my law degree. The possibility that some dissatisfied client might one day turn nasty. But I never thought—I never imagined it would ever happen to me. Or realised how awful it would feel if it did.'

'Joey—'

'I *spoke* to him, Gideon!' Her voice broke emotionally, and her eyes were wide with distress now as the trembling intensified. 'I stood in front of him in the coffee shop, and when he came outside he deliberately engaged me in casual conversation. And all the time he— It can't have been a coincidence, Gideon. He must have been watching me. Must have followed me to the coffee shop! Deliberately stood behind me in the queue—oh, God…!' The trembling became full-blown shaking as the enormity of that supposedly casual meeting hit her.

Gideon had become so accustomed to Joey's perky self-confidence, the way she usually had an answer to everything and everyone, that for a few brief seconds he could only stand and stare at her rather than respond. Until those tears swimming in her jade-green eyes began to cascade over her lashes to fall hotly down her cheeks.

'Oh, Joey!' Gideon gave a pained groan as he stepped forward to enfold her in his arms and hold her tightly against him.

Joey clung to Gideon, knowing she had never felt so scared. Never felt as if her life, what was going on around her, was so totally out of her control.

How long had Richard Newman been following her? Just this past week, since she'd come to work at St Claire's? Or had it started before that? Had he been secretly watching her for weeks? Just waiting for the chance, the opportunity—

'Don't let your imagination run away with you, Joey,' Gideon advised evenly.

'Well, at least I can claim to *have* an imagination!' She moved back to glare up at him.

Gideon's mouth thinned as he recalled their conversation on Monday morning, when Joey had last accused him of lacking in imagination. 'Resorting to insulting me again isn't going to help this situation.'

'*Nothing* is going to help this situation!'

'I'll deal with it.'

'How?' Joey challenged. 'How will you deal with it, Gideon?' Her voice rose emotionally. 'I realise you're one of the invincible St Claires, but even so—'

'*Joey.*'

Joey stared at him for several long seconds before drawing in a deep, controlling breath. Gideon had only spoken her name, in that cool and calm way of his, but nevertheless it was enough to halt her rising hysteria.

'I'm sorry.' She released a shaky sigh. 'Instead of insulting you I should really be congratulating myself—the fact that Newman only punctured one of my tyres to your two would seem to imply that he only hates me half as much as he hates you,' she explained ruefully when Gideon raised questioning brows.

'Glad to see you're getting your sense of humour back!'

he murmured as his arms dropped back to his sides and he stepped away from her.

'That's me.' Joey nodded self-derisively. 'A laugh a minute!'

Gideon wasn't fooled for a moment. He had seen yet another side of Joey this morning. Beneath that tough exterior she chose to present to the world there was a woman every bit as soft and vulnerable as her twin. The woman who kept a golden dragon on her desk because her twin had given it to her. For good luck, she said. And the woman with a singing voice an angel would envy, which she chose not to share publicly. Knowing what he did of her now, Gideon was sure there was a perfectly good reason—an emotional reason—why that was.

Joey McKinley was the most complex and by far the most fascinating woman Gideon had ever met...

That alone was enough to set off alarm bells inside him. The emotions she displayed were enough of a warning to keep his distance. Gideon had managed, for over twenty years to avoid all emotional entanglement, apart from with his close family, and the complex and deeply emotional Joey McKinley was in danger of breaching that carefully built-up detachment.

Gideon had learnt at a young age, after the break-up of his parents' marriage when he was ten years old, of the complexities and the danger of feeling emotion—particularly romantic love—for another person. His mother Molly had loved his father Alexander—only to learn, after thirteen years of marriage and the birth of three sons, that her husband had been in love with another woman for twenty years. The woman Alexander had eventually abandoned his wife and sons to be with.

Oh, Molly had seemed to finally come to terms with that when Lucan had announced he was marrying the granddaughter of the 'other woman' in that love triangle. But Gideon still clearly remembered the heartache his mother had suffered when she and Alexander had parted so acrimoniously. In all these years she had never even thought of falling in love again—let alone remarrying. It was a lesson in 'love' that all three of Molly's sons had taken to heart.

The fact that Jordan and Lucan had both succumbed in the past two months, and subsequently married the women they'd fallen in love with, in no way shook the decision Gideon had made over twenty years ago *never* to put his own heart into someone else's keeping just so that they could trample all over it.

He certainly wasn't about to break his own rule of re-maining detached by allowing himself to feel any sort of emotion for the unpredictable Joey McKinley!

Apart, that was, from the desire that raged through him every time he so much as looked at her...

He moved to sit back behind his desk before Joey could become aware that he was once again aroused. 'I believe the best way to deal with this is for me to contact the police and tell them what we know. Once I have, they will prob-ably want to talk to you, too.'

'I'm not going anywhere.' Joey had no idea what Gideon had been thinking about for the past few minutes, but what-ever it was they hadn't been pleasant thoughts.

Not surprising, really, when the two of them had the problem of Richard Newman hanging over their heads like the Sword of Damocles. But, awful as that situation was, Joey felt a certain relief that it had at least diverted attention from their earlier passion.

That whole situation was getting completely out of hand—or *in* hand, as it had turned out; Joey wondered if she would ever be able to banish the memories of touching

Gideon, and having him touch her as intimately, completely from her mind!

But she was going to have to do just that if she was to stand any chance of getting through the next three weeks of working with him so closely.

She straightened. 'I suggest we refrain from telling Stephanie or Jordan anything about this for the moment,' she said briskly. 'They can't do anything about it, and it would only worry Stephanie, and no doubt Jordan too, if they knew about it.'

Gideon raised derisive brows. 'I believe I have enough intelligence to have worked that out for myself.'

Joey had never doubted his intelligence—only his ability to empathise with other people. Although even *that* was questionable after the way he had kissed and caressed her to the brink of release earlier.

Her traitorous body still ached for that release. Her breasts chafed uncomfortably inside her bra, and her panties were damp and uncomfortable against the sensitive skin between her thighs...

She nodded abruptly. 'I'll leave you while you call the police.' She turned swiftly on her heel to walk to the doorway between their two offices.

'Joey...'

She came to an abrupt halt, determinedly schooling her features into mild curiosity before she turned back to face Gideon. 'Yes?'

'It's going to be all right, you know.' He gave her a reassuring smile. 'I'm not going to let Newman anywhere near you,' he added gently.

That gentleness was almost Joey's undoing, and as she once again felt that emotional lump rise to constrict her throat. She could deal with Gideon's coldness, his sarcasm, his detachment, even his unexpected passion, but his gentleness was something else entirely...

'We'll see,' she managed, before finally escaping into her own office.

Before she broke down a second time and decided to run back into the security of Gideon's protective arms and blubber all over him like a baby!

CHAPTER NINE

'I STILL think this is unnecessary,' Joey muttered grump-
ily as she got out of her car and locked it, before turning
to face Gideon as the two of them stood in front of her
apartment building.

'You heard the police advice.' He shrugged unapologetically as he joined her on the pavement, his own car parked
directly behind Joey's. 'For the moment there's safety in
numbers—which means I don't intend letting you drive to
or from work again on your own, or indeed anywhere else,
until they've managed to locate and question Newman.'

Yes, Joey had been present in Gideon's office when the
two police officers, after learning of the events of the past
few days, had offered that advice. She had even appreciated the practicality of that advice at the time; if she never
went out alone then Newman wouldn't be able to accost her
again, as he had at the coffee shop on Monday morning.
But appreciating the practicality of the advice and actually
living with it were two distinctly different things!

Especially now, after a day of having Gideon insist on
accompanying her to the coffee shop this morning to collect her hot chocolate—with less than flattering remarks
about the immaturity of the poor guy serving behind the
counter!—and then again to the park nearby when she went
out to eat her sandwich at lunchtime. Now, finally, he had

followed her home in his own car to make sure she arrived safely.

All this 'togetherness' certainly wasn't going to make it any easier to forget what had happened between them that morning!

She pulled the strap of her bag firmly up onto her shoulder. 'I'm home now, Gideon,' she said pointedly, not feeling in the least reassured by the way he had locked and walked away from his own car just now.

His eyes narrowed. 'Are you intending to go out again?'

'What if I am?' Joey frowned. 'You aren't coming with me!' she exclaimed as she saw the determined expression on his face.

'That would depend on where you intend going, now, wouldn't it.'

Joey snorted her frustration. 'And if I'm going out on a date?'

Gideon's brows rose. 'Are you?'

'As it happens, no,' she said. 'I usually go to the gym on a Friday evening,' she added grudgingly.

He nodded. 'Then that's where we'll go.'

She sighed with impatience. 'Newman is hardly going to follow me there. You have to be a member to get in, for one thing—'

'Joey.'

Again Gideon only said her name—but it was done in such a way as to convey to her that he had no intention of doing anything other than what he chose to do. And at that moment he was choosing to accompany her to the gym.

'We haven't so much as set sight on the man for the past two days—'

'Which in no way guarantees that he won't decide to follow you again tonight,' Gideon reasoned.

'This is utterly ridiculous!'

Gideon had to hold back a smile at Joey's obvious frustration with the situation. Not that he found the reason for this caution in the least amusing, but her response to it certainly was.

She had been obviously uncomfortable that morning, when he'd accompanied her to the coffee shop and given his opinion on the 'buff' young god serving behind the counter. She'd been equally ungracious when Gideon had chosen to eat his own lunch in the park with her—and then teased her mercilessly about illegally feeding most of her sandwich to the ducks. And he had to admit to enjoying her discomfort now, at the idea of his accompanying her to the gym.

Obviously his spending all this time in her company was far from ideal, after his earlier decision to keep his distance from her, but other than assigning her a bodyguard—something Joey would no doubt find even more unacceptable than their present arrangement—he couldn't think of any other solution to their present problem.

So, until the police had found and at least spoken to Richard Newman, the two of them appeared to be stuck with each other. And she would just have to accept it.

'How about I take you out to dinner afterwards?' he cajoled.

'Isn't that rather defeating the object of going to the gym?' Joey asked.

'Not if you have something healthy to eat, no.'

He was being deliberately irritating, Joey decided shrewdly. He was patently enjoying himself far too much—and at her expense! 'Look, Gideon—'

'No, *you* look, Joey,' he interrupted calmly. 'You and I both know that Stephanie would never forgive me if I didn't make sure nothing happens to you.'

Damn!

Damn, damn, *damn*!

Joey glared at him. He *would* have to invoke the 'Stephanie' word. A tactic that Gideon knew very well was guaranteed to silence all her protests. Much as Joey liked her independence, she would never do anything to disturb or disrupt her twin's newly married bliss to the gorgeous Jordan.

She couldn't help thinking that, for twins, the two men didn't look or behave anything alike. Jordan was dark-haired and golden-eyed, and Gideon had blond hair and chocolate-brown eyes; Jordan was effortlessly charming, while Gideon's charm was much more subtle.

So much of Gideon, it seemed, was hidden beneath the surface. That deep love for his family. His concern two months ago for Stephanie. The way he was insisting on taking care of Joey right now...

Whatever the reason for Joey's attraction to him—and the more she came to know him the deeper the attraction became—she hoped that the police managed to find and talk to Richard Newman very soon. Because she wasn't sure how much of this togetherness with Gideon she could take without succumbing to the desire that raged through her every time she looked at him—when she wasn't annoyed with him, that was...

She gave him a reproving frown now. 'That's emotional blackmail.'

He appeared unconcerned by the accusation. 'So?'

Joey grumbled, 'It's absolutely shameful to use my love for Stephanie in this way.'

'Is it working?'

'Yes.'

'Mission accomplished.' Gideon gave an unapologetic smile. 'I'll wait here while you go up and get your things.'

Wasn't this going to be a lot of fun? The whole point of Joey's thrice-weekly workout was to keep her fit, but it also involved her becoming hot and sweaty. Not something she particularly relished with Gideon looking on.

'You're wasting time, Joey,' he drawled mockingly, as if well aware of her discomforting thoughts.

Which no doubt he was! 'How about I sign you in as my guest, and you can join me instead of just keeping an eye on me?'

'Good idea,' he agreed. 'I usually go to my own gym every morning before work, so my stuff from this morning is still in the boot of my car.'

Well, that little ploy hadn't worked, had it? She should have guessed Gideon worked out in a gym on a regular basis; he obviously hadn't acquired that muscled chest and the taut power of the rest of his body, just by sitting behind a desk five days a week.

'Unless you think Jason Pickard might object to us spending the evening together?'

Joey's gaze sharpened suspiciously as she looked up at Gideon, but she was unable to read anything from his politely enquiring expression.

She wasn't deceived. 'I've already told you—you have completely the wrong idea about my friendship with Jason. It isn't like that.'

'You seem very determined that I should believe you.'

'Probably because I don't want you to go around thinking I allowed you to…to kiss me when I'm already involved with someone.'

Without breaking Jason's confidence, Joey had no way of convincing Gideon of that; Jason might have chosen to confide in his parents now about the true nature of his relationship with Trevor, but that didn't mean he wanted his very private life revealed to anyone else.

'I don't think that at all,' Gideon said. 'I believe I know you well enough by now to realise that double-dealing and two-timing just isn't your style.'

'Then why do you keep mentioning Jason?'

'I didn't realise you had the monopoly on teasing...'

Teasing? Gideon had been *teasing* her?

Joey stomped off, muttering, 'I've created a monster!'

Gideon's smile was rueful as he watched Joey from between narrowed lids as she walked to her apartment building, very aware of the sexy sway of her hips and silkily shapely legs before she opened the door and disappeared inside. In much the same way Richard Newman had been aware as he'd watched her walk away from the coffee shop on Monday morning...

Gideon's smile faded. Just thinking about the other man having been that close to her was enough to strengthen his resolve to protect her in spite of herself. He had been stating the truth when he'd claimed that Stephanie would never forgive him if anything happened to her twin sister, but it was equally true that Gideon would never forgive himself, either...

'Ready!'

Gideon focused on Joey with an effort as she appeared beside him in the promised five minutes, his eyes widening as he saw she had used that time to change into a fitted white T-shirt beneath a black sports cardigan, and baggy grey tracksuit bottoms that rested low down on her hips above white and purple trainers.

'You really are short, aren't you?' he commented. Once again, she reached only as high as his chin.

'Or you're just exceedingly tall.' She shot him an

annoyed glance as she unlocked her car and threw her sports bag onto the back seat.

'Or I'm just exceedingly tall,' he allowed dryly as he dug his car keys out of his trouser pocket. 'You lead and I'll follow.'

'Now, there's an interesting suggestion,' she jeered.

'I think we've exhausted "interesting" for one day, don't you?' Gideon's smile was wry as he remembered the awkward way in which things had ended between them this morning.

'Probably.' She grimaced as she opened the driver's door of her car. 'I'll see you at the gym.'

Joey was very aware as she drove, as she had been earlier, of Gideon's car a short distance behind her own—probably to ensure that no one cut in between their two cars; she could clearly see Gideon in the driving mirror every time she glanced at it. In fact, she was so focused on Gideon driving behind her that she doubted she would have noticed Richard Newman if he had been sitting beside her!

Much as she might protest the necessity of having Gideon accompany her everywhere like this, she was grateful to him for bothering—even if his only reason for doing so was because Stephanie would never forgive him if he didn't.

She felt less grateful for that attentiveness an hour and a half later, when they met up in the bar for a reviving fruit drink at the end of their workout, and saw that he had barely broken a sweat despite the rigorous routine that she had witnessed surreptitiously as she'd moved around the apparatus in the gym—whereas Joey was dripping wet and very red in the face from her own exertions.

Looking at Gideon, dressed in a black vest top that showed the width of his shoulders and the defined muscles in his chest, and a pair of long black shorts that emphasised the muscled length of his legs, wasn't doing a lot to moderate her heart rate, either!

Several other women in the bar were eyeing him appreciatively too. Glances that Gideon, admittedly, seemed completely unaware of as he sipped his orange juice. Although she very much doubted that was because he was bowled off his feet by her own sweaty appearance!

'Have you heard from Lucan at all?' Joey abruptly filled the silence that—for her at least—was starting to stretch awkwardly between them; in contrast, Gideon seemed perfectly relaxed and at ease as he sipped his juice.

Gideon raised mocking brows. 'He's on his honeymoon, Joey. Of course I haven't.'

'Well…yes.' She felt warmth colour her cheeks—as if they needed to be any redder! 'I just thought…' She grimaced; she hadn't been thinking at all. Of *course* Lucan was on his honeymoon—and recalling the broodingly sensual way in which he had been looking at his bride at their wedding, they had probably spent all of the time so far in bed!

Gideon took pity on Joey's discomfort as he chuckled softly. 'You just thought, because Lucan has always been a workaholic, that he wouldn't be able to resist telephoning me to check on things, anyway?'

'All you St Claire men are the same when it comes to your work.'

He shrugged. 'I'm guessing the beautiful Lexie has given my big brother a different perspective on what his priorities are in life. Just as Stephanie has Jordan,' Gideon added with a frown, knowing he was still coming to terms with those particular changes in his two brothers.

For so long it had been just the three of them, united against the world during those long, interminable visits to their father—until they'd reached an age where they could choose not to go, and didn't. Then the years they had spent at university and the three of them had been there for each other when they'd entered their chosen careers. Then Jordan had fallen in love with and married Stephanie, and Lucan had met and fallen in love with Lexie. Giving Gideon's brothers a different focus in their lives in an incredibly short space of time.

It was utterly ridiculous of Gideon to feel as if Jordan and Lucan had somehow left him behind. Especially when he had no more interest now in falling in love or getting married than he'd ever had—which was no interest whatsoever. He sincerely hoped that the desire he now felt for Joey was only a temporary aberration...

But desire her he did. Even now, obviously hot and glowing from her time in the gym, Joey somehow managed to look desirable, in a fitted white sports top that clearly defined her bared breasts beneath, and left a six-inch expanse of her flat stomach bare. She had removed the grey sweats to reveal black Spandex sports shorts that clung to the slenderness of her hips and thighs and the tautness of her bottom; he obviously couldn't see the latter at the moment, but he'd had plenty of opportunity to watch her earlier, as she'd moved around the gym. It was an opportunity he had taken full advantage of, admiring the slender curves of her body as she exercised—

Damn it—that was enough!

'Time we both showered, I think.' Gideon sat forward suddenly, and placed his empty glass on the table.

Joey couldn't speak for several seconds as she was instantly assailed with an image of the two of them together in the shower, completely naked, as she lathered soap over every delectable inch of Gideon's muscled body...

Which she was pretty sure wasn't what he had meant at all!

Joey gave herself a mental shake as she placed her own empty glass on the table beside his. 'Good idea. I'll meet you downstairs in Reception afterwards.'

She stood up to hurry away to the ladies' changing rooms—before Gideon had the chance to notice, and question, the sudden heat that had returned to her cheeks.

What was wrong with her? She couldn't seem to spend a single moment in his company any more without her thoughts turning to the bedroom—or, in their case, the bathroom!

Get a grip, Joey, she instructed herself firmly. Gideon was only spending his leisure time with her because he felt a family obligation to keep his sister-in-law's twin safe. It wasn't Joey personally he was concerned about. It was just that strong St Claire gentlemanly code of honour dictating that he ensured no harm came to her. Something she would do well to remember...

Joey felt refreshed and fortified by the time she rejoined Gideon in Reception fifteen minutes later. Her hair was still damp from the shower, and falling softly onto her brow and nape, but she felt far less exposed in a cream fitted sweater and figure-hugging low-riding jeans than she had in her sports gear.

Gideon, on the other hand, was once again dressed in the tailored business suit he had worn to work earlier. Although he *had* left off the tie and unbuttoned the top two buttons of his white silk shirt.

Joey felt a little self-conscious. 'I think I'm a little under-dressed to go out to dinner.'

'Or I'm over-dressed.' Gideon smiled.

Joey's stomach lurched, and her heart pounded loudly

in her chest. So much for fortification—Gideon only had to smile at her and she was once again a quivering mass of desire!

'Maybe I should go home and change first?' he added at her continued silence.

She shrugged. 'I can always meet you somewhere—'

'Not an option, I'm afraid.'

'But—'

'Come with me.'

Joey blinked. 'Come with you where?'

'To my apartment, of course.' Gideon looked down at her, noting how soft her red hair was without the gel she usually applied to achieve that wispy style. Her face was bare of make-up too, after her shower.

Although he wasn't quite sure about the horrified expression that had appeared on her face at his suggestion that she accompany him to his apartment to wait for him while he changed before they went out to dinner!

It probably *wasn't* a good idea, now that he thought about it. In fact he had no idea why he had even suggested it in the first place; he didn't take women to his apartment. *Any* woman. Not even one he had offered his protection. Most especially when Gideon had the distinct feeling that *he* was the one Joey might need protection from once they were alone together...

'Never mind,' he said. 'We're only going to grab something quick to eat at a bistro, or somewhere equally as casual, before I make sure you get home safely, so I don't suppose it really matters what I'm wearing.'

'No! No, I— It's fine if we go to your apartment first,' Joey said, slightly breathlessly, her curiosity about Gideon's home overriding her good sense in regard to whether or not it was actually a good idea for her to go anywhere near the privacy of his apartment with him.

She was curious to know if his home was as lacking in complications as the rest of his life appeared to be...

'I can guarantee you won't like the white decor, or the chrome and black furnishings in my apartment,' Gideon said with a brief smile, guessing her thoughts.

'You don't sound as if you like them very much yourself.' Joey looked up at him thoughtfully as they stepped outside. Gideon's face appeared grim in the single spotlight illuminating the Tarmacked area behind the gym where they had parked their cars earlier.

'It was already decorated that way when I bought the apartment.' He gave a dismissive shrug. 'It serves its purpose in giving me somewhere to lay my head at night.'

'And is that—'

'It's functional, Joey, which is all I've ever needed or wanted it to be,' he said with finality, before striding across the Tarmac to his car.

Definite end of subject, Joey acknowledged ruefully as she followed more slowly, knowing a sense of disappointment that Gideon's home was as sterile of sentimentality as she had imagined it might be.

'Damn!' Gideon's angry outburst interrupted Joey's thoughts. 'Damn, damn and double damn!'

'What is it?' She hurried over to where he stood beside his car. 'What's happened—?' She broke off abruptly as she saw for herself exactly what had happened: a single, long and jagged gouge had been made all the way down the driver's side of his car. 'Oh, no!' she breathed.

'Oh, yes,' Gideon confirmed grimly as he turned his attention to Joey's car parked beside his own.

He came to a halt as he saw there was an identical gouge, deep and jagged, on the driver's side of her Mini.

Gideon was pretty sure they both knew who was responsible for the damage....

CHAPTER TEN

'DRINK up, Joey,' Gideon encouraged as he handed her one of the two glasses of brandy he had just poured. 'You'll feel better if you drink all of it,' he instructed firmly when she only took a tentative sip.

It was over an hour since they had left the gym and discovered the damage to the cars. An hour, during which the same two policemen they had spoken to earlier had driven out to the car park to assess and give their professional opinion of this second act of vandalism.

The use of the St Claire name earlier today had obviously had some effect on their efficiency.

The policemen had then offered their regrets that they obviously hadn't yet managed to locate Richard Newman, let alone talk to him; that apology seemed to confirm that they also believed the man to be responsible for the deep gouges in the paintwork of the two cars.

By the time the police left, Gideon had seen that Joey didn't look at all her usual perky, confident self: her face had been pale, her hands—all of her, in fact—trembling almost uncontrollably. Her distress had been confirmed by the fact that she had raised no objections to his suggestion that they leave her car where it was for the moment and he would drive them both back to his apartment.

Despite his earlier aversion to that idea, it had seemed

the wisest choice in the circumstances. His apartment building had a doorman downstairs and security cameras installed, and Joey's obviously didn't. Besides which, Gideon had no idea whether she had any reviving brandy in her apartment, and there was no doubt they were both in need of something after the shock of finding their cars deliberately damaged.

The red of Joey's hair was the only real colour in the Spartan comfort of Gideon's sitting room. It comprised a glass and chrome coffee table sided by a black leather couch and two chairs, black and white prints in chrome frames hanging on the white-painted walls, a chrome and onyx standard lamp behind the couch, and a matching light overhead in the centre of the room.

His own and Joey's apartments were as different as the moon from the sun. Hers had all the warmth and comfort that made it a home, rather than just somewhere to store clothes and sleep at night…

Joey shook her head. 'I don't understand why Newman has waited until now. If it is him doing these things— and I'm inclined to think that it is—' she shuddered as she once again remembered actually talking to the man on Monday morning '—it's been over two months since we—well, mainly you—' she shot Gideon a rueful glance '—extracted Steph from any involvement in the Newmans' divorce.'

Gideon nodded grimly. 'I didn't understand the timing of this thing either, so I did some checking earlier today. The Newmans' divorce went to court last Friday. Rosalind Newman went for everything she could get—including custody of the two children, with only agreed access for Richard Newman. It would seem to be a case of "hell hath no fury" etc…'

'I'm inclined to think Rosalind Newman's fury was

justified where her ex-husband is concerned!' Joey exclaimed, the brandy having revived her somewhat.

Enough for her to recognise that he had brought her
back to his apartment after all...

An apartment that, with its white decor and black and
chrome furniture, was as impersonal as Gideon had warned
her it was. She *loathed* it!

'So am I.' Gideon began to pace the room. 'Unfortunately
Newman hasn't been able to find another job, either, since
being so suddenly "let go" from his last one.'

Considering that Newman had been involved in an
affair with his boss's wife, that 'letting go' wasn't so
surprising!

'I hope you aren't expecting me to feel sorry for the
man,' Joey snorted. If it hadn't been for Gideon's involvement, Stephanie might have been damaged professionally
as well as personally by being wrongly accused as 'the
other woman' in the divorce. 'As far as I'm concerned,
hanging, drawing and quartering wouldn't be enough
retribution for the extent of his deceit!' Joey announced
forcefully.

'Remind me never to get on the wrong side of you,'
Gideon murmured.

She smiled. 'Too late!'

Gideon found himself returning the easiness of that
smile. 'I'm afraid if you want to eat this evening we'll
have to send out for something. I rarely eat at home,' he
explained, 'so there's nothing in the kitchen apart from—
oh...a loaf of bread, some butter, milk to put in tea and
coffee, and maybe a few eggs. And a packet of smoked
salmon,' he remembered belatedly. 'My mother brought it
down for me from Scotland last week.'

Joey looked amused. 'Must be nice to have smoked

salmon brought down from Scotland, or to be wealthy enough to order a takeaway or eat out every night.'

It could be a little tedious, as it happened, Gideon recognised with a frown. He hadn't realised the limitations of his chosen lifestyle before Joey had breezed into his life almost a week ago. He'd ceased to notice the cold sterility of his apartment, the impersonality of eating out at the usual restaurants four or five nights a week. Unless he was actually seeing someone, it hadn't even bothered him that he often dined alone; the management and staff of all those restaurants recognised and spoke to him, so what did it matter if he ate alone?

But bringing Joey here, seeing his apartment through her eyes, made Gideon all too aware that the lack of any personal items or photographs, and the monochrome decor, gave it all the warmth and appearance of a hotel rather than a home.

But it had been deliberate, he reminded himself impatiently. As a child, he'd had years of shunting backwards and forward between his mother's home in Edinburgh, his father's estate in Gloucestershire and the boarding school he'd attended in Shrewsbury, and then he'd had several temporary digs in London during his student years. All of which had resulted in him keeping his personal possessions to a minimum, on the basis that it was easier that way when he needed to transport them to wherever he lived next.

Gideon just hadn't realised until now that those personal possessions were almost non-existent...

'Did it ever occur to you that I can't cook, either?' he rasped.

'Surely I didn't hear you correctly?' Joey taunted. 'I'm sure I couldn't have heard the self-sufficient Gideon St Claire admit that there's something he can't do proficiently, if not better than the next man?'

Gideon frowned. 'I have no idea where you gained this impression that I'm somehow all-powerful, Joey, but I can assure you that there are a lot of things I can't do—proficiently or otherwise.'

She gave him a searching look, recognising from his closed expression that, although it had been his decision that they come back to his apartment, he was far from comfortable with allowing her this window into his private life.

'I'm feeling better now, so maybe I should just go.'

Gideon scowled darkly. 'Go where?'

Her brows rose. 'Home, of course.'

'I don't think that's a good idea.'

Joey blinked. 'Sorry?'

'I'm sure you noticed the doorman downstairs when we arrived, to screen non-residents? The security code to enter the lift? The cameras inside the lift and on individual floors?'

Joey's stomach did a lurching somersault as she began to have a dreadful inkling of exactly what Gideon was about to say. 'Yes…'

'I think, until the Newman situation has been sorted out, that it would be better if you stayed here with me.'

'No way!' Joey surged to her feet even as she frantically shook her head in protest. 'I've already had to put up with you following me about all day—'

'It works in reverse as well, you know—I've had to put up with following you about all day!' he retorted.

Her cheeks warmed at the rebuke. 'That was your choice, not mine.'

'I have a responsibility,' he came back icily.

'Because of Stephanie,' she acknowledged heavily. 'I'm sorry, Gideon, but there is no way—absolutely no way—that I'm going to… Look, I realise that I—that we—

behaved less than discreetly this morning, but that doesn't mean I'm going to just move in here with you.'

Gideon recoiled as if a snake had lashed out and sunk its fangs into him, a nerve pulsing in his tightly clenched jaw. 'Having you move in with me was the last thing I was suggesting.'

Obviously. He looked so horrified at the mere thought of it! 'Then what *did* you have in mind?' Joey challenged. 'That I just share your bed for the night?'

Blond brows lowered over glittering brown eyes. 'I don't think I care for the accusation in your tone.'

'Tough!' Joey snapped, and she was the one to now pace the room. 'I have no idea what you think I am, Gideon, but I'm definitely not easy.'

'Oh, I can vouch for that,' he muttered harshly.

Joey glared. 'You know exactly what I meant—'

'And you,' Gideon cut in coldly, 'are deliberately choosing to misunderstand what *I* meant!' He sighed. 'I'm not intending the two of us to share a bed. You can have the bedroom, and I'll sleep out here on the couch.' And very uncomfortable it was likely to be, too, considering it was only a two-seater sofa and he was six foot three inches tall!

But did he get any thanks for having his life disrupted in this way? Any appreciation for inviting Joey into his home when he never invited *anyone* here? Any consideration of his own discomfort?

No, all he received for his trouble was her suspicion and distrust. Which was damned insulting, to say the least!

'I'm not staying here with you,' Joey insisted.

Gideon drew in a frustrated breath. 'Then I guess I'll just have to come back to your apartment with you.'

'Any more than I intend inviting you to spend the night at my apartment with me!' Joey finished determinedly.

'I'll be sleeping on the sofa—'

'I don't care if you're sleeping outside in the hallway—the answer is still no!' she said, her voice rising in her agitation.

'And if Newman chooses tonight to decide he isn't satisfied with just damaging our property and decides to make it more personal?'

Joey looked frightened. 'You think he might become violent towards you or I?'

Gideon's mouth thinned. 'I think he's already violent—it just hasn't manifested itself yet into outright physical assault.'

Joey felt her face go pale and an icy shiver run down the length of her spine as she once again recalled Richard Newman standing close behind her in the queue at the coffee shop on Monday morning—the way he had deliberately stopped and spoken to her. As if he didn't care if she recognised him, or had perhaps even wanted her to.

Gideon regretted being quite so blunt when he saw the way her eyes now looked dark and haunted against the pallor of her cheeks. 'I didn't mean to frighten you.'

'Well, you succeeded!'

He ran a hand through his hair. 'Let's just calm this down a little, hmm?' he encouraged.

'And how do you propose we do that?' Joey asked.

'We would probably both feel better—less agitated—if we had something to eat.'

'You mean *I* would, don't you?' she challenged. 'I've yet to see you act as anything other than Mr Calm!'

Gideon refused to be distracted by her obvious determination to have another argument with him. 'If you don't feel like ordering food in then we could make scrambled eggs to go with the smoked salmon, with maybe some toast on the side?'

'Neither of us can cook, remember?'

'I believe, if you can handle putting some bread in the toaster, that my culinary skills might stretch to making scrambled eggs and opening a packet of smoked salmon,' Gideon said dryly; he had lived on eggs at one point during his student days, when his monthly allowance had run out before the next one was due. He preferred more sophisticated fare nowadays.

She raised auburn brows. 'Really?'

'I believe so, yes.'

'Perhaps you should go and change out of your work clothes before you start cooking?'

Gideon was still wearing his white shirt and the dark trousers of his suit. 'Into what? I don't even own a pair of jeans, Joey,' he explained as he saw her frown.

'Why on earth not?'

Gideon shrugged. 'I'm simply not a jeans sort of person.'

Amusement now glittered in those jade green eyes. 'In that case—lead on, MacDuff!'

Gideon was smiling at Joey's return to good humour—at his expense as usual, of course!—as he led the way to his kitchen. A kitchen, he realised uneasily, that with its black, lemon and chrome decor, and uncluttered and virtually unused work surfaces, was as impersonal as the rest of his apartment.

Which was exactly the way he liked it, Gideon reminded himself firmly. He moved across the room to take eggs, milk, butter and smoked salmon out of the fridge, suddenly uncomfortable with the idea of preparing a meal with Joey. Of preparing a meal with anyone. He rarely put himself to the bother of cooking at all—let alone for some cosy twosome with a woman he had previously considered to be both annoying and irritating.

Exactly when had he ceased thinking of Joey as being either of those things?

Oh, he was still frequently annoyed and irritated in her company, but not in the same way he had been before; now that annoyance and irritation was directed more towards himself—for allowing his attraction to her to become such a big part of his life.

'You were right. I do feel much better now that I've eaten.' Joey sat back on the stool opposite Gideon's at the black marble breakfast bar where she had insisted they had to eat—rather than in the formal dining area of that cold, impersonal sitting room.

The two rooms of the apartment she had been allowed to see were both lacking in warmth. In fact they lacked any evidence at all of the personality of the man who actually lived here.

The top of his desk at St Claire's was kept similarly devoid of any evidence of the type of man who worked there each day. Admittedly he was working in Lucan's office at the moment, rather than his own, but earlier in the week Joey had needed to borrow a legal book from Gideon's office farther down the hallway. Joey had unpacked those boxes of personal items she had brought with her on Monday, and placed them about Lexie's office to make her feel more comfortable for the month she would be working there. But Gideon's office, where he had worked every day for years, was as lacking in any warmth, let alone comfort, as his apartment.

Who lived like this?

Well…obviously Gideon did. But *why* did he? Was it just another manifestation of that 'aloneness' that helped to keep him removed from emotional involvement of any kind?

The same aloneness that now, in his allowing Joey into his apartment at all, was in danger of being demolished?

Joey had been too distracted earlier to appreciate that fact, but...

'Please don't think that I'm ungrateful for your suggestion earlier that I stay here with you tonight.'

His mouth compressed. 'A suggestion you totally misunderstood.'

'Yes, and now I'm attempting to apologise for it,' she said evenly.

Gideon gave her an assessing, narrow-eyed look. 'Don't let me stop you,' he drawled finally.

Joey chuckled huskily. 'Aren't you supposed to be a little more gracious about it than this?'

Gideon's gaze became mocking. 'I'm enjoying the novelty of having the outspoken Joey McKinley apologise to me far too much at the moment to even attempt to be gracious.'

She grinned across the breakfast bar at him. 'I'm not sure, considering how rude we are to each other, how we ever came to be caught in such a compromising position earlier—' She broke off, her cheeks warming uncomfortably. 'What I meant to say was—'

'It's okay, Joey. I know exactly what you were trying to say,' Gideon acknowledged wearily—he had been trying to make sense of it all day himself. The only explanation he could come up with was that it had to be an attraction of opposites.

Joey was the warmth of sunshine to his cool of the moon. Was openly emotional to his icy reserve. Heatedly outspoken to his calm caution. Casually feminine—when she wasn't in work mode and presenting a much tougher look—to his stiff formality.

Opposites, indeed.

And yet their attraction to each other was most definitely still there…

He frowned. 'This morning was—'

'I hope you aren't about to insult me again, Gideon?' Joey eyed him warily. 'Because, the way I remember it, it was a mutual ripping off of clothes.'

Total opposites, Gideon acknowledged with a wince at her frankness. And yet that honesty was also commendable. It was even amusing on occasion. In fact he had found himself laughing out loud several times during the past week at some of her more candid comments.

'We didn't rip each other's clothes off—'

'As good as,' she insisted bluntly.

Gideon's mouth quirked. 'No clothes were actually ripped. And in my own defence I would like to state that I usually exhibit better control than I did this morning.'

'Oh, believe me, you give a whole new meaning to the word *control*,' she assured him.

'Which is why this morning's…lapse was regrettable,' he finished.

Joey gave him an exasperated look. 'Tell me, Gideon, do your relationships usually last very long?'

He looked taken aback by the question. 'Sorry?'

'I asked do your relationships usually last very long?' Joey repeated unapologetically; Gideon might be as handsome as sin, and an erotically accomplished lover, but she couldn't see too many women putting up with the need he felt to analyse and dissect every aspect—particularly the physical part—of a relationship. She certainly found it less than encouraging.

Which was, perhaps, the whole point of the exercise?

Gideon frowned his displeasure. 'I have always found it advisable to be completely honest when it comes to what you choose to call "relationships".'

Joey quirked auburn brows. 'And what do you *choose* to call them?' she asked curiously.

He looked irritated now. 'An arrangement of mutual needs.'

She gave a splutter of incredulous laughter. *'An arrangement of mutual needs?'* she howled. 'It sounds more like you're discussing a business deal than a relationship!'

'Probably because that's how I prefer to think of them.'

'And how long does it usually take you to put your "mutual needs" card on the table?'

That irritation flickered again across his brow. 'I can always tell after a first date whether I want to see a woman again.'

'Go to bed with her, you mean?'

Gideon's mouth firmed. 'Yes.'

Joey stared at him in wonder. 'No wonder you're still single at thirty-four.'

'I'm still single at thirty-four, as you put it, through *personal choice*,' he bit out tightly.

'Keep telling yourself that, Gideon,' Joey teased as she stood up to begin loading the plates from their meal into the dishwasher. 'Personally, I'm surprised any woman ever agrees to go out with you a second time after you've given her your "mutual needs" speech!'

Gideon had no idea how this conversation had shifted to the way he conducted his personal relationships. Although why he should be surprised he had no idea; he could never predict or anticipate what the outspoken Joey McKinley was going to do or say next.

As demonstrated by her next statement!

'I suppose I should feel grateful that you haven't suggested having a "mutual needs" relationship with me.'

Gideon's expression became guarded. 'What would your answer have been if I had?'

She looked across at him. 'Guess!'

Gideon continued to look back at her for several long, searching seconds, knowing by the angry glitter of her eyes and the flush to her cheek, exactly what her answer would have been to any suggestion on his part that they satisfy their physical desire for each other within the guidelines of his usual businesslike relationships.

He gave a tight smile as he stood up. 'I'm not sure your answer is humanly possible.'

She laughed softly. 'Probably not.' She straightened as she finished clearing away. 'Now, if you could just drive me back to the gym so that I can collect my car...'

'I can do that, yes,' Gideon said. 'But only if I then either follow you back to your apartment and stay the night with you there, or alternatively we both come back here.'

'Gideon—'

'It's non-negotiable, Joey,' he stated.

Joey could see and hear that in the implacability of Gideon's expression and tone. And, much as she didn't relish the idea of him spending the night in her apart-ment—her 'mutual need' for Gideon might just rage out of her control if she knew he was laying naked in the room next to hers!—she appreciated the offer. Even if that offer *was* being made to Stephanie's sister rather than to Joey personally...

'Fine,' she accepted finally. 'But don't expect me to play the gracious hostess and offer to let you sleep in the bed while I sleep on the sofa, because it just isn't going to happen,' she warned caustically.

Gideon gave a derisive smile. 'I never expected anything else.'

She gave a sweetly saccharin smile. 'I'm so pleased I didn't disappoint you!'

He was frowning distractedly as he went to his bedroom to collect the things he would need for an overnight stay at her apartment.

Joey never disappointed him. She surprised him, deliberately shocked him on occasion, and evoked an uncontrollable and inexplicable desire in him, but nothing she did or said ever disappointed him...

CHAPTER ELEVEN

'ARE you sure you're going to be comfortable sleeping on here?' Joey frowned down at the makeshift bed she had made for Gideon on the sofa in her sitting room; the only bedclothes she had been able to find were a spare set of sheets, two old blankets and one pillow.

'Probably not,' Gideon drawled as he dropped his overnight bag down beside the sofa, before taking his mobile and wallet from his trouser pockets and placing them on the coffee table. 'Which will no doubt make your own dreams all the sweeter as you sleep in the comfort of your bed.'

She somehow doubted that. Especially when he was only putting himself through this discomfort in an attempt to protect her. Something, despite her earlier apology, she knew she really had been less than gracious about.

'Perhaps I should be the one to sleep on the sofa, after all—'

'I'm just teasing you again, Joey.' Gideon dropped lightly down onto the sofa and grinned up at her. 'I'll be absolutely fine sleeping here.'

'If you're sure?'

Somehow, now that the time had come for Joey to go to her bedroom, she was reluctant to leave… She doubted she was going to get any sleep anyway, knowing he was only feet away. Possibly naked!

Good Lord, wasn't she a little young for hot flushes and heart palpitations?

'I'm sure,' Gideon answered gruffly. 'Just go, hmm?' he urged firmly when she still made no effort to leave.

Joey looked at him from beneath lowered lashes, noting the gold glow of his eyes—as a sign of his own physical awareness of her?—and the slight flush on the sharp blades of those sculptured cheeks. She moistened suddenly dry lips before speaking. 'I feel very guilty taking the bed and leaving you to sleep on the sofa.'

'Good.'

Her eyes widened. 'Gideon!'

He arched mocking brows. 'As I told you earlier, you have to learn to take it if you're going to give it.'

'Okay, point taken.' She nodded. 'There's coffee in the kitchen if you wake up before me in the morning, and—'

'And here I imagined you'd be bringing me breakfast in bed.'

Joey eyed him uncertainly. 'You're kidding again, right?'

He smiled. 'What do you think?'

She gave a grimace. 'I think you're going to be waiting a very long time if you expect me to bring you breakfast in bed.'

'Another of life's little disappointments.' He gave an exaggerated sigh.

Joey wasn't quite sure what to make of Gideon in this teasing mood. It was disconcerting, to say the least!

'Goodnight, Gideon,' she said stiltedly as she turned away.

''Night, Joey,' he called softly.

She closed her bedroom door firmly behind her before leaning back against it, aware that her heart was pounding, her cheeks flushed.

This was utterly ridiculous. She was twenty-eight years old, and a lawyer of some repute—not some inexperienced eighteen-year-old lusting after a man she couldn't have! Even if that last part *was* true. She *did* lust after Gideon and she knew she couldn't have him—on his terms, at least. She wasn't interested in a temporary fling just to scratch an itch.

Gideon's good humour had left him the moment Joey closed the bedroom door behind her, and he gave up all pretence of being relaxed as he stood up restlessly to begin pacing the room.

How the hell was he supposed to spend the night sleeping on the sofa when he knew that Joey was only feet away? Possibly naked!

Did she sleep naked...? Just the possibility that she might was enough to cause Gideon's thighs to harden to a throbbing ache as he imagined those lush, full breasts, her slender waist and invitingly curvaceous hips and thighs, sprawled across silken sheets—

Gideon turned sharply as he heard the bedroom door reopen, schooling his features to casual uninterest as he looked across at her enquiringly.

'I need to use the bathroom,' Joey said huskily, and she came out of the bedroom wearing an over-large white T-shirt that reached down to her thighs.

So much for imagining her sleeping naked, Gideon mocked himself once Joey had disappeared into the bathroom down the hallway. Although the T-shirt did have a certain appeal, as it hinted at rather than outlined those softly luscious curves beneath...

Who was he trying to fool? She could have been wearing a sack and he would still have found her sexy!

''Night, again,' she murmured, her gaze averted as she went back into the bedroom and closed the door.

Gideon was once again consumed with frustrated desire as he stood in the middle of the room staring at that closed bedroom door for several long seconds. Knowing Joey was just behind that thin veneer of wood. That he now ached to kiss her softly pouting lips. To take her in his arms and mould her soft curves against his own. To caress every inch of her until she was as aroused as he was.

Oh, to hell with this!

He moved to grab his overnight bag before marching down the hallway to the bathroom. He needed a cold shower. A long—very long!—cold shower. For all the good he expected it to do…

If Joey had ever suffered a more restless night's sleep in her life then she couldn't think when. Surely nothing could ever have tormented and disturbed her as much as knowing that Gideon was asleep on the sofa in her sitting room?

She had actually got out of bed half a dozen times during the night, with the intention of either joining him on the sofa or inviting him to share her bed, her body aching, longing, to finish what they had started earlier that morning.

Somehow she had resisted each and every one of those longings. Forced herself to return to bed alone. Only to get up again minutes later when she was once again consumed with the same desire.

It was a relief when early-morning light started to permeate her bedroom curtains. A glance at the bedside clock revealed that it was almost seven-thirty. Surely a respectable—acceptable—time for her to get up?

Whether it was or not, Joey knew she'd had enough of lying in the tangle of her own bedclothes. A trip to the bathroom to clean her teeth was in order, before she went into the kitchen and made herself a pot of tea. A *large* pot of tea!

She achieved the first of those tasks by simply not look-ing at Gideon as she moved quietly down the hallway, but she couldn't resist on her way back. She glanced across to the sofa, her breath catching in her throat as she saw him lying sprawled face-down on the sofa, with only a sheet to cover his nakedness. At least she presumed he was naked beneath that sheet; his back was certainly bare, as were his long and muscled legs.

Joey couldn't resist padding softly over to look down at him, her fingers aching to reach out and touch the fall of golden blond hair across his forehead. His lashes were long against the hardness of his cheeks, his lips slightly parted as he breathed in and out.

If Joey bent down just slightly she could kiss those lips—

'I don't smell any breakfast cooking!' Gold eyes gleamed at her wickedly as Gideon suddenly raised those long lashes to look up at her.

Joey almost tripped over her own feet as she jumped back guiltily. 'I thought you were still asleep!' she accused, her cheeks burning with embarrassment at being caught in the act of ogling him while he slept. Correction, while she had *thought* that he slept!

'Obviously you thought wrong.' Gideon took the sheet with him as he rolled over to look up at her. He was very aware that a certain part of his anatomy had woken up before the rest of him, and that looking at a sleep-tousled Joey was only increasing that throbbing ache between his thighs.

A fact she was also aware of if, the way her eyes had widened as she glanced at that restless bulge beneath the sheet was any indication!

'What can I say? Part of me is very pleased to see you,' Gideon drawled ruefully.

Joey's cheeks were still flushed, but she quirked mocking brows. 'And how does the rest of you feel about it?'

Gideon put an arm behind his head as he relaxed back on the pillow. 'As I said, I don't smell any breakfast cooking.'

Just as he had thought, sleeping on the sofa hadn't been his main problem last night. It had been forcing himself to resist knocking on her bedroom door and then joining her in bed that had proved the most difficult.

The cold shower he'd taken had been a complete waste of his time once he'd lain down on the sofa. His mind had worked overtime as he'd imagined kissing Joey, making love to her, having her make love to him...

One look at her this morning, red hair soft and tousled, those jade-green eyes heavy with sleep—or lack of it?—and all those erotic imaginings had returned with a vengeance.

'And, as I told you last night, you won't either,' Joey assured him. 'There's toast or croissants in the kitchen if you're hungry, so just help yourself.' She turned away.

Gideon reached out and lightly grasped her wrist. 'Where are you going?' his voice was husky.

She was very aware of his fingers curled lightly about the slenderness of her wrist. Of his nakedness beneath the thin sheet. Of the long length of his arousal poised beneath that sheet...

She swallowed hard. 'I thought I'd go into the kitchen and make some tea and coffee.'

Gideon gave a light tug on her wrist. 'Weren't you about to kiss me good morning a few minutes ago?'

Her eyes widened in alarm as she realised how easily she had given herself away. A sudden but unmistakable sexual tension filled the room...

'Don't be ridiculous—'

'Don't lie to me, Joey. Or yourself,' he added softly.

Joey tried to back away. 'I'm not lying—'

'I think you are.'

'No—'

'Yes!'

Gold eyes blazed up at her as Gideon's fingers tightened about her wrist before he gave a second, harder tug, and succeeded in unbalancing Joey.

She could feel herself starting to panic as she tumbled towards him. 'Stop this, Gideon,' she instructed firmly as she tried to regain her balance, but instead she found herself sprawled on top of him, only the thin material of the sheet and her T-shirt between them.

Which was no barrier at all. Joey felt the hardness of his shaft pressed against the softness of her thighs, her breasts crushed against his chest, and their faces were now only inches apart.

She lay unmoving, not breathing, as her body was suffused with heat. That heat was centring, pooling between her thighs as the intensity of his golden eyes held her captive. 'I don't think this is a good idea, Gideon,' she said.

He released her wrist to bring his hands up and cradle either side of her face, thumbs moving lightly against the shadows beneath her eyes. 'Did you sleep at all last night?'

'I—no, not really,' she acknowledged with a grimace.

'Neither did I,' he admitted quietly.

The tip of her tongue moved nervously across the sudden dryness of her lips. 'This isn't the answer, Gideon.'

He gave a rueful smile. 'Well, it certainly isn't the question!'

Joey breathed shallowly. 'Then what is?'

Those golden eyes held her mesmerised. 'The question is, can either of us stop what happens next?' Gideon shifted slightly, nudging her thighs apart. Her core was now pressed against his unrelenting hardness. 'Can you?' His hips flexed to rub that hardness against her already throbbing nubbin.

Joey gave a little whimpering moan, her eyes closing as pleasure coursed through her. She felt herself start to moisten between her thighs, her nipples peaking, hardening to an aching throb.

'Joey?' Gideon prompted throatily.

She raised emerald-bright eyes. 'Can *you*?'

Gideon shook his head. 'I don't even intend to try,' he admitted gruffly, knowing he had lost this particular battle the moment he'd heard her leave her bedroom earlier. He'd watched from between narrowed lids as she'd moved stealthily down the hallway to the bathroom, her breasts twin peaks beneath her T-shirt, her legs bare and silky. Knowing she was completely naked beneath that inadequate garment had only made Gideon desperate to remove it.

He did so now, and her thighs straddled his as he sat her up, slowly lifting that T-shirt, revealing auburn curls between the slim thighs that he longed to plunder, the slenderness of her waist, and finally the full thrust of her firm breasts, tipped with dusky rose nipples that were already pouting at him, begging to be kissed.

Gideon's gaze held hers captive as he parted his lips to reveal the soft moistness of his tongue and the sharpness of his teeth. 'Bend down and put your nipple in my mouth, Joey.'

Every breath she took lifted her breasts in invitation. Her nipples were so hard and aching now they were almost painful. A pain that she knew only Gideon's waiting tongue and teeth could assuage.

Her position of power was too much temptation, her

need too great, too immediate, for her to do anything other than what he asked. Her hands moved to rest on the pillow either side of his head as she lowered her breasts and instantly felt the sharp sting of pleasure as he took one of those fiery tips deep into the heat of his mouth, while his hand cupped its twin to allow his fingers and thumb to pluck and roll the hard and aching nipple.

Moisture flooded again between Joey's thighs and she moved against him restlessly. Gideon groaned low in his throat even as he continued to pay attention to first one nipple and then the other, teeth gently biting, tongue rasping, driving her higher and higher towards the release that was becoming a desperate need.

'I've waited so long for this,' Gideon gasped as he kissed his way across the slope of her breast before moving up to capture her lips with his.

They kissed long and deeply, desire blazing, heightening their senses to fever-pitch.

'I can't wait any longer. I need to be inside you now.' He moved quickly, rolling to his side with Joey beside him as he threw the sheet aside, before moving up and over her to hold himself poised above her parted thighs, his face savage. 'Take me in, Joey!' he urged fiercely, his lips against her throat as his hands cupped her bottom, preparing her to receive him.

Joey needed Gideon inside her just as much as he wanted to be there. Her fingers were a light grasp around him as she reached between them to guide him, groaning low in her throat as she felt him carefully enter her before sliding deeper, stretching her, filling her inch by pleasurable inch.

Joey stiffened briefly in pain, her fingernails digging into the flesh of Gideon's shoulders, when she felt his hardness surge past the barrier of her innocence to fill her totally as he buried himself to the hilt before becoming strangely still, unmoving.

'Gideon?' she prompted uncertainly when he continued to lie there.

'What the hell—?' Gold eyes glittered dangerously, and there was a flush to his cheeks as he raised his head to look down at her. 'Damn it—tell me I'm not your first lover!'

Joey felt her heart plummet even as she knew her face paled at the accusation she could read so clearly in Gideon's expression. 'I— Does it matter?'

Did it *matter*? Gideon's shattered thoughts echoed chaotically.

Did it matter that Joey had been a virgin? Did it matter that he had just ripped through the gossamer barrier of her innocence? Did it matter that, virgin or not, he had obviously hurt her? Hell, yes, it *mattered*!

His expression was fierce as he took her by the shoulders. 'You can't possibly be a virgin!'

'Well…not any more, no,' Joey acknowledged softly.

Gideon growled low in his throat as his thoughts became even more disjointed. 'But everyone knows—you and Pickard. The two of you were seen together for months!'

She shook her head. 'I already *told* you. We were *never* lovers.'

'But you must have been out with other men over the years?' he persisted disbelievingly.

Had Joey ever suffered through such an embarrassing conversation in her life before? Somehow she doubted it very much!

They were both completely naked, his hardness still buried deep inside her, and he wanted to talk about why she hadn't been to bed with any of the other men she had dated. It could only happen to her!

She moistened dry lips. 'Could we talk about this later, do you think, Gideon?'

His face darkened angrily. 'We'll talk about it *now*!'

Joey couldn't quite bring her gaze up to meet the glittering gold of Gideon's accusing eyes. 'It's a little…awkward at the moment, don't you think?'

He wasn't capable of thinking at all right now. Was too stunned, too shocked by the discovery of her previous physical innocence, to think coherently. It was a bewilderment his manhood obviously echoed as he felt himself softening in readiness for withdrawal. Taking his previous desire to its conclusion was the last thing on his mind right now.

Gideon moved up and away from Joey, to stand beside the sofa and look down at her. She quickly pulled the sheet over her nakedness. But not before Gideon had seen the telling smear of blood between her thighs.

He closed his eyes briefly, before turning away to run his hand through the thickness of his hair. He really had just taken Joey's virginity. Indisputably. Irrevocably. Unknowingly.

But *she* had known…

Gideon turned to look at her through narrowed lids. 'None of this makes any sense.'

Joey looked up at him. 'None of what?'

'You. Me. The fact that you were still a—a—'

'A virgin,' Joey finished helpfully—Gideon still seemed to be having trouble with the concept.

'Yes!'

What had she expected? Joey wondered wearily. That the two of them would make love and it would all be wonderful?

Well, until Gideon had discovered her virginity it *had* been wonderful!

Then it had turned into something of a nightmare because of his shock. His anger.

And Joey's own realisation that she had fallen head over heels in love with him...

CHAPTER TWELVE

HER eyes narrowed. 'Exactly what is your problem with us having made love, Gideon?' she questioned slowly as he turned away to pull on a pair of black figure-hugging boxers.

He was still too stunned to know what he was thinking, let alone what was coming out of his mouth. A part of him felt as if he was burbling a lot of nonsense—and the rest of him knew that he was.

How could this possibly be? Joey was a sophisticated twenty-eight-year-old woman who gave every impression of being worldly-wise. Damn it, how *could* she still be a virgin?

And yet she was.

Had been...

And Gideon had no idea how he felt about it.

The wary expression on her angrily flushed face told him that perhaps he should keep his mouth shut until he *did* know.

'Joey—'

'I would rather you didn't, Gideon,' she warned evenly, and she moved to the end of the sofa when he would have reached out to her, all the time clutching that crumpled sheet in front of her, the knuckles of her hands gleaming white beneath her skin.

Gideon's hand fell back to his side, a scowl darkening his brow at her rejection of his touch. 'I'm not going to hurt you—well, no more than I already have.' He gave a pained frown. 'If I'd known—'

'I really don't want to talk about this any more, Gideon.'

'It doesn't just come down to what *you* want—'

'As far as I'm concerned, that's exactly what it *does* come down to!' Her eyes flashed a warning as she stood up to wrap the sheet tightly round her. 'I'm going to take a shower now. My advice to you is to leave before I come back.'

'You know I can't do that,' he rasped. 'Not with Newman rampaging about.'

Joey eyed him scathingly. 'He's hardly *rampaging*, Gideon. And even if he were I have no intention of going out today—so there's no problem, is there?'

No, the problem appeared to be totally between the two of them. And Gideon knew that he was the one responsible for it. If he had only reacted differently once he'd realised... But how could he be expected to have done that when he had been shocked to his very core by the discovery of her innocence?

'Why has there been no one else for you, Joey?' he asked quietly.

She regarded him pityingly. 'Well, Gideon, that really isn't the right question to be asking, is it?'

'Then what *is* the right question?'

Joey gave a humourless laugh before turning to walk away. 'I'm going to take a shower. Lock the door behind you on your way out.'

Gideon gazed after her in frustration, knowing by the stiff set of her bare shoulders and the straightness of her spine, that it would be a mistake to push her any further right now.

But, damn it, he had no idea what the right question should have been!

Joey had no idea how she made it as far as the bathroom before the tears began to fall, but she somehow managed to get inside the room and lock the door firmly behind her before they cascaded hotly down her cheeks.

What a mess!

She had fallen in love with Gideon. With a man who had made it patently clear he never intended falling in love with *any* woman!

Even so, she should never have allowed things to go as far between them as they had. Should never have given in to the desire—no, the *love* that had kept her awake and wanting him for most of the night.

But she *had* given in to it—had wanted and welcomed his lovemaking only to have the whole thing fall apart when he discovered that she was a virgin. If she had known it was going to cause this much trouble then she would have made a point of losing it years ago.

No, she wouldn't. She and Stephanie had grown up in a loving family. Their parents were even more in love with each other now than they had been on their wedding day. And somehow that love and total commitment to each other had become a part of both Joey's and Stephanie's psyche— so much so that neither of them was willing to settle for anything less. To the extent that going to bed with a man they weren't in love with had become complete anathema to both of them.

Well, Joey had realised she was deeply, irrevocably in love with Gideon—she had just overlooked the fact that he wasn't in love with her too. In fact she had made a complete mess of things. To the point where she wasn't sure how she was even going to face him again, with the knowledge of her lost virginity hovering between them like some ghostly spectre.

It was small comfort that he was so out of touch with emotion that he obviously had no idea she was in love with him—that the question he should have been asking was why had she chosen *him* to be her first and only lover?

Gideon was still here. That was Joey's first thought when she emerged from the bathroom half an hour later and caught the smell of toast and coffee coming from the kitchen.

He obviously hadn't taken her hint earlier for what it was: a need on Joey's part not to see or speak to him again for at least the weekend. By Monday morning she might— just might—be able to face him again with some of her usual self-confidence.

As it was, it appeared that another confrontation was going to happen much sooner than she would have liked.

Her shoulders straightened determinedly as she disappeared into her bedroom to dress in faded jeans and a green jumper, running a brush lightly through the dampness of her hair, not even bothering to apply any make-up, and then marching back out to the kitchen—before she had time to change her mind.

Only to come to an abrupt halt in the doorway as she saw that he had set two places at the breakfast bar. A pot of tea and one of coffee were already there, steaming, along with mugs and milk and sugar, and warm croissants and toast were arranged temptingly in a basket.

'What are you doing, Gideon?' she demanded coldly.

His expression was as guarded as her own. 'Making breakfast for both of us, of course,' he said casually as he carried the butter over and placed it on the breakfast bar with the rest of the food. He was now dressed in a brown cashmere sweater and tailored brown trousers. 'I know that you prefer tea, so—'

'You proved earlier that you don't know *anything* about me, Gideon.' Joey's teeth were so tightly clamped together her jaw ached, and her hands were bunched into fists at her sides, her fingernails digging into her palms.

There was a responding glitter of displeasure in the dark brown of his eyes. 'Obviously not,' he bit out tautly, only to give a weary sigh as she became even more tense. 'Look, I don't want to argue with you, Joey—'

'Oh, there isn't going to be time for an argument, Gideon,' she informed him. 'Because you're leaving. Right now!' She looked utterly fierce and determined. 'I gave you every opportunity to do this graciously, and just leave while I was taking a shower, but now I'm telling you outright to go!'

Gideon bit back his impatience, knowing it would only make the situation worse than it already was. If that was even possible! 'I don't want to leave things between us like this,' he explained, keeping his voice deliberately even. 'Don't you see that I need to understand why you—'

'How can you possibly begin to understand anything, Gideon—about anyone at all!—when you have all the emotional warmth of an automaton?' she said vehemently. 'Your apartment is as impersonal as a hotel suite. Your office looks like no one works there. Your personal life is just as uncluttered by sentiment. No one lives like that.'

Gideon did. Through choice. Because he had seen exactly how it had destroyed his mother to lose both the husband and the home that she'd loved twenty-five years ago. Gideon's decision never to become attached to people or things, apart from his immediate family, was based entirely on witnessing the complete devastation of his mother's life.

Nothing had changed in the years of his adulthood to shake that conviction. Except he found he absolutely hated the very thought of Joey believing he lacked emotion...

'I don't believe you can accuse me of being unemotional half an hour ago,' he pointed out.

'That wasn't emotion, Gideon. It was just a natural physical reaction between a naked man and a woman,' she dismissed flatly. 'Anyone with blood flowing through their veins has those!'

He drew his breath in harshly. 'So you're saying what happened between us earlier meant nothing to you?'

Joey stiffened as every barrier inside her, every defence mechanism she possessed, sprang into place; it was one thing for her to know she was in love with Gideon, but something else entirely for him to realise how she felt about him. She deserved to leave herself with some pride after this morning's humiliating experience, surely?

'We weren't discussing me, Gideon. And we aren't about to, either,' she added firmly as he would have spoken. 'Not now. Not ever. Now, I really would like you to leave.' Her gaze met his unwaveringly, her chin held high in challenge.

Gideon had never felt so impotent, so incapable of knowing what to do or say next. Except he knew that he had to do or say *something*. That he couldn't leave things so strained between himself and Joey.

'Why don't we just sit down and eat breakfast? You felt better last night after you had eaten—'

'Feeding me isn't going to change a damned thing this time,' Joey declared. 'Right now all I want is for you to just *go*.'

'I can't leave you like this.' Gideon's mouth firmed in frustration. 'We went to bed together this morning—'

'Technically, it was a sofa,' she cut in icily. 'And I've already told you I don't want to discuss that any further today.'

'You are the most stubborn, difficult—' Gideon broke off abruptly as he heard the ringing tone of the mobile he had left on the coffee table in the sitting room, along with his car keys. 'That could be the police with news on Newman.' His expression was grim as he brushed past her on his way out of the kitchen.

Joey breathed a little easier once she was alone. She knew another reason to avoid physical relationships in future; when love wasn't reciprocated, the conversation afterwards was just too embarrassing. In Gideon's case he wasn't even aware of the *concept* of loving someone, let alone capable of realising that she had fallen in love with him!

Joey's legs felt shaky as she moved to sit down on one of the stools beside the breakfast bar, her movements a little awkward as she became aware of the slight soreness between her thighs. Yet another embarrassing aspect of having made love with Gideon earlier. Especially as that lovemaking had been cut so unsatisfactorily short...

Was there a book on the etiquette of the morning after? Or in this case the hour or so after? Joey wondered. If there was, then she badly needed to get herself a copy! Although she doubted she would ever be in need of it again after today, so perhaps not.

'It was my mother, not the police,' Gideon said tersely as he strode back into the kitchen.

Joey gave him a sharp glance as he commenced pacing the kitchen restlessly. 'Is everything all right?'

Gideon ran an impatient hand through his hair. 'She

would like me to fly up to Edinburgh for the rest of the
weekend.'

Gideon was going to Edinburgh for the rest of the
weekend. Why, when Joey had told him to leave earlier—
repeatedly—did that knowledge cause a hollow feeling in
the pit of her stomach?

'That's nice,' she said noncommittally.

'You think so?' Gideon scowled darkly beneath lowered
brows. 'She says there's something important she needs to
discuss with me, and she would rather do it in person.'

'Oh.'

Gideon gave a humourless smile. 'Sounds a little omi-
nous, doesn't it.'

Joey shrugged. 'Maybe, with both Lucan and Jordan
away, she's feeling a little lonely?'

He gave a snort. 'She's hardly had time to miss any
of us—she only went back to Edinburgh on Monday! Or
is that just me exhibiting another example of having the
emotional warmth of an automaton?'

That comment seemed to have struck a nerve, Joey acknowledged with a frown. It was true, of course, but maybe
she shouldn't have said it...

Too late now!

'A weekend in Edinburgh sounds like fun.'

Gideon looked grim. 'I'm glad one of us is looking forward to it.'

'What do you mean?' Joey gave him a bewildered
look.

He raised blond brows. 'You're coming with me, of
course.'

'I'm—? I most certainly am not!' she assured him
indignantly.

Gideon stopped his pacing to meet her gaze with his
own implacable one. 'Joey, nothing that happened between

us this morning changes a single thing about the Newman situation. He's still out there somewhere, probably thinking up his next malicious act, which means I have no intention of going to Edinburgh for the weekend without you.'

Joey ignored the wincing pain between her thighs as she stood up. 'And I'm certainly not going to Edinburgh with you!' She shot him an incredulous look. 'What would your mother think if I were to just turn up with you?'

'I've already told her you'll be accompanying me.'

'You've done *what*?'

Gideon shrugged unconcernedly. 'My mother is expecting both of us later this afternoon.'

'I— But— Did you tell her about Richard Newman?'

'Of course not.' Gideon looked appalled. 'There's absolutely no reason to worry my mother with any of that.'

'Then what reason did you give her for me going with you?'

Joey was the one to pace the kitchen restlessly now. Gideon was insane. He had to be. Because there was no way—absolutely no way—that she could go with him for the weekend to visit Molly St Claire at her home in Edinburgh.

'I didn't.'

'You *didn't*?' Joey squeaked. 'You just told your mother that I would be accompanying you without giving her an explanation as to why?'

Gideon looked down the length of his arrogant nose at her. 'Why should I have done?'

Well, Joey knew for a fact that if she took a man with her to stay at her parents' house for the weekend they would draw their own conclusions. 'Because your mother now has altogether the wrong impression of us!'

He didn't look at all bothered by that. 'I'll explain to her once the Newman situation has been resolved.'

'And in the meantime she's going to draw all the wrong conclusions,' Joey muttered disgustedly. 'No, Gideon, I *refuse* to go with you.'

His eyes narrowed. 'You've already told me you have no other plans for today.'

'That doesn't mean I want to waste half my day in an airport, waiting to get on a flight to Edinburgh. A flight I have no wish to take in the first place,' she snapped exasperatedly.

'There won't be any sitting around waiting for a flight, because I'm going to fly us up in the St Claire helicopter.' Gideon easily shot down that objection.

Joey abruptly stopped her pacing. *'What?'*

He gave a crooked smile at her scepticism. 'Don't worry, Joey. I assure you I have a valid pilot's licence.'

'Well, that's a relief—I thought perhaps you were going to fly a helicopter on the basis of owning a dog licence!'

'I actually don't have one of those,' Gideon drawled. 'Probably because I don't own a dog.'

Of course he didn't own a dog. A dog was a living, breathing being, in need of the love and nurturing that Gideon avoided at all costs!

Joey had a vague recollection of Stephanie mentioning something about Gideon flying her and Jordan back to London last year, from the St Claire estate in Gloucestershire, after there had been a health scare concerning Molly St Claire. A scare that had been alleviated once Molly had visited a specialist in Harley Street. Which was probably why she had completely forgotten that Gideon could fly...

She remembered with a vengeance now, though—and Joey had no intention of flying anywhere in a helicopter!

'Sorry, Gideon, but you can count me out.'

'If you won't agree to go, then I'm not going either,' he said, just as determinedly.

Her cheeks were flushed with temper. 'You're being totally childish about this.'

'Either we both go or neither of us does,' Gideon repeated grimly. 'I'm not leaving you here unprotected, Joey, and that's the end to the subject.'

'In your opinion!' She faced him challengingly. 'Which means diddly-squat to me!'

'I take it that's a euphemism for you not caring for my opinion?' He arched mocking brows.

'You can take it to mean what you damn well please,' Joey told him heatedly. 'I've said I'm not going to Edinburgh with you, and that's the *end of the subject* as far as I'm concerned!'

CHAPTER THIRTEEN

'YOU can either wipe that smugly superior smile off your face, or I'm going to take it off for you!'

A statement that achieved completely the opposite effect on Gideon as he now felt an uncontrollable urge to laugh.

Joey had been utterly resentful as she threw some clothes into a bag, and bad-tempered when Gideon drove them to the private airfield where he kept the helicopter. She had maintained a stubborn silence during the flight up to his mother's home just outside Edinburgh, and been stoically tight-lipped as he'd set the helicopter down on the custom-built pad in the extensive grounds. That resentment had now finally turned to belligerence as they walked the short distance to the house.

She had eventually given in with bad grace and agreed to accompany him to Scotland, after all—but only, she had assured him firmly, because his mother so obviously wanted to see him. Gideon had so far managed to resist commenting on any of Joey's moods. Obviously she had taken exception even to his silence!

'It's not smugness, Joey,' he told her. 'I'm just relieved to find there wasn't any snow and we could land safely.'

'Was it ever in doubt?'

Gideon shrugged. 'It's February in Scotland.'

Joey gave him a sceptical glance, not fooled for a

moment by his excuse; there had been a definite air of smugness about him from the moment she had agreed to come to Edinburgh with him after all. A decision she certainly hadn't made for Gideon's benefit; if Joey had her way she wouldn't see him again until she was old and past caring for or responding to him!

But Joey had liked Molly St Claire from the moment she'd met her at Stephanie and Jordan's engagement party. Molly's love and pride in her three sons had been obvious, and it was a love and admiration that was reciprocated; the three St Claire brothers obviously adored their beloved mother.

The fact that Molly had so unexpectedly asked Gideon to visit her in Edinburgh this weekend was unusual; Joey knew from Stephanie that the older woman simply wasn't one of those clingy, suffocating type of mothers. Gideon's stubbornness in refusing to visit his mother unless Joey accompanied him had placed her in a difficult position. One that, despite her protestations, she had known could ultimately have only one solution.

Which was why she was now in Scotland, approaching the huge oak front door of Molly's manor house home, with Gideon strolling along casually—and triumphantly, damn him!—at her side.

Explaining exactly why she was here with him was Gideon's problem, she had decided when she'd agreed to accompany him. And if he thought his mother wasn't going to demand an explanation at some point then he was in for a surprise!

'Now *you* appear to be smiling smugly.'

'Do I?' Joey glanced sideways at Gideon. Both of them were wrapped up warm against the cold, Joey in a thick duffel coat over her jumper and denims, Gideon in a fine woollen caramel-coloured coat over his jumper and trousers. 'I can't imagine why.'

Neither could Gideon. But he had no doubt it would involve laughing at him in some way.

Joey was back to being her normal perky, outspoken self, he realised ruefully. Almost as if their making love this morning had never happened. As far as Joey was concerned perhaps it hadn't...

Gideon wasn't having the same success in blocking the vividness of those memories from his mind as she appeared to be. In fact he had thought of little else since it happened.

He most especially wondered what the 'right question' should have been...

If Gideon were the sort of son who confided in his mother then he might have discussed it with Molly. No, he probably wouldn't; he didn't exactly feature in a good light in what had occurred!

It was frustrating as hell, for a man who was always in control of every aspect of his life, not to know what was going on. Although he should be used to it by now; Joey had had him wrong-footed in one way or another since the moment he'd first met her!

And yet Gideon knew that he was enjoying having her with him. That, bad-tempered or otherwise, he was never bored in her company. In fact—

'Gideon!' His mother had opened the door before they could even attempt to ring the bell—evidence that she had been looking out for them. She gave Gideon a brief hug. 'And Joey,' she added warmly as she clasped both Joey's hands in hers. 'Do come in and warm yourselves by the fire. Did you have a good flight?' she asked once they were in the hallway taking off their coats.

Joey shot Gideon another sideways glance before

answering dryly, 'Not having flown in a helicopter before, I have nothing to compare it with.'

'Oh, Gideon is a very good pilot,' his mother said with an affectionate smile in his direction. 'I have everything ready for tea, if you would like to come through to the sitting room?'

Gideon's mother couldn't have been more welcoming, and yet Joey still felt uncomfortable about being here. 'It's very kind of you to invite me to stay, too, Mrs—er...' Joey gave an awkward wince at her inability to address Molly St Claire, who had divorced her husband twenty-five years ago.

'Please call me Molly,' she invited with a smile—a beautiful woman in her late fifties, with dark shoulder-length hair that was inclined to curl, and warm brown eyes. Gideon's eyes...

'Shall I take our bags upstairs before we have tea?' Gideon asked. He was somewhat surprised, considering the urgency he had sensed in his mother's request that he come to Scotland as soon as possible because she had something important she needed to discuss with him, that she seemed so relaxed.

'Oh, yes—do,' Molly answered. 'I wasn't quite sure what to do regarding sleeping arrangements for the two of you, so I've put you both in the blue bedroom for now, with the option that one of you can move into the adjoining room if that's what you would prefer.'

If Gideon had expected Joey to be embarrassed by his mother's assumption that the two of them would be sleeping together, then he was sadly disappointed. Instead, Joey looked fiendishly delighted as she turned to look at him with a pointedly mocking expression in those cat-like green eyes.

Gideon's mouth thinned as he turned to answer his

mother. 'I'll put my things in the adjoining bedroom.' He marched out of the room without so much as a second glance in Joey's direction.

'Did I say something wrong?'

Joey felt a certain amount of sympathy for Molly's obvious bewilderment at her son's behaviour. 'Much as I enjoy seeing Gideon less than his usual confident self, I think you should know that he and I aren't a couple,' she said.

'You aren't?' The older woman looked disappointed. 'Why aren't you?' She rallied briskly. 'It seems to me that you're exactly the type of young woman to shake my son out of his complacency.'

Joey chuckled softly. 'Oh, I definitely rattle the bars of the comfortable cage he's created for himself.'

'Then might I suggest you keep on rattling them until the cage falls apart completely?' Molly advised.

Joey grimaced. 'I could be old and grey by the time that happens.'

Molly moved forward to briefly squeeze her arm. 'I love all my sons equally, Joey, and have every confidence that Lucan and Jordan have made wonderful marriages—marriages that will last and blossom. But I do worry so about Gideon—he was a very loving little boy, you know.'

Joey couldn't imagine it. Actually, yes, she could... She could almost see Gideon as a golden-haired little boy, his eyes glowing gold with happiness rather than anger, knowing he was loved as much as he loved, his world totally secure...

'He was the closest to Alexander. My ex-husband,' Molly provided unnecessarily; Joey was well aware of who Alexander was. 'When the marriage disintegrated...' She shook her head sadly. 'All the boys were devastated, but Gideon was hit the hardest. It's made him very suspicious of love, I'm afraid.'

Joey was aware that it wasn't only love Gideon was suspicious of—it was any and all emotion. 'You really are mistaken about the two of us, Molly. We're not together in that way.'

'Don't give up on him, Joey,' the other woman urged huskily as Gideon could be heard coming back down the stairs. 'The fact that he brought you here with him is significant, you know.'

Joey shook her head. 'There is a reason for that, and it isn't the one that you think—' She broke off as Gideon came back into the room.

His eyes narrowed guardedly as he moved past them to stand in front of the fire to warm himself.

'Would you mind if I gave tea a miss and went upstairs to rest instead?' Joey ignored Gideon and spoke to Molly. 'I didn't sleep too well last night and I'm feeling a little tired.' She also thought it would be better if she made herself scarce so that mother and son could have their talk...

'Of course.' Molly smiled warmly. 'Gideon, would you—?'

'I'm sure I can find my own way if you just give me directions,' Joey said, deliberately avoiding Gideon's gaze as she sensed rather than saw his amusement at her remark about not having slept well. Let him be amused; he was only feeding his mother's curiosity, if he did but know it!

But Gideon wouldn't know it. Because Gideon never thought in terms of real relationships with women. Only those relationships of 'mutual needs' that Joey wanted no part of.

'It really isn't that bad, Gideon.' Joey looked up at him with concern as he stood so tall and remote in the hallway outside her apartment, after their return to London late on Sunday afternoon.

Gideon looked down at her blankly. 'Sorry?'

'I thought Angus Murray seemed like a nice man when we met him at dinner last night,' Joey said. 'And he obviously adores your mother.' She smiled at him encouragingly.

To Gideon's surprise the news his mother had wanted to share with him was of her intention to marry a laird of the clan Murray—a man she had met at a dinner party a year ago. Angus Murray had an estate near Inverness, and the wedding was to be in the summer, after which Molly intended moving to Angus's home in the Highlands.

Joey and Gideon had met the older man the evening before, when he'd joined them for dinner—a bluff, gruff Scottish widower in his early sixties, with admiration and love for Molly shining brightly in mischievous blue eyes.

Gideon realised that Joey had the impression he had a problem with his mother's intention to remarry, but she couldn't have been more wrong; he was more than pleased that after twenty-five years of being alone his mother had finally found someone she loved, who obviously loved her in return, and with whom she wanted to spend the rest of her life.

It was the fact that his mother, after all these years, felt *able* to love again, to make a future with another man now that the past had finally been laid to rest with Lexie's marriage to Lucan, that had thrown Gideon's own years of cynicism towards love and emotion into question.

He nodded. 'They make a great couple.'

'They do. And the fact that the police telephoned this morning and told you they have Richard Newman, and that he's admitted the vandalism, means you no longer have to feel obliged to spend any more time with *me*,' Joey pointed out happily.

Ah.

Now, *that* was a problem for Gideon.

In fact he had thought of almost nothing else since receiving that call from the police...

'What do you think will happen to him?' Joey prompted wistfully; Newman was currently 'helping the police with their enquiries'.

Gideon shrugged. 'He'll probably end up seeing the same psychiatrist as his ex-wife.'

Joey grimaced. 'There you go—yet another example of what marriage can do to you!'

'What a *bad* marriage can do to you,' Gideon corrected.

'I didn't think you were aware there was even a distinction?'

He gave a rueful grimace. 'Maybe the obvious happiness of the rest of my family has changed my mind.'

'I somehow doubt that,' Joey dismissed lightly. 'Still, the main thing is that the Newman situation is over.'

Gideon had believed he would feel relieved when his enforced time with Joey came to an end. Had thought he wanted nothing more than to get back to his own ordered life. That, once the situation with Newman was settled, he would be more than happy to walk away from her.

In fact, he didn't feel any of those things...

Gideon had no idea exactly what it was he was feeling, but it certainly wasn't the relief he had expected.

'I'll see you at work tomorrow, then.'

Gideon refocused on Joey, not in the least reassured by her wary expression as she looked up at him. He had been proved wrong, time and time again about his first— and stubbornly held—impression of her as being a hard-mouthed sophisticate who'd had any number of sexual partners. An impression he now knew to be totally wrong because she had been a virgin until yesterday morning.

'Gideon?'

He blinked as he shook himself out of his own thoughts. 'Yes, no doubt we'll see each other at work tomorrow.'

Joey had no idea what he had been thinking about just now, when he'd frowned so darkly, although she could guess: he was obviously still troubled by his mother having announced that she was to remarry in the summer. Joey knew from that brief conversation with Molly yesterday, while Gideon took the bags upstairs, that with Jordan and Lucan now married and starting out on new lives together with the women they loved, Gideon was Molly's main concern.

Although the other woman's hopes of a relationship developing between Joey and Gideon were pure fantasy!

She turned and entered her apartment. 'Goodnight, then.'

'Joey...'

'Yes?' She looked up at him quizzically, the door already half closed.

Gideon drew in a harsh breath, not sure what he was doing, only knowing that he didn't want to say goodbye to her just yet. That he didn't want to say goodbye to her at all! 'I hope you'll have a better night's sleep tonight.'

Joey gave a rueful smile. 'All that clean Scottish air knocked me out for eight hours last night.'

'Still...'

Why didn't Gideon just go? Joey wondered, knowing that if he didn't do so soon she was going to be tempted into giving in to the impulse she felt to invite him into her apartment. Into her bed! An invitation that would only end up in her feeling totally humiliated when Gideon refused...

'Drive safe,' she told him lightly.

'Do you want me to pick you up in the morning?'

'Gideon, will you just go?' Joey finally snapped. 'The strain of us having to be polite to each other for the past twenty-four hours for your mother's benefit is definitely starting to get to me—even if it hasn't got to you!'

Of course it had, Gideon realised. What could he be thinking of, trying to delay their parting in this way?

For once in his life he wasn't thinking, only feeling, he acknowledged wryly. Quite what the reluctance he felt to go back to the cold impersonality of his own apartment told him, he still wasn't sure...

His mouth twisted. 'In that case I should thank you for so successfully keeping your aversion to spending time in my company from my mother.'

'You should, yes.' Joey looked up at him quizzically. 'Well?' she prompted as he remained silent.

Gideon smiled tightly. 'That is all the thanks you're going to get, I'm afraid.'

Joey gave an answering small smile. 'Goodnight, Gideon.' She closed the door decisively in his face.

Only to sit down abruptly on the sofa once she reached her sitting room.

The strain of having been constantly in his company for the past forty-eight hours had not arisen from being with him at all—she loved being with him—but from having to hide the love she felt for him...

CHAPTER FOURTEEN

'GIDEON, it's *two o'clock in the morning*!' Joey stared up at him disbelievingly, having opened her apartment door in answer to the doorbell ringing and once again found him standing outside in the hallway.

'Yes.' He didn't even bother to glance at the watch on his wrist to confirm the time.

He was still dressed in the black jumper and trousers he had been wearing earlier, with blond hair seriously tousled—as if he had been running agitated fingers through it constantly for the whole of the last eight hours.

In contrast, Joey was wearing another overlarge T-shirt to sleep in, of pale green this time. Not that she had actually been asleep when Gideon pressed so persistently on her doorbell, but that wasn't the point. At two o'clock in the morning, he had to have *known* she would have already gone to bed.

'Gideon—'

'Why me?'

Joey blinked. 'Pardon?'

'The question I should have asked you yesterday morning was why me?' he repeated, dark eyes compelling. 'Why choose *me* as your first lover?'

Joey felt the colour drain from her cheeks, and she

leant against the edge of the door as her knees felt weak. 'Couldn't this have waited until morning?'

'No,' Gideon said determinedly, and he stepped forward into the apartment before firmly moving Joey away from the door and closing it behind him. 'Why me, Joey?' he prompted again huskily.

She swallowed hard. A lump seemed to have lodged in her throat, and her lips felt stiff and unyielding. The chances of him ever realising what question he should have asked yesterday morning had been pretty slim in her estimation. She wouldn't have mentioned it at all if she hadn't believed that.

She moistened the dryness of her lips. 'Well, I had to start somewhere—'

'Don't!' Gideon rasped harshly, and reached out to firmly grasp the tops of her arms, that compelling dark gaze holding hers captive. 'You're twenty-eight years old, very beautiful, with a keen sense of humour, fun to be with—'

'Much as I'm enjoying this paean of praise, Gideon—'

'So why, when dozens of men must have wanted to make love with you,' he continued, talking over Joey's attempt at mockery, 'did you wait until I came along to make love for the first time? With a man who more often than not annoys you intensely?'

This was a continuation of her nightmare, Joey decided. She had fallen asleep after all, and this was a really bad dream. A very realistic bad dream, admittedly—Gideon's fingers felt firm on her arms, and she could feel the warmth of his breath ruffling her own tousled hair—but he couldn't possibly really be here in her apartment at two o'clock in the morning—nor could they be having this conversation!

'I think it's probably overstating it slightly to say that dozens of men have wanted to make love to me—'

'Joey, I realise this is how you normally get through your day, but for once will you just stop making a joke out of everything?' Gideon's expression was fierce as he shook her slightly.

Should she be able to feel those fingers holding her arms if this was just a nightmare? And should she be feeling slightly dazed from Gideon shaking her if she was actually asleep?

If the answer to both those questions was no, then Joey was in serious trouble!

She eyed him guardedly. 'You're really here, aren't you?'

Gideon's answer was to pull her hard against him as he lowered his lips to capture hers in a kiss that was as intense as it was punishing. His eyes glittered deeply gold when he finally lifted his head to look down at her. 'Does that seem real enough to you?' he demanded gruffly.

Yep—she was in serious, serious trouble!

Gideon gave a rueful laugh as he saw the sudden panic in Joey's expression. 'Shall we go into the sitting room and talk about this?'

'As I've already said, it's two o'clock in the morning—'

'I've already conceded that it is,' Gideon drawled, and turned her in the direction of the sitting room. 'If you want to wait until morning to continue this discussion, then fine. I'll just sleep on the sofa again.'

'I can't possibly go back to my bedroom and fall asleep knowing you're out here on my sofa!' Joey returned sharply, obviously horrified at the very thought of it.

Gideon tilted his head in consideration. 'Why can't you?'

'Because— Well, because— You can't stay here again tonight,' she insisted firmly.

'Tell me why not?'

Her mouth firmed. 'I don't have to tell you anything except goodbye!'

'Would my telling you that I've fallen in love with you make the prospect of my staying here tonight more or less horrifying?'

Gideon held his breath, all the uncertainty, the disbelief, the fear that he had known as he'd paced his own apartment earlier, trying to make sense of his own feelings and finally succeeding, coming back with a vengeance.

What if he had totally misjudged this situation? What if the conclusions he had come to about their lovemaking yesterday were completely wrong? What if he had just made a complete idiot of himself by telling a woman who cared nothing at all for him that he had fallen in love with her?

So what if he had?

He had spent the last twenty-five years being emotionally restrained. Never really making a home out of any of the apartments he had lived in. Dressing conservatively. Driving equally unimaginative cars. Choosing friends who demanded nothing of him and women who demanded even less.

Making an emotional fool of himself was long overdue!

Although Gideon really hoped—prayed—that it wasn't going to happen with Joey...

She eyed him warily as she slowly moistened her lips again with the pink tip of her tongue. 'And are you actually telling me that? That you've fallen in love with me?' she said huskily.

Gideon returned her guarded gaze. 'Oh, yes.' The admission was accompanied by a smile, which turned rueful as he obviously saw her complete shock.

'I— But— You *can't* have fallen in love with me!' she protested incredulously. 'You think I'm outspoken. And rude. And pushy. And—'

'Yes, I did think you were all of those things.'

'But you don't any more?'

'No, I don't. What I think—know—is that I've fallen in love with you. That I want to ask you to marry me.' Gideon held his breath once more as he waited for a response.

It was that very self-consciousness that gave Joey the hope that she wasn't dreaming this after all. Surely even in a dream Gideon wouldn't look this uncertain of himself?

If not, had he really just said he was in love with her? That he wanted to marry her?

Gideon reached out and clasped both her hands in his. 'I realise this is too sudden for you—that I've done very little to endear myself to you. Hell, I've done very little to endear myself to *anyone* for the past twenty-five years,' he acknowledged in disgust. 'But if you'll let me—if you'll give me a chance, Joey—I swear that I'll do everything possible, whatever it takes, to help you fall in love with me too.'

She could only stare at him, sure that the strain of the past few days must have sent her completely out of her mind. Gideon loved her and wanted to marry her? Maybe if she kept saying it over and over again to herself she might actually come to believe it!

She swallowed hard before taking in a deep, determined breath. 'You asked why you, Gideon,' she reminded him.

'You don't have to answer if you would rather not,' he assured her hastily.

He was still massively uncertain, Joey realised wonderingly, totally incredulous that Gideon, a man always so sure of himself, was obviously completely unsure of her and how she felt about him.

Novel as that was, Joey found she didn't like it. She didn't like it at all!

'The "why you" is easy, Gideon,' she said softly. 'It's true that when I first met you I believed you to be arrogant, aloof, superior, sarcastic—'

'Stop, Joey!' he groaned.

'But I also thought,' she continued firmly, 'that you were the most gorgeous, sexy man I had ever set eyes on. I wanted us both to rip our clothes off right then and there and lie naked together on white silk sheets.'

'Red. The sheets were always red satin in *my* fantasies about the two of us,' he explained self-consciously at Joey's questioning look.

'You've had fantasies about us making love too?' Joey stared up at him in wonder.

Gideon nodded. 'I've spent the last week doing little else,' he admitted. 'In every venue and position possible— and some that probably aren't!'

'I'm shocked, Gideon!' Joey gave a choked laugh as she finally started to believe that he really *did* love her.

Gideon loved her!

He really loved her!

'No, you aren't,' he shot back.

'Well...no, not really. Perhaps *hopeful* best describes it?' Her eyes shone a mischievous green.

'Hopeful?' He looked even more uncertain.

'Gideon, haven't you realised yet that I've fallen in love with you too?' She finally allowed her eyes to glow with the emotion.

He looked down at her searchingly, wanting to believe, but afraid to hope that he really had just heard Joey say that she was in love with him. At the same time he knew that she couldn't possibly love the emotionally repressed man he had been for so long.

'Don't even try to make any sense out of it, Gideon,' Joey advised him huskily. 'I've discovered that falling in love isn't rational. Or logical. Or even sensible. It just *is*.' She gave a joyous laugh. 'And I happen to love you very, very much. So much so that if you don't soon finish what we started yesterday morning, then I really will have to start ripping your clothes off!'

Something seemed to swell in his chest—to break loose, to shatter—and as he felt his love for Joey expand and grow, filling the whole of his being, he realised that it was the shield he had always kept around his heart.

'I love you so much,' he choked out emotionally as he pulled her into his arms, burying his face in the silky softness of her hair as he held on tightly. 'Will you please marry me?'

She clung to him just as tightly. 'Maybe I should just check out that experience over stamina theory before I give you my answer?'

He gave a triumphant laugh, knowing that he would always treasure the love and laughter Joey had so joyously brought into his life.

'Mmm, I think you might be right—experience is so much more...*delicious* than stamina,' Joey murmured a long time later, nestled in Gideon's arms, her head resting on his shoulder, in the aftermath of lovemaking beyond her wildest dreams.

He quirked blond brows. 'I'm willing to give you another demonstration if you still have any doubts?'

Joey laughed huskily, completely satiated. 'I don't,' she said softly, fingers playing lightly with the dusting of hair on his chest.

Gideon settled her more comfortably against his shoulder. 'Are you going to tell me now why you deliberately chose not to sing professionally?'

Joey's breath caught in her throat. 'You realised that, hmm?'

Gideon turned to face her and ran a finger lightly over her flushed cheek. 'You have the voice of an angel.'

'I wouldn't go that far.'

'I would.'

Joey grimaced. 'I made a promise to myself—a vow— that I wouldn't.' She shook her head. 'I loved singing. When I was younger it was my vanity, if you will. But then Stephanie was injured in a car accident when we were ten years old. She couldn't walk. And I—I made a vow that if she could just walk again—'

'You would *give up* singing?' Gideon realised incredulously. 'That is so—so...'

'Stupid?' Joey supplied ruefully.

'So typical of the warm and generous person I know you to be,' Gideon corrected. 'You were willing to give up something you loved very much if your twin could walk again.'

'Well...yes. Because I loved Stephanie more,' she explained.

Gideon had already known that from their conversation this past week. He hadn't believed he could love Joey any more deeply, but in that moment he knew he did.

'I believe it was your singing voice that I fell in love with first,' he murmured. 'When I heard that voice rising to the roof of the church at Jordan and Stephanie's wedding I really thought I was listening to an angel.'

'Stephanie asked me to sing at the wedding, and I—well, I thought that as it was for her it wouldn't be breaking my promise.' Joey smiled tremulously.

His arms tightened about her. 'Will it be breaking your

promise if you sing just for me sometimes, Joey? And for our children?'

Her eyes widened. 'Our children?'

'Half a dozen of them, I think.' Gideon nodded. 'All with your beautiful red hair and green eyes.'

'If some of them are boys they might just have something to say about that!'

'They'll love you so much they won't care,' Gideon assured her indulgently.

'You really want half a dozen children?' Joey repeated wonderingly.

'Well…maybe just four—if you think six is too many?'

Joey thought six children sounded perfect—all with their father's blond hair and warm chocolate-brown eyes.

'Of course you'll have to marry me first,' Gideon insisted.

'Of course.'

'Is that a yes?'

Joey reached up to coil her arms about the bareness of his shoulders. 'That's most definitely a yes!'

There was another lengthy silence while Joey showed Gideon just how much she loved and wanted to marry him.

And Gideon immediately reciprocated by showing Joey—time and time again—just how much he loved *her*, would always love her, for the rest of their lives together.

Six weeks later

'Did I ever remember to thank you?' Gideon murmured softly.

Both Lucan and Jordan were standing beside him in the church to act as his best men, all three waiting for the moment when the organist would begin to play and Joey would enter the church, followed by Stephanie and Lexie as her bridesmaids.

Lucan raised dark brows. 'Thank us for what?'

Gideon gave a rueful smile. 'For knowing before I did that Joey was the one woman in the world who could make me feel complete.'

His older brother returned that smile. 'She's wonderful, isn't she?'

'Well, of course Joey's wonderful,' Jordan put in. 'How could she be anything else when she's Stephanie's twin?'

'I think he's slightly biased,' Lucan murmured dryly. 'But I'm glad it's worked out for you and Joey, Gid,' he added warmly, and the organist began to play in announcement of Joey's arrival.

It had more than worked out for Gideon and Joey. The past six weeks had been the best of Gideon's life. And today was their wedding day. The very first day of the rest of their lives.

As he turned to watch the woman he loved with all his heart and soul walking down the aisle towards him, looking stunningly beautiful in her long flowing white wedding gown, and with that same certainty of love shining in her eyes only for him, Gideon had absolutely no doubt that they would spend the rest of their lives together, blissfully happy...

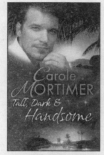
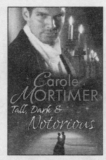

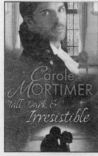

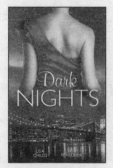